FATAL EQUATION

Fatal Equation

By

Gethyn Jones

Edition 1

ISBN: 978-1-3999-4794-7

1

So here we go again – a filthy, dimly lit alley on a cold, damp night in Portsmouth – scaring the life out of some poor sod, whose only crime was to get behind with the rent. Talk about heavy-handed. The guy is clearly traumatised as Ali Kurmi pushes him against the wall, leans into him, teeth gritted, fingers tightening around his collar.

The lad lets out a pathetic whimper.

In the nearby harbour, a ship's horn moans over the background drone of the carrier Queen Elizabeth's generators, that relentlessly tick over. The pungent smell of diesel fuel taints the salt-sea air, adding to the heavy atmosphere.

Pay up or get hurt – simple as that. Ali's ruthless father demands it, and Ali and his two cousins deliver, with force if necessary, whenever the call comes.

It could be Portsmouth, Southampton, Bristol or Brighton – Liverpool, even.

Patriarch Javed Kurmi has properties wherever there's a university – he's certainly cornered the market in the south. The trouble is, there are always some students who piss their rent money away rather than setting it aside for their landlord. So they … need a little visit.

Ali's cousin, Hammad, looks scary – he's tall and he works out. You can see that. You wouldn't want to argue with him, that's for sure. The same goes for Kamran – high octane, high alert.

Hammad pushes Ali out of the way and kicks the guy's legs from under him. Down he goes, begging to be spared – promising to pay up soon. Kamran steps in for good measure, kicking the student on to his side – placing a foot firmly on his neck.

'Listen, want to keep that handsome face – you pay up now. Understand?'

'I can't,' splutters the lad, 'I haven't got any money on me.'

'So what are you going to do?'

'I'll pay – I will.'

Kamran presses his foot down harder; 'When?' he demands.

'Please, please don't,' the lad begs. 'I'll get the money. I will.'

'How?' asks Hammad.

'My Dad.'

'Oh yeh?'

Ali is standing a few metres away, squirming. This is so not him. What the hell is he doing here anyway, having sworn he would never do it again?

'Alright! That's enough,' he says, unable to watch any more.

'Ease up. He'll pay up – won't you?'

'I will, tomorrow – honest I will.'

Kamran slowly and reluctantly lifts his foot, sneering at his cousin.

As far as Hammad and Kamran are concerned, it's just routine. No cuts, no scars – just a few bruises to act as a reminder never to mess with the Kurmis again. And it works every time, in spite of their cousin.

They know only too well that Ali isn't up to this job. His mind is elsewhere. It always is. He just hasn't got it. They laugh at his futile attempts to disguise himself by turning up his collar whenever they're on a job. What's the bloody use of that? But family's family,

Ali's their cousin and Uncle Javed pays them well. So, they play ball and don't ask questions.

Yet again, Ali is crippled inside. He feels nothing but shame and disgust. He's raging with resentment and frustration, most of it towards his father, the rest at himself.

Although he's said it many times before, tonight *will* be the last time.

Kamran kicks the hapless student in the thigh, hard. The student rolls over and groans, cursing into the evening air as the three Kurmis slouch away.

Another dirty deed for the boss. And another very bad day for Ali's karma.

2

If he actually smoked, now would be the time to light up and inhale deeply – but he's never touched the evil weed. So instead, Ali calms his troubled thoughts with the night-time view across the harbour and all its twinkling lights. There's hardly anyone about – just a rough sleeper outside the bus terminal on the Hard. He leans forward and looks down over the railings into the murky darkness below. The tide's out and he can just make out the small fishing boats sitting askew on the mudflats. It's time to go home – finally time to get things sorted out, once and for all.

Ali Kurmi has another life, which couldn't be more different from that of unofficial bailiff. Whilst he certainly looks the part – tall, strong and toned – he's no tough guy. He's actually very shy and sensitive; kind and respectful to his friends and, ironically, hates any form of confrontation.

He's also a very capable musician and songwriter and has big ambitions to find a place in the harsh and fiercely competitive music business. He lives modestly and invests most of his earnings in professional recordings of his songs, at a local studio.

As well as creating original music, Ali is also a popular Events DJ on the corporate circuit, thanks to his 70s/80s niche tastes. The work is enjoyable and well paid and he's built up a good reputation with event organisers across the South.

But at the end of the day, it's the song writing and producing that consume Ali's mind, 24/7.

His style of writing is inspired by the retro music he loves and it's a quirky combination. An Asian guy producing this kind of music is somewhat unusual. However, he's hoping that this might give him the edge he needs, to break into the massively competitive music industry.

So what's holding him back?

Ali detests the work he's obliged to carry out for his father's company, Kurmi Properties Limited. Chasing rent defaulters and roughing them up is not exactly his first career choice but, unfortunately, he doesn't have an option. Javed Kurmi, holds that extremely large trump card and Ali is forced to follow his father's wishes or face further public humiliation. It's nothing short of blackmail. He concludes that his father has never forgiven him for what happened all those years ago.

The big Kurmi shame and Ali's to blame.

*

He sits up, swivels his legs around to the side of the bed and leans forward to pick up his boxer shorts. Becky reaches out with her left arm and affectionately pats his back. As he stands up, his tummy gurgles loudly with last night's kebab – bad idea. He turns around and half smiles as he looks at her naked body.

Home for Ali is a two-bedroom terraced house in Southsea, Portsmouth. It's been his base for all his adult years and is one of his father's many properties in the city. For years, he shared the place but as his passion for music developed, he needed more space to store his gear. Bedroom two is now piled high with lights and speakers that comprise his DJ rig. It's also where he does his song writing.

Even before the dark days, music was his passion and soon became an obsession. From the moment he first tuned in to those retro radio chart shows, he was hooked on 70s/80s music, much to the amusement of those around him. Teaching himself to play the guitar and piano was inevitable. He stepped innocently into another wonderful and potentially life-changing world. He persisted in developing his musical skills – particularly when he was first sent away to Portsmouth. Immersing himself in music enabled him to block out the harsh realities of his life.

'Was it no good for you last night?' asks Becky. 'Did I do something wrong?'

'No, no, it's nothing to do with you. It's me, I'm sorry. I've got to do something about all this shit,' he says, jerking the coffee grinder into action.

'Ah …' says Becky, shouting over the noise.

'Yeh, the poor bastard. The bloke was scared shitless. I should be used to all this by now – but I'm not and I never will be.'

He turns the grinder off and decants the powder into the percolator.

'Was he hurt?'

'Luckily, no, but I tell you what – I've had enough of all this. My father can go screw himself. I don't care what happens. He can do or say what he wants but I'm not having this anymore.'

'Oh Ali … you can't go on like this, that's for sure you'll make yourself ill.'

Becky Davies is 26, bright, determined, and clever too. She didn't fancy launching straight into a law career after getting her degree and has had a string of temporary jobs ever since. She's currently biding her time waiting tables at a Mexican restaurant. She has long jet-black hair and is fortunate to have the most amazing smile that is her natural resting expression. Consequently, a lot of people smile back at her and surprise, surprise, she gets great tips at the restaurant.

She enjoys spending time with Ali – it's an arrangement that suits her very well. She likes the fact that he's considerably older than her and she admires his general take on life. They share a similar sense of humour, both like good food – and meet up when one or the other feels like it. Nice and casual. She's got too much going on in her head at the moment and doesn't need the complication of a more formal relationship.

She hasn't had the pleasure of meeting Ali's father. Thank God. But she has a good mental picture of the man, having endured Ali's many rants since they hooked up last year.

Ali looks up and turns off the bubbling percolator. Becky is keeping him together at the moment – along with his music. Well, to be honest, the music's his first and only real love. Becky's a great mate and they have great sex together but they both know that romance is never going to be on the cards.

Deep down, he'd love to find his soulmate, someone to cherish and share his interests and dreams. But for now, it would seem, he has the practicalities of life and burden of his father to deal with – thankfully, with the support of Becky Davies.

'I really am going to tell him it's over. I can't believe I've left it so long.'

'Yeh?'

'Yeh! It's time to focus seriously on the music. I'm going to have a proper go at it.'

'I'm sure he'll have something to say about that, won't he?'

'Sod that. I've got a conscience – I can't sleep properly, and I bloody well deserve it. Hurting and humiliating people like we do – it's immoral as well as illegal. Look at me, I'm bloody 35 – heading for 36 – and living on my effing monster of a father's blood money!'

Ali's teenage and adult years have been a rollercoaster – emotionally and physically. However, with all that he's had to endure, particularly the scandal, he's not only survived, but developed into a remarkably strong, ambitious and determined man. Despite being denied any formal education from the age of sixteen, he's done a pretty good job in educating himself. He's quick to learn, reads voraciously, loves maths and is a complete sucker for a good Sudoku. He's proud of his personal achievements – but he'd feel an awful lot prouder if he was free of his father's stranglehold.

*

The twittering tune of an excited blackbird breaks the pre-dawn silence – its voice, jubilant and hopeful. Laura O'Brien smiles and listens intently to its complex tune and marvels at the bird's obvious joy at something as simple as the start of a new Tipperary day.

She's spent many nights lying in bed, impatiently waiting for first light, and Mr Blackbird lightens her heart as he ad-libs his way through his repertoire.

She softly smiles. Things are on the up, at last.

Not long ago, she dreaded night time and those long hours of tossing and turning, unable to settle, unable to sleep. All those crazy unlinked random thoughts flying in and out of her brain, taunting and punishing her for her stupid self-indulgence.

But at last, her shattered sleep pattern – thrown into disarray by her drinking, is slowly getting back to normal. She's recently been re-training her body to rest at the times nature intended. Finally, she's beginning to have better nights. She's off the grape juice and is beginning to think more clearly again, and Mr birdie-dick outside is her new best friend.

Sadly, she's been in this place before but, to put it into perspective, it was a long time ago. She thought she had alcohol under control but, "once an addict, always an addict" – that's what they say, isn't it? She thought she had the booze licked.

The past few months have been a nightmare, dealing with Frank's sudden death and all those people wanting her to do this and do that, sign here, sign there. All that money. Whenever she sought peace and quiet there was always someone hovering, wanting something from her. It completely befuddled her, and her emotions have been all over the place, struggling to process that traumatic event. In the end, the lure of the bottle was too strong – and it won. For a while anyway.

Then something happened to change in Laura O'Brien's corner of the universe. She can't explain it but she caught a glimmer of hope and snatched at it with excitement and relief.

This is now her second major recovery and she's proud that she's turned things around, largely through self-determination, a lot of help from AA and devoted guidance from her mentor, Alice Kingston.

Back in the room. The blackbird's solo performance has now ended and the general avian chorus has started. Another day has begun and for the first time in ages, Laura O'Brien is feeling a little more in tune with the world.

*

'That sounds really cool,' says Becky. 'You're so lucky being able to play an instrument. I wish I could.'

Ali is in front of his computer in bedroom two, with his guitar on his lap and a midi piano keyboard in front of him – it's his little home studio and he's in love with this gear. You can do amazing things these days with DAWS (Desktop Audio Workstations). They're fully professional recording studios combined with a selection of synthesisers, all rolled into one piece of software. In theory, you can turn out your own fully professional rock classics from the comfort of your home computer.

'That looks so complicated. I don't know how you manage to make such brilliant songs from a tiny laptop.'

'I love it – it's all I want to do Becks – write and record music.'

He puts the guitar on its stand and looks up. 'So, what do you really want?'

'What do you mean?'

'Well, you know what I want, a career in music. But what do you really want, for *you*?'

'Well, that's a big one,' she sighs. 'I'd like to stay healthy, that's the first thing … and I'd like to be happy.'

'That sounds pretty good to me.'

'But … *the* most important thing for me is nothing material – it's simpler than that. It's stability. That's what I need. To feel safe and secure. Yeh, I've never had that and I reckon it comes from my parents. I'm sure they don't love each other – haven't done for years – and I'm convinced they've only stayed together for me and my sister. Whatever, that emptiness has rubbed off on to me, leaving me feeling insecure. And it's not very nice.'

'Does your sister get the same vibe too?'

'Dunno, I haven't discussed it with her. But I don't feel complete or whole. Does that make any sense?'

'I know *exactly* what you mean. Don't forget, I was removed from my family when I was 16, so I know precisely what you're saying. I think we both probably crave the same thing. A solid, loving, secure life where we feel needed and safe. It's not a lot to ask for, is it?'

'No, I don't think so.

'As for a career? I don't know. I'm still thinking about it. The jury is out on my law degree … did you hear that?'

Ali stands up grinning.

'So, Becky Davies … will you marry me?'

'Fuck off, Ali Kurmi. Not in a million years.'

'Alright, enough of all this ribaldry. I have a suggestion.'

'Oh yes?' giggles Becky. 'What might that ribaldry be then?'

Ali smiles too and puts down the mouse with a sweeping flourish.

'I'll give you a clue. It's got nothing to do with marriage, music – or parents. Follow me please, this way – and don't worry, I'm now a kebab-free zone.'

*

Javed Kurmi is a BIG man. *Big* is the word. Big ego, big business, big appetite and a big belly. Oh, and bad breath too – that's a *big* problem.

He's used to getting his own way – with just one possible exception – his son Ali. God knows he's tried to support him ever since that crisis all those years ago. But Ali prefers to waste his time being, of all things, a DJ.

A DJ, can you believe? Playing moronic music to mindless idiots. Javed just doesn't get it. Why would anyone turn down the chance to become a major part of a thriving business, with all its rewards? He finds it hard to accept that Ali isn't like him in any shape or form, repeatedly defying his demands to return to Bromley and "settle down".

But he also takes comfort in knowing that he has the ultimate leverage over his wayward son – and he won't be afraid to use it, probably sooner rather than later.

'When is Ali coming over did you say?' he shouts up the stairs, looking at his phone calendar.

'They're all coming for lunch next weekend. That's what you wanted isn't it, the whole family?' calls Namita.

'Yes, of course. I just wanted to double check.'

Namita is now on the landing at the top of the stairs.

'What are you up to Javed?' she says, concerned.

'I'm going to sort him out once and for all. He's been away for far too long.'

'Oh dear, not again. You want him to come back to Bromley? Why would he, why should he? You threw him out!'

'I did NOT throw him out!' shouts Javed, indignantly. 'I did what any father would do – I protected my son.'

'Oh yes? You protected yourself, more like. You can be a very selfish man, Javed Kurmi.'

'How dare you! I've done nothing but put my family first, throughout my life, and look how I've been rewarded? A son who is wasting his life away, at my expense, playing music in nightclubs and orgies. Portsmouth was never intended to be a permanent arrangement anyway. As for you – you never support me on this, you're always on his side.'

'Oh Javed, you haven't got a clue have you? Ali has turned into a good young man and he's carved out his own life - without you, Javed. He hasn't had a normal family life and I think he's managed incredibly well, under the circumstances. And I've had to watch all that from a distance. Do you know how hard it's been for me, not having my own son living at home with us?'

'Yes, well he brought it on himself and I don't agree with what he does down there. His priorities are all wrong. I believe in loyalty and tradition – the family. I've listened to you for long enough. I want him back here to take responsibility and help with the business, full time. I have plans and I need him. Portsmouth is over for him and that's the end of the matter.'

Javed Kurmi's worked hard to get where he is – his empire of flats, bedsits and houses didn't come overnight. It required not only capital but imagination, skill and strong nerves. The property market isn't for softies if you're playing the big game. You have to be tough and ruthless when required.

Javed can't put an exact figure on his properties but it's in the hundreds and they're all carefully managed and maintained to keep the money flowing.

He knows how to keep his properties rentable, without wasting money on unnecessary comforts. Some of his tenants would probably dispute that, but Javed is used to the usual complaints about dampness, dodgy boilers and peeling paintwork. There's no room for sentimentality in business if you want a decent return on your investments.

He has success alright, and the wealth that comes with it. He's proud of his organisational skills and of his network of employees across the south where he has the bulk of his properties. It's a system he set up, and it works like a charm – most of the time.

He runs Kurmi Properties Ltd., from an office in Bromley, helped by various members of his family for whom he shows little gratitude or respect. Namita used to work with him in the office but was relegated to the role of housewife, cook and cleaner some years ago. A health scare presented Javed with the opportunity to get her out of his way.

Javed Kurmi is text-book, old-style male chauvinism personified.

3

Laura O'Brien is 52, but she really doesn't look it. To say she's beautiful would be an understatement – tall, proportionally shaped, glistening dark brown shoulder-length hair, spell-binding green eyes – and it doesn't stop there. As well as being a stunner, she's clever, degree-positive, cultured, well-read, and witty. All this is combined with an air of vulnerability – and it's a mesmerising mixture that draws people to her. Laura is also a fighter and is more than familiar with misery, despair and depression – she's learned life's lessons the hard way.

As she wanders around her luxury Tipperary home in Ireland, she's on her phone to her friend and former AA mentor, Alice Kingston.

Alice is video calling from Wickham in Hampshire. She is bright and bubbly, persuasive, a bit new age and unmistakable, with her cascade of flowing golden ringlets. She's pushing Laura to up sticks and relocate to Hampshire, just as she did herself. She's been dry for many years and is convinced that her friend could get over the trauma of her husband's sudden death and start a new life, if she makes the move too.

Alice is a brilliant organiser, with a heart of gold and a deep sense of compassion. She's a born networker and promotes her beauty business on social media – Facebook, Instagram and whatever pitches up next with street cred.

'Hey Laura, how are you, my love?' she asks.

'Could be worse I guess,' says Laura, reservedly. 'I still can't take it all in – which is ridiculous when you think how long it's been now, 18 months, but I'm OK thanks, what about you?'

Alice has become a lifeline for her friend since Laura's husband, Frank, died of a brain aneurysm. The fire service had to smash down the bathroom door.

'Never mind me – it's you I'm interested in – you're looking well. I hope you're still taking everything one day at a time. You had such a shock. Have you been to plenty of meetings?'

'I have – as often as I can, and it feels like I'm back on track. I'm not craving anymore – and I'm eating well, which a big step forward, considering the amount of weight I lost,' says Laura. 'Most important of all, the intention's there – and I'm keeping busy. And Mary's been an angel. She's so much more than a housekeeper and she's been about the only one I can really talk to – she's been great. She's on my side.'

'Unlike those other two, eh?' says Alice. 'You should do as I suggest and just get out of that place. It might be a palace, but living there is doing you nothing but harm.'

'It's not a palace, Alice,' smiles Laura, amused by the accidental rhyme. 'But I take your point. I'm going to have to do something soon because Stephanie is being so unkind. She really hates me, Alice. She won't leave me alone for five minutes.'

'That woman is poison, and you don't deserve it. You already know what I think. You should distance yourself from people who deliberately set out to do you damage. Frank's children will just carry on eating away at you. Leave Stephanie to get on with her own horrible life, swat her and her brother away. But better still. Come here!'

'Ha – if only it were that simple. But I agree, Stephanie is certainly a one-off. A beauty she may be but I've never met anyone carrying so much hatred.'

'It's all about money, my love – that's all she's interested in, she's greedy and nasty. For God's sake, hasn't Frank already left a fortune to her and Richard? Why does she want even more? You really need to abandon that place. Bring the lovely memories of Frank with you and leave all the rest behind.'

'She wants more money, Alice. My money, and she wants me out of the business completely.'

'But you said she's not even interested in horses, so what's that all about?'

'I know, but she wants my share of the stud. She won't let go. She's impossible. I don't actually think I've ever told you the full story. Do you know, Frank was even considering cutting them out of his will completely?'

*

Frank O'Brien had been incredibly well-organised and proud of his stud farm. It had made him a legend in the equine racing world, as well as a very rich man. He was also aware of his mortality. He realised that if he were to die unexpectedly, everything he'd worked for would inevitably be swallowed up by a hovering competitor or simply fizzle out.

He was acutely aware that his children Richard and Stephanie had never shown any genuine interest in it, so as a precaution, with the help of his accountant Seán Ryan, he'd put in place the financial mechanism to set up a trust to keep the business afloat for two years. Thereafter, it would be sold and the trust dissolved. The trustees would be guided by his mentor and stud manager, Joe Kelly.

This way, his loyal staff, many of whom he looked on as almost family, would have sufficient breathing space to make their own arrangements or be taken on by the new owner.

All this would only happen in the event of his death, obviously. And that wasn't going to happen any time soon, was it?

*

'It's always money, isn't it?' says Laura, continuing their conversation. 'Where there's money and particularly, a will, there's a relative!'

'You said she's already received more money than most people can only dream of.'

'Yes she has, they both have, but to be fair,' Laura is obliged to point out, 'so have I – but she can't bear the thought that I'm getting more than her. Here's the thing. Frank's instruction to the trustees is that at the point of sale, half of the profits will come to me and the other half will be *shared* between Stephanie and Richard.'

'Laura, just leave it to the legal people. That's my advice. I don't want to become a pain to you, but you do trust me, don't you? We've been through so much, you and me – and for goodness' sake, you've helped me more than you'll ever know. You really have. But please think about it – there are places to rent over here that are wonderful. You can come over, take your time to regain your strength, have a long think and start over again. You'll love it. Spring's coming, the sea's nearby, the village is beautiful and, if you need it, London's only just over an hour away. It's fabulous!'

'Listen, I promise I'll think about it,' says Laura, winding things up and turning towards the huge window overlooking the grounds. More than a few seconds go by. Then Laura sighs:

'You know I really did love Frank, don't you?'

'Yes my love, I do.'

'I never wanted all this money – I just loved him. And he really did love me. It wasn't a fling or sudden decision.'

'There's nothing that can take all that away from you. It happened. You loved each other, and Stephanie and Richard, or anyone else for that matter, can't change the facts, no matter how they'd like to. You were actually blessed, both of you, to have that love even if it didn't last as long as you'd expected.'

Laura says goodbye, hangs up and steps through the bi-fold doors and into the chilly, dazzling winter sun that sits low in the sky. She closes her eyes and takes a long slow breath. She knows a decision has to be made and it has to be made soon. She's done absolutely nothing wrong and deserves better than the treatment she's getting from Frank's children. The friends she's made since coming to live at the house, have slowly melted away. She doesn't really blame them – what can they say or do? Anyway, they're all so much older than her.

They've been kind enough, but now it's time for her to step forward on her own and make some more bold decisions.

For the first time in what seems an age, Laura feels that old positive energy returning. She's dug herself out of misery before and she's just done it again. All by herself.

She's finished with being pitied and patronised – it's time to take the reins with both hands.

4

Ali is sitting in the colourfully lit control room at Jim Sexton's Key Studios, where for the past two years he's been investing in making high-end recordings of his songs. He's serious about building his music career and is setting about it in a methodical and professional way.

The studio is impressive from first sight, situated inside a living, breathing church – a community church where people come and go all the time. The imposing, stained-glass windows in the main part of the building create a moody atmosphere when the sun is in the right place, throwing huge shafts of light and shadows across the interior. It's a wonderful vibe, and that, together with the fab people who run it, makes the studio a unique creative space that musicians love. It inspires Ali and he loves working here with Jim.

'Hi. How's it going?' he asks.

'Yeh – fine thanks.'

Jim's in his customary position, at the mixing desk in front of a very wide, curved computer screen and a battery of different size speakers. Jim and Ali have a lot in common. Same age, similar ideas on life, music – most things, actually. Considerably tattooed and standing a little over six feet, Jim has short, forward-combed hair; he's a vegan, a conspiracy theorist, a brilliant musician and an extremely clever sound engineer. He keeps himself fit by running at dawn every morning along the nearby coast. His daily efforts are recorded on social media, and he is rewarded with a rock-solid body.

And waddya know, Jim also grew up listening to 70s and 80s music – thanks to his dad who was in a band whilst also running the local musical instrument shop. Together, they talk of their dreams and what they would do with success. They're also painfully aware of how the music business operates and how difficult it's always been to penetrate. Like Ali, he loves music passionately and, whatever the odds, he too will never give up.

'You went for your run this morning then, I saw on Facebook.'

'Yeh, I need energy to work with you,' smirks Jim. 'What are we doing today?'

Ali brandishes his portable hard drive and grins broadly. 'Some more backing vocals to add, plus a piano part.'

'*I Keep Walkin*'? OK, let's get it up,' says Jim, taking hold of the drive.

The control room door opens and Jim's partner, Carl, steps inside as they listen to the track.

'Liam's got a great voice, hasn't he? Anyone for coffee or tea? Kettle's boiling.'

'No thanks, Carl, I'm fine. How are you?' says Ali.

'We manage,' says Carl. 'Still get a few calls thinking we're a Christian music recording studio. Can't blame 'em I suppose – it is a church after all. Anyway, when all your songs are Number 1, you won't forget us will you?!'

'Hah. I'll make a generous donation to your collection at the end of the session, Carl.'

'Gratefully received dear boy. Have you decided what you're going to do with all these tracks?' he says, nodding at the studio monitors.

Ali fidgets, 'Good question. It's not Top 40 music – that's more Jim's market. I'm aiming for the wider 40-plus audience. The trouble is, they're not all glued to Spotify – and with radio in decline, it's not easy reaching them.'

'Well, they say there's a market for everything. I'm sure you'll find a way,' says Carl, as he leaves.

'I'm going to make some big changes,' says Ali, turning back to Jim. 'It's time to start getting organised with all this and stop pissing around. We've got some decent songs here and it's time to get them out there.'

'Right ...' says Jim, having heard all this before – from every band and artist he's ever recorded. Everyone wants to be a star.

'How are you going to do that then? Feeling lucky?'

'I know, I know, but I'm going to start right here, right now,' says Ali tapping his temple. 'Get into the right frame of mind, get into that vortex and start believing in myself, completely. I know what you're thinking, that you've heard it all before a million times. But I genuinely believe something very good is about to happen. It's just a question of being in the right frame of mind to receive it.'

I'm looking at my life – hopin' for the best,
I'm thinking long and hard,
To see what comes up for me next,
I'm in the vortex – I'm in my space,
I'm in the here and now - living in the now.

5

Berners Street in London is home to the headquarters of the Performing Right Society that is running workshops for unsigned, ambitious songwriters.

PRS collects and distributes money on behalf of songwriters and composers, for the use of their musical works when they are publicly performed, or recordings of them are broadcast, streamed online or played in public spaces.

Ali is attending today's workshop. He knows London quite well, but he still needs an app to get around. He's on time, despite a delay on the train service from Portsmouth. It's all been a bit of a rush to get here but he's looking forward to getting some constructive feedback from some music pros.

It's a small room with a round table where he and three other hopefuls are sitting with the PRS rep and three professional songwriter-producers. The rep introduces the panel and Ali's immediately disappointed that he's never actually heard of any of them. *No worries, it'll be OK*, he reassures himself.

First up, is the guy on his left, who looks incredibly straight and the last person you'd expect to be sitting here touting pop music. He looks more like an accountant. He gives his name as Paul and his song starts – a gentle acoustic number which sounds incredibly like Harry Nilsson's, *Everybody's Talkin'*. Ali thinks that it's a bit familiar – that they'll never go for it, surely. It's way too derivative.

But to his amazement, they really like it.

'It's cool, bro – good vibe, like the feel. I could really hear that covered by quite a few artists. You know what I mean?'

'Good for sync too,' adds one of the other panellists. 'I know a few ad agencies and music supervisors, who use stuff like that. Good one, bro.'

And they go on to give him more advice.

Now it's Ali's turn. He clenches his buttocks tightly and cautiously introduces himself, aware that these guys, from what he's just heard, are very unlikely to have any interest in him or his track *Ozone*. But he's come a long way today and the song means a lot to him, so sod it.

It was one of his first serious master recordings. It's all about the incredible spiritual high he gets from a stunning panorama, standing alone, at dawn, on a beach near his home, in Gosport. The wide view extends from Portsmouth and the English Channel to the left, panning right across the Solent, taking in all of the Isle of Wight up to Cowes and Southampton Water on the right. It is truly breath-taking and takes him into another zone. Hard to do justice to, but the song has a go at it.

The technical guy presses the play button on the iPod.

God, this is excruciating. Ali can't look at these people. The song gets past the brass introduction and first verse and into the chorus. It then moves into the middle section, and finally into the last powerful choruses, and out with the ending he'd so carefully thought about. Gently fading away with the choir sounding like voices slowly mingling with the waves as they land on the shore. Genius, he reckons.

'Oh man,' says one member of the panel, shaking his head, 'nobody writes songs with fades these days. Sorry bro but you need to know, this is so not happening.'

'It ain't gonna cut with any playlist curator - it doesn't fit any genre,' says one of the other writers.

Ali's not sure which one because at this stage he's cringing with embarrassment and shock.

'Why did you write a song like this, bro – what is it – gospel, man?' he sneers. 'Who's gonna pick up that kind of cut? You need to check out what's goin' down, man.'

Ali swallows hard and sits back, humiliated and flat. That, in its grim reality, was his first and probably last, workshop.

Everyone has heard about how difficult it is to find success in the music business, and Ali has had his fair share of slammed doors. But armed with a stubborn determination and a fair degree of wishful thinking, he intends to see it through.

He knows that his song writing is never going to set the world aflame for innovation and win awards. He isn't looking to become a legend among the all-time greats, but he firmly believes he still has a part to play on this exciting and ever-changing musical roundabout. He writes catchy tunes that he knows the masses would like, if only he can find someone in the music business to back him and get them out there.

Context is what it's all about – and of course, Sudoku.

6

Ali is a big fan of Yotam Ottolenghi. The man can do no wrong in his eyes. He avidly reads his online column and tries his recipes. He loves food and much to his friends' amusement is coming down with cookery books that he never has time to use. Ali's taste in food is eclectic, like his taste in music – there are no traditional rules and boundaries; he likes anything and everything. Mixing things up.

He has of course his mum to thank for all this – her cooking is the best he's ever tasted.

Today, Ali's attending a family meal in Bromley that includes his older brother and two sisters with their partners/spouses/children. He's expecting the usual pressure and contempt from his father to abandon his dreams and return to Bromley. But this time he's prepared.

Ali loves his mother, Namita – just about gets on with his patronising older brother, accountant Mohammed, and is fine with his sisters Rani and Basma – but his relationship with his father is as fraught as ever.

There are thirteen, including four children, seated around the enormous dining table and the room is echoing with animated conversations. Ali is at the far end, not saying much, just listening to his brother and sisters talking about ... to be honest he hasn't the faintest idea what they're all banging on about – because he isn't listening.

He's rehearsing over and over again in his head what he's going to say to his father. This is not something he's been looking forward to because, at the end of the day, Ali doesn't like confrontation of any kind. But enough is enough. He's come to abhor his father's hypocrisy – of being a mosque-attending Muslim whilst at the same time beating the shit out of people simply because they're struggling in life.

'What's wrong, Ali?' asks his mother. 'You normally wolf your food down.'

Ali grimaces and prods at his food. 'It's fine Mum, lovely.'

'It's that tacky lifestyle he has in Portsmouth, Mum, catching up on him. Aren't you fed up living in that crap place?' sneers Ali's brother, Mohammed.

'You have no idea what you're talking about.'

'I do. I've been there plenty of times,' laughs Mohammed. 'It's a shit hole.'

'Do you mind, Mo? Don't speak like that here, please. Show a little respect for your family,' says Namita.

At the head of the table, Javed Kurmi just grunts something inaudible and continues to concentrate on his food. He will speak when he's finished his meal, but not before.

'Portsmouth's a fantastic place to live,' says Ali. 'It's got everything – the Spinnaker Tower, The Mary Rose, HMS Victory, the seafront, theatres, arts centres, gyms, clubs and great places to eat. Oh, and yes, we own a lot of properties there – that pay the wages.'

The giant, Javed Kurmi, finally stirs in his chair and wipes the perspiration from his forehead. 'Ali, you and I are going next door for a good chat. There are things we need to talk about.'

'Talk here Dad – I know what you're going to say anyway.'

'I doubt that very much and I don't want to embarrass you and your brother and sisters, or your mother, by talking in here.'

Rani and her sister Basma hurriedly herd their children out of the room.

'With respect Dad, the only embarrassment is you,' says Ali, taken aback by his own assertion.

'Respect? How dare you speak to me like that! You owe me and this whole family everything. For years you've had your own way. How dare you. I've even spent a fortune on buying you all that music equipment – God knows what you do with that. I've done so much to help over the years. But now – now what are you – 35? 35 years old, wasting your life away and doing the bare minimum for the business. It has to stop.'

Ali is now furious, too.

'So, you want me to beat up even more struggling students and other innocent people, do you?' he says, looking around the table directly at his mother, brother and sisters, who've just returned without the children.

'Yes, dear family, did you know that our father orders me, Ham and Kam to beat people up when they don't pay their rent on time? Do you realise what a heartless bastard he is? The man who goes to mosque and prays – he's a complete hypocrite. Look at him. Be honest, you've never forgiven me for 2004 have you? Well, you can stick yourself right up your own backside. I'm out. As from now. This minute.'

He suddenly stands up, catching the tablecloth, up-ending several glasses on the table.

Amongst shocked, stifled howls, Ali takes his leave. His father screams after him but he is quickly and dramatically out of the door.

7

Wickham, Hampshire, is about 12 miles from Portsmouth and 15 from Southampton. It couldn't be more different from urban Portsmouth. It's a picturesque village and boasts the second largest medieval square in England.

It's surrounded by historic buildings, preserved in a conservation area. There are a lot of wealthy and professional folk living nearby, and along the adjacent Meon Valley. It's sought-after and very expensive. And bucking national trends, it's a thriving community that is determined to maintain tradition – whilst simultaneously looking to the future.

It's also a bit different. There's the annual Wickham Festival, which has become an important part of the British rock and roots music calendar. Great bands, great food and a great atmosphere.

And once a year on May 20th the village plays host to the Wickham Horse Fair, dating back to the 13th Century. It's an historic event, where the travelling community in their hundreds descend on the village to sell and race ponies and horses. For a couple of days, the village is a very different place that some approve of – and some, inevitably, don't.

Whatever. Wickham is a very nice place to live, in a very nice locality.

Alice Kingston lives compactly in a modest semi, just outside the village.

Childless and divorced 15 years ago, after a rocky marriage to an Irishman, which fell apart because of his infidelity and her drinking, she upped and moved to Wickham, where she quickly settled and started a business offering beauty treatments to locals, from her home. Take a bow, social media.

Like her friend Laura O'Brien, who's just moved to the area from Ireland, she too is a recovering alcoholic and has been dry for years. Having such a close mental and spiritual bond, the two have stayed in touch, despite the physical distance between them. She first met Laura at an A.A. meeting in Dublin and became Laura's sponsor – over 20 years ago.

Taking Alice's persistent advice, Laura made the difficult decision to relocate to Wickham. Whilst she's left Ireland behind her, she brings with her many happy memories of her short but happy marriage to one of the world's most successful horse breeders. When Frank died suddenly, leaving her to cope with the fallout – which included his two resentful and unpleasant children – she really struggled. They never approved of her from the word go, and have mercilessly tormented her ever since. It was only her remarkable inner strength and resolve that saw her through. That and the sure knowledge that her marriage to Frank was a genuinely good one.

Alice Kingston is now not only a neighbour but an entire support system for Laura.

Laura is currently renting and looking to buy a property nearby. The move from Ireland to Hampshire was a culture shock, to put it mildly. Not quite traumatic, but getting close.

Leaving your home country is no small step at any time, but when you're carrying the weight that Laura has been shouldering for what seems forever, it's a very big deal indeed.

She'd been living her life stumbling through each day in an alcoholic haze, in the mistaken belief that it would expunge all those bad thoughts hurtling around inside her head.

Luckily, in a moment of desperation she called Alice, a move that consequently enabled her to turn her life around, again. Alice was in close enough contact to help her break the cycle, and their frequent phone and video calls equipped her to slowly accept that, once again, she needed proper help.

Laura needed to drag herself back to some meetings and start the A.A. ball rolling again. She'd done it before, all those years ago – she could do it again and crucially, she wanted to do it again.

And so, at last, the healing process began.

Today, happily, Laura is living in a brand-new environment, off the bottle, in surprisingly good health, stable and ready to start thinking about her future again.

She's been introduced to Alice's circle of friends – a mixture of middle-class housewives, neighbours and others who share Alice's interest in things spiritual and facial.

Laura is out of the mire and ready to start anew. She has the means to do so and plans to put a good proportion of her immense wealth, to philanthropic use. They're just vague ideas at the moment but she's determined to see it through and put her money to good use.

Probably best not to share that with her baying stepchildren.

8

Ali is standing on the bench at the back of the control room at Key Studios, his arms windmilling like Pete Townshend at the Hollywood Bowl. His air guitar is taking a battering as they listen to the playback of his latest song, *In Paradise*, which is turning into an epic production with heavy guitar power chords and an orchestra – giving the song stadium rock status.

Heavy rock is just another facet of music that Ali loves to embrace when writing songs – nothing in the musical spectrum is off-limits.

Today, the air guitar has replaced the more sedate Sudoku puzzle, his usual aid to concentration. He makes no apology for his mathematical obsession, either. Music is all about beats per minute, time signatures and formulaic progressions, so it's all very logical and structured – mathematical, even if he doesn't fully understand *how* it all fits together.

'Nice job, mate. Sounding good, very happy with that. Let's have an ear break,' Ali says, looking up when the track finishes. He strokes his chin, as his thoughts return to the real world.

'I've fallen out with my dad again.'

'Oh dear, what happened?' asks Jim.

'In a nutshell, I told him where to put it! That I was quitting.'

'Blimey. And have you?'

'I'm not sure to be honest. I suppose I'll find out soon enough …'

'Are you OK? Do you want to talk about it?'

He looks up at Jim and re-focuses. 'Thanks, but no, I don't want to waste any more time on my bloody father. Let's finish this.

Much better idea. Hey, it's sounding good mate. Can we listen to your guitar solo again? Then I think we're done.'

'Almost ready to mix, dare I say,' says Jim. 'Ian's vocals are spot on. What are the plans for this one?'

'I thought it would be a great sync track for a TV drama.'

Jim presses the play button again.

'Yeh, it's got drama alright. Very passionate. Autobiographical by any chance?' says Jim, beaming and edging the volume up.

'This wouldn't sound out of place on the Pyramid stage at Glastonbury you know,' he yells, leaving the volume up and then slowly bringing the level down.

'How are things with you and Becks by the way?'

'Why do you ask? There isn't a *you and me* thing going on. Becks is a pal, that's all. Well, and a bit more,' he smiles.

'She's fab but she has her own dreams and I have mine. We respect each other but we don't love each other in a romantic way. Mind you, I wouldn't do anything to hurt that girl. She's very special.'

'Go on, play it again, give it another whirl. Let's hammer those speakers of yours!'

*

The roar of the hovercraft is deafening. Quite a sight for the uninitiated – as it hurtles up the shingle on Southsea beach. There's little wind but the giant engines at the rear of the craft create a whirlwind as the vessel finally sinks on its skirt and halts. The engine noise gradually subsides, and the ground crew gets ready to open the door to let the Isle of Wight passengers disembark.

The spectacle still excites Ali, even though he's seen it a hundred times. He's walking along the beach with his sister, Rani, who's visiting to try to patch things up; he complains about his father's lack of understanding and respect for what he does.

'I'm 35, almost 36, for God's sake. I want to make my own life but he's hell-bent on stopping me. He's a bastard. A nasty, vindictive man. For my entire life he's picked holes in me. Nothing, and I mean nothing, I do is right for him.'

'Oh Ali, I do know – he's very single-minded and stubborn. But he's not all bad, and he is our father.'

'You're kidding? Not bad? The other day we flattened yet another guy who'd taken on more than he could manage. And last week a woman and her kid in Southampton – we really roughed her up, Ran. It was pitiful and you could see she's struggling. Are you honestly telling me that's OK, because it's just business? It's so not. It's disgusting. And it's Dad's hand.'

'No I'm not. But I don't want you to end up in trouble – you know Dad well enough. He could cause you a lot of grief.'

'Oh yes, drag that up why don't you. Did he send you here to threaten me? 'Cos if he did, Ran, you can fuck off right now.'

'No! He didn't Ali – I came here because you're my brother. I love you and I don't want to see you get hurt.'

Rani steps closer. 'I want to help Ali, please let me. Think about what you're doing – because from where I stand, you'll end up hurting yourself more than him. What's the expression? Don't cut off your nose to spite your face? He's in one of his moods right now and I don't want to lose you, Ali – and neither do the others, I'm sure, particularly Mum. Do you really want to lose your family – completely, this time?'

'Of course not.'

'I totally understand that you hate the horrible work he makes you do, but now is not the time to be virtuous. Another thing, how much does it cost you to record all these songs of yours in the studio?'

'I know what you're going to say …'

'I bet it's a lot and I bet you can't finance it with your DJ earnings – without working for Dad.'

'Not fair, Ran. I work hard, gigging.'

'Enough to pay for your music recordings, the house, all the amenity bills and everything else that goes with your lifestyle? If you upset him and leave the business, he would cut you off in every way – where would that leave you? And then of course, on top of that, there's the other matter to consider …'

'The bastard – he's a total bastard,' splutters Ali, frustrated by reality.

'Think about it Ali – just play along with it. Play the long game. You can avoid a big showdown – and a potential family disaster – and carry on with your music. I'm just trying to keep the peace and our family together.'

Ali calms down and gives his sister a gentle hug. He doesn't like losing his temper – and rarely does. He's not so much angry with her – more frustrated about his predicament. How the hell is he going to break free once and for all? In the meantime, it would seem, he's totally stuffed, and will no doubt have to face his father – yet again, and carry out his dirty deeds with his cousins.

'Come on, let's go to Gunwharf for some caffeine. Jim and Becky are there – I want you to meet them,' says Ali.

The sun, which has been hiding behind the clouds for most of the day, now comes out – changing the mood on cue. The two siblings make their way along the prom, down Penny Street and into Old Portsmouth, the posh part, along to Gunwharf Quays and the imposing Spinnaker Tower.

It's bustling with activity, as usual. It's the South Coast's leading designer shopping outlet, comprising oh-so-tantalising top brands. Home to the well-heeled and to those who want to look well-heeled. It's also packed with eateries and cafés. It used to be a Royal Navy base, HMS Vernon, where minesweepers tied up. How times change.

The harbour is humming with marine activity, as usual. Jim and Becky are already enjoying their coffees, looking at the luxury yachts moored in the marina. After the introductions and debating the rights and wrongs of the super-rich and their lifestyle trappings, Ali steers the subject of conversation round to music.

'Sorry folks, I probably spend too much time in music forums. But come on, enough is enough. I'm so angry that the music industry has all but closed its doors on new talent and it would seem that no one can make a living out of song-writing nowadays – unless they're already successful. How can that be nurturing music?'

'I'm no expert on music as you know, but shouldn't all types of music be subsidised by the Government – pop and rock music, EDM … everything?' suggests Becky. 'They subsidise opera, ballet, classical music and the like, so why not pop music? It's art.'

'It wouldn't even scratch the surface, Becks – the money would just go to the chosen few! At the moment, the big stars get richer and richer and the new blood – people like us, are not welcome.'

'It could be argued that things are actually better than ever, because literally anyone can release a record – without the need for a record company,' Jim says.

Ali again disagrees. 'Do you know – over 60,000 tracks are uploaded to Spotify every day – probably many more – and 99.9% of those disappear without trace. Releasing songs and getting them streamed to a decent-sized audience, is pretty much a waste of time, especially if you're expecting to earn any money; and actually selling records is very unlikely. Call that progress?'

Becky chips in again. 'I hate to say this, all this talk of making money from music – shouldn't music be free anyway? It's a talent, not a bloody commodity.'

'That's ridiculous. It costs a lot of money to record quality music. Art costs money and it needs investment. The world only goes around because of money – didn't you do economics at school? Take away money and capitalism, and people would starve, and we'd be back in caves. It creates order.'

Jim tries to sum things up, 'Listen, I don't think we can do much about it can we? Let's just hope that someone will wake up and put things right someday soon and make the big boys pay musicians and songwriters properly, and let them earn a living. In the meantime, all we can do is enjoy what we do best, making that music.'

'And don't forget the other thing we do best,' adds Ali.

'We dream. Whatever we do, we must never stop dreaming.'

The station ident plays, Mandy Steele gives a time check and segues straight into *I Keep Walkin'* by Coolstar. Ali settles himself into the guest chair opposite the presenter and the two catch up, off-mic. It's Ali's second interview on Mandy's show.

Mandy loves her job in local radio, especially this show, where she gets to play and interview local musicians. She's a real supporter of local talent which is good news for bands and singers trying to get noticed. Radio audiences are dwindling but it's still a way to get your music heard – and you never know who might be listening in.

The studio red light comes on. 'That's *I Keep Walkin'* by Coolstar kicking off the second part of tonight's show,' says Mandy.

'I'm pleased to say that Ali Kurmi, the man behind Coolstar is with us again tonight. Hey Ali.'

'Good to be here,' says Ali.

'Another great track,' enthuses Mandy, 'and so different to the songs we played last time you were in ...'

'Thank you,' says Ali, his face lighting up, 'that's the whole idea – doing something completely different every time.'

'Who's singing this one? What a voice!'

'That's Liam. He's great isn't he? Sounds like he really means it when he sings.'

'So, is it a song about hobos and homeless folk?'

'It is about that, yeh – but it's also a song about determination, keeping going with whatever's in your mind. Not looking back, look ahead, keep walking.

'That's what I'm doing really, and it's hard,' he chuckles.

'It's tough out there for new bands and singers. Is it worth the effort do you think?'

Ali smiles his disarming smile. 'No offence, but I wouldn't be sitting here now if I didn't believe in possibilities and dreams, even if they seem unreachable. It's probably a bit of a cliché but I believe failure is an option – not a given. Failure only happens when you give up. And so far I have no plans to do that! I just keep walkin'!'

9

The sound system is deafening and the crowd at Ocean is starting to build up. Ali is gigging locally tonight. He likes Ocean because, although the pay's a bit of a joke, the club's just around the corner and the only equipment he needs to bring with him is a USB memory stick.

Ali is an experienced Events DJ and gets paid a lot of money – when the corporate gigs come in. His retro music is his USP – which means his gigs are a little thinner on the ground than if he were playing mainstream, so he's happy to keep the coffers topped up with smaller gigs like this one. Tonight it's EDM and the playlist is already sorted for him, so it's just a question of getting up there and doing his thing.

Ali's achieved mascot status with the regulars and with the staff. He heads for the bar which is already busy and noisy. Sarah is serving a group of two guys and three girls to her left. They're unfamiliar and she's looking at them curiously. They've obviously had a few drinks already and they're laughing and a touch unsteady on their feet. She watches them more closely as she prepares and serves their drinks. One of the guys particularly draws her attention. He looks cocky and occasionally stares back at her. It unsettles her. She really doesn't like him. She moves back to serve Ali and her face turns into a smile as she hands him his usual drink. Not to everyone's taste – pomegranate and lime soda, but he loves it. She has a soft spot for Ali. She's a good few years older than the rest of the bar staff but she's great fun, knows her cocktails, and Ali likes her a lot.

'Hi Ali, how are you?'

'Yeh, all good thanks. I don't know how you do it, Sarah,' he says looking to his right. 'Some people are so horrible when they get rat-arsed. Where do you find the patience?'

'I get paid Ali. It pays the rent.'

She pauses and looks back at the group of young men.

'They were playing games with me just now – got me really confused with their order. I'm sure they did it on purpose. Anyway, here's yours. I'll have another one waiting for you later.'

'Bunch of prats if you ask me. Cheers Sarah.'

Ali takes a sip and heads back towards the stage to begin his set. As soon as he starts, the floor instantly fills up and the lights start flashing and the music pumps even louder.

The suspect group is now sitting at the back and they keep looking towards the stage. Ali notices that one girl in particular seems familiar. He instinctively keeps his head down.

As the tunes follow one another seamlessly, he works his crowd and in no time, they're loving every minute. He knows his stuff. The lights are mesmerising and Ali's effects are working well with them. Another great Ali Kurmi show.

He keeps glancing over at the group – that girl could easily be a pissed-off tenant he's previously had to "have words with" – a hazard he's constantly paranoid about. Thank God she looks totally pissed.

The music plays on, the crowd is happy and slowly Ali starts to forget about the troublemakers and feels a lot better, in the moment – in his element.

But during the classic, Animals by Martin Garrix, Ali frowns and takes an unsteady step backwards. He ignores it, finds his balance again and places one side of his headphones to his right ear and listens. Not long afterwards he looks confused again and starts to shake his arms and hands to assist circulation.

Woah there, he wonders. What's *this*? He wobbles on his feet, feeling giddy and slightly nauseous, and very quickly notices that his knees are starting to give way.

What the fuck is happening here? Something is very wrong.

In just a few short moments, he's feeling so dizzy, that his knees completely go – and he collapses behind his console, gasping for breath.

'Help me, please', he splutters, hidden from view.

His breathing becomes difficult, and he starts to panic. His heart is pumping violently. The music seems to get louder, the lights flash faster – then comes dazzling white light. He squints, tightly screwing up his face.

And then, all of a sudden ... silence.

After that ... darkness.

10

Portsdown Hill sits immediately north of Portsmouth and on a clear day you can see – no, not forever – but you can certainly see for many miles. It's one hell of a sight.

Alice Kingston has been dying to show Laura the view.

'See what I mean?' she says excitedly. 'Smell that sea air – even up here. It's incredible. I still can't believe how awesome this is, and I've been here loads of times. Just look at it!'

She points to her left, 'Portsmouth looks so small, even the Spinnaker Tower – and Hayling Island. There's Gosport – and over there, beyond it, the Isle of Wight. To the right, you can just see Cowes, and Southampton Water, even. It's amazing – right up there as far as panoramic views go. What do you reckon?'

They gaze in silence for a few seconds, breathing slowly and deeply.

'We've got some pretty stunning coastlines back home on the west coast but this is very different. It's beautiful.'

'Have you ever been to Australia?' says Alice.

'I wish,' chuckles Laura.

'I have, just the once. We went to the Blue Mountains and the Three Sisters rocks. That has to be right up there too, as far as awesome vistas go. I don't see how you can fail to be moved by it. It actually made me cry. How can something as massive as that just be a natural fluke?' she says. 'Trust me, we are just part of a much, much bigger picture.'

'It certainly makes you think, doesn't it? I'm not religious, as you know, but there sure is some clever stuff going on around us all, and that's way beyond my understanding.'

They walk slowly along the pathway and the conversation turns to more material matters. Laura has explained to Alice that, already very rich, she stands to inherit the remainder of her late husband's fortune in 12 months' time – and it's likely to be a very large amount of money. Consequently, she's been considering ways of putting the money to good use. She particularly wants to give something back to the wider community as a way of thanking Alcoholics Anonymous.

'I do genuinely believe in being kind to people. Being horrible doesn't get you anywhere in the long run. I've learned that for sure. That's why I'm still thinking along the lines of a support centre for abused men and women.'

'That's an interesting choice – why not alcohol abuse? Wouldn't that a bit closer to home?' says Alice.

'I did think about it, but there's quite a bit of support already in place, isn't there?' says Laura. 'It's why I'm looking at abuse. Most people tend to think it's just women who suffer but there's newer evidence that indicates that it affects all genders.'

'So I understand, sadly. It's a great idea – but how hard would it be, to get that off the ground?'

'Very hard I'm sure. I know it's a lot to consider, but it's something I'm definitely going to take a closer look at. I can't just sit around with all that money in the bank. I couldn't live with myself.'

'You're a good woman, Laura O'Brien. I admire you; I really do. A woman who's been through the mill and come out the other end, much stronger and more independent. Good on you.'

A dog walker passes by, with a miniature dachshund trailing behind her. Laura and Alice smile.

'Don't you just love those dogs? They're so intelligent.'

'And very naughty,' the passer-by adds, with a grin.

'Now, are you doing anything next Saturday evening?' asks Alice, abruptly changing the subject.

'I don't think so, why?'

'I've told you about Finn O'Donnell, haven't I?'

'Remind me.'

'You'll love him – he's in events – and his wife, Samantha, is a client of mine. They live up the road, at Soberton. Quite a place. They're having a party next week and Sam wondered whether you'd like to come too. I told her a little bit about you. I hope you don't mind.'

'That's very sweet of her. Will there be a lot of people there? I'm not too good with crowds just yet.'

'I don't know for sure, but I seriously doubt it – they're so nice. You must come.'

'Remind me, what does he do?'

Alice explains that Finn O'Donnell is an organiser of corporate events and team-building exercises. He's ex-Royal Navy, a Commander before retiring, self-assured, hearty and friendly, with a dry, quick and very cheeky sense of humour.

'He's a good man and I dunno, I just have a strong feeling that you should meet him.'

They turn away from the Solent view and get back into Alice's car.

'He sounds interesting – I'd love to come,' says Laura. 'It'll be good to meet new people.'

'Good decision. You never know, you might even meet the man of your dreams there!'

Laura, horrified, turns to face Alice.

'If you think I'm going to put myself through any more emotional carnage, you must be mad Alice Kingston. I've had my fill of men. They always leave me in the end – one way or another.'

11

Ali blinks, slowly opening his eyes, and is blinded by the brightness. He shields them with his right hand, squints and mumbles.

'Lights ... turn them off ... please, the lights are blinding me.'

The sound system is still pumping out music and Ali recoils at the physical pain of the thudding bass.

'Is there anything we can do about those lights and the sound?' says the paramedic, leaning over Ali, who is flat out on the floor, still behind the DJ console, and now dribbling.

The paramedic dabs Ali's mouth, at the same time holding Ali's wrist with his other hand.

'Already across it,' says Dom, the club manager. 'We're clearing the hall right now.'

The paramedic speaks slowly and clearly, 'The ambulance should be here any time now, sir. Can you tell me your name please?'

'Ali Kurmi. What ... what's happened?'

'OK Ali, you're in safe hands; there's nothing to worry about. But we need to get you to hospital to get you checked over. Can you see my fingers OK? How many are there?'

'Yes I can, three.'

'That's good, how much alcohol have you had Ali?'

'None. I don't drink.'

'Are you taking any prescription drugs?

'No! What's happening?'

'I'm just going to move you now Ali. Tell me if anything is hurting.'

Dom turns to his colleague, Rob. 'Take a bow – Ali owes you Rob. Without you, no one would have known it had happened.'

'I saw him go down,' says Rob. 'I was collecting glasses and he just went, dropped like a sack. I dialled 999 straightaway, then called you.'

'Good on you mate. You did the right thing.'

*

'You had us worried there, I thought I'd lost my best DJ.'

'Yeh, very funny,' says Ali lying in Ward E5 at the Queen Alexandra Hospital, struggling to get his words out, from an extremely dry mouth.

'Pass the water can you. I'm parched.'

'Sure, there you go, how's that?'

'Thanks Dom. What the fuck happened?'

Ali is slowly coming round after a long sleep. He's been joined at his bedside by Becky and Dom. They've been told by the nursing staff that he's ingested ketamine – but that he's recovered amazingly well.

'We're not a hundred per cent sure but it looks like someone spiked your drink. I'm sorry mate but the police want to have a word when you're feeling up to it. It's kind of out of my hands. Rob and I have already given statements. Can you remember anything that happened mate?'

'Yeh, and I've got a bloody good idea who it might have been. Bastards. But for Christ's sake, I don't want the police involved.'

'I don't think you've got a choice, mate.'

'Has anyone contacted my parents?'

'No, we haven't got their numbers – do you want us to call? We thought about looking on your phone, but of course we can't get in,' says Becky.

'NO! For God's sake, no. Don't do that. That'll be just what my dad wants to hear. No, definitely not.'

'The police have already taken our CCTV drives so let's hope they get the bastards,' says Dom.

Ali begins to process his confused thoughts. Damage limitation is required here, that's for sure, as he knows only too well that this would only fuel his father's arguments against his DJ work. And if he's right and that crazy group of twats did spike his drink out of revenge, it could open up a huge can of worms. If the police start digging, it will bring the work for his father out into the open, and things could get very awkward indeed for everyone, particularly Ali.

He's definitely going to have to play the whole thing down.

What he doesn't know, lying there in bed, feeling sorry for himself, is that he's not in as much control of events as he'd like to think. Far from it. And it's not just this current club incident. His whole life is about to change in the most profound way – and whether he approves or not, there's absolutely nothing he can do about it.

12

'Laura, how good of you to come. I'm so pleased you could make it. Come in - welcome aboard!' says Finn O'Donnell, nodding gently and stepping back to let her in.

'How do you do,' says Laura, with a wide smile.

They move into the large living room, where groups of guests are engaged in lively conversations. For a barely perceptible moment, the room quietens – and all eyes follow Laura, as she and Finn cross the room to the window.

'I understand you've not long moved from Ireland?'

'That's right. Blame Alice, she bullied me into coming!'

'I'm pleased she did,' Finn smiles. 'We like Alice. Good sort. I believe she's in the kitchen with Samantha. Anyway, how are you settling in – how do you like the area?'

'It's lovely from what I've seen so far – I'm looking forward to exploring.'

'We're very lucky round here – it's got everything, in my humble opinion – and there's the coast nearby. And London, if you need it, is only a hop, skip and a jump away. Oh, and the locals are very friendly too!' he says, indicating with his arm and looking around the room.

Laura smiles again. 'Your name - O'Donnell, that's a good old Irish name.'

'It certainly is. Donegal is where it all started I think. But I'm afraid I let the clan down a bit, joining the Navy. O'Donnells tended to be soldiers.'

Finn cuts an imposing figure – tall and upright in stance, as you'd expect from an ex-Royal Navy officer, and impeccably presented. He commands respect and attention – qualities earned from treating others in exactly the same way. Amongst his many duties in the RN, he was responsible for organising a range of events – on several occasions, functions involving members of the Royal Family. Moving into corporate events was a natural progression when he left the Navy, and his business is a great success.

He's sharp and he knows his business inside out. Which is presumably why he lives in a very large country house, in one of the most expensive areas of Hampshire.

He and his wife Samantha have invited Laura to their drinks party after hearing about her from their mutual friend, Alice Kingston. Alice explained that she was trying to help her bereaved friend settle in the area and the O'Donnell's immediately suggested inviting Laura to their do.

'Sam, my wife, has given me a bit of a briefing, hope you don't mind. Can I say how sorry I was to hear about your husband? It must have been a terrible shock for you.'

'That's very kind of you, I'm much better now thanks. It's actually been a while,' says Laura, prepared for such a comment.

'You're renting I believe?'

'Yes, for the moment. I'm looking around for somewhere permanent.'

'Hello Laura,' Finn's wife, Samantha, joins them, with Alice trailing. 'I'm so pleased you've come. I hope you're settling into your new home.'

'I am, I was just telling Finn, I'm looking for somewhere to settle.'

'Horse breeding, wasn't it?' says Finn, raising an eyebrow.

'It was indeed, but that was really my husband Frank's world. We were only married for four years, so I suppose I was only a spectator, a novice.'

'So what's happened to that – are you still running the business?'

'Not exactly, Frank's manager is running it with a trust – for the next year or so, and then it's hopefully going to be sold. It's all got to be sorted out.'

'Sounds like you had a wonderful life in … Tipperary, wasn't it?' says Samantha.

'It was wonderful, even if it didn't last as long as I'd expected. But that's the tough old world we live in, isn't it? It can be very cruel. But I am grateful for the time we had together and I try to focus on that.'

'How did you meet your husband – if you don't mind me asking?' says Finn.

'I met him on an assignment. I was a journalist. We met and we just clicked. It was very sudden and unexpected for both of us. But it really worked until ...'

Finn kindly interrupts, 'Alice here, has hinted that you might be looking for something to keep you occupied, yes? I haven't got any call for a journalist, or anything full time, but I could do with somebody I can rely on with a bit of maturity and authority, from time to time. What do you think?'

'Gosh, I'm not sure about the authority part, I'm sure.'

'Tell me more about your time as a journalist.'

'I worked for the News, in Dublin, for years on and off – and in the end, I worked as a freelance.'

'Yes, I know the News,' says Finn, admiringly. 'Good paper.'

'I covered everything in my time there, as you do on such papers. From dog fouling in public spaces to international politics! I think I had the best of it, though. Lord knows what's going to happen to papers like that, now everything's online.'

'Love it, myself. Online stuff, computers, iPads and all that - I've even got ear buds.'

'A lot of people don't. Especially more mature folk,' says Laura.

'Well, I made a decision some years ago to embrace it – not fight it,' says Finn. 'Now I actually find it quite fun – there's an app for everything, isn't there? And my phone is my office!'

'I agree,' says Laura. 'As long as you don't let it take you over, it's a great thing. But I do feel sorry for young people who've known nothing else. They're totally consumed by it all.'

Laura looks for somewhere to put her empty glass. 'Anyway, what about you?' Tell me about your business. What do you actually do?'

Finn enthusiastically explains how it was a natural transition from Royal Navy to Civvy Street, setting up his events business that he runs from home. Calling on a wide group of experienced professionals to assist, he's able to stage a variety of functions: corporate business gatherings, large-scale weddings, exhibitions and, increasingly, bread-and-butter team building weekends – on-sea, on-land, on-anywhere. Up a mountain if necessary. You name it, Finn can arrange it.

'Luckily, I'm not too shabby in the planning department,' he says, 'thanks to the Navy. But more to the point, I love it. That's the secret. If you love what you do, the chances are you'll do OK. Well, it's worked for me anyway.

'Listen, going back to what we were talking about earlier, I don't know if all this will interest you but I'm looking for someone to act as a sort of liaison officer – a posh term for meeter and greeter, I suppose. I can't be in every place at every moment, when we put on of these events, and I could do with another pair of hands to look after clients and contributors. Would you consider helping out? Or at least give it a try?'

'I'm very flattered, I'm sure,' says Laura. 'Can I have a little think about it?'

'Yes of course. You must. Just to let you know – next month we have a large event up the road at Alresford. Watercress country. Do you know it? Steam trains, Watercress Line and all that? It's a private party for a lovely couple who want a very special 'do' for their 40th wedding anniversary. They've ordered the full works. All in their grounds, open air – weather permitting – huge marquee, hundreds of guests, side shows, go-karting, balloon rides, live band and a top DJ. Big job and no expense spared.'

'Sounds impressive,' says Laura, as they turn and go back to the party inside.

What a nice man, she thinks. No sides, no hang-ups, no issues, just plain polite and courteous.

Just like Frank.

13

Eighteen months ago

Laura is frantically banging on the bathroom door.

'Frank! Frank are you in there? Frank! Please.' She continues hammering with her fists at the solid oak door. No response.

'For God's sake Frank, please open the door, I'm scared.'

Half an hour later, although it seems a lot longer, the fire service and an ambulance arrive. They get a quick summary of the situation from a panic-stricken Laura.

'He's in there. He won't come out. He's not answering. Please can you do something?'

One of the men asks for Frank's name and bangs firmly on the door. 'Mr O'Brien – are you in there? Could you open the door, Mr O'Brien?'

'OK Ma'am, I'm afraid we're going to have break the door down. Please stand right back and put these on.'

The other fireman hands her a pair of goggles. It takes a whole minute for them to beat that mighty door until it slightly opens. They find Frank O'Brien half-dressed, lying on the floor. The paramedic is straight in and administers an IV. He's checking for signs of a heart attack or a stroke.

Laura looks on in horror at the scene inside the bathroom.

The paramedic says, 'Sorry Ma'am, please, move out of the way. We must get him to hospital as soon as possible. Mind out please.'

Housekeeper Mary arrives at the scene, looking bewildered. 'What in heaven's name is happening here?' she asks. 'I only popped out to the shops.'

The ambulance crew is now wheeling Frank O'Brien out of the house. The firemen gather their tools and make an attempt to tidy the pieces of splintered door.

Frank O'Brien is unconscious but breathing when he reaches the General but the outlook is grim. After an initial assessment, he is taken down for a scan and then put in Intensive Care. When the results come back, they reveal a massive bleed on the brain caused by an aneurysm that they inform a stunned Laura, is inoperable.

Frank O'Brien, one of Ireland's true racing greats, died later that day.

The next morning, back at the house, Laura is still numb from shock. The tears have yet to arrive. She is having trouble taking in the fact that she's lost her husband of just four years. Mary is being as attentive as ever, and doing her best to chivvy her along. But what do you say to console a woman who's lost her beloved husband in such a sudden and ruthless way?

Frank's children, Stephanie and Richard, are both prowling around the house. Richard appears genuinely shaken but Stephanie looks her usual composed, coiffed, cold, calculating self – devoid of any human emotion.

'Where the fuck was security – where was Bill?' she growls.

'It was his day off, apparently,' says Richard.

'You're kidding me. All that fecking money we pay for security and the man isn't here the one time he's actually needed. How ridiculous,' she spits.

Stephanie is full of anger-fired bravado, but the events of the past 24 hours have shaken her to the core, and although she'd never admit it, she's really struggling. Her part of the cosmos has just been shattered into tiny pieces and she hates the feeling of being out of control. Her brain is awash with the full implications of her daddy's death. Not least his money.

Richard announces that he will deal with registering the death and after finishing a coffee, leaves.

Stephanie just sits in the drawing room staring out of the window.

It's difficult to know what could be going through her mind at this moment but it's likely to be something vitriolic.

She hasn't even spoken to Laura yet and she probably won't.

14

Ali, Kamran and Hammed are travelling down the motorway heading for Southampton – to visit another rent defaulter. Ali is sitting in the back of the car, silent, muted by the shame of going back on his own words – of vowing never to do this again. He hasn't spoken directly to his father since walking out of the family meal. He thought he'd had the upper hand at the time – but things seem to have slipped back to normal.

Ham is at the wheel, dressed in his signature leather jacket, silk scarf and shades – Kam, in T-shirt and Everlane shorts – always shorts. Ali is grateful that Ham isn't once again verbalising his hatred of anything Tory or Liberal. Ham hates people who represent anything right of left, politically. He's a very angry socialist and rants frequently on social media. It doesn't take much to trigger his political beliefs into a diatribe and these car journeys are often his opportunities to spout. However, the subject of conversation in the front is lighter today – appraisals on the current forms of Man City and Arsenal. Ham and Kam tease each other about their chosen teams but rarely bother to involve Ali in any form of conversation – and that suits him fine. They don't have much in common anyway. Ali isn't a sports fan. Sure, he has an interest in the big events like the Olympics or the World Cup – and has even been known to watch the FA Cup final, especially if it's a David and Goliath scenario. But generally speaking, he can take it or leave it.

However, he is fanatical about writing music and it's never far from his mind. Ham and Kam wouldn't even begin to understand, so he doesn't bother to share. They live in their world and he lives in his.

Today, they're heading for a place called Shirley in Southampton where many of the houses have been turned over to multiple occupancy student accommodation. Javed Kurmi has many properties in the area and they form a significant proportion of his portfolio.

Rent payments are well monitored by the Kurmis at their HQ in Kent. The system is conducted online via standing orders – but far too often, these payments don't happen and that's when Ham or Kam is charged with the task of 'persuading' the defaulter to pay up. If said defaulter persists, Ham and Kam, along with cuz Ali, will visit personally. Things can – and very often do – get very nasty.

In a change of strategy, instigated by his father, Ali has now been reassigned to playing good cop, while Ham and Kam play bad. Whatever, it'll probably still involve some form of violence. It sickens Ali and it looks like it's about to happen all over again.

Kam starts to hand-roll another cigarette. Ali watches his cousin from behind.

'Do you have to?'

Kam turns and sneers – jabbing at the window button. It drops a couple of centimetres.

'Wonderful,' says Ali.

'You and your dad OK now?' asks Hammed.

'What do you mean?' says Ali, defensively.

'We heard about the big showdown at the lunch.'

'You told him where to shove it, then,' says Kam, sarcastically.

'It's not funny. You guys know well enough, that I've had it up to here, with all this. I just want to do my music. This stuff – I'm not even any good at it, so what's the point?'

'Yeh, yeh, yeh,' says Ham. 'And you're still here.'

'I know,' says Ali.

'Don't worry, cuz. Change of plan today. You play the nice guy – then we step in and … bam!'

'You guys really are total shit. '

'Hey cuz.'

'I don't know why you play along with him.'

'He pays the wages,' says Ham.

'Seriously, Ham, how long are you going to carry on doing this – hurting people? How do you deal with it?'

'I have my plans, you'll hear about it when I'm good and ready,' replies his cousin, dismissively.

'Oh yeh? And Kam, what does your good lady think about what you do? I bet she doesn't even know.'

Kam turns his head suddenly and glares at Ali.

'You leave her out of this or I'll fucking …'

'You'll what, Kam?' Ali interrupts. 'You'll beat the fuck out of me too?'

Ali, flops back into his seat, sighs deeply and checks his phone. He mournfully looks out of the car window, as they drive down Shirley High Street.

He shakes his head and notices that everyone looks bloody miserable today – it must be in the air. How the hell has he allowed himself to be bullied into this pit of complete and utter stinking shit?

15

Max and Christine Walsh were married in 1982 and to celebrate their milestone ruby wedding anniversary they've decided to go the whole hog and throw one of the biggest parties seen in Alresford for many a year.

Status in these parts tends to be based on the number of watercress beds you have – rather than Range Rovers.

So here we are on party day. The contractors have finished preparing for the main event and the stage is set. The grounds are alive and buzzing with people going about their different tasks.

It's a lavish display of opulence – all stage-managed by Finn O'Donnell and his team. Finn has been joined today by new recruit, Laura, who has been briefed by him to look after the entertainers and their various entourages.

Her presence hasn't gone unnoticed. Wherever she moves, heads turn and follow her. She carries a strong air of confidence, whilst maintaining an element of vulnerability. It makes the combination irresistible.

'Are you OK for the band and DJ?' says Finn, on the phone.

'Yes, all good – I've spoken to the band and I've left a voicemail for the DJ; they all know where to come and I've told them to text me when they get here,' she says.

'Splendid. Tell you what, come over to the catering tent when you're ready. You can't work on an empty stomach. See you in a bit.'

Finn is a happy man when things run smoothly and today is looking good. He and the Walshes decided on Thursday, to run with Plan A for the party. Plan B was to be put in place in the event of rain. Today, the gods are smiling down and it's non-stop sunshine, and it's a very pleasant outlook for the party, which gets under way at 4 o'clock.

Guests will be welcomed with champagne; and for those feeling adventurous, there's Karting, Bubble Walking on Water, Archery and a Micro Fun Fair for the youngsters and oldsters. Circus performers will be walking around mingling with the guests, too.

After a lavish dinner inside the main marquee, the music will begin – there's a disco with a Top DJ and a live band to keep the show rocking and rolling until midnight. Even the Walshes think that's probably late enough to be disturbing the residents of Alresford and beyond.

They have been very specific about the music for the event and the theme is 70s and 80s – not just disco and soul but also music by some of the greatest rock bands: Genesis, Pink Floyd, The Who, The Stones, The Foo Fighters, and others. The Walshes are big music fans and used to go to all the main festivals. They like nothing more than a bit of "Glasto".

Finn knows his job and he's booked Ali Kurmi for the DJ gig.

Ali has a great reputation and, hey presto, he specialises in this very kind of music. So, he'll be providing the background music throughout – as well as putting on his special show later in the evening. The live music will be from Brother Soul – a band that loves to party and has a big following for live gigs. Ali has worked with the band many times before and he's persuaded them to play one of his numbers tonight.

So, let the party and the show commence.

Ali follows the directions in the text message and parks his van on the grass behind the main marquee in the fenced-off area, where all the service vans are parked. There's a mini marquee too, which has been set aside for the band and Ali. A further large one, obviously for the catering, is to the rear and connected to the main marquee. Outside, a young man in chef's whites with bright copper coloured hair, shaved at the sides, slouches against a tent prop as he squeezes the filter of his cigarette. He inhales and slowly blows out a cloud of smoke as he turns to take in and wonder at the grounds and house.

The side of the main house is visible, and it would appear to be neo-Georgian in style. From where Ali's standing it looks as though it's been built with exceptionally good taste; *no tack here*, he thinks.

He looks back at his van, glad that he doesn't have the whole rig to carry in, and is looking forward to the gig immensely.

The great thing about corporate work is that you seldom get any aggro. The worst that can happen, usually, is dealing with a few posh drunks. Anyway, he looks at his phone again. He needs to find a woman called Laura O'Brien.

Laura steps out of a door to the side of the main house, where Finn O'Donnell and his team have their modest quarters. The sun is high in the sky and the grounds look incredible. She's just had a text from the DJ to say that he's arrived, and she's off to meet him in the service car park.

Ali waits patiently by his van and does a 180-degree pan, looking out for the woman he's just texted. Towards the house he sees someone moving and heading in his direction.

It's definitely a lady. My God, it's certainly a lady. She's dressed in tight, light blue jeans and a white, red-trimmed jacket, with short sleeves. She's coming towards him and the closer she gets, the harder he stares. This lady is gliding across the grass and Ali is transfixed by the sheer presence and elegance of her movement.

He can see that she's considerably older than him, but is completely bowled over by her looming beauty.

Wow – what an amazing figure! She is advancing, beaming with the biggest and loveliest smile Ali has seen in his whole life. And, beautiful penetrating eyes. Another wow.

This woman must have a very happy partner.

'Ali, is it?' says Laura, still smiling and holding out her hand.

Ali nervously wipes his right hand behind his back and offers it to Laura, immediately realising the naffness.

'Pleased to meet you,' he bumbles, in awe.

Still smiling, Laura says, 'Follow me and I'll take you to Finn. You two know each other quite well I understand?'

'Yes, we've worked together before.'

'Oh that's good. Have you eaten by the way?'

'Yes thanks,' says Ali, who is actually starving, having skipped breakfast.

'Let's go this way. Here's my card, with my number if you need it and I'm not around. Just give me a shout.'

Ali clutches his man-bag and follows Laura, admiring her from behind.

What the hell is happening here? This woman is gor-geous.

They step inside the house, eyes adjusting to the change in light, and walk down to Finn's 'Ops room' door.

16

Richard O'Brien and his sister Stephanie are sitting in their solicitor's office, sipping cups of tepid instant coffee. They've already explored all avenues with their father's accountant Seán Ryan, to no avail. They're desperate and they need legal advice about their father's estate.

Frank O'Brien had made provision for his business, worth billions, to be run by a group of trustees for two years, and then sold by auction. The profits would be shared equally between his widow, Laura, and them: 50% to Laura and 50% to Stephanie and Richard. They are, to put it mildly, indignant about what they see as an unfair split.

They never liked Laura O'Brien from the time she was introduced to them by their father, resentful that she sneaked into their lives, stealing what they see as their rightful inheritance.

In their eyes, she's nothing but an opportunistic gold digger who has already pocketed millions that she doesn't deserve. And there's even more, a lot more to come.

What they didn't know, was that Frank O'Brien had never forgiven them for their hostile attitude to Laura and had even considered removing them from his will.

Alas, it's not good news for them, as solicitor Kellie Gibson explains.

'There are four ways to challenge a Will under Irish law: first, the Will is invalid; second, the testator was placed under undue influence; third, proper financial provision has not been made; and fourth, prior agreements have not been met what is known as "estoppel". Having looked at your father's Will, I'm afraid I can't see anything worthy of a challenge. He was very thorough. I can see that very clearly.'

'But surely, there has to be a way. I won't let this happen. Laura O'Brien is nothing but a bitch and a cheat. She can't possibly inherit after only four years of marriage,' retorts Stephanie, slowly realising how desperate she sounds.

'I'm sorry, Ms O'Brien. I don't think there's anything you can do.'

Devout Catholic, Stephanie O'Brien at 38, is slightly younger than her brother, Richard. She married another O'Brien, much to everyone's amusement. Still, it saved her a lot of hassle not having to change her name.

She's a tall, striking woman who mastered the art of turning men's heads, many years ago – more often than not taunting, teasing and snubbing admirers on approach. She knows how to work men and gets whatever she wants – and that includes her long-suffering her husband, Séan. How or why he agreed to marry her is a mystery to many.

She carries herself with a slight limp, the result of a childhood illness but she's never considered it a disadvantage ¬– on the contrary, she views it as a way of gaining more attention.

Stephanie O'Brien doesn't do weakness, full stop. She pays great attention to her appearance, from her eyelashes to her toenails – and everything in between. Her beautiful face, high cheekbones and a perfect set of white teeth disguise her true unfriendly and bitter persona.

She may not win any popularity stakes but she's a certainly a successful businesswoman. She owns and runs several popular bars in County Tipperary and is a tough operator. She's driven, ambitious and heartless – which goes a long way to explaining why she is such a loner.

She showed no interest whatsoever in her father's passion for horses and horse breeding when he was alive. Now he's dead, she's suddenly become very interested indeed.

When he announced his marriage to Laura, she was horrified and set about undermining Laura in any way she could. She made Laura's life very difficult and it prompted many stand-up rows with her father. Their relationship had always been difficult but Frank's beautiful new fiancée brought it to a new low. She was like a crazy dog with a rag. She wouldn't let go.

So determined was she to hurt her stepmother that, out of sheer spite, she hired a private investigator to dig for dirt. He found out about Laura's infertility, about her drink dependency and AA – and about her mentor, another alky, Alice Kingston. She'd hoped for more – but at least it was something to work with. She'd never heard any mention of drink problems from her father – so gambling on the likelihood that Laura had kept quiet about it, she planned to confront her father with the evidence.

Unfortunately for her, she left it too late and missed the opportunity. After her father's sudden death, she was spitting broken glass at the thought of losing anything that belonged to him or her mother, let alone sharing any of her father's multi-billion-Euro business.

Brother Richard, by comparison, is a pretty weak and inconsequential character. At 40 years of age he's a bit of a spineless toady and, like his sister, he has no interest in horses. But he is obsessed with money and the more he can get, the better. He's a lazy man and was only able make a good start in business thanks to his father's generosity. He's become a wealthy man as a result. He too is married and childless. He spends much of his time keeping in with the local council and playing golf with other local influential businessmen and women.

The pair of them, mainly fired by Stephanie, are completely toxic.

17

Brother Soul are busy setting up their equipment on the stage when Ali returns from the house. Greetings are exchanged and it's confirmed that tonight the band will be playing one of Ali's songs called *Alright*. Ali takes some photos. He's excited about this, as most of his creative work is done in the insulated world of the studio. But tonight, he gets to see and hear how one of his songs sounds played to a live audience.

At four o'clock the party gets under way and guests start to arrive. Ali has the music pumping out at a gentle level all around the grounds. He's put a lot of time and energy into compiling the Walshes' playlists.

The partygoers are a real mixture; young and old, some very young. Some have partied at the Walshes before but many haven't and they are going to have one hell of a good time with everything that's being laid on for them. Real Go-Karting, water games, a fun casino with a burlesque croupier; a mini fun fair and a whole lot more – it's all there to be enjoyed. And the champagne, the real stuff, is flowing.

Whilst Ali's pre-prepared playlist can be heard all over the site, he takes a walk and finds himself smiling at almost every turn. There's such a lot going on. It's clearly a feat of organisation and he has to take his hat off to the retired Commander. He's done a brilliant job.

He's standing by the mini fun fair watching the penalty shoot outs, and for a moment he's tempted to have a kick, but his thoughts are interrupted.

'Hi, how are you doing, Ali? Go on, back of the net!' comes a voice.

It's Laura.

He looks at her again, eyes widening, butterflies fluttering, struggling to comprehend just how beautiful he finds her. He's never looked at an older woman before – well not in that way. But this woman has him spellbound. Once again, he checks himself, sure in the knowledge that she must be happily partnered or probably married – and WELL out of his league.

'I probably won't,' he grins. 'I don't want to show them up! I'm not really a footballer. I'm happier on a rowing machine in the gym to be honest.'

'I can see that,' says Laura, cheekily.

'Anyway, I suppose I should be getting back to my humble console.'

'I'll come with you. I'm going that way too.'

As they head towards the main marquee area, they're stopped in their tracks by two very tall, imposing and fabulously made-up circus clowns, in full costume. They look incredible in the blazing sunshine. However, for just one eerie moment they look sinister, as clowns can.

Before Ali has time to react, his face is suddenly dripping with something cold, wet and very sticky. The bastard clown has shoved a whole ice cream cornet in his face. Ali staggers backwards in shock, covered in goo.

Laura is stooping, holding her knees. She is crying – no, howling with laughter. She slaps her thighs and looks up at Ali.

'I'm SO sorry. I shouldn't laugh but you look SO funny. You should see yourself.' She carries on laughing. A small crowd gathers, much to Ali's dismay.

'I should see myself?' he says, so not amused by what has just happened.

But in a matter of moments he realises that he too is beginning to smile, as he attempts to wipe the slime from his face. His tongue can't resist sampling the cold, sweet confection. Laura's hysterics are so infectious that Ali starts to laugh out loud too.

For a brief moment, he is almost overwhelmed. He feels blood rushing to his face and he knows he's going to blush.

'Come on let's get you cleaned up,' says Laura, and they head off towards the house.

He obviously can't count them up, but Ali reckons there are probably a good 400 people at the Walshes' party, and he wonders what it must be like, to be able to afford putting on something like this. He's behind his console, coming to the end of his first set, and he has the partygoers in the palm of his hand. They're just loving the music – all those great tracks, masterfully mixed and blended by Ali. He takes more photos of the crowd. He's pretty good at spotting good shots and there are plenty here that'll soon find their way on to Instagram and Facebook.

Then it's time for the live music and Ali introduces Brother Soul to a huge cheer from the crowd. The band launch into their opening number which is a frantically-paced medley of classic songs given their soul treatment. The brass section hammers out the riffs from *Hold on I'm Coming, Gimme Some Lovin', Time Is Tight* and *Little Sister.* The crowd is going crazy – they're ready for this and the band doesn't disappoint.

Then comes Ali's big moment – his song, *Alright.* Thankfully there are no introductions – the band simply play the song and the audience keeps on dancing. *Yes! Yes,* thinks Ali. *I like this. I like this a lot.*

A drunken woman is standing in front of the stage, shouting up at Ali, still behind his console. He can't possibly hear what she's saying, so he just smiles back. She's looking very wobbly and sure enough, down she goes. Ali can't stop himself laughing at the ungainly tangle of limbs. Up she gets and carries on wobbling. She continues to beckon to Ali but is soon pulled away by some friends. All good fun and no harm done. The dancing continues and the hits keep coming.

It's been a great evening and the whole event has been a massive success. Ali's now winding the crowd up for the grand finale. But he's also scanning the marquee for signs of that amazing lady, Laura. He can't get her out of his mind but, unfortunately, she's nowhere to be seen. Never mind, he must pull himself together and concentrate on the job he's being paid a great deal of money to do.

The atmosphere is fantastic and the Walshes have joined the crowd for the last few numbers. From the look on their faces, they're also having a great evening. Ali finally gets the cue to start the fireworks music. It's a perfect clear night – but not for long, because the display commences and the sky lights up in technicolour. The music blasts out all the usual fireworks favourites, *Carmina Burana, Star Wars, Ode to Joy, We Will Rock You.*

Ali looks around at the party-goers, still led by their hosts, the Walshes, all enjoying the spectacle and, just as he's about to give up all hope of seeing her again, there she is.

Laura is walking towards the display from the house and is heading towards him.

18

Ten months ago

She's sitting in her garden, shaded by a large parasol on the patio; it's noon. The gentle sound of the fountain in the background adds a soothing accompaniment to the stillness. It's ironic that the weather is so beautiful at a time when Laura's world has been obliterated. She sips gently from her Pinot Grigio and it's not her first of the day. Not by a long chalk.

Housekeeper, Mary, is watching her through the living room windows. She too has had to grieve the loss of her employer but she's of the generation of folk who keep their thoughts and feelings to themselves. However, her heart bleeds for Laura. She's finding life difficult at the moment, trying to run the house when there's such a bad atmosphere. Not from Laura – but from Frank's two children, Stephanie and Richard.

Richard's not so bad but Stephanie is off the scale.

Mary remembers how different she was, as a young woman, when she first came to work for the O'Briens. Something happened, that's for sure, because somewhere along the line, Stephanie turned into a monster, albeit a beautiful one. Mary thinks it was likely to be the death of her mother that kicked it off, or possibly it was something more deep-seated. Whatever the trigger – now, she's lost her father too – and sad as that is, it's no excuse for being so beastly to everyone, especially Laura.

'Is there anything you want?' Mary asks,' stepping into the sunshine. 'Can I get you some lunch?'

'No thanks, Mary; I'm not in the mood.'

Mary knows that it's pointless trying to talk Laura round. It's been the same every day since the funeral. Laura has slowly descended into an alcoholic quagmire that only she can claw herself out of.

She slurs, 'Mary, don't worry yourself about me, I'm doing OK – I just need to be on my own.'

Mary knows that in just a couple of hours Laura will be asleep, anaesthetised by the white grape – only to wake up a couple of hours later and head for a refill and start all over again. An endless, crazy cycle of nothingness.

At 4 o'clock she knocks gently on Laura's bedroom door to announce that Stephanie has arrived and is asking after her.

'Oh Lord,' says Laura, 'not again. Where is she?'

'In the kitchen,' says Mary. 'Can't you hear her? She's grinding coffee beans.'

'That bloody woman,' mutters Laura, pulling the duvet away from her face. She steps out of bed, still fully clothed and walks over to the dressing table and tentatively looks in the mirror. She doesn't like what she sees.

'What does she want now? Can't she just leave me alone?'

As Laura walks unsteadily into the kitchen, Stephanie looks up.

'Just look at you. You should be ashamed of yourself. Have you no respect?' she snaps.

'Respect?' mumbles Laura thinking that, no, she hasn't actually, not for herself – or Stephanie.

'For the dead. My father. Your fecking husband. The man who wasted all his money on you. For what? I knew all along that you were just a money-grabbing drunken slut.'

'Stephanie ...' Laura tries to speak.

'You're nothing but a thieving whore and we want our money back. You're a miserable thief and I'm going to make you pay, if it's the last thing I do on God's earth.'

She's really spouting now.

'Look at yourself – WHAT are you doing here? It's our family home and you have no right being here. You never loved Daddy, admit it. You saw an opportunity and you took advantage of a wonderful man's kindness.'

'Stephanie, I can't be doing this. I'm too weak. I loved your father ...'

'How DARE you say that,' yells Stephanie. 'I know all about you anyway. You've been an alcoholic for years and you lied to Daddy – you kept that from him, along with all your other lies. You're just complete trash.'

'I'm sorry, I can't talk to you like this. I want you to leave please. Please GO. Now.'

Incandescent with anger, Stephanie reluctantly turns to leave, with a parting salvo.

'You just wait – you're going to regret ever setting eyes on my Daddy when I'm done with you. That's a promise.'

As she leaves, Laura heaves a great sigh, opens the fridge door, removes a bottle and pours herself another glass of numbness.

Meanwhile, in Wickham, Hampshire, Alice Kingston's whale ringtone announces a call. She answers.

It's Mary in Ireland reporting back again, as planned.

19

Laura picks up her phone and the display reads, '*Unknown*'. She goes ahead anyway.

'Hello, who's calling?'

'Hi Laura. It's me, Ali. Ali Kurmi, the DJ at the Walsh party.'

'Oh, hello Ali. Hang on a moment while I go somewhere quieter. I'm doing the laundry!'

She's taken off guard for a moment and moves to her living room. She's found herself repeatedly thinking about this young man who's now on the line calling her – with that wonderful voice. He's considerably younger than her and she feels a bit uncomfortable about it. But she can't deny that she's pleased that he's called. At the Walsh event, she was enchanted by his strikingly attractive good looks. Those amazing dark brown eyes. Very magnetic, very sexy.

'OK, that's better. This is a pleasant surprise, what can I do for you?'

Ali is taking a massive gamble with this call. He's been agonising over whether this amazing woman is or isn't attached. He noticed on Saturday, that she was ringless, but accepts that that doesn't mean much these days. He just has a feeling that it's right to make contact.

'I was wondering if you'd perhaps, er – come for a walk, a walk along the seafront sometime,' he says, in the hope that his approach is a bit different.

'Well Ali, I don't know, I'm sure. That sounds lovely but ...'

'Please just say if you're married or already spoken for. I know I'm being a bit forward, so just tell me to go away and I will.'

'Actually, I'm not as it happens but …'

'Really? I know I'm much younger than you but it was so nice talking to you on Saturday – could we perhaps just have another chat, a little walk? Without the ice cream this time!' he asks, trying not to sound too desperate.

'I don't know where you live but perhaps you'd like to come to Portsmouth? I live near the seafront – and the beach and the prom are fantastic for walks. Please come. I could collect you.'

Still a little confused but flattered, after a pause, Laura responds.

'Well then, this is a surprise, isn't it? A bit unexpected. A walk and a chat? Well why not, eh? Why not indeed? Yes, that sounds very nice, so thank you. Invitation for walk accepted. However, I insist on driving,' she says. 'Let me know where to meet you and I'll find my way there. I haven't been to Portsmouth before, but it's on my list.'

'There you go,' says Ali, 'Perfect. We get to chat and I get to show you around Pompey. How good is that?'

The conversation continues, the rendezvous is arranged and they both ring off.

'Yes.' says Ali, 'Re-sult.'

Laura, steps outside, closes and locks her front door with a smile on her face. What has she just done? She gets into the car and heads for Wickham Square and her appointment at the hairdresser. The journey isn't far but it passes particularly quickly as she spends the time picturing the young man she's just accepted a date with. She realises that she's still smiling from ear to ear.

Laura's hair is important to her and she's very fussy about who cuts it. She cannot believe how lucky she's been on this score. Any lady who respects and looks after her hair properly will tell you that finding a good hairdresser who'll do things your way is no easy thing. She got lucky with Andrew – and he does foils.

Three hours later, and she's back in the car, looking a million dollars, and she decides to call in on Alice on her way home. She's excited and she needs to share.

'Is it ridiculous? He's so much younger than me. What an earth is he doing asking me out for a walk? It's a different approach, I'll give him that. None of your drinks and candle-lit dinners. We're going for an effing walk on the prom!'

'How old is he?' asks Alice.

'I don't know! In his thirties, I'm guessing. '

'Nothing wrong with that my love, just enjoy. We're not on this planet for long, so embrace it while you're fit and healthy, that's what I say.'

'I'm nearly old enough to be his mother!'

'Rubbish. When was the last time, you know …?'

'Alice! I haven't even dated him yet!'

'I know, but we women have our needs … don't we?'

'And he has this most wonderful voice. No wonder he's a DJ.'

They both giggle and Alice thinks it's brilliant news.

'I think it's amazing. What does he look like? Is he handsome?'

'Yes, he is! He has the most amazing dark eyes. He's Indian, I think, his name points that way. Ali.'

'Ooh, Laura, get you. When are you meeting him?'

'Thursday morning at 11 near the fun fair – on Southsea seafront. Do you know it?'

'I certainly do,' says Alice.

‘Isn’t this bizarre? At my age. Who would have thought?’

‘Wow,’ says Alice, ‘this is such good news, Laura. But listen here, take a look at yourself in the mirror. That’s pure unadulterated gorgeousness you’re looking at, lady. You are fabulous and you are still in the prime of your life. Embrace. Go and have fun on the dodgems.’

20

Ali is back in the studio with Jim and they catch up. Ali tells Jim about the amazing party at the weekend. He shows him some of the photos he's taken. Jim knows that Brother Soul were going to try out Ali's song *Alright* at the gig.

'Cool. How did it sound?'

'Really good,' says Ali, 'it was such a buzz to hear the song played live.'

'They're a good live band.'

'Guess what? I met THE most amazing woman.'

'Ooh, that sounds good too,' says Jim.

'What's she like?'

'Where do I start? It's impossible to do her justice. And I didn't take a bloody photo. She is a-mazing. She's got long hair down to here. She's beautiful and has the most exquisite body, sorry, figure I've ever seen. And she's incredible fun too. She was working for the organiser.'

'You sound "got".'

'I am. Here's the thing – she's quite a bit older than me.'

'Yeh? How much older?'

'No idea, but a fair bit.'

'So you're a toy boy then.'

'I guess so. I don't care!'

'Fixed a date?'

'Yeh, this week.'

'Blimey you don't waste any time do you,' says Jim. 'But what about Becky?'

'Ah … yes,' says Ali pausing thoughtfully. 'I know ... but you wouldn't believe this woman. I can't tell you how stunning she is. She's unreal. I don't know what's hit me.'

Jim is still grinning broadly and winking, staring at Ali, teasingly trying to catch his eye.

'Stop it. This woman is class.'
'What do you know about her?'
'Nothing really. She sounds quite posh – she's got a slight accent but I can't place it, Irish possibly? I dunno,' Ali smiles again.

'As I said, all I know is that she works for the guy who organises events so she must live somewhere round here. Anyway, isn't it very strange that we're working on a love song called *The Longest Summer!*'

'Yeh, but it's about a summer romance that ends in tears, isn't it? Not a good omen.'

Jim hits the play button on *The Longest Summer* and they listen to the work they've done so far on the track.

'I know it's a bit reminiscent of ABBA – but that's precisely what I wanted. Every songwriter likes Benny and Bjorn, don't they?' says Ali. 'Even if you're not an ABBA fan, they've written some classic songs and they know their art – those songs in Mamma Mia, they're so feelgood and so cleverly put together. Even if they are a bit cheesy. I'm not copying them – it's more of a tribute to genuine song-writing craftspeople. And I'm sure some TV producer or music supervisor could use some retro music.'

'There have been some crappy ones too, if you dig back through their albums,' says Jim.

'You're right, unfortunately, but there are more than enough good ones to enjoy.

'And that's what we're trying to produce here, Mr Sexton; a good old cheesy, feelgood summer song. Bugger what the snobs say. What's wrong with writing a simple catchy ditty?'

'Nothing at all. Did you know, in the old days, I mean, really old, back in the 50s and 60s – I read that they used to write songs that the butcher's boy could whistle. How weird is that?' says Jim.

'You're kidding.'

'No it's true. If the butcher's boy can whistle it, it must be a hit.'

'Wonderful.'

'Anyway, I've got another song idea for you. Great title too.'

'Yeh? What's that?'

'Granny Snatcher!'

21

Laura is driving into Portsmouth in her black Range Rover and turns the radio down so that she can concentrate on the satnav instructions. She's been Googling the history of the port and it's a place she's looking forward to exploring. There's so much more to it than the Mary Rose and HMS Victory, for sure. Her first impression of the city is mixed. The ferry port on her right looks very impressive but there's some architecture on the left which doesn't fit in at all, depressing really. In the distance, the iconic Spinnaker Tower, a landmark in southern England, stands proudly – welcoming all.

She's feeling a bit flustered because she hasn't dated anyone since Frank – and even that wasn't conventional. She spent a considerable time this morning umming and ahing about what to wear – and settled on her scarlet Bobbi Brown jacket, red blouse and jeans. Striking but not over the top. She checks her makeup in the mirror. All OK.

She's glad she's using the GPS because she hasn't the faintest idea where she is.

Eventually, the road widens and the buildings are set further back – and ahead, beyond the parked cars, she spots the sea.

'You have arrived at your destination,' her satnav proudly proclaims.

'Hi there,' says Laura stepping down from her car, with fashion model deportment.

'Hi,' says Ali, highly impressed. 'You made it. You look amazing.'

'Thank you,' she says. 'You don't look too bad yourself.'

‘That’s some car you’ve got, I like it.’

All over again, Laura has Ali shaking his head in wonderment. Her penetrating green eyes are so come-on and so sexy. It feels like she’s looking deep inside him, into his soul. Ali’s stomach feels like it did when he took school exams – and his driving test. Full of butterflies.

‘So here we are – Southsea. What do you think?’ says Ali pointing towards the Solent.

‘What a view! I didn’t realise.’

‘Let’s go this way.’

Laura follows, still slightly bemused but beginning to feel more relaxed.

‘This is my second favourite view in the world,’ says Ali, as they sit on a bench on the promenade facing the sea.

‘It’s lovely,’ says Laura, looking around. ‘I love the sea. So, what’s your first favourite view then?’

‘It’s my personal idea of heaven on earth,’ says Ali. ‘It’s a little bit like this actually, just around the headland from here, across the harbour, in Gosport,’ he says, pointing to his right. ‘It has what I think is the most wonderful, spiritual, uplifting view. I believe it can change you, if you go at the right time.’

‘Wow, that sounds like some place.’

‘It is. It’s wonderful. I even wrote a couple of songs about it.’

‘Songs?’ says Laura. ‘You write songs?’

‘I do,’ says Ali, proudly. ‘And I record them at a studio in Gosport. Special place is Gosport.’

‘I’ve never met a songwriter before,’ says Laura, ‘and I’ve only met one DJ before.’

‘Oh, who was that?’ asks Ali.

'You,' she smiles. 'You're very good, by the way.'

Ali groans, slow off the mark. This lady is smart.

'So you're a singer/songwriter?'

'No, I'm not a singer. Whatever I try to sing comes out like a dreadful, cheesy cabaret crooner. My voice is not good. I get other people to sing my songs.'

'Gosh, I'm impressed … and a DJ too …'

'Yeh, I enjoy that. I do quite a bit of corporate work. Well I try to. It's better paid than the usual gigs.'

'Is that full time?'

'Yep. I'm out gigging a fair bit at weekends.'

'Do you have to go far?'

'Where the money takes me,' he says. 'Mainly from London, down across the South East.'

'Good on you.'

'But I also do smaller gigs, like Ocean, here in Portsmouth. You'll have to come along one night!'

'It's been many years since I went to a club disco,' Laura smiles.

'I must ask you,' he says, 'your accent is amazing. Where are you from? I can hear one, can't I?'

'You can, but I didn't think it was that noticeable. It's Irish, Dublin originally, but it's gradually faded over the years. Too many years,' she laughs.

'You're joking,' says Ali, stopping suddenly. 'You look great.'

'I'm 52,' she says, getting the awkward issue out of the way as quickly as possible.

'You're what? I don't believe you.'

'I am.'

'I'm not just saying it, I'm absolutely amazed. I was thinking early 40s but ...'

'That's very sweet of you. How old are you, if you don't mind me asking?'

'Mind? Of course not, I'm 35.'

'Well then, there's a thing now – there's a thing,' says Laura, looking ahead and smiling yet again.

'You talk about my accent – but what about yours, eh? You've got a lovely voice. I can see why you're a DJ.'

Ali is familiar with this kind of comment – he's well-spoken and it often raises eyebrows – but it doesn't really bother him – in fact he quite likes the attention. He just smiles.

'It is real,' he says, 'I didn't spend years cultivating it!'

They stand up, chuckling, and carry on walking along the prom. Ali nods and says hello to a passing couple and smiles at another.

'You know quite a few people round here, then,' says Laura.

'Can't help it really,' says Ali. 'I've been here a while. Most folk are nice.'

'Where are you from originally?'

'Bromley in Kent. This is much nicer though. I love the sea.'

'What about you? How come you're in these parts then?'

'It's quite a story I'm afraid, but I'll try to condense it as best as I can, if you're interested.'

'I am,' says Ali brandishing his best white-teeth smile.

Laura, tells Ali about her bereavement and relocating to Hampshire and her work for Finn O'Donnell. But she stops short of giving too much detailed information. It's too soon to be talking about her problematic stepchildren and her equally bad relationship with alcohol. She doesn't want to talk about the negative stuff. She's decided to be very upbeat today.

Ali is very open about his DJ work and musical aspirations – he also talks about his work for his father. But he, too, decides to go soft on the details. Now is not the time to be talking about how he hates his father and the reality of the violent work he has to do for him. Christ, she'd run a mile.

'Look at the time,' says Ali. 'We've been talking for so long I've forgotten about food. That's very rude of me. We could eat out or I could make us something back at my place. What do you fancy?'

'I really don't mind,' says Laura. 'I'll do whatever you choose. I don't need much. A snack would be just fine. I'm easy.'

Ali is now floating and loving every second of being with this very classy lady. She's so self-assured and confident, speaks so nicely and he finds himself checking his own grammar.

As they cross the road, from the prom to the common, Laura starts to giggle.

'Did you see that man?'

'Which man?' replies Ali grinning, but not having the faintest idea of what she's on about.

'That man over there – he just tripped up, stepping off the kerb. It was so funny. I'm sorry, I have a weird sense of humour, Ali. It takes a bit of getting used to I'm afraid. Do you like the old Norman Wisdom movies?

'Who?' says Ali.

'Norman Wisdom. He was a very funny comic actor from the 1950s and 1960s – black and white movies. SUCH a funny man – if you like all that slapstick stuff.'

'You surprise me, I thought you'd be more into intellectual humour, wittier stuff.'

'Me? No. Give me a banana skin any day.'

Ali smartly adds, 'And an ice cream in the face presumably – especially if it's a clown and it's my face!?'

'Yes,' snorts Laura.

She loops her arm though Ali's and they make for the café just ahead. They order coffee, and a sandwich to share and sit outside.

'I'm glad you like good coffee,' says Ali. 'Don't laugh, I grind my own beans. And I'm a bit of a foodie.'

'Oh yes?'

'Hmm, I'm afraid so. I can't stop buying books and I look at all the cookery programmes. Mind you, I struggle with a Dorset Knob. What's that all about?'

'I've no idea – but I won't laugh about your grinding, Ali – or your Dorset Knob! I like a real coffee too, even if it can make one a bit hyper. And I love good food. Good food, good mind, good body.'

Ali pauses and smiles. 'Thank you for coming today. I'm really enjoying myself.'

'That's nice, Ali. I'm enjoying myself too,' says Laura, looking directly into his eyes.

'I'm a firm believer in proactively making things happen. I have a friend called Alice. She's more than a friend really. She's actually the reason I'm here. She persuaded me to come over and relocate to Wickham.'

'I like this lady a lot,' says Ali.

'She's very spiritual – but not in the conventional sense, if you get my drift. I'm actually a Catholic girl but I'm afraid I lapsed many years ago. Anyway, she has some very wise ideas and I love her to bits. She's introduced me to loads of interesting concepts and I find it all very fascinating. For example … I know it's not exactly a new idea, but do you know anything about the Law of Attraction?'

'Yes, I've watched some YouTube videos about that. I often joke about stepping into the vortex but it's only meditation really, isn't it? Emptying the mind. Do you do that stuff?'

'I do, when I remember to.'

'So do I, when I can quieten myself down enough. It's quite a discipline, isn't it? Clearing the mind of all that clutter. It's hard.'

The two of them make their way slowly, back along the prom, to the funfair that's dominated by the big wheel, rotating noisily with screaming people. They stand and watch and are still talking an hour later. Laura looks at her watch.

'Ali, if you don't mind, I'd better be moving on quite soon,' she says. 'It's been lovely. You really do make me smile and laugh.'

'I suppose that's a good thing, I hope so,' says Ali.

'It certainly is. Anyway, I'd like to get back before the traffic builds – I'm not too fond of city driving if I'm honest.'

'Sure,' says Ali.

He escorts Laura back to her car, walking on the outside of the pavement. It's something he's never actually done before, but he's trying it out and it feels very good, playing the perfect gentleman.

Should he take a picture? Nah. Too pushy.

'I love this car,' he says, looking all over it. 'I'd love one of these.'

'You'll have to manifest it then, won't you.' says Laura. 'It's certainly done me well – coming over from Ireland and that. Mind you, getting it relicensed here with DVLA wasn't much fun.'

Ali reaches to open the door. 'Can we do this again?'

Laura steps into her car, and with her arm on the open door, she looks down.

'Well, I don't know about that.'

She leaves another agonising pause.

She slowly lifts her head, beaming with a heart-melting smile. She leans forward and very deliberately kisses him on his left cheek.

'Yes, of course we shall – let's do this again, Ali Kurmi.'

22

In the years following the Millennium, organised crime, racketeering and gang warfare, particularly involving drugs, has been a serious problem on Merseyside. Many places in Liverpool and surrounding areas have been become no-go areas at certain times.

A number of high-profile arrests and court cases saw some individuals put behind bars, as police changed their tactics to combat the problem. Today, some of the drug barons are living in exile but others have moved in and the problem still continues. The gangs trade in fear and violence to get what they want.

More recently, there's been a change in the way the gangs operate and County Lines trafficking has spread outwards from the city.

There's a move towards gangs working together; unheard of until now. The reason is, quite simply, bigger profits. More gangs across the UK have combined to add greater strength when negotiating for bigger shipments of drugs like cocaine and they're dealing with bigger organisations like the Mafia, who have tougher demands.

Two Merseyside gangs who have been fighting bitterly in more recent years, have caught wind of the trend and have been making noises about talking to each other. They're rapidly expanding and want in on the County Lines operations.

Until now, nothing concrete has been realised and nobody has been sure that there's even a will on either side, to take this forward.

Tonight, the two sides are finally meeting face to face. They've agreed to explore any common ground to pursue the initiative and get things moving.

There are six men at the meeting, which is taking place at a large, rented property they've commandeered for the evening. A Javed Kurmi property. It's clear that the building, used by students, has been evacuated hastily, given the worse-than-usual untidiness. No matter – they won't be there for long. One of the housemates does a little dealing, so it was no trouble getting him to clear the house for a few hours. This last-minute tactic combined with an unremarkable location, reduces the risk of the meeting being picked up by anyone unwelcome, particularly the police.

No weapons are being carried and the talking is to be between the heads of the two gangs.

Both sides know how much damage in-fighting causes – and the police have recently scored some high-profile convictions with long prison sentences.

The two bosses sit nervously staring at each other. Shaun James is facing Brian White across a tatty coffee table, littered with empty mugs. The atmosphere is very heavy. But at last, they begin speaking, in their strong scouse accents, and slowly the tension eases. As they begin to feel more relaxed – a conversation clumsily begins.

They both know they have a mountain to climb to earn each other's trust but they slowly begin to make some progress.

'So are we OK?' says Brian White.

'Yeh, OK,' says Shaun James.

They agree that pointless deaths could and should be avoided in future. They're not only a waste of money but also draw unwanted attention. But even more importantly, they're distractions from a much better use of their collective time. Making more money. They're both very keen to expand and make some big money. The pair along with their respective Scouse acolytes have no moral compasses. They couldn't give a shit about dragging young children into their world of drugs, violence and profits. Big money requires big supplies and taking bigger risks. They all have to step up to do whatever is required, regardless of the collateral damage.

Two men are keeping a look-out at the window and are peering out from time to time.

'We're serious about this … how can we be sure you are too?' says Shaun James.

'You can't,' says Brian White, smugly. 'Don't worry pal, we're in.'

Shaun stares at him, straight in the eyes, looking for some small indication of sincerity. Unfortunately, at that very moment, there's an unexpected interruption.

In a gap between curtain twitches, Ali Kurmi and his two cousins Hammad and Kamran, lope up the short path to the front door of number 29 and rap loudly. They've come to see Dominic Radley who is behind with the property rent and has cancelled the standing order to Kurmi HQ.

Hearing the knock, the gang leaders in the living room look up startled and freeze.

'What the fuck?' says James.

'Fuckin' 'ell,' says White.

They came to the meeting unarmed but one of White's gang produces a short knife from nowhere.

'Who there – no need for that, man,' says James and turns to his lookout. 'Who the fuck is it, can you see?'

'It's three guys. Can't see very well because of the angle but they don't look much …'

'Get rid,' says James.

Brian White quickly retorts. 'Are you fuckin' mad, man – we're outta here – was this you? Is this a set-up? You'll fucking pay for this.'

He leaps to his feet, glaring threateningly at James – and with his sidekicks, hurtles out of the room, through the kitchen and into the back garden.

At which point, James's lookout opens the door and pointing his phone, immediately takes a series of rapid photos of Ali and his cousins.

'What choo want?' says Jason Brand, smiling to reveal a frightening set of braces.

Ali, taken aback, says, 'we're here to see Dominic Radley – about the rent. It's overdue. Please can you get him?'

'Who? He's not 'ere.'

'Please don't play that game,' says Ali. 'We're not stupid.'

'No, but you'll be fucking dead if you don't fuck off now. Hear me?'

Before Ali or the others have time to react, he slams the door. Kam takes over and hammers loudly on the door telling the guy to come out. Ali joins him and the pair keep banging.

Ali shouts through the door. 'This is our property you're in. We have every right to ...'

The door opens again.

'To ... what?' says Jason Brand, jabbing at Ali, 'You. Have. Fucked. UP.'

'But ... you're trespassing on private property.'

'You are so fucked. Fuck off.' He suddenly runs at Ali and with his shoulder, slams into his chest sending him flying backwards on to the path. Staring angrily at Ham and Kam, he turns round, walks back and slams the door behind him again.

Lying on the ground and in shock, Ali is winded and unable to speak. Ham and Kam quickly pull him to his feet and drag him towards the road. Ali gradually recovers his normal breathing rhythm.

'Oh my God,' he says, keeping his voice down – who WAS that guy? What the fuck?'

'We're not banging that door again, that's for sure,' says Kam. 'Let's get out of here. Let's go. NOW!'

The Kurmis retreat with half the street watching them.

There hasn't been as much excitement in Grove Avenue since the water main burst five years ago.

23

Javed Kurmi is squinting in front of his computer screen at his Bromley office. There was a time when he struggled with technology but he's taken things slowly and he's made the effort to learn. In the not-too-distant past he would have laughed at the idea of a spreadsheet. In fact, he wouldn't have known what a spreadsheet was. But his children persuaded him and now he actually prefers working digitally.

The business is a real family affair and they're all on the payroll; his daughter Basma and nephews Ham and Kam, his sister, Sunita – and Ali, when called upon. Ham and Kam's father, Malik, Javed's brother, is a sleeping partner and just takes his share of the profits. He has his own business interests. He and Javed see each other regularly and attend the same mosque but Javed has slowly come to resent sharing the proceeds with his brother and is planning to cut him out.

Javed likes getting his own way and generally speaking, he does – in business and in family life. But he's grown increasingly concerned about Ali's recent outbursts of contempt for him and the business. It's a problem he intended to sort out some time ago, but Ali's persistent defiance has surprised and angered him.

He sent him to live in Portsmouth to avoid the scandal, believing it was the right thing to do at the time. But that was a long time ago and he now wants his younger son to get more involved in the business again and help with his expansion plans. Unfortunately, he hasn't factored in how Ali has not only survived but flourished since moving to Portsmouth. In exile, he reinvented himself, and has his own independent life and ambitious plans.

This is of no consequence to pompous Javed Kurmi. He's the head of the family and while he draws breath, he calls all the shots and he wants Ali back in Bromley, as soon as possible. No arguments – end of.

And he knows exactly how to do it.

Javed is proud of his successful business and he puts it down to basic hard graft – and thrift – exercising caution with capital outlay and avoiding any wastage. Having had so little money when he started the business, as it steadily grew he learned to truly appreciate its value.

Fate has also been kind. Thanks to Tony Blair, he built his booming business based on the politician's insistence that all young people should be able to go to university. They'd of course need somewhere to live. Ker-ching!

In rare philosophical moments, he does wonder whether higher education degrees are really worth anything, at the end of the day. But … who cares? Students have made him a wealthy man.

Most of his houses are in the southern counties but he has around 40 properties in Liverpool. He's just sent the boys there to sort out two defaulters and to do routine checks on the other properties in the city.

His phone rings.

'Mr K, we got a problem.'

Nephew Kam is calling from Liverpool.

'Did you get the money?'

Kam relates the drama of the previous night – the strange guy at the door and Ali being pushed over. He describes the man, his scary teeth braces, how he attacked Ali, the photos he took and the threats.

'OK Kam, obviously, don't go back there. I need to make a call. But can you still cover the other work?'

'Sure,' says Kam, 'but I've got a bad feeling about this guy, Uncle Javed. He looked like that guy Jaws from that Bond movie.'

'OK Kam, I'll look into it. Don't worry, I'll speak to you soon.'

The fact that his son was attacked and might have been in serious danger doesn't even cross his mind. He's more concerned about the identity of the person with the crazy teeth braces and what he was doing inside his property. He certainly isn't a student. He calls Raj, one of the few people he can genuinely call a friend. He might know something about this very distinctive-looking guy.

In less than an hour, Raj is back on the line and the news isn't good.

'OK thanks, much appreciated. Yes, loud and clear. Got it. Be well my friend – bye.'

Raj has said that from the boys' description, it's very likely that they accidentally had a brush with gangland Liverpool and that they got off very lightly, given what could have happened. If he's right, the guy is a member of one of Liverpool's most-feared drugs gangs, and rumour has it he's been involved in more than one suspicious death in the city and is a very dangerous character.

Javed stares blankly out of the window. Time has proved that Ham and Kam are more than capable of looking after themselves, so to hear that they felt scared and threatened, has set off alarm bells. At first, he was furious that one of his houses had been taken over, even briefly, but when Raj went on to elaborate about the gang and their reputation, his anger switched to fear.

24

Laura is standing naked in front of the cupboard looking straight at Ali. She exudes the confidence that only comes from someone at home with their body. Her hair is slightly ruffled, her shoulders are relaxed and her breasts are proportional to her gently curved hips and long legs.

Laura O'Brien is in perfect shape and Ali, also naked, is doing his best to control his passion. He isn't going to ruin this most wondrous moment in his life by getting excited too quickly. Laura transfers her weight to her left leg and places her hand on her right hip and looks *alluringly* at Ali.

Arggh, what a sight. Am I big enough for her?

It's the usual male insecurity.

She's obviously happy with what she sees as she steps towards Ali with her arms outstretched. Ali quickly moves forward and in a split second they are kissing and holding each other tightly. Ali lifts his hands to her face and whispers.

'This, is the most wonderful, exciting moment, in my whole life.'

Laura responds with a soft groan and intensifies the kissing.

They manoeuvre themselves, glued together, to the bed, still kissing – and gently fall on to it, Ali first. He's on his back and Laura raises her leg, swivels round and squats, hovering over him. Gently, she lowers herself as he slowly slides into her – he groans with pleasure and starts a rhythm that gradually gains momentum. He cannot believe the intense pleasure he's experiencing and is only able to express himself with a soft *fucking hell.*

They roll over carefully, still linked together, and now Ali is on top and props himself up on his hands and looks into Laura's eyes.

'I love your eyes. This is so wonderful, you're so beautiful,' he says.

'Shh,' whispers Laura, '… don't stop.'

'What are you thinking about?' she says softly, as they lie side by side. 'You're not still thinking about Liverpool are you?'

'No, not all, don't worry. Far from it actually. I don't know … no, actually, I do know,' says Ali immediately correcting himself.

'Nothing. Right now, I'm thinking about nothing – I'm just, you know, being. Floating. Gentle and happy.'

Laura tilts her head and kisses his cheek. 'Isn't it wonderful?'

'It's lovely, and I have *never* experienced an orgasm like that in my whole life.'

'Really?'

'No. Believe it or not, I haven't slept with that many women and not one single time was like that. That was so much more than something physical. God, doesn't that sound shitty?'

'Oh Ali, that is so beautiful. It was lovely for me too. You're very good! But you don't think I've been too forward, do you? It's only our second date. I don't want you thinking I do this sort of thing lightly.'

'Are you kidding?' he says, turning and propping his head up with his hand.

'I don't know how to describe it. It was just, I don't know. Perfect.'

In Laura's kitchen, Ali is padding around in his boxers looking for the tea. He looks at the flowers he brought with him, lilies from the florist – not forecourt flowers – and smiles to himself. He's never spent more than a tenner on flowers for a woman before.

'How do you like it?' he calls loudly, up to the bedroom.

'Builders,' comes the distant reply.

When Laura told Ali she was renting somewhere temporarily, he'd automatically assumed it would be something modest. But here he is, standing in the luxury kitchen of a very large five-bedroom detached house, at the end of a winding lane, surrounded by fields, populated with horses. He looks out of the window, raising his eyebrows. He hadn't expected this and he definitely hadn't planned on making love – but lust had taken over both of them, and right now he finds himself in a state of euphoric contentment. His whole body is still gently humming.

Laura joins him, wearing a light cotton dressing gown. His shoulders slowly sag at the vision. He kisses her gently on the lips, steps back, and passes her the mug of tea.

'Tell me more about what happened with your husband. If you don't mind talking about it, that is.'

Laura picks up the story and tells Ali about how her husband Frank's death almost did for her. She also tells him about Frank's business and how important he'd been in the horse breeding world, producing many famous international champions.

Slowly the penny begins to drop and Ali realises that the grandness of this property is less surprising given the way Laura is now talking. This lady must be pretty rich.

'Do you like the house? Nice, isn't it?'

'It certainly is; it has the wow factor, for sure,' says Ali looking around the room again.

'I'm looking for something permanent so if you know of anywhere, do let me know,' she says, cheerily.

'Ha. As if,' says Ali.

'I'm looking for somewhere with a swimming pool,' says Laura. Ali swallows hard. 'A swimming pool?'

'Yes, and it has to be indoor. It's one of the things that kept me alive last year. Swimming for an hour every day.'

'You had an indoor swimming pool? '

'We did,' she smiles. 'And I miss not having my daily dip. It keeps me in trim.'

They return to the bedroom with their teas and sit propped-up on the bed.

'It's a bit late to ask this, isn't it – but haven't you got a girlfriend? A handsome man like you must have a queue of girls waiting, surely.'

Ali, swallows hard. 'No, as I said earlier, I haven't had many proper relationships, I'm actually a bit shy. Although I do tell a slight lie. I do have a very good friend, called Becky.'

'Oh yes?' says Laura smiling, 'Becky, is it?'

'She's just a good friend.'

'Good friend?'

'Well, a bit more. We have an understanding.'

He shows Laura a photo of Becky Davies on his phone.

'She looks lovely,' says Laura. 'Why aren't you a proper couple then?'

'Nah. Not Becks.'

'Do tell. Is that how you like things, then? Informal.'

'No, not at all,' says Ali firmly. 'We get on well but there's no romance. I haven't met anyone *that* special yet. I've had a couple of kind-of-serious relationships, but neither of them worked out.' 'Oh. You haven't met anyone special then!' laughs Laura.

'Argh, you got me. That's not fair.'

He sips his tea. 'Anyway, what about you? The most beautiful woman on earth. Surely you must have someone special.'

'Oh, that's very sweet of you. But the truth is, I've had a very tough time, Ali.'

'Of course you have, I'm sorry. But I can't believe you haven't had millions of guys queueing up to take you out.'

'It's OK. Yes, there have been a few men who magically appeared on the scene to show concern when Frank died, but you can spot them, the predators, a mile off. To be perfectly honest I haven't really given much thought to relationships. I haven't been looking. I've just been sorting myself out. I'll tell you all about it one day. Maybe!

'But let's talk more about your music, I know how important it is to you.'

Laura isn't familiar with the ins and outs of the music industry and listens, fascinated, as Ali talks enthusiastically about his ambitions,

'You must carry on with that dream, Ali. I'd love to hear your songs. What sort of music do you write?'

'Everything and anything. Rock anthems, ballads, funk, brass rock, country rock, modern pop – you name it. I like and write all types of music.'

'Can we listen to some?'

'I tell you what I'll do. I've got them all on a SoundCloud Playlist. I'll send you the link and you can dip into them at your leisure. There are too many to listen to in one go. I wouldn't expect you to do that.'

'I shall make a point of doing exactly that. Soon as.'

Laura smiles, pauses and looks aside.

'I have to confess that us meeting – and today, you know, this closeness – has taken me a bit by surprise. I'm still working out what a young man like you, sees in a woman like me. I'm 52 for goodness sake.'

'What?' shouts Ali, 'What are you talking about? Please allow me to demonstrate my response to that ludicrous question.'

'Oo, yes please.'

Laura is completely bowled over by this beautiful and talented young man – his wide-eyed youth and innocence are very attractive. She's bewitched by those large, dark brown eyes, glistening, bright and so exciting. She wants to make love to him and mother him, all at the same time.

She slips down the bed and pulls the duvet over her head. She rolls on to her side and presses herself against Ali's firm body and starts moving gently. In a split-second Ali responds and once again they lose themselves completely in pleasure.

An hour later, they stir and Ali looks longingly at Laura's breasts. They are full and firm, a perfect size he thinks and he can't resist the urge to touch them and kiss them again. Her nipples are obviously very sensitive and Ali's warmth triggers another wave of pleasure that spreads down her body. Laura groans and the two share a very long, lingering kiss.

It's now early evening and the couple are cuddling in the sitting room.

'Shouldn't we be making love in the kitchen, with you sitting on the counter and your legs wrapped around my waist?'

'What?'

'That's how they do it in all the TV dramas these days, isn't it – haven't you noticed? The woman's always sitting on the counter!'

They laugh and Laura mock-punches Ali.

'Let's have another tea,' she suggests, 'all this physical exercise has made me thirsty. I'll make it.'

She soon returns and kisses Ali on the top of his head as she passes behind the sofa and puts the mugs down on the table.

'I haven't told you about my dad yet, have I?' he says, looking serious. 'I need to tell you this.

'We've kind of fallen out. Mind you, we're always falling out. He just doesn't get me. He's old-school Muslim and he'd rather I settle down with a nice Muslim girl, have Muslim babies and run the business with him.'

'That's me finished then.

'No, seriously, I'm sorry to hear that and I hope you can patch things up. It's not good to have break-ups within families.'

'I know, that's what everyone tells me, but you don't know the full details.'

'What business would that be?' says Laura, genuinely interested.

'Property,' says Ali. 'He owns hundreds of properties and rents them out, mainly to students.'

'Gosh.' says, Laura.

'I work for him part-time,' says Ali. 'But I hate it.'

'Oh, why's that?' says Laura, adjusting the cushion.

'It's my job to chase up people who don't pay their rent on time. Nice.'

'Right …' says Laura, 'a bailiff type of thing?'

'Yeh, but sometimes it gets heavy. Very heavy. We – me and my 'cousins, that is – threaten them with force sometimes and it does my head in.'

What kind of force?' says Laura, nervously.

'They get hit,' says Ali, distress beginning to sound in his voice. 'I don't do it, but Ham and Kam, my cousins, do. They don't ever take no for an answer.'

'That's sounds dreadful. And your father?'

'He's the one behind it. The bloody hypocrite. I'm so sorry, I expect you hate me now. But I've got to be honest with you and I can't tell you how upset I am about it all. I want to get out but I'm trapped. He's got a hold on me and he won't let me go.'

Tears begin to well in Ali's eyes and Laura puts her arm around him and pulls his head towards her.

'Everything can be fixed, Ali. If you want to get out of this situation there will be a way. You just need to dig deep, find some strength and take control.'

'Easier said than done, I'm afraid – you don't know my father.

'What really worries me is that there must be a part of me that's naturally violent – a dark side. And that scares the shit out of me. I don't want to be schizophrenic like that.'

'Listen, you're not a violent man, I can tell that. I've met schizophrenics and I can assure you that you have nothing to worry about. But please, all this violence and unpleasantness – how far does it go back? Has it got something to do with why you ended up in Portsmouth?'

'Mmm, kind of …' says Ali, keen not to be drawn too far into his past.

25

Stephen Wilkins is the Music Supervisor at Satellite Television. He and his teams at the headquarters of the TV giant are responsible for selecting a huge range of music tracks for use across the whole TV platform. They're the snippets of music and songs that crop up in TV dramas, programme trailers, films and advertising.

Stephen's teams audition music for inclusion in their library which they can draw upon when a producer is in need of specific music for his or her production. Getting a song featured in such a broadcast is highly desirable for music producers, composers, bands and singers – and Ali.

It's an avenue that he's been exploring as a way of breaking into the music business – and being paid for the pleasure. Unfortunately, he is not the only one with this intent and the competition is fierce.

However, the seemingly impossible can sometimes happen.

His phone rings and it's Stephen Wilkins from Satellite.

'Hi, Al Kurmi?'

'Yes, hi,' answers Ali.

'It's Stephen Wilkins from Satellite TV.'

Ali swallows hard, trying to sound confident.

'Great, how can I help?'

'Well it's more a case of how I can help you. Thanks for sending the links to the two tracks – *Homeland* by Coolstar was it – and *Healer* by Coolstar – I've listened to both. And yes, *Homeland* has a nice rousing emotional feel to it. Our teams don't make many pieces with that rockier type of tune, but I could see it fitting in in certain places – for example in Rugby VTs. The other one, *Healer,* has a more modern general feel which could fit anywhere. Yeh, I like them. Let's see what happens. We'll put 'em in.'

He continues, 'You know about all the admin stuff, do you? You might need this information. When it comes to commercial tunes, all the broadcasters have blanket licences. Have you registered the tracks properly with PRS and PPL?'

'Yes I have.'

'OK, that's great then. Send along a .wav file of the tunes plus instrumental versions for me to add to our library and we'll take it from there. Good luck.'

And with that he hangs up.

'Wow,' says Ali. 'Wow, effing wow!'

*

'You're in a particularly good mood today,' says Laura, as they stroll hand in hand past the shops in Albert Road, Southsea. It's bustling with pedestrians – and parked cars line each side of the street. Business is good in these parts.

'I am. I've had some good news about a couple of songs. They might be used on TV.'

'Wow. That's great news, but before you say anything,' she says, tugging Ali's arm and bringing them to a halt. I must tell you something. I love your music! I'm not just saying it either. I really mean it. I haven't gone through your whole playlist, but I tell you, you've definitely got something.

'Which ones are they interested in?'

'*Homeland*, the rocky one, and *Healer*. I'm not a hundred per cent sure of what they'll do, but it could be good.'

He recounts the conversation he had with Satellite TV.

'At least it's a start, something to build on,' he says.

'I'm so pleased for you, that's great news.'

They're now standing outside a steak house.

'How d'ya like yer steak?' he asks, in his best Australian accent.

Laura giggles. 'That's a dreadful Aussie accent, Ali. I don't eat much steak really. How do you like yours?'

'Just whip off its horns, wipe its arse and slap it on the plate, mate!'

Laura snorts. 'That's disgusting, horrible. Where on earth did that come from?'

'Sir Les Patterson.'

'Oh, Barry Humphries. He's a bit old fashioned for you, isn't he?'

'No, not at all. He's vulgar, clever and absurd and I love that – the ridiculous.'

'Me too!'

'I remember you saying how much you like slapstick. Well, I like verbal slapstick I guess, like Les Patterson. But I also love other types of comedy like Omid Djalili, Romesh Ranganathan, David Mitchell … and er, I like Katherine Ryan. Peter Kay, is amazing – did you see *Car Share*?'

'I did,' says Laura. 'It was brilliant. And what about *After Life* with Ricky Gervais?'

'Wow yes, I loved that too, but isn't that a bit, well you know – a bit raw for you?'

'Surprisingly it wasn't. I can take or leave Ricky Gervais but I have to hand it to him, I binge watched *After Life*. It was utterly brilliant. Having fun with bereavement. Whatever next! I didn't get upset at all,' says Laura.

'I totally agree – that dog.'

'Most people expect me to have a more sophisticated sense of humour. I don't know, perhaps it's the way I look. But as you know, I'm on the floor with Norman Wisdom – and Tommy Cooper doesn't have to say a word and I'm in stitches. I love him.'

'People love to pigeonhole, don't they?'

'They certainly do, Ali. If you don't fit into their pre-conceived stereotypical image, it un-nerves them.'

'You're absolutely right. You wouldn't believe how many people are puzzled by my voice – they presumably expect a strong Indian dialect. And then there's music. For example, I love church choral music – how left field is that? And I never miss Johnnie Walker's Sounds of the 70s.'

'There's nothing wrong with that either.'

'Because I'm Asian, or more to the point, look Asian, they immediately think I'm into Indian hip-hop or Bollywood pop. And everyone thinks I'm posh because I speak without an accent. I don't conform to a lot of things. I don't go to mosque. I love roast beef (just pink). I don't watch Man U at the pub. I'm not politically correct. I could go on. I don't do lots of things people think I should.'

'And good on you Ali. Quite right. Each to his own or her own – or their own. You're a wise man for your age and I love the sound of your voice. It's not posh, just well-spoken. It's very classy and *very* attractive.'

As they turn into his road making for the seafront, Ali says, 'I want to buy you a present. When's your birthday?'

'End of June – you've just missed it!'

'You're kidding me, what date?'

'28th.'

'No! Mine's June 30th. Wow, that's weird, so close. We're both Cancerians. Do you go in for the stars, astrology?'

'Only when it fits!'

As they head towards the common, he lifts up and waves his phone. 'What about social media? I see you're on Facebook.'

'I am, but as you can see, I haven't touched it for ages. I did use it a lot before I met Frank but more recently, I must confess I haven't really used it. There hasn't been much to celebrate in recent times. Most of the stuff I've been going through would be a tad depressing to post about, I think.'

'I'm sorry that was a stupid question,' says Ali.

'Not at all – I don't mind. I see you post quite a bit.'

'Goes with the job I suppose,' says Ali, as they continue to stroll.

'I hope you don't think I'm prying but tell me more about your family.'

'OK. Well, there's mum – she's called Namita – and I love her, whatever. I just feel sorry for her as she's controlled completely by my father. He just uses her.'

'I have an older brother called Mohammed, who's alright but can be a patronising bastard. And I have two sisters, one older and one younger, Basma and Rani. They're both good.'

'Do you see much of them?'

'Not as much as I probably should – but it's difficult. They're so busy with their families … '

'You said you'd tell me how you ended up in Portsmouth.'

Ali spots a difficult situation. 'I did, didn't I? Well, my parents thought it would be good for me to go and live with friends. Good for my development.'

'That's a bit unusual, isn't it? How old were you?'

'Sixteen.'

'Gosh that's young isn't it? What about school and leaving home, that sounds tough?'

'It was, but I didn't have a choice in the matter and that helps doesn't it? But it was actually OK, I'm not complaining. Looking back, apart from working on the market every day when I first came down, I loved living with the Patels. They were really kind to me and whilst I don't see so much of them now, we do keep in touch. Anyway, after a couple of years living with them, my father allowed me to move into one of his properties down here which I shared with various people over the years. It was all OK. It made me the man I am!'

Ali beams at Laura, pleased with the way he's just handled her tricky question.

They cross the common at the end of Ali's street and head into a café.

'The coffee's good here,' says Ali. 'I hate that High Street stuff. It's never strong enough.'

They pick a table and Laura heads for the bathroom before they settle down.

'Won't be a moment,' she says.

Ali just smiles and pulls out his phone, seizing a Sudoku opportunity.

'I knew I'd find you doing that,' she says, on her return.

'I'm an addict! Thank you for listening to me banging on about my family, by the way. I don't want to bore you to death.'

'Ali, you don't bore me, I promise.'

'Anyway, what about you? It's your turn now. Tell me more, you've only told me about the more recent heavy stuff.'

Laura briefly looks towards the beach and takes a slow deep breath.

'So that's the Isle of Wight then, is it?' she says, buying herself a little time.

'Yeh, part of it. The eastern end. I'll take you there one day. If you'd like.'

'And what's that round thing in the middle of the sea?' she says, pointing.

'It's a fort,' says Ali. 'Spitbank Fort.'

'A real one?'

'Yep. One of Lord Palmerston's follies, to be precise. There are four out there. Built to keep the French out, but never needed, I believe. That one's a hotel now, I think. I'm not sure if I'd fancy it though, would you?'

'Staying there? Yes, I'd give it a go – as long as you're paying!'

Laura returns to Ali's original question.

'Right then, here goes. Me, then. Well, I grew up in Dublin with my mum and dad. Dad was a printer and ran his own business. Mum helped him with that and they were a very tight unit. I was the only child. I don't know if that was intentional or not. I would have loved a sister or a brother, but it wasn't to be.

'I think it made me more independent so that's not a bad thing and I've always managed to pull through when I've had to, during tough times.

'Anyway, I went to a decent school, and did OK. Middling to average, that's me all through, to be honest. Although my parents were fairly well off, they weren't rich. They were Catholic, of course, and when I was younger we went to church regularly, but for some reason that all stopped in my early teens. Almost overnight, and I never got to the bottom of it. Anyway, after school I wanted to study journalism and, luckily, I won a scholarship which got me to London. Now, that was a big deal for a young Irish girl, I can tell you.

'I absolutely loved it there, the freedom, the people – and the music. I had a boyfriend too, Declan. He was also from Dublin. Funny that we had to go to London to meet. Anyway, we did and fell in love and did everything together, and later we got married.'

She stops and looks at Ali.

'You weren't expecting that Ali, were you? I'll tell you more about that in a minute. So, I got my degree and decided to stay in London because I got an internship on a weekly paper in South London. I'd only been at the paper for a couple of weeks and got the news that both my parents had been killed in a car accident.'

'What! The. Fuck.' says Ali, stunned. 'That's terrible.'

'I know. Sorry to sound so abrupt and dramatic, but that's exactly what it was. It changed my world. Instantly.'

'I bet it bloody did,' says Ali. 'Oh Laura. Both parents – how the hell did you cope with that?'

'It was more than a shock, that's for sure. It was like a nuclear bomb going off. I was unable to function for a while.

'Declan was amazing, I have to say that. I could have gone under, but somehow he managed to keep me together. So, we went home, and I had to sort out all the mess. It was an absolute nightmare. All that work we had to do – well, I had to do, on top of the grieving. My aunts and uncles, friends and neighbours all offered to help, but it's not something you can delegate, is it? Funerals, probate and all that paperwork. It was horrendous.'

'But both your parents … how on earth did you cope?'

'I just had to Ali. I didn't have a choice. It's amazing what people can do when they don't get to choose. You said it yourself, just now.'

'Oh my God, all that and the later death of your husband. That is so unfair. It's more than that, it's cruel. I'm so sorry. I'm amazed that you've got through all that

– and look at you. Just look at you. You're amazing.'

'One of the reasons I pulled through, and it pains me to say it, is I drank. I drank a great deal and despite all the hangovers and the dark days, alcohol got me through my parents' deaths, my marriage break-up, which I haven't told you about yet – and to an extent, Frank's death. But please, please, please don't think I'm condoning it – I wouldn't recommend the same path to anyone else. It's a very slippery slope – and I've been down that slope, headfirst, two, possibly three times. I'm afraid I have an addictive personality.

'My marriage to Declan was a huge mistake. Oh my word, it was a disaster. We should never have done it but I was still young and bewildered by my parents' deaths. I still shudder thinking about those times. I became a drunken beast.'

26

Fifteen years ago

Laura opens the front door to the flat and carries in her shopping bags, putting them on the counter in the kitchen, bottles clanking. It's 5.30 pm and it's another cold and damp day in Dublin. Declan will no doubt be working late again, she's thinking. So, no change there then. He's cut himself off from her, and these days he just looks at her with contempt. And it's really pissing her off.

She checks in the fridge before opening another bottle of white wine and looks around towards the door. Good, no empties lurking. She may be a tad forgetful, but she keeps the empty bottles well and truly recycled – or out of sight.

Laura and Declan have so far failed in their painstaking attempts to have a child, including IVF. It's the Noughties and Laura is approaching the dreaded 40 and has all but given up on the idea. Declan, who has always been very supportive, has recently changed. And it's taken Laura a bit by surprise. She's really struggling and is reminded of her parents' deaths.

Her way of dealing with crises lies inside the fridge, where there are always a couple of chilling bottles of Pinot Grigio, waiting to cheer her. For a while.

Declan still works at Pfizer, where he's successfully climbed the promotion ladder, and is clearly not going to budge from, as he's doing so well. He's also thrown himself into a local amateur dramatic group, on his own. Acting is his thing.

Meanwhile, Laura is holding down her sub-editor's job at the Dublin News.

At the moment though, she's unaware that quiet comments are being made about her timekeeping and the smell of alcohol that fills the office in her slipstream.

To make matters worse, she's beginning to dislike her work and as a result she's cutting corners – and standards.

If this persists there could be trouble ahead. The crazy thing is that she knows all this, but unfortunately, she doesn't have the capacity, or the inclination, to put it right.

Laura has a serious drink problem, and she needs help.

Tonight she's thinking, she's going have it out with Declan. It's time to order a takeaway and talk.

Shortly after 8 o'clock, later than usual, she hears the key in the door as Declan returns. He goes directly into the bathroom where he seems to spend an age before emerging, expressionless.

'Hi. You OK?' he grunts.

'Yes thanks. You?'

'I can see I don't need to get you a drink. How many is that then?'

'Fuck you, Declan. Shut the fuck up,' yells Laura.

'Don't shout, Laura. Let's not go through all that again.'

'Sarcastic bastard. I hate you.'

'Thank you very much. That just about sums things up, doesn't it? You've only got swearing and insults left to throw at me. Is that what we're going to do for the next hour? Until you pass out.'

Laura rages, 'You're so fucking smug.'

'I tell you what Laura. I was going to sit down and try to have a talk with you this evening. A talk about us and how we might fix this effing problem we've got. But now, before we can even start I can see it's pointless, because you're completely drunk. Again. I'm going out.'

Declan picks up his coat and strides towards the door.

'Declan, please. Don't go. I'm sorry. I'm sorry.'

He turns. 'Laura I'm finding this very hard indeed. I can't stand coming home to find you wasted and slurring your words anymore. Night after night. I have no idea how you function at work, given how much you're putting away. You'd better watch it, or you'll be thrown out. And to be honest, I'm beyond caring. You need to get some professional help Laura and VERY soon. I can't help you anymore.'

He pauses as Laura sits silently.

'Do you want to help yourself, Laura? Do you? Because you realise that you've single-handedly wrecked this marriage with your selfishness.'

'You bastard,' says Laura raising her voice again. 'You just blame me for not providing you with your precious child. That's all you think about. That and your fucking theatre company. Never a thought for me and what I'm going through. Well, I'm sorry I can't give you what you want. If you'd told me that years ago, I'd never have married you, so you can fuck off. Go and play fucking tragic Hamlet and screw Cordelia.'

This time Declan reaches the door and leaves.

Laura unsteadily refills her glass and bursts into tears. She's never felt so miserable. Even the death of her parents. Her anger and frustration pour out as she lets go of what's left of her inhibitions. Even the booze does nothing to quell her feelings of desperation. Her body refuses to provide her with a child and now she's punishing it with alcohol.

She dabs her nose gently with a tissue and reaches into her handbag and pulls out a ragged scrap of paper.

Alcoholics Anonymous. Has it really come to this? She calls the number.

*

It's all drama at Kurmi HQ. Raj is back on the line by late afternoon with an update on the recent Liverpool situation.

'I was right, Javed. It was the gang. Apparently, your tenant and his housemates were threatened and forced to hand over the house for the evening. They don't know why but they didn't argue. Just as well, from what I know. You don't mess with these people. They're not petty criminals Javed. They're gangland killers. I think you just got unlucky my friend. It's the way they operate up here. If they need a meeting place, they just take over somewhere without any warning; they just barge in and clear off when they're finished. That way, no one knows what they're up to in advance.

'But the good news is, there was no damage to your property or anyone. If I were you, I'd leave it at that, I really would Javed.'

Javed grunts in his usual way, wipes his forehead with his handkerchief and thanks Raj for all he's done. But he's not done with this, just yet. He can be recklessly stubborn in his determination to get what he wants.

He sits quietly for a few moments, twiddling with his pen and then opens the Tenants Excel file on his laptop. He finds Dominic Radley's contact details, phones him, and gets through after three rings. Not even gangland Liverpool is going to stop Javed Kurmi collecting what's due to him. The direct approach really is better sometimes.

The young man is surprisingly polite and clearly very upset when Javed refers to the night in question without going into any detail. The conversation ends with a promise from Radley to re-instate the standing order and settle the rent arrears by the end of the week.

Under the circumstances, Javed believes him.

27

Ali and Laura are standing on a bridge that runs over the disused railway line near Laura's Wickham home. Once upon a time, Queen Victoria would have frequently passed here in the Royal Train, heading for Gosport pier, where a boat would take her and her entourage to Osborne House, her Isle of Wight retreat.

'I'm damaged goods I'm afraid Ali. I've been through the mill a bit. Do you still want to date a 52-year-old woman whose shoulders are almost scraping the ground with the weight of the baggage she's carrying around?'

'There you go again! You must be joking. If you're damaged goods I'm certainly not sending you back.'

'That's so sweet of you to say that, but you're so much younger than me and all this has happened so quickly. You'd be far better off with someone nearer your age. Someone you can settle down with and have children. I can't do all that for you.'

'We've hardly started dating and you're already trying to get rid of me. Please don't Laura, I *really* like you. Please don't spoil it all.'

Laura looks uncertain and turns to look at the view from the bridge, down to the lush water meadows where the River Meon meanders its way to the coast. They look so beautiful and peaceful. The whole summer stretches ahead and it's another sunny day. Although she's wary about embarking on a relationship, she has an undeniably warm feeling being around Ali and she likes his company. And the sex is wonderful. So, for the time being, she checks herself.

'Sorry about me. I'm still a bit unsure about everything. Mind you, I do have to say, I love your music, Ali. I've listened to all your songs now and I didn't appreciate how good you are. Some of those could be hits, I reckon. Do we still have *hits* these days?'

'Thank you. I don't quite know what to say. That means a lot, it really does.'

'Which do you prefer – cooking or composing?'

'Composing of course. I love cooking but when you've eaten it, it's gone isn't it? At least with song-writing there's something that lasts,' he says smiling and hugging her tightly.

They look at each other intently and kiss.

Two walkers pass by and glance over at them, smiling, but Ali and Laura are otherwise occupied.

'I really am an addict, you know. Hopefully a recovered one. It's something I'd like to talk to you about. Do you mind me talking about the booze again?'

'Of course not.'

'I don't want to hide anything from you. It's not something I'm proud of,' says Laura. 'It was both my salvation and my downfall.'

'Talk about it as much as you like, I don't mind.'

'Well it certainly got me through my crises. Numbed everything out of the way. But it presented me with a different and even bigger problem. Being dependent on it. I couldn't function without a glass of wine. It's something that only drinkers know the horror of, Ali. Sometimes I turned into a beast, a real howling bitch. Please, please, don't ever go there.'

'I don't drink, as you know. I just hate the taste of alcohol. I'm lucky I guess.'

'That's good. Yes you are lucky, you really are. Being stuck in a cycle of feeling physically sick if you don't top up – and still feeling sick when you do, is the most terrible place to be. Believe me.

Anyway, the first time it happened seriously, when my first marriage broke down, I met Alice who I've told you much about, at AA – and she mentored me. We go back a long way Alice and me, and that's why we're almost joined at the hip. I slowly pulled myself together, and got clean and mentally stable. Thank God.'

'Well done. And well done Alice. I can't wait to meet her. It must have been so hard.'

'It was very hard. So what do you think? You've hooked up with an ex-alkie. What do you think about that then?'

'Listen, I don't care what you did in the past. It's what you are now. That's all I care about.'

He momentarily cringes at the realisation of his own skeleton in the cupboard. That one's certainly going to have to stay put for the moment.

'It was a repeat performance after Frank died. But that time I managed to pull myself together a lot quicker. But hand on heart, that's me done with the booze. I know it's famous last words with drinkers, but I know it deep down this time. No more vino, goodbye Pinot. Farewell. Bon Voyage. That ship has sailed.'

Ali, leans on the bridge parapet and hugs and kisses her again, a long slow and passionate kiss.

'Don't you have to be at the studio?'

'I do, but this is much more importa ...'

*

'I've got some great news,' proclaims Ali, in the control room at Key Studios.

'Yeh?' says Jim.

'*Homeland* and *Healer*. I had a call from the Music Supervisor at Satellite TV. They've accepted the songs for their 'library'. I just hope they actually use them.'

'Wow, how did you manage that?

'I just took a punt.'

That's amazing. Will they let you know when they use them?'

'I have no idea, mate. But hey, it's the first good thing that's happened for me and it's just the start, isn't it? I'm chuffed.'

'What do they want to use them for?'

'Trailers I think – you know, those spots where they promote upcoming programmes …

'Anyway, back to today. I've written a song about a young man and an older woman.'

Jim immediately turns round from his mixing desk with a huge grin on his face.

'Seriously? And what might that be about then?'

They both laugh.

'It's called *May December*.'

'Oh yeh?'

'That's what age gap relationships are called – honestly.'

'In the States they are. Anyway, I can just hear Erin singing it. It's very passionate – of course – and she has just the right voice. I can also hear a heart-tugging sax part in it too. Tell me what you think. Play it.'

'She's rich then?'

'Who, Erin?'

'No, you prat, Laura.'

'Oh, so you've heard. Yeh, she's pretty wealthy, I think. But I promise you I didn't know that when we met and started going out. To tell you the truth, I'm still trying to get my head around the whole thing. I seem to be in the middle of an enormous dream. But I tell you what, I like it very, very much.'

'A whirlwind romance, eh? That's cool and I look forward to actually meeting her. She sounds amazing.

'So, shall we make some more music? Let's hear this demo then,' Jim grins again.

Once again, Ali hands over his home recording of the song they're going to transform into a finished professional production. Some of his playing will be used in the final mix but there's much to be done here at the studio.

'I like it,' says Jim, after the playback. 'Definitely 80s in the overall feel. I see what you mean about a sax, I can hear that too.'

After a couple of hours the pair take an 'ear break' – a phrase that Jim has coined.

'What's the idea with this then – release it as a single?'

'Don't know. Is there any point? Let's see how it turns out. But it's the usual issue, it's not current Top 40. It's … I don't know what it is. It's just me writing a nice tune, I guess. It's what comes out. Is that so wrong, not writing to a Top 40 formula?'

Ali sits up and straightens his back. 'You know, those record company guys think they know everything. They're self-proclaimed music experts and force their mistaken ideas on the public. They presume that everybody is passionate about music and all music must be defined and categorised by genres. Well, they're missing the fact that the majority of the public aren't glued to their headphones all day searching Spotify for playlists. The masses are only marginally interested in music and frankly don't give a toss about genres. These people used to access music easily, listening to the radio, and if they liked a song they'd just go and buy it. They just dipped in and out.

'Music's been divided up into genres, just so these shirts can identify them and market them easier. Like sodding soap powder.'

'Or sudding soap powder?'

'Thank you. As for bringing on new talent, they're only interested in how many Instagram followers this act or that act's got. What's that got to do with the price of fish, for fuck's sake? That's not music – it's statistics which can of course be manipulated. It's just cold marketing. Now artists just seem to be pushing fashion or sexuality on Instagram and TikTok – what happened to the music for God's sake?'

Ali stands up and bows.

'You finished?' says Jim.

'Enough. I have spoken.'

'I do know what you mean, though,' says Jim. 'Sometimes I don't know why we even bother. It's a good job we enjoy what we do, isn't it?'

They chuckle again. Regardless of what happens to Ali's tunes, the two of them love the process of creating quality music from what were originally rough musical doodles. The joy is in the creation.

Well, that's what they would say to anyone asking, but don't be fooled by the smiles – not far down, under the surface, these two are fiercely ambitious young men, determined to make their marks in an industry that seems to be doing all it can to keep them out.

May December
We just fell in love
Ah – they say we're acting like fools
May December

Our hearts don't tell lies
Ahh – we know we've broken the rules
But come on – we've been thinking it through

28

The May-December couple that is Ali and Laura, grows stronger every time they meet – and that's becoming frequent. There is a powerful dynamic energy between them and it's expanding.

Laura has pondered over the fact that, correspondingly, Ali is as much younger than her – as Frank her late husband, was older than her. Crazy. Ali, on the other hand, is less analytical and is happy just to savour his good fortune.

He is acting as tour guide today and Laura is doing the driving. They're on the car ferry to the Isle of Wight, with the intention of doing a spot of sightseeing. Ali has planned a tour, which includes Queen Victoria's Osborne House – for a bit of history and culture, followed by lunch in Cowes and an afternoon driving around the island.

They're sitting in the café area as the ferry throbs its way over the Solent and Ali leans in and kisses Laura on the side of her forehead. She's reading a discarded newspaper, looks up and returns the kiss.

'Do you ever wear skirts or dresses?'

'Ha, where did that come from? Sometimes I do, but most of the time I'm happiest in slacks or jeans to be honest. It's easier, certainly when I have to drive.'

'You look wonderful in any clothes, but I do look forward to seeing you in a skirt. You have superb legs. And yes, sorry you're lumbered with the driving.'

'That's fine, I like driving. As long as you tell me where I have to go and give me plenty of warning.'

'Have you ever made love on a boat before?'

'Stop it,' says Laura, smiling. Then she gives him another peck.

Ali has been completely taken over. He adores Laura. He's appalled by her tragic past, which adds to the mystique, but it's not the only reason he's fallen head over heels for her. He loves her warmth, her smile, her sense of humour, her knowledge, her wisdom and her strength – and her body. She's the one thing on his mind, 24/7. He can't quite believe how she has changed his life so completely in such a short time. The age difference is of absolutely no consequence and he's pretty sure the feeling is mutual.

Laura looks up from the Daily Mail.

'Which paper do you normally read?'

'I don't look at the papers much, to be honest. I mostly get the news from my phone. But I like the puzzles in the Mail, and The Guardian, as well as online. And the Sudoku!'

'What about politics?'

'Groan, I'm sick of how aggressive it all is – particularly in the media. People get so angry, don't they? Mainly in social media.'

'I totally agree. I don't use it much at the moment but largely speaking, I think it's a good thing, where everyone gets a voice. But the down side is that it also gives a voice to nasty, spineless people who just use it to snipe or be vicious,' says Laura.

'I used to be a real stroppy left-wing socialist, but not anymore – looking at how it's been inflicted on nations over the years, it's menacing and it's thrown up its share of dictators, hasn't it? How did they get there? The Putins, Kim Jong-uns, the Mugabes, Idi Amin … I've never understood that.'

'We've got a few of our own haven't we!'

'Hah – not quite as bad, but I think there are too many self-serving people in government. How many are really there to run the country on our behalf? Not many, I reckon. Left-wing or right-wing, they're all the same. They're more interested in party politics and furthering their careers. They just don't care.'

'I agree, you need statesmen, people with good hearts, to run countries,' says Laura. 'I could tell you a few things about politics. Remember, I was a journalist for many years. You wouldn't believe some of the things I covered.

'It's not all bad though. I'm glad there's been a lot of progress in things like racism and gender issues. And I'd like to see that develop. But I'm not a supporter of woke. That's taking things too far. It stifles debate. Cancelling history is just foolish, in my humble opinion. History is there for us to learn from. Ignore it and you're missing a big point. That's how societies move forward – learning from mistakes. Mistakes are a good thing in that context. There. I've finished.' Laura concludes.

'I so agree with all that. Talking of controversies, you realise where we're going, don't you? What do you think about the Royal Family?'

They drive off the ferry and it's just a short distance to Osborne House, Queen Victoria's palatial holiday home that she loved so much and shared with Prince Albert, their children, and grandchildren.

'I expect you think it's a bit weird – me bringing you here, but I actually love this place,' says Ali.

'Whatever you think about the monarchy, Prince Andrew, Harry and Meghan and the like, it exists and so does its history – right here in this place. It's fantastic and I just get a very good vibe from it. I think they must have been a happy family and I want to share that with you. See if you feel the same.'

'That's very cute,' says Laura. 'I can't imagine what some folk back in Ireland might say, given the historical relationship between Ireland and England.'

They wander through the gallery at the start of the tour and Laura gazes up at the huge painting of Gan (Queen Victoria), and smiles. The children's nursery at the top of the house is a poignant place for her and Laura is rather taken by the rows of specially made little beds. Apparently made by Prince Albert. Then it's off to Victoria's private rooms, complete with one of the first flushing lavatories.

'This place is amazing. You're right, and I love it, thank you so much,' says Laura as they step back outside into the sunshine after the tour. They saunter, hand in hand back to the car park.

'Where now?'

'We're off to Cowes, where the rich come to play with their yachts, and hopefully, a nice spot of lunch. The restaurant's got some good reviews on Trip Advisor.'

*

They're sitting, shaded from the sunshine, outside a small restaurant in Cowes, overlooking the Solent – devouring all they can about each other.

'This is beautiful. So many yachts and boats,' squints Laura, taking in the bustling atmosphere in the harbour and the Parade.

'You should see it during Cowes Week, it's mental. The world's yachties descend. It's complete madness. But it is very exciting. Definitely a sport for the rich.'

'Would you like to have a yacht like one of those, if you could afford one?'

'Nah, too much like hard work. And dangerous. I don't want to go missing at sea.'

He turns back to face Laura.

'You're not still having second thoughts about all this are you? You know, us, you and me. I've never felt like this before to be honest, and if you left me, I don't think I could cope. There, I've said it.'

Laura slowly smiles. 'Where on earth did that come from?'

Ali pouts.

'I'm getting used to it – I suppose!'

She's teasing him, because she too, has been taken aback by the feelings that Ali stirs in her and it's not just physical attraction. She's fascinated by her young man and the effect he's having on her, and it's a very pleasant surprise. Her early doubts seem to have vanished.

'I'm very happy, to be perfectly honest. Is that any good? Stop feeling so insecure, Ali Kurmi. We're fine. Where are we going next?' she asks.

'I was going to suggest Blackgang Chine at Ventnor – it's on the south of the island. It's an amusement park. They've got a ride there called the Vortex Tunnel which I thought might amuse you, given your obsession with the Law of Attraction, but I don't think we've got the time.'

'Excuse me please! Obsession? I'm not obsessed and I do get it, you know – vortex, the law of attraction. And you wrote that song about it. It is such a good song Ali. You're so clever. So I suppose I'll excuse that cheap shot.'

Laura is referring to one of Ali's newest songs called *Living In The Now,* that he's recorded and added to his creative stockpile, ready to unleash on the world when the right moment comes along. Ali just smiles.

'One of your best, from what I've heard so far. As I've already told you, I like everything I've heard on your playlist. It's a good mix – I like that – and different singers.'

‘Thanks, that’s the general idea. Variety. Why keep on churning out the same old thing, time after time? Leave that to the Top 40 acts.’

‘You’re a clever boy, Ali. Anyway, I suppose we should get going again, yes? Have we got room for a cream tea?’

‘Bugger the cream tea, let’s find a quiet field and have a little mingle,’ says Ali, leaning in and kissing Laura’s neck.

‘How dare you. A mingle indeed, whatever that is. What kind of a girl do you think I am? ‘

‘A very beautiful one,’ mumbles Ali, still buried under her hair.

29

Javed Kurmi strides into his house at a brisk pace, wipes his forehead, clears his throat loudly and deliberately slaps his keys on the hall table. This is a familiar warning sign to Namita that all is not well in her husband's world.

The Kurmis live in an affluent area just outside Bromley, less than 12 miles from the centre of London. Javed, wealthy and proud of his property empire, recalls only too well how his early days in the business were financially tough. The family somehow managed to squeeze themselves into a terraced house down the road, without murdering each other in the queue for the bathroom. Now he lives in a huge detached house that's coming down with bathrooms – but the children are long gone. Times have changed.

In those days, he spent a lot of his time on the road, looking for and purchasing suitable properties. He would often, single-handedly, convert them into multi-occupant dwellings – fitting them out as cost-effectively as possible, with the basic requirements.

His foresight was impressive. When expanding his portfolio, his preference was to purchase properties as closely together as possible – handy for ancillary help, when it was needed down the line – and for routine inspections. These days, that's Hammad and Kamran's domain, but in the early days, Javed Kurmi was a real grafter and did everything himself.

Eventually, Namita became actively involved in running the business but after a subsequent cancer scare, she was forced to step down. Now, fully recovered, she bides her time with the grandchildren, looking after their home, reading, cooking, and generally enjoying the comforts of life at her enviable address near the Manor. Javed has never asked to her to return to work.

The family workforce operates from an office in the town centre. Eldest son, Mohammed, is the company accountant of Kurmi Properties Ltd., and his daughter Basma works alongside her aunt, Javed's sister, Sunita.

They work hard for Javed and since they temporarily stopped expanding their portfolio five years ago, the workload has been more manageable. However, Javed has new plans which will change that, so they're bracing themselves. But he's going to have to play it carefully because he's secretly planning to oust his sister Sunita's husband, currently a sleeping partner, and he might find it trickier than he thinks.

Sunita's sons, Hammad and Kamran, are also on the payroll and play a big part in handling the not insignificant maintenance side of the business. This keeps them pretty busy, given the number of properties the company owns, and the age of the buildings. They've established contractors all over the south, to call on when in need. But they're more than capable of rolling up their sleeves to fix things if they can – particularly when it comes to the collection of unpaid rent. Javed relies heavily on these two and if he ousts their father, he might find things very difficult.

The last person directly involved in the business, is Ali. Ham and Kam consider him to be a complete waste of space, but their uncle insists on him being involved in *rent default solutions* – a phrase coined by Ham, so they just play along. They reckon it's their uncle's attempt at toughening up his wayward son.

It's very rare for them to run into difficult situations when chasing defaulters, like the recent fiasco in Liverpool, but there's a first time for everything. Generally though, the business runs very smoothly, without any major problems.

Meanwhile, Namita is presently concerned that with the way things are going – not for the business but with the big wide world – her current happy domesticity is under threat. With more and more people working from home, she fears that it won't be long before Javed abandons the office model and works from home himself.

She tolerates her husband and all his huffs and puffs – and distance between them during the day has been a very workable arrangement for her. But she isn't ready to have her husband around her all day and every day. No thank you.

'You look stressed. Is there anything I can do to help?' says Namita.

Javed ignores his wife's concern and picks up a post-it note with Ali's name written on it.

'You've spoken to him?' he asks sharply.

'Yes, he called yesterday.'

'What was he after?'

'He wasn't after anything – he just rang to say hello and to see how we all are. He's a good boy, Javed.'

'He's had long enough. And he's not a boy anymore. It's time to make some grown-up changes.'

'Oh Javed, don't do anything rash.'

'I've been putting the word out again to see if there might be someone acceptable to us – but it's been tricky.'

'Marriage? You know that I don't think that's a good idea,' she says, biting her bottom lip in anticipation of the Kurmi temper.

'I don't care what you or he think,' says Javed, raising his voice. 'He's had years to get over it. And anyway, what about us? We've had just as much to live down – if not more than him. No, enough is enough. It's time to restore the reputation of this family – and it's common sense.'

'Ali is different from his brother and sisters', says Namita. 'He's more sensitive.'

'He's lazy, you mean.'

'Come on, he's just different. He's very talented at music and his DJ work is quite successful, I understand.'

'A DJ? That's not a proper job. A man needs self-pride and that only comes from working hard. Not playing around.'

Javed hands Namita his phone. 'There she is, a doctor. A professional and, amazingly enough, she hasn't been married. What do you think?'

Namita looks at the photo briefly. 'She looks very nice Javed, but ...'

'The family is fully briefed and aware of Ali's background and I think she will be very good for him.'

Namita knows that she has little hope of persuading her husband to see it from Ali's point of view.

He believes in his version of Islamic tradition and will not be challenged, despite the rapidly changing world in which he lives. He's made up his mind and, as far as he is concerned, that is the last on the matter. He's far too stubborn and set in his ways and is unlikely to change his views.

Namita also knows from bitter experience, that despite her husband's strict authority and confidence, this latest plan is likely to run into problems and her husband is going to get all worked up again and into another big sweat.

Still, at least she knows what's coming. Sort of.

30

In Portsmouth, Becky Davies is walking quickly towards Gunwharf Quays, on her way to work, when her phone vibrates in her back pocket. In a hurry she fumbles for it and answers without stopping.

'Hi Ali. Long time, no see. Yeh, fine thanks. Can't talk now, I'm just on my way to work. Can I call you after my shift? OK, speak then.'

'Damn it,' says Ali, picks up his keys and heads out of the door and off to the shops. He has a difficult task ahead of him and he still doesn't know how he's going to play it, let alone know how it'll go down. But he's determined to do the right thing and tell Becky about Laura. She's going to find out soon enough, and he wants to get to her first.

He approaches one of his favourite restaurants, Koh Thai, and peers through the window. Becky loves Thai food and his first thought had been to bring her here to explain things. But he's now thinking that if things don't go well, it might be easier to pick somewhere with a quicker escape route. He decides to ponder over it during a workout. That usually does the trick.

It's one of those fitness places where you can just turn up with your key fob and train whenever you feel the urge to get physical. He likes the flexibility and has been known to train in the middle of the night. He's got a training programme, but he prefers his own customised version, which works very well for him. He loves the feeling after a good session – the natural high, his entire body tingling with a combination of exhaustion and contentment. It's physically and mentally challenging – and it's money in the good health bank.

Workout over and suitably humming with muscular and mental energy, he feels well prepared for his rendezvous with Becky later, at his now chosen venue, the Tap Room.

Ali buys the drinks, and they sit together at one of those high round tables for two.

'Any good?' asks Ali. 'I don't know anything about real ale but the guy says Block Island is good.'

'Fab,' says Becky, taking a large mouthful. 'Nice and strong. Like you! Are you trying to get me pissed?'

'No, I just feel a bit guilty for not being in touch. How'd it go today?'

'OK thanks, busy as usual. No morons today.'

'Becks, I've got something I need to tell you.'

'I know, Ali.'

'Sorry?'

'I already know. About your new friend.'

'Oh shit.'

'It's OK. It's fine. It was going to happen one day, wasn't it? I mean we've never exactly been an item, have we? You just beat me to it.'

'I know, but I feel awful Becks. You're my best mate and I love you dearly. I really do.'

'And you're mine too. And that won't change … unless you want it to?'

'What? No, of course not. So, you're not angry?'

'Not at all. It's time I got myself sorted out, anyway. I've been drifting for far too long. You don't exactly need a law degree to serve enchiladas, do you?'

'So any ideas about what you'll do?'

'Well my mum and dad want me to complete all the law training. But it'll take years and I don't want to end up as some bloody ambulance chaser. The world seems to be full of money-grabbing lawyers and solicitors. It's so dull.'

'You could earn loads of money.'

'So they say, but so much law work is in the gutter. There are a lot of immoral legal people out there hiding behind the letter of the law. Some would sue their own grannies if they saw a financial opportunity.'

'So, will you stick around here, do you think?'

'I dunno. Do you remember Dominic, my uni friend?'

'Possibly, you may have mentioned him,' says Ali.

'He's a bit of a case too but we do keep in touch and last time he suggested travelling a bit, Thailand possibly. I said no at the time, but I might just change my mind.'

Becky takes another long drink. 'Enough of that. Tell me more about this lady then – I've only heard bits and pieces.'

Three Block Islands later, the two are still sitting in the Tap Room chatting ferociously – and at closing time Becky, somewhat unsteadily, stands up.

'Time to go then my old *mate*!'

'Indeed *mate,* time to call it a day', says Ali, stone-cold sober.

Becky is completely pissed and Ali helps her outside, still giggling and chattering away.

'So I suppose it's farewell then. I'd better say goodnight,' says Becky, wobbling and looking deeply into Ali's eyes.

'Absolutely not, I'll walk you home.'

Becky's not listening.

'A frightfully f-fond farewell then,' she says.

They stand staring at each other. For a very tangible moment they almost kiss but at the crucial moment when they might engage, they're rescued by the noisiest moped in Portsmouth as it screams past, howling deafeningly, at 15 mph.

Ali mouths the words fucking *twat*, as the youngster disappears slowly, but at full throttle – close to breaking the sound barrier.

31

Alice Kingston is removing a bowl of lightly pickled carrots and red onion from her American fridge and as she lifts it on to the dresser, she leans forward for a gentle sniff.

'Won't be long – I just need to grill the salmon. The rice is already done.'

'Smells lovely, Alice. Where on earth do you find the time to cook from fresh, what with running the business?' says Laura, looking around approvingly again at Alice's compact designer kitchen.

'No, don't you worry, I leave plenty of time for myself.'

Laura has a complimentary facial tonight, a CACI – but it's a light dinner first.

'How's Ali? You're hiding him from me. I want to meet him – soon.'

'He's fine thanks – he's got a gig tonight.'

'You don't go to those, do you?'

'I don't think he really wants me to. And to be perfectly honest, it's not really my thing – probably standing around a lot. But I love the music, don't get me wrong.'

'No that wouldn't be much fun would it. How often does he work?'

'He's quite busy at weekends and sometimes during the week.'

'That's a shame – for socialising, going out together, I mean?'

'Not really, the nice thing is, he's around quite a bit during the day, so we actually see a lot of each other.'

'What about you and him generally … is everything still good?'

'It's lovely. I know folk still think we're the odd couple but we're very happy thank you. He says he wants to protect me. Isn't that the cutest thing?'

'Protect you from what? What a cheek, you're an independent woman.'

'No, don't get me wrong. He means well.'

'I suppose that is sweet. And he does all this other music too. He must be a busy man. Tell me about it – you know, his song writing and producing thingy. What's that all about?'

'Alice, he's absolutely brilliant. I mean it. I'm not just saying it. He really is very talented. You should hear some of the songs he's recorded. I'm no expert but I think they sound as good as anything you hear on the radio.'

'I'd love to. Where or how, can I hear them?'

'Well you can't really, at the moment – although he did release a couple of singles a while ago, I think. He's storing them up and trying to get some sort of deal. I don't exactly know what. It's all a bit complicated to me. But the songs are great and they're really varied which I like – they don't all sound the same. I've got a very talented toyboy. I'll send you a link to his song playlist, I'm sure he won't mind.'

'Yes please, I'll have a listen. I'll look forward to that. Now then, are you ready for this? I have something to tell you, Laura O'Brien. I've met a man.'

'Wah … that's great. Where did you find him? Do tell all.'

'His name is David, he's local and he owns the wine bar in Wickham. And his aura is e-normous!'

'Oh no. Alice you have to be kidding me!'

'I know, I know, sounds risky doesn't it? But he's very nice. It's early days anyway. But it's looking OK. I've done a card spread and that was good.'

'Does he know about your hocus pocus world and your unfriendly relationship with booze? A bar manager, for goodness sake Alice.'

'He knows I don't drink but I haven't told him why yet. I'll just see how it goes.'

'Easy on the eye?'

'I think so! He has very long sideburns, which is a bit different. But I don't mind a bit of facial. Helps me exfoliate!'

'How old is he?'

'A year younger than me.'

'Ha. So, you've got a toyboy too. Gosh, synchronicity in action.'

'Certainly is my dear, the stars are aligned.'

They chuckle and continue eating.

'He's handsome and he's very funny and he's divorced. No nasty surprises around the corner. I hope. And he has two motorbikes.'

'I can't wait to meet him. Tell you what, let's organise an evening, so everyone can meet up. I agree with you, it's high time you met Ali properly.'

After their meal, the pair move outside to Alice's treatment room in her garden. There's a side gate for her clients, which is ideal and protects her privacy. It's a celebration of space conservation and clever design; she's got everything set up efficiently, with hot and cold running water, and a small bathroom. Her significant client base indicates that she's definitely doing something right.

Alice prepares her machine whilst Laura settles herself for the treatment – and a good old natter with her pal. Laura has a remarkable complexion for her age, but she puts the effort in and has no shame in shelling out on preventative care. A girl needs to look after herself.

*

'How are you – my gorgeous, gorgeous Laura?' he whispers into his phone.

'What time is it?' says Laura, waking from a deep sleep.

'Late.'

'Where are you?'

'Home.'

'What are you doing? Are you safe? There's nothing wrong is there?'

'No, relax. Everything's fine, the gig was great – I just wanted to mentally climb into bed with you and make love with you.'

'Oh Ali. It's one o'clock.' Laura let's out a deep breath. 'Shit, Ali.'

'I can't wait until morning.'

'You'll have to – I need to sleep, so go to bed Ali, be a good boy. Do as I say. I'll see you in the morning.'

Inevitably, Laura cannot immediately go back to sleep, so she just lies there looking into the darkness. Eventually she settles and smiles, as she drifts off thinking about him, grateful that she seems to have manifested herself a new life and a brand-new start – with a very handsome young man. So far, so good. So very good.

Ali is still buzzing from the club, so he sits up in bed and switches on his tablet. His first thought is a touch of Sudoku, but he decides against it. He's recently been looking at more YouTube videos about that bloody Law of Attraction – as prompted by Laura a while ago. He likes the idea of only attracting things that you really want in your life. Who wouldn't? He watches a few videos – or at least parts of them, as they're all quite long. He's already grasped the principles, but he can't make up his mind whether it's a huge pile of pretentious shit – or whether there's something he's missed and needs to explore further.

He wonders if he attracted that call from Satellite TV, offering to use his songs? He hadn't formally sat in meditation specifically asking for the songs to be used, but yes, he did wish for them to be taken up. So maybe it did work like that?

Whatever, he doesn't come to any conclusions because the next thing he knows is, it's morning and he's decided that regardless of any supernatural laws, he will mindfully guarantee that only good things happen today.

32

Five years ago

Laura walks into the large function room with husband Frank at her side and she's beaming and looking beautiful in her favourite Dior number, and hair up. There's a lot of flashing as the press and guests start taking photos. They're not really pointing at her – it's her celebrated husband they've come to see. But Laura does scrub up very well and tonight she's looking very much the movie star.

It's a charity fundraiser and the great and good are all here for a charity auction. Laura and Frank have only been married a few months and there are plenty of folk curious to see what the new Mrs O'Brien looks like in the flesh.

She's nervous and light conversation doesn't come easily to her so, instead, she does a lot of smiling. The organiser of the event, Niall Byrne steps forward and steers the couple towards a large group who are waiting to meet the great Frank O'Brien in person. Frank is something of a national treasure and his rise to fame and great success touched the nation's collective heart. His professional and personal life has been well scrutinised by the press for years – he's always been good for a few column inches or the modern digital equivalent. Frank mingles happily with the group and makes a point of introducing Laura to everyone.

They finally seat themselves for dinner with a diverse collection of tablemates. A haulage boss, who's looking extremely uncomfortable, as he repeatedly tugs at his shirt collar. To Laura's right is a plastic surgeon, who she later learns, specialises in all things breast and is, judging by the loudness of his voice, much like his implants, over-inflated. She makes a mental note to steer clear of him.

Going round the table, there's an undertaker, a leisure centre manager, a doctor, and a plumbing and heating engineer who's obviously a big local spanner, because Laura's seen his vans everywhere.

It's all men getting the limelight and they're dutifully accompanied by their supportive ladies. Laura wonders how many here tonight are female entrepreneurs.

She chuckles to herself – the doctor's wife clearly had a couple of gins before coming – she's pissed already and sharing her opinions very loudly. Her husband is visibly wincing and fidgeting in his chair.

Two tables away, sit Richard and Stephanie O'Brien, their spouses and other guests. Laura tries to avoid looking over, but she feels the stares of Stephanie from time to time and it's very unsettling.

After dinner, the auction takes place, conducted by a brilliantly funny character called Joe Carroll. He's the perfect auctioneer. He has the crowd in stitches with his witty patter, whilst subtly taking all their money from them. He knows exactly what he's doing.

When the sale is over, it's time for the band – a real old-fashioned Irish showband who sound absolutely brilliant to Laura. She sticks to her chair, petrified that someone ghastly will ask her to dance.

Frank is across the room, socialising – he clearly knows most of the people in the room and Laura is delighted at how well presented her husband is. Frank is by no means vain but he takes good care of himself and he has plenty of female admirers hovering around him tonight.

She can see he's torn between duty and his obvious love for her. He keeps looking across at her, eyes glistening with pride. Frank knows he's one hell of a lucky guy to have found this staggeringly beautiful young lady. Just look at her. Bejesus, how did he manage that?

*

Eighteen months previously ...

Laura Conran arrives at Silver Beeches, having followed the satnav instructions, which have run out as she and her cameraman approach Frank O'Brien's residence, outside Tipperary. They have to guess the last bit and turn off the road, at which point they're greeted by two huge gates with imposing brick and flint pillars.

Laura, as a freelance journalist, working for the Dublin News, is doing a feature spread on Frank O'Brien, one of Ireland's most successful horse breeders with countless Group and Grade I winners. She's done her homework and whilst she has little interest in horses, she's confident that her professionalism will see her through the assignment.

Damien, the photographer, does the honours and speaks over the intercom. The gates slowly swing open and they drive in and follow the road, whilst admiring the impeccably maintained fenced fields that lead up to a grand brick and stone-built house at the end.

Laura scans both sides as they drive towards the house. The property is naturally secluded by the gently undulating land and some thoughtful tree planting. She can see why a wealthy man like Frank would choose this large, verdant hideaway. There's a large circular turning area in front of the house with a horse sculpture at its centre. Surprisingly tasteful, she thinks.

'Some place this,' wonders Damien. 'What a house.'

The period building is covered in wisteria and boasts a large green front door with wide stone steps leading up to it.

'You'll get some good photos here,' says Laura, 'but have you noticed anything? Can you see a single horse anywhere – apart from the sculpture? Because I can't.'

'They've got security cameras instead – they're all over the place. It'll be a photo-finish.' quips Damien.

A mature, well-dressed and friendly-looking woman, steps out of the front door.

'Hello and welcome to Silver Beeches. Ms Conran, isn't it? And?'

Damien holds out his hand, 'Damien'.

'You've had quite a drive, haven't you? I'll find you some refreshments presently.

If you'd like to follow me, I'll take you to the garden room to meet Mr O'Brien.'

As they walk through the house, Laura likes what she sees. This man has taste – or someone does. The house is richly but subtly decorated.

'Welcome to Silver Beeches,' says Frank O'Brien, getting up from a seat in the bright naturally lit room. He shakes Laura's hand and smiles warmly at her. He's dressed casually, in a blue cashmere jumper and plum chinos, and has a full head of well-maintained salt and pepper hair.

'Ms Conran, isn't it?'

'Please call me Laura.'

'Pleased to meet you too?' he says, turning to Damien.

'It's Damien, nice to meet you.'

'And this is Mary,' he says looking across the room. Mary looks after this place and me too. Can we get you anything? I'm going to have a coffee – what would you two like? Thank you, Mary.'

'I thought we should start here and then I'll take you both down to the stud. Plenty of good pictures there of course. But I thought I could give you the background here.'

'Forgive the impudent question Mr O'Brien.'

‘Frank, please.’

‘Frank, I don’t see any horses outside.’

‘Ha! We have plenty of horses don’t worry – they’re best looked after down the road, at the stud.’

‘Of course,’ says Laura, feeling a little foolish. ‘And I expected to find you surrounded by security people. You’re tucked away here, aren’t you?’

‘We are, but we have cameras everywhere. The very latest technology. Very discreet.’

‘Oh I see,’ says Laura, looking around, wishing she hadn’t asked that question either.

‘And we do have Bill lurking in the background. He looks after us too. I’m sure he’s not far away.’

Laura switches on her recorder and the interview begins. Frank starts his story – recounting how he was a successful property developer, who entered the horse-racing world after buying a couple of horses, just for the fun of it.

‘There’s no doubt about it – or shame – I was a successful businessman and I had money to spend and invest. But to start with, it was an amusement really. It was a way of entertaining business associates at the races. I didn’t really know anything about horses. My father was a straightforward working man and enjoyed a bet on them. Nothing more serious, though. But I got hooked.

‘It wasn’t until I bumped into Joe Kelly that I realised there was a business opportunity as well. Joe was, and of course still is, a big name in racing circles as a trainer and he told me I’d soon be wiped out if I didn’t change my ways and create some form of plan. He told me that the real money in racing lies in breeding and stallions. So, on a handshake we decided to work together – and the rest as the well-worn saying goes, is history.

'Happily, we became a bit of a national success story.'

Laura is enjoying listening to this hugely successful man talking so modestly. She likes the way he speaks, with a hint of self-deprecation. He has a light in his eyes that shines bright and deep. He clearly takes pride in his appearance and his aftershave smells divine. She gets the feeling that there's a lot more to Frank O'Brien than making money.

'Shall we think about going to the stud?' he eventually suggests.

Mary leads Damien off to take some exterior shots and as they walk through the house, Laura compliments Frank on the décor.

'Ah, that's all down to Catherine. I can't take any credit.'

'Catherine?'

'My late wife. She died of breast cancer four years ago. Wonderful woman.'

'I'm so sorry, that was very insensitive. There was no mention of her in the press release.'

'That's alright my dear,' says Frank. 'The tears have dried up now. But we were a good team.'

'Do you mind me mentioning her in the article?' asks Laura.

'Not at all – mention away. She was a huge part of me and for a long time I thought about giving everything up. Grief does that to you, doesn't it? But I didn't do anything rash. And I'm very pleased I didn't,' says Frank.

They're now in the hallway. 'What about you? You're married?' he asks, spotting her wedding ring.

'I'm so sorry I shouldn't have asked that – I'm being intrusive. That was very rude – please forgive me.'

'No, don't worry yourself. I really don't mind,' says Laura looking straight at Frank.

'I was married, but I'm afraid it ended in tears. I keep a ring on that finger to stave off unwanted attention.'

'Oh dear, that puts me in my place doesn't it?'

'No not at all,' says Laura hastily. 'You're a welcome exception!'

'I'm truly sorry to hear about the marriage, though – divorces are messy things.'

'Yes, I'm afraid you're right there.'

'Cruel things do happen alarmingly often, don't they? At the time, they hurt and don't make any sense. But later you find yourself on another path that wouldn't have appeared without the upset or tragedy having taken place. Do you know what I mean? Or am I rambling?'

'No, you're not and that is so true. We can never be sure what's round the next corner. Or indeed why it's round there.'

'Agreed, and when unexpected opportunities present themselves, you need to be able to recognise whether or not they're right for you, and if they are, go with them. That's my philosophy,' says Frank as they make their way outside.

The three, along with security man Bill, sitting next to Damien in the back, drive down to the stud in Frank's top of the range black Range Rover, with Frank at the wheel. After less than a kilometre, they turn off the main road and follow a long tree-lined driveway, at the end of which they park up in a huge yard. It's surrounded by stained timber and stone buildings that turn out to be the stables. Stable Block A to be precise.

There are three more yards, Blocks B, C and D, just out of view, and Laura and Damien are taken aback at the sheer size of the place.

Colourful, weedless, raised flower borders surround the whole of Yard A, softening the symmetry.

Laura is thinking that this looks more like an upmarket holiday village. It's enormous.

'Impressive, isn't it?' says Frank, 'and the beauties inside are treated better than humans. I tell you. You'll meet them in a moment.'

'Ah, here he is. This is Joe – Joe Kelly.'

'Joe, this is Laura – and Damien, from the Dublin News. They're doing a feature about our work so we must be very nice to them.'

'Sure we will,' says Joe stepping forward with a wily smile. 'Let's take a look around. Have you been to a stud before? '

'No, never.'

'Well, there's a lot more going on here than you probably imagined, we have dozens of full-time staff and twice as many again of specialists who come and go when required. These horses get 5-star treatment 24/7 and believe me that takes some fair work. So, if you're ready, let's go.'

And that's how the going got good for Laura Conran and Frank O'Brien.

33

'What do you think about this one?' asks Laura, handing Ali an estate agent folder, labelled 'Meon Lodge'.

'What do I think? It looks incredible,' says Ali. 'You've started looking then?'

'I have and I want to get this right. Much as I like it here, it's time to get things moving. Here, take it. It rather takes my fancy. Will you come and view it with me?'

'Sure, let's see,' says Ali, reaching out for the details. 'When are you going?'

'I've booked a viewing tomorrow morning.'

'OK. Yeh, sure,' Ali repeats. 'You don't hang around, do you?'

'Look, it's Georgian with 1.5 acres, six bedrooms, a luxury kitchen, a garage block, a stable and mainly lawned grounds. But. Wait for this. It has … an indoor swimming pool. Hey.

'Look at that hallway, and I love that wide staircase. The conservatory has got a jacuzzi, three of the bedrooms have en-suites and take a look at that kitchen, Ali Kurmi – could you cook in there?'

'Wow, that's pretty impressive. A steam oven too and built-in microwave. How much is it, if you don't mind me asking?' says Ali.

'Just over 2 million,' says Laura without even lifting her head from the details.

'As good as your place back in Ireland?'

'Nothing like it. That would be far too big – and anyway, that was then and this is now.'

Ali looks at Laura who's deep in thought again, and his heart flutters. He loves the warm tone of her voice with just that slightest hint of an accent. He adores her soft eloquence and confidence, combined with that sense of worldly experience. Being with her makes him feel supremely proud and incredibly energised. One thing's for sure, she's not frightened of making big decisions either.

He picks up his guitar, removes the plectrum from between the strings and puts it between his teeth as he flips the instrument over a couple of times. He's normally bashful about playing in front of others but with Laura he feels completely relaxed.

'That's nice,' she says, 'a lovely sound – not that I know anything about guitars.'

'I'm very fond of it,' says Ali. 'It's been a good friend to me.'

'You know, I don't talk to you about your music nearly enough. I'm so sorry. How do you actually write your songs?'

'Whoa, that's a hard one to explain simply. I just pick up my guitar or sit at the keyboard and let my fingers run free – doodling, I think is the best way I can put it; it's a leap of faith if you like.'

'Religious faith?' Laura raises an eyebrow.

'I don't know, could be I suppose. It comes from somewhere – I mean tunes or phrases just pop into my head without me making any effort.

'I'm not brilliant on the guitar or the piano or keyboard or whatever, but I learned to play by ear when I was young, and I just strum away. I dunno, suddenly a string of chords will just grab me, and I keep going until the sequence starts to feel good.

'So, yeh, I suppose it's faith that it'll turn into something decent. Mind you, anyone listening in would think it's a pile of rubbish – but you have to trust yourself to continue until the chords hopefully start to sound good.'

'What about the tune? How do you get that?'

'The tune comes from the same unknown place. The chord sequence inspires me to start humming or singing nonsense words and somehow a tune, or part of one, will emerge. I always have my voice recorder on the phone handy, which is great to keep all my ideas on. It's so easy to forget them.'

'I think you're amazing Ali – having heard some of the songs you've written. To think they start out like that – and the lyrics too. I have to say, I simply adore *In Paradise.*'

'Yeh, lyrics take me a quite a bit of time to get right and they usually come after I've written the main tunes.'

'Are you ever scared you might accidentally steal someone else's song?'

'Ha, every songwriter's continuing nightmare. I'm constantly paranoid about that. I expect you're thinking about Ed Sheeran's court case?'

'Yes, and George Harrison over My Sweet Lord.'

'It's always a worry, but I can honestly say, hand on heart, I've never sat down to copy anyone else's song deliberately. I once caught an interview with Paul McCartney and he put it the best way. He said he had no shame in admitting that many of his songs were often inspired by other artists he'd listened to and had always loved. You can't help absorbing what you listen to, can you? Even the great classical composers must have studied the music of their own musical heroes, and you can be sure that something will have rubbed off.

'But the best thing of all, is that I can write absolutely anything. I love all types of music – Carmina Burana to Stormzy, The Beatles to Snow Patrol – from Genesis to Dua Lipa. I love all those amazing bands and singers like Tears for Fears, Eurythmics, Depeche Mode, The Clash, The Buzzcocks, and the Ramones. And then there's the Who, The Stones, Jethro Tull, Pink Floyd, and all those iconic stadium bands. I don't copy them but I am influenced by them. But nothing more than that.'

'Can you try something now?'

'What – compose now?'

'Yes.'

'I'd rather not, if you don't mind. No offence, but the way I write is very private – which is why I'm hopeless in today's music scene, where dozens of people end up writing bits of songs. It's like pass the parcel. I can't do all this with someone else listening. I have to knock it into shape first.

'Anyway, I've got a crap singing voice – I need other people to sing my songs. I'm not like Michael Bublé, Michael McDonald or Paul McCartney – they could sing any old rubbish, strum a few ideas and still sound brilliant – and Beyoncé, Craig David, Elton John or Phil Collins and Paul Carrack – all these folks' voices sound great singing anything. So I have to play it a different way – forgive the pun.'

'You've got such a lovely speaking voice, isn't that strange? Anyway, you're pretty good on the guitar.'

'I'm OK but, like the piano, I wish I'd stayed with the lessons. Never mind.'

He continues doodling on his guitar.

'Feeling hungry?'

'I am,' he says, giving Laura an overly large smile.

'No, food, you fool. Shall we eat soon or ...'

But before Laura can finish her sentence, Ali has put his guitar down and she finds herself kissing him, her arms dropping limply to her sides. She's got those twinges again, spreading down through her body – and already she's leading him off, still kissing him. She giggles and tries pulling him towards the door, with upstairs in mind, but Ali clearly has different ideas and in this intense moment, she really doesn't mind. All she wants right now is to feel him inside her again.

And so they end up sprawled across the sofa attempting to undress each other as they go. They get halfway before Ali is now kissing and licking her nipples as Laura takes hold of him and guides him into her.

'Oh Ali,' says Laura groaning with pleasure, 'this is so unexpect ...'

'Laura, I love you. I love you so much, it hurts,' he whispers.

Laura squeezes her thighs together tightly and he recoils with pleasure.

'To the stars and back?'

'Around the universe and beyond that, five times, and then back again,' Ali says.

And so it goes, they linger in their own passionate paradise, until they're both physically spent.

Ali stays inside her and continues to gently move while Laura lies, entranced. She's just enjoying the moment and thinking about how much this man is making her happy. She realises that she too has fallen hopelessly in love.

'I love your body,' says Ali. 'I worship everything about it. It is perfection.'

Laura groans with pleasure.

'How do you manage to look so perfect?'

'No children. That feels so-o good. Don't stop. Ever.'

I'm so happy – I am complete,
I was worried – now I'm free,
Floating ... Rising through the air,
I tell you there ain't no one comes close to you – you are my light,
Right here inside,
In paradise.

34

Richard O'Brien is on the 12th green at Ballynamon Golf Club, and he's been missing his shots all morning, so it'll be back to the range for him, to improve his swing and pitching. He's playing a round with a regular group that includes businessmen like himself, a couple of county councillors and a planning officer who's active on the current 'Shaping Our Future' development plan.

Richard goes to great pains to keep in with the movers and shakers, who have enabled him to expand his own property development business in Tipperary and nearby counties. It's the way the system works, and Richard plays it to a tee.

He's married and childless, but his work is pretty much his life and he has just one person to thank for this. His late father, Frank O'Brien. Frank's name opened all the doors, and business opportunities came Richard's way, without him having to actually graft for them. The power of fame and success.

Since his father's death, Richard has become acutely aware that he's going to have to work a bit harder on polishing up his people skills. Trouble is, he finds it hard to get on with these people in the way that his father did, so effortlessly – it doesn't come naturally to him.

Nevertheless, people remain nice to him – presumably because of his wealth. So, it's still boom time for him, at least for the foreseeable future.

It doesn't help that his sister is currently distracting him with her obsession to bring down their stepmother. Short of murdering the woman, he fails to see what his sister can do. She's gone completely mad, he thinks. Well, madder. She's always been crazy in his mind. Mind you, he doesn't say anything to her face. She actually scares him – always has. It's easier to follow the line of least resistance and let her get on with it.

After golf, as arranged, he duly meets Stephanie at one of her bars. When he arrives, he texts, and she opens up for him and they walk through to her office.

'Coffee?'

'No, I'm good thanks. You've cleared up then,' he observes.

Stephanie is still smarting from a break-in at the bar two weeks ago. The place was ransacked but thankfully nothing of great value had been stolen. The Garda still haven't turned anything up, despite their efforts and they're being quietly suspicious that the break-in is probably related to something that Ms O'Brien isn't disclosing. Like most people, they're confused by the woman. At first glance she looks beautiful and charming but the reality is very different. Stephanie O'Brien is a cold, aloof, abrasive and manipulative schemer.

'We need to do something about that woman,' she growls, referring to Laura.

'Kill her off, her you mean?' says Richard, sarcastically.

'Listen you,' she says, pointing aggressively at him. 'You stand to gain as much as I do, so for fuck's sake Richard, stop making idiotic comments. God in heaven knows why Julie married you.'

'You're in a good mood today, dear sister. What about her boozing, can we work with that?'

'Are you serious? It would have the reverse effect, you idiot. People would be sympathetic and more likely impressed by how she's dealt with it. No, we need to do something much more drastic. I'm working on it.'

'Oh Steph, why are you so angry? Do we really need to be going to all this trouble? We've already done pretty well.'

'Trouble? What have you done, you fat fucker? Fuck all.'

She stands up and strides aggressively to the window.

'Don't you worry, fat boy; I have a plan.'

She hasn't shared her intentions with her brother and that's exactly how it's going to stay.

Stephanie is a successful woman in her own right and a shrewd operator – she likes to do things herself. She owns a string of bars that she set up from scratch, and she manages them with a cold heart and an iron fist. She's ruthless and with the help of her accountant, turns in a good profit. She's unpopular with her staff and, frankly, she couldn't care a fig – despite being aware of their feelings towards her. But she's very careful not to put a foot wrong, legally.

In the early days, she had everyone working part-time to keep the wage bills down, but the laws changed, and staff became better protected. But she still does the absolute minimum required by law. However, she can turn on the charm if it's absolutely necessary; she certainly uses her looks to cosy up to staff at The National Excise Licence Office.

She's already benefited from her father's demise, but the scent of even bigger money – and her hatred of Laura – has driven her to a frenzy. This kind of money is life-changing and Stephanie has decided to really go for it and expand her empire – create her own brand and franchise it across Ireland. It's a big ambition, requiring BIG money and taking BIG risks. Therefore, she'll need even more money – as much as she can get. So Laura can go and fuck herself.

She has this plan and she believes it'll work – as long as she can find the right people to help her. This time, she's going to need more than a private eye.

The kind of people she needs are not exactly found in a Google search.

Instead, Stephanie will be prowling the dark web.

35

'Shouldn't you be working, writing some music?' teases Laura, as she lifts herself and rests on her elbows and turns to Ali who is lying by her side. Once again, she's thinking that he is the best looking, most perfectly shaped man she has ever set eyes on. Her very own, personal Adonis. Ali, with his jet-black hair and fabulous glistening dark brown eyes and rock-solid body from top to toe. It's a sight to behold and cherish. She loves this man for his mind – and his wonderful body.

They're at Ali's house, in Portsmouth.

'Bloody cheek,' says Ali. 'I give blood for my art, my music.'

'I know you do,' she smiles cheekily. 'You work very hard and I really do admire you.'

Ali stares lovingly back and has to pinch himself for his good fortune in lying next to, in his opinion, the most exquisite human being on the planet.

Thank you, Finn O'Donnell, the finest organiser of events in the world. Thank you for July 12th, the day I met Laura O'Brien.

'I'd like to run a couple of things past you. And please don't just say No. Hear me out.'

'That sounds extremely worrying,' says Ali.

'I know we've only been together for a comparatively short time, but you do know how much I love you, don't you?'

'Yes … I do … and I love you too, babe. Where's this going?'

'Well, I know some people still find it a bit odd, you know, us and the age difference – and that this is all too quick – but I want you to know that I am the happiest woman in the world right now and there's stuff I'd like to talk about. So, are you ready?'

Ali turns and kisses Laura full on her lips.

'Babe, stop just for a second …'

Ali kisses her again.

'For God's sake Ali, I want us to live together! And you never know, one day ... we could … you know …'

Ali kisses her yet again and then pulls back.

'Yes? Go on.'

'Make it official, you know.'

'Get married you mean?'

'Yes, one day.'

Ali kisses her again. 'I've been thinking exactly the same thing. But do you think it would work? Don't you think we could have a problem with being so unevenly balanced?'

'No, I don't. And what do you mean by unbalanced?'

'I mean, I can't offer you anything financially. It's all you. I've read so many stories about couples who, with the best intentions, still break up because one is the giver and the other one just takes. And I'm the taker here, aren't I?'

'All I can say is what I believe now. That is, that I love you and I want to be with you all the time.'

'But after a while won't you get pissed off with being the main money provider?'

'Ali, the question is – could you hack it? Because I couldn't give a damn. You know, this money isn't the real me. I never had any before I met Frank and if it all suddenly disappeared now, I'd still feel the same about you. I haven't had all this for that long.'

'That's incredible. I don't know what to say.'

'But it's not going to be like that. I'm not going to lose that money – we're going to enjoy it together; have the time of our lives, and I'm going to put it to good philanthropic use, too. How's that for putting out a good intention to the universe?'

'Er ... yes please, I think so.'

'Only think so?'

'No I don't mean it like that. It's just that I've got the situation with dad and mum. I haven't even told them about you, and we've been going out for months. I'm not sure what to do. It could ruin everything.'

'What's the problem? They might resist at first but we'll show them.'

'Where do I start? My dad would not be happy about us. End of. Which is why I haven't told them.'

'I hate to sound cold, but does that matter, Ali? It's your life, not your father's. You're not ashamed of me are you?'

'Christ, no. For God's sake, I am massively happy.'

'So, do it. Tell them and have done with it. They'll get used to the idea. I'll protect you. We can do this, together. The new house is finally sorted now. I love it. You love it. So, let's do it.'

Ali thinks very hard. He knows exactly how news of his love with an older white woman is going to go down in Bromley. Like a giant bag of sick.

Strangely, though, not telling his family – in particular his father – has empowered him. For once he's felt in control. He's spoken on the phone many times to his mother and his sister Rani, but he hasn't let on about Laura.

'OK I'll sort it, somehow,' he says, unconvincingly.

Laura is standing, still undressed, by the side of the bed and sits down again.

'And now. The other thing.'

'There's more?' says Ali, reaching out to pull her back into bed.

'Yes, there is. Stop it, Ali. Stop that now.'

She continues, 'I'm not an expert on music like you, but I do know that you've got talent and that your gift on its own, is not enough to be successful in show business, right?'

'Music business,' corrects Ali, smiling. 'But yes, you're right.'

'Whatever. What would you do if you had unlimited funds at your disposal? If you could wave a magic wand – what would you do, to further your musical dreams?'

'Oh Laura, I'm not sure I know. I'd have to think. Why do you ask?'

'I'd like to help you really get going with your music. If it takes money, well, I'm coming down with it and we must use it to help you.'

'That's incredibly generous but it could be pouring money down the drain. So few people make it into the big time.'

'Hey, stop it you. Cancel that negativity. That doesn't sound like a positive-thinking man standing in the vortex, believing in himself, ambitiously driving forward with every breath, does it? Come on Ali, think like a star. You've got to imagine you're already a success and you're *already* enjoying how it feels. Knowing that you are a success. That's how it works I'm told. I manifested you, for God's sake!'

'Did you now? Have I been lurking inside your private vortex?'

'You have!'

Laura climbs back into bed beside Ali and cuddles up to him. 'Seriously, what would you do?'

'I want to concentrate on syncing for TV and film, as I've told you, but if I could release a single with the proper backing it would certainly be worth trying. I'd pick my most commercial song and get a really professional video made to go with it. No amateur phone camera shit. And I'd hire a proper, experienced publicist to promote it like a top professional artist would. That's the proper way to do it. The singles I've released already, *Ozone* and *When You Walk In*, disappeared the moment they came out. I'm a songwriter and producer for God's sake, not a merchandiser.'

'Yes, but would that help your career *significantly*?'

'Well, it would certainly be a big step forward, if we did it really well.'

'Then let's do it,' says Laura excitedly and squeezing Ali's arm. 'Let's make a video and hire a publicist.'

'Wow,' says Ali. 'Is this real? In half an hour, I've suddenly got a hinted-at marriage proposal and a colossal boost for my music career.'

'Just one condition though. When you're famous, you must NOT run off and leave me behind. That is NOT allowed! OK?'

'OK.'

Ali's phone rumbles on the side table and he looks at the display.

'Oh no.'

'What's the matter?'

'It's Ham. That can only mean one thing.'

'You should answer it.'

'No, it'll mean another job.'

'Answer it, Ali. It's not going to go away. Go on, do as I say.'

'Yes, Miss.'

*

Ali looks up from his tablet and smiles. He's just finished an incredibly useful video call with one of the most successful executives in the music business, Stephen Gretsch. He's the friend of Ali's new publicist, Alvin Spear, who managed to swing 15 minutes of the big man's time.

Stephen has been very upfront about the harsh realities facing Ali in his quest for success – and because the music business is now completely unrecognisable from what it was just a few years ago, he warns Ali that even he's not the best man to advise. But he does offer Ali some crumbs of hope.

'As far as I can see, your music isn't Top 40 material. More adult pop/rock, right?'

'Yes, some is and some isn't, which is why I have this problem. Being so diverse.'

'Well if you want to compete with everyone else, whether you like it or not, you're going to have to conform. Define your genre, build your social media up, big-time, and pump out tracks consistently to your fan base. Heard that before Ali?' says Stephen, chuckling.

'Just a bit, yeh. But that's not where I want to be.'

'OK, so what do you want? Do you want to be a hit songwriter and producer? Because if that's so, what I just said, is your way to go.'

'No, I don't want to sit at home churning out dozens of formulaic songs on a production line for a music publisher, no thanks. And I don't want to be a performing artist. I'm a songwriter and producer and I invite guest singers to perform my songs. Each song is different. My songs, I hope, appeal to an older, wider audience if only I could reach them.'

'OK, a BBC Radio 2-type audience, probably.'

'Yeh, but they only play a handful of new tracks every week and they're always by established artists.'

'A warm welcome to show business, Ali.

'I haven't heard your music yet, but Alvin tells me it's very good indeed. So, my BEST advice to you Ali, is to determine your own context. Create your own platform. I think you could spend hundreds of hours on social media and streaming and probably pick up a few thousand streams and YouTube views. Pretty much a waste of time, isn't it? You need millions just to make a small amount of money.

'Why don't you think outside the box and conjure up a completely different way for your music to be used – something that's kind of unique to you? I don't know, write a musical perhaps, or a TV drama. Something that will feature your music. Think bigger and bolder. It sounds like a long shot but, to be honest, no longer than the original alternative. In fact, if you do a good job, you might be surprised that the right folk might sit up and listen.'

'Wow, that's an amazing idea. I'd never have thought of that.'

'Well do give it some thought, Ali. Remember, Andrew Lloyd-Webber can't sing either! Whatever you do, take your time to get it right. People are cautious about newcomers and it's very, very hard to make progress without huge backing. But I genuinely wish you luck, sir. If you've got something good, keep at it, and never give up. Remember … context.

'Oh … and hold on to your publishing – don't sign anything away before you have your first Number 1!'

36

In Toxteth, Liverpool, Jason Brand is sitting on a bench, staring at the phone photos of that Indian bastard and his mates the other week. The night the big meeting went badly wrong and he practically got the blame for it. He was only the lookout, for fuck's sake.

Jason's boss, Shaun, is still furious – and so is the other gang leader, Brian White, who initially believed Shaun had set him up. Shaun managed to calm White down but he's still got a lot of work to do to regain his trust – so the Asian needs sorting. Jason took an instant dislike to the guy. He looked smug. So in his mind, he's already dust.

His phone rings. 'Job,' says Shaun and immediately hangs up. The usual procedure. Nothing is said – nothing to trace.

Jason's had a pretty tough life. After leaving school and having failed his exams, for three years he worked for his cousin who runs a heating company, mainly installing central heating systems across Liverpool. He seemed keen at first, but he started to lose interest when he got in with a different crowd from Toxteth – and they smoked a lot of weed, so he eventually quit.

Since then, he's never really had a formal job, nothing longer than a few weeks, so he's existed on the occasional burglary, benefits, and working for cash when *business opportunities* arose.

He's had several brushes with the law and as a result has form. He spent six miserable months in prison for assault, which he's keen never to repeat. So, hooking up with Shaun, one of the big boys, has been a real turn-up for the books and lifted his profile in the "community". He just happened to be in the right place at the right time, when Shaun was "recruiting", and he's happy to plod along, doing what he's told.

He cuts an imposing figure on the street and most people step back when they see him coming. He doesn't care and even the scars on his arms and stomach are something he just accepts as part of the life he leads. His teeth braces are a fashion accessory rather than a dental correction. He likes the look. No one else does and that's pretty good in Jason's mind.

He knows there are big plans afoot and that the disastrous meeting that they went to was important, because Shaun said so.

Shaun is still very unhappy, so Jason's feeling very unhappy too. For the moment though, he's earning his wages and he's got another drop off.

He doesn't touch the drugs he peddles. He tried weed for that short time, but since then he's seen too many mates end up floating in the nearby Mersey.

Jason is a complex character and seems to function best without doing too much thinking.

In reality, he doesn't know if he's happy or sad.

What the fuck are happiness and sadness when they're at home?

37

'It's been a long time since I got up before dawn,' says Laura stifling a yawn. They're in Ali's van driving down the A32 in Gosport, towards the coast.

'It's the best time to come to Gosport,' says Ali. 'The roads here are jammed at commuter times.'

'This had better be good for me to lose my beauty sleep.'
'Don't you worry my lovely lady – all will be revealed in a very short while. As I've told you before, you're going to have the full *Ozone* and *In Paradise* experience.'

'Such good songs,' says Laura, 'very spiritual.'
Ali's hoping that he's got his timings right. Gosport is very close to Portsmouth if you look at it on the map – just across the harbour. Quick on the ferry, but by road, being a peninsular, it takes a while to get here.

Stokes Bay is the destination. Ali has quite a few friends living in the town, and he's spent a lot of time here over the years. But it's one thing in particular that he's brought Laura to see – and the weather has to be exactly right.

This morning is one of those magical summer mornings, when the UK is sitting under a static high-pressure area that isn't budging – and squats, delivering day after day of sunny, still, blue skies.

Ali's van rounds the corner, and suddenly the Solent, in all its magnificence, appears in front of them and there's not a soul about. The Isle of Wight looks so close, you'd think you could walk to it.

It's breathtaking.

‘Here we are,’ says Ali parking the van. ‘We’ve arrived – this is what the songs are all about.’

‘Wow,’ says Laura slowly scanning the view from one side to the other. ‘This is something else.’

In front of the couple, is a wide panoramic spectacle of still blue sea, bathing in the brightest, clearest sunlight that pinpoints even the smallest features on the horizon, whichever way you look.

‘Listen to that,’ says Ali. ‘Silence. And the tide’s just right too.’ He points towards the island. ‘See over there, slightly to your right – see that huge white/cream building? That’s Osborne House – that’s where we went. We stood on the beach there looking over to here. How good is that, eh?’ he beams.

‘It’s beautiful Ali – hardly a sound and from the far left round to the far right, you just get this beautiful wide, wide crystal-clear picture.’

Laura is mesmerised. ‘And there’s nobody here. Where is everyone? If I lived here, I’d get up at dawn every day.’

She points to a couple of small boats in the distance.

‘You can’t even hear their engines. And the smell. What is it? Seaweed, I suppose. It’s not strong, just natural. It’s lovely.

‘It’s a shame we can’t record smells, isn’t it?’

She reaches for her phone. ‘I must take a photo.’

‘Waste of time.’

‘Why?’

‘I’ve tried. Many times. The problem is, you can’t get the depth of field and you can’t include the peripheral vision that you only get from using your eyes.’

‘What a shame.’

'I know. It doesn't matter though, let's just stand here and enjoy it in real time for a while, not speaking, and breathing in and out. Meditate. You can almost go into a trance,' says Ali.

They stand together in silence for three or four minutes.

'A couple of years ago I came here and did exactly what we're doing now – standing and wondering at the enormity of it all. And then suddenly, directly in front of me, just a couple of metres off the shore, up popped this little furry head. So close. He or she looked at me as if to say *good morning* and then swam along by the shore looking this way and that. It was a baby seal, all on its own, looking for breakfast, I guess. It wasn't remotely freaked out by me being there. I wanted to call out to someone to share it but of course I was all on my own. It was so beautiful.'

'Do you know what I love about you, Ali Kurmi? Well, one of the things. I love the fact that you aren't afraid of your feelings. I know that sounds like therapy speak. But it's true, you really are in touch with your feminine side.'

'Oh yeh? Maybe. I definitely can be a bit emotional, and I'm happy with that.'

'How far away is the island?'

'About three miles from here, I think. It doesn't look like it, does it?'

'I totally get why this place is so special to you. It's beautiful.'

'But here's the thing, it can also disappear.'

'What?'

'Yeh, just a bit of mist – that's all it takes and you wouldn't know the island's there. And in winter this sea turns a browny-green colour and the whole place turns very menacing. Madness.'

Ali sighs contentedly. 'Let's just enjoy it a little longer before the dog walkers and joggers pitch up. Breathe in.'

Open up your arms and smile,
Pull the power deep inside,
You'll never have to feel alone,
When you breathe in ozone.

38

Alice Kingston and David Draper have had a couple of dates, both at Dave's wine bar, so perhaps calling them dates is stretching it a bit. But Alice has been there as a result of a direct invitation from him, so that'll do for her. They were dates!

She's been out with a few men since she settled in Wickham, but nothing that has lasted. The men are either just looking for sex, plain boring or downright ugly.

Dave Draper is different; he's easy on the eye for a start, he dresses nicely and he's a bit of a biker, it would seem – with not one, but two motorbikes in his garage. He has a bit of life about him, is interesting to talk to – and he doesn't leer. A lot of plus points there, Alice thinks.

There's a large grapevine growing profusely in the garden at the back of the wine bar, and its triffid-like growth is a frequent topic of conversation.

'We're going to pick those grapes in October and tread them with our feet,' proclaims Dave from behind the bar, to his regulars, who have gathered nearby. Alice is amongst them sipping her fruit juice.

'What did you just say?' says one of the ladies fighting the noise.

'Yep, we're going to make Wickham Wine Bar wine. I'll get a big barrel and we'll have a big grape-treading ceremony.'

'No thank you,' says another in the group, 'I wouldn't fancy that at all.'

'OK, I'll do the bloody treading on my own, then,' says Dave, proudly.

'What? With your athlete's foot, Dave? No thanks,' another cackles.

'Alright, I'll wear socks.'

'Argh.'

'Sterilised surgical socks then.'

Alice likes coming here. The people are uncomplicated and they're good fun – and Dave is a good host. All she knows about him is that he's divorced and has clearly taken a shine to her. She's very happy to go with the flow.

He leans across the bar.

'Can you hang around later this evening?'

'I don't know, I ...'

'Please stay if you can, it would be nice to talk to you without all this going on,' he says, pointing towards the animated group.

'Well, for a little while I suppose but I have got a full diary of appointments tomorrow, so I don't want to be late.'

'I know, I won't keep you up,' he says. 'Promise. I was hoping we could meet up one night – away from here. What do you say?'

'That sounds lovely, let's sort it out later, shall we?'

'Absolutely,' says Dave, twinkling.

'Have you got a crash helmet?'

*

A couple of miles away, Laura and Ali are still at it, shifting boxes. It's a good job Laura knows what she's doing, because Ali hasn't got a clue.

Most of her worldly possessions have been in storage since she moved from Ireland and today they're stacked in tall piles, in her brand-new home, Meon Lodge.

Ali's excited. 'Hey, look what I've found. A stereo system. Blimey, I haven't seen one of those for years. Wow, a CD player with twin cassette players for copying.' Ali is delighted with his finds.

'Don't laugh. You're holding my precious past there. Those boxes over there have got all my CDs and vinyl.'

'Yes Ma'am, re-spect. Actually having something to hold and love.'

'You can go through them tomorrow if you like but right now, I'm shattered. That's enough for one day,' says Laura.

'We've done well,' he says.

'We have indeed,' and she gives him a big kiss on his cheek.

'When are you going to speak to your family about us? You haven't said anything since our discussion.'

'I know, I've been so busy with the gigs and the studio, I just haven't had time.'

Laura gives him a *look* and doesn't need to say a word. He gets the message.

Ali has yet to work out how he's going to explain to Laura to his family – well, to his parents, without triggering a family holocaust.

'I do hope you will. Soon.' She gives him another kiss and turns back to look at the mountain of boxes.

'I know it looks like I've got a lot of stuff, but I actually left most of it behind,' she says. Stephanie and Richard would only have created a fuss. They'd accuse me of theft. So, they can have it all, as far as I'm concerned.'

'They sound absolutely vile,' says Ali.

'I'm afraid I have to agree with you there.'

She looks around. This house is going to take some filling up, I reckon. But I have plenty of ideas. We're OK for the time being, though. Yes, I'm very happy indeed.'

Ali yawns loudly.

'We've got a lot more to do tomorrow, so let's get some sleep.'

They trundle up the stairs hand in hand and Ali starts singing in a high voice.

'I need some peace, Mr Kurmi!'

'I just wanna tell you baby, I'm finding things inside me, I don't know what's going on, maybe … Lavender.'

'*Lavender,* what's that? A new song?'

'Yes indeed. Did you know that lavender is part of the mint family? Lavandula, in Latin.'

'Thanks Ali-babe, I'll keep that uppermost in my mind.'

39

'This is sounding pretty good already,' says Jim, as the pair listen to a playback of the bare bones of *Lavender.* Ali is hoping to use this new song for his first big promotional push – a new single, backed by the services of an experienced London publicist – and a professionally shot video by a recognised videographer. He's excited and has a very good feeling about the song.

But even if the worst happens and it disappears without trace, he has a plan to focus on writing music for TV dramas, commercials and films. And then there's the other plan. The idea of writing a musical which has come from his recent conversation with music mogul, Stephen Gretsch. It's given Ali a new sense of purpose and fired him with enthusiasm. But he's following Laura's advice to keep it to himself for the time being. It could so easily fail to materialise and the fewer people who know about his plans, the better, at this early stage. And that includes his pal, Jim.

'I love it when the backing chorus comes in. Sounds like a nice tight choir. Sounds really good,' says Jim.

'I sang all those parts with a bath towel over my head,' says Ali. 'To keep the echoing down.'

'Professional sound proofing,' chuckles Jim. 'Not. But it's absolutely OK, we can use this.'

'And you're OK to sing it?'

'Yeh, I'll give it a go.'

'I wrote it in a slightly different way from how I usually write – an airy-fairy idea to be honest. After I'd put the chord structure together on the piano, I just sang the first tune and words that came into my head and recorded it all. Believe it or not, it hasn't changed much from the first take. In literature they call it stream of consciousness. I think.'

'OK I'll take your word for it,' says Jim, 'sounds crazy.'

'It was, but here we are.'

Jim and Ali start experimenting with different instruments and sounds, to add to the track. Ali loves this part of the process and the morning speeds by.

Then it's back to reality and a cloud of disillusionment returns to Ali's thoughts.

'Do you mind if I ask you something?' Ali says, during a break. 'A bit of advice, actually. Non-musical.'

'Oh yeh. What's that?'

'You know that Laura and I are getting on really, really – really well?'

'Yeh, I had noticed.'

'The problem is, I haven't told my family about her.'

'Is that a big deal? Do you need to?'

'Yes I do actually, but I've got some careful juggling to do. It's my dad. I haven't told you any of this but he's threatened to disown me if I don't give all the music up, settle down and marry a Muslim girl of his choice. There's no way I'm going to let that happen of course but I've got to play it very carefully.'

'You what? That's outrageous! I'd tell him to fuck off if it were me. Sod that – it's your life.'

'It's incredible isn't it? I'd love to do that and I might well do so. My mum would probably come round eventually, but he's so old fashioned and stubborn he'd probably try to cut me off from the family completely. For the sake of Laura, I could handle that, but

I don't think my mum and sisters would deal with it at all well. But there's even more to it than that. It's way more complicated – unfortunately, my father has got something big on me.'

'What's that then?'

'I'd rather not say if you don't mind – I'll tell you one day.'

'Sounds like a nightmare,' says Jim. 'Families.'

'How can I do it for God's sake?'

'Why don't you talk to your sister about it? She seems pretty cool from what I remember when we met and she might have an idea or two, no?'

'Yeh, I suppose so. A problem shared and all that. but I'm not holding my breath.'

*

Rani and her family live in Beckenham, another London dormitory, a short drive from her parents' house in Bromley and her siblings. Conveniently close, but far enough away to enjoy some independence.

Without any intention, her role in life seems to be that of general shoulder-to-cry-on – peacemaker and patcher-upper, when things go wrong, especially in her family. It's the price she pays for being a good listener.

Of the three siblings, she's closest to Ali, in age and thinking. She admires how he's turned his life around and totally understands why he doesn't get on with their father. Ali has the same respect for her and appreciates how hard she's had to work to maintain her dignity after being so unfairly pressured by their father into settling down and raising a family.

Whilst Ali has been blessed with musical talent, Rani is the most exquisite artist – not just a painter working with oils and other media – she has a natural flair for many things, like ceramics and making jewellery. She went to art college but after getting her degree, her father insisted that marriage was to be her first priority. Since then, and having her own children, she's had little opportunity to express her gifts.

She's talking to Ali on the phone while preparing the family tea.

'My God Ali, you don't half drop some bombshells. I didn't see that one coming. I could understand if it was you and Becky. Wow, wow, wow … how long have you been going out with this woman?'

'Her name's Laura,' says Ali, firmly.

'OK, sorry – Laura.'

'Quite a while.'

'Gosh, why didn't you tell me?'

'Because I can't let it get back to him. Can you imagine what he'd say? More to the point, what he'd do. I couldn't burden you with lying for me. I'm scared shitless, Ran. Not of him, but of losing Laura. I love this woman and I don't want to lose her but if she gets to hear about everything – I reckon it would be too much for her. She's had a stack of her own issues to deal with and I think that this, on top, would be too much and she'd walk.'

'Are you sure about that? I think you should just tell her.'

'It's too risky, Ran. Plus, there's the ongoing issue of an arranged marriage – which of course I have no intention whatsoever of agreeing to.'

'There has to be a way.'

'I can't tell you how awful it is carrying all this around in my head, deceiving the woman I love. I can't handle it, I'm a complete bundle of nerves.

'If there's anyone up there … please help me!'

40

Laura and Ali are dining at Alice's house – and Alice being Alice, it's not the usual bill of fayre – they're having raclette.

Alice grins widely at Laura. They're both in a good place. Even a short glance speaks volumes with these two. Interocular communication at its best.

'Have you had it before? It's French, I think,' says Alice. 'Don't be afraid, it's ever so simple and great fun.'

'No double dipping please,' says Laura, studying the two-layered device.

Ali is glad to be distracted from his agonising preoccupation. He gets the hang of raclette quickly, relaxes and starts to enjoy himself.

'Love that cheese,' he says.' It really works.'

'So Ali, we finally get to spend some quality time together,' says Alice. 'Laura's told me so much about you but whenever we meet it's always, *Hi* and *Goodbye*.'

'Uh-oh, what's she been saying?'

'You won't be surprised to hear that it's all good.'

'I'd better be on my best behaviour then.'

'No David tonight then, Alice?' says Laura.

'Not yet, he's at work. That's the drawback of running a bar, isn't it? Getting time off is difficult. But he said he'd try to pop in later, if we're still going strong.'

'It's going well, then? You and David.'

'Yes, so far, so good – when I can get him on his own.'

Alice turns to face Ali and theatrically wiggles her head.

'So, your music Ali. Laura sent me the link to your songs. I hope you don't mind.

'Well. I have to say, I am totally gobsmacked! I wasn't expecting that kind of music.

'That didn't come out right, did it? Please don't get me wrong …'

'That's very nice of you, and thanks. It's what most people say. Don't worry, I'm used to it. I know – the face doesn't match the music!'

'I'm a bit of a head banger for my sins so I like the rockier ones – and country rock! I absolutely adore *How Could I Be So Wrong.* And OMG, who's that fiddle player? He's brilliant!'

'That's Graham, he's amazing isn't he? He's done quite a bit for me. He's almost part of the family.'

'And who are the singers?'

'That'll be Liam and Lily. Liam's done a few songs for me. A star in the making. And Lily's got that great sassy sound. She's a real country gal.'

'What's it about?'

'Ha. Good question. It's about those stupid arguments when both people think they're right and refuse to back down. One person accuses the other – who turns the accusation right round. You did that! No I didn't, you did! I did not, yes you did! You get the picture …!

'I also really like *Homeland* … and, *In Paradise* – I love those orchestral bits at the beginning of them leading into the heavier sound. *In Paradise* is epic. Is *Coolstar* a proper band by the way?'

'It can be!' says Ali smiling. 'If Michael Eavis calls to book us at Glastonbury, yes, we're definitely a band. It's actually my band name and my brand name if you like. You've got to call yourself something.'

'Tell me, why don't you sing on your songs?'

'I do actually. I do the backing vocals – hidden away. Seriously, if you could hear me singing, you'd know why I ask other people.'

Alice turns to Laura, grinning approvingly.

Ali continues, 'Laura tells me that you have a strong spiritual side. Is that personal and private or do you talk about it?'

'I LOVE talking about it,' says Alice enthusiastically. 'Are you?'

'A bit, I think. Like most people, I'm curious about how we all got here and what happens when we die. But I'm not in the Big Bang camp, I don't think. There's too much clever stuff going on for things to have been random.'

'I agree,' says Alice. 'I think some force, something very intelligent, created our world with humanity and the animal kingdom. To even begin to understand and appreciate that, we need to strip everything right back to basics.

'For instance, have you ever stopped to consider the number of actions and functions taking place in your body when you just sit still in a chair doing nothing? Thousands, maybe millions. It's SO complex.'

She's now in full swing.

'You need to stop, think slowly about what's really happening around you and in you, at that very moment. If you do, I guarantee that you'll look at the world very differently. We're all moving too fast to see what's really going on under our noses. We need to slow down the vibrations – to see things as they really are – at their pace.'

'Interesting, that sounds like meditation,' says Ali.

'It is. As for a God of creation, I don't believe in the conventional white-bearded God, and I don't go with any formal religions like Catholicism, Church of England or Islam. I do, however, think there is an energy, a higher force if you like, that we have no scientific understanding of. Yet.'

So far, Ali is OK with what Alice is saying. He'd expected to be wearing his sceptic's hat before now – but so far, so good.

'Do you believe in ghosts and an afterlife?'

'Maybe and yes,' says Alice. 'I don't know about ghosts but yes, I'm convinced there's life after death. I've been to several *proper mediums*, who've given me information that I believe is a validation. Hand on heart Ali, I was a 100% non-believer, until I started delving into the subject deeply.'

Concerned that this may be a theory too far for Ali, Laura joins the conversation.

'I've been trying to explain the Law of Attraction to Ali but he's on the fence with that one. I suppose I don't blame him. It's not easy to grasp, is it?'

'Have you tried it?' Alice asks Ali, keenly. 'It's very powerful.'

'I don't know. I dream of having a successful music career. I'm very determined about that. But I'm not stupid enough to believe that things happen just because you simply wish them to.'

'I know – but do you actually *believe* in the outcome of those wishes? Feel that they've already happened, Ali. Do you feel success, already? That's what you've got to do.'

'Hmm,' says Ali. 'I've just had a break with a couple of songs I sent to Satellite TV – they said they're going to use them. Maybe I attracted that. But I didn't sit down formally to request it.'

'But you're missing the point, Ali. You must have attracted them by already BELIEVING they are successful. So, yes, you did attract it. Wishing needs to be replaced by believing and feeling. But as long as you continue wishing, that's where your dreams will always stay – just out of reach, waiting to happen, pending. My advice to everyone is to meditate, clear the mind and start believing your dreams – live in the now.'

Ali smiles to himself. He thinks he understands, but he's not completely convinced and politely says how fascinated he is by the idea.

'I definitely get the living in the now bit – stopping to smell the roses and all that – that's good sense. I've even written a song called *Living in the Now*?!'

'There you go. More synchronicity. I haven't heard that one yet – I look forward to hearing it.' enthuses Alice.

'Wait a second, let's get a group selfie.'

There's a tap at the front door. Alice quickly responds and David Draper enters the room brandishing a bottle of wine, smiling at everyone.

'Sorry it's not our own Wickham vintage – but we're working on that,' he grins.

'Had a good evening, all?'

'Yes thank you,' comes the chorus.

'There's some raclette left, if you want it,' says Alice, pecking him on the face. 'I'll get you some.'

David sits down, and twists the bottle top off.

'Anyone need topping up? No one else drinking tonight? What a good lot you are. Do you mind if I do?'

Alice introduces her friends and wonders if they'll all get on. As yet, she hasn't had the chance to get to know David properly. He doesn't strike her as being particularly spiritual, so she thinks it's probably better to move on from that topic.

'How was tonight?' she asks.

'Busy and noisy. It's nice to come here for some peace and quiet,' he smiles at Alice and raises his glass. Here's to us.'

'To us.'

'Wait a second,' says Alice, taking another quick photograph. 'Thank you, ooh yes, that's a good one.'

'You're better at this social media stuff than I am,' says David. 'I've got a page for the wine bar but I never remember to do anything with it.'

'Easy to put right, my dear, just keep taking photos at the bar and post them,' says Alice. 'It's just a habit you need to get into, you can do it without thinking.'

'Hmm, not sure about that,' says David.

'You'd better do as she says, David. Alice knows best and she can be very persuasive,' Laura chips in.

Alice rolls her eyes.

'OK you guys, time for introductions. I'll go first. I'm Alice, I'm English and I'm happily divorced. Reborn in Hampshire. I'm teetotal. I run a beauty business with loads of nice clients, and I believe that nothing happens by accident.'

'Hey!' They all cheer loudly.

'Ta da! I'm Laura, I'm from Ireland. I now live in Wickham. I'm looking for kindness, harmony and happiness. I want to help people if I can and have a great deal of fun too,' turning pointedly to Ali.

'I'm Ali Kurmi. I'm English and I'm of Indian descent – there's a clue,' as he points to himself. 'I'm definitely up for some fun too. I'm a songwriter, producer and DJ. I want to continue writing tunes that people will like and I want world leaders to wake up and start thinking more about their people and the planet. Not just about themselves.'

'Hooray!' they all shout, banging the table with their hands.

'And I'm David, I'm Welsh. I run the Wickham Wine Bar. I don't play golf. I don't smoke. I like the occasional red and the odd burn-up on my bikes. I'm divorced and I reckon things have just changed for the better.'

'Hooray!'

41

'Do come in, Laura, how nice to see you. How are you?'

'Fine thanks, Finn.'

Laura has asked Finn O'Donnell for some business advice. Accommodating as ever, he's agreed and she's driven over to meet him in his home, at his invitation.

'Let's step into the kitchen and have a brew. What can I get you, tea or coffee?'

'Tea please, builders for me.'

'Coming right up.'

'It's good of you to see me,' she says looking around. 'I love this house; it's got such a warm feeling. It's a happy house, I can tell.'

'That's kind of you Laura, indeed we're very happy here,' he says passing her mug.

'So, how can I help?'

'I just want someone mature, with a bit of business experience and common sense to bounce some ideas off and to give me some good old grown-up advice.'

'Not sure I can give you that,' Finn winks, 'but I'll give it a go.'

'I won't take up too much of your time, don't worry.'

She gently bites her lower lip. 'I don't know how much I've already told you, but I'm pretty sure I told you about my husband passing away and how I ended up here.'

'You have my dear, all very sad.'

'I thought so, but what I didn't tell you is that I'm – how can I put this without sounding pompous? I find that I am a … woman of some means. In fact, I have a lot of money and there's the prospect of a great deal more money to come in the next few months.'

'Heavens. Perhaps you need a financial adviser, Laura.'

'That may well be the case, but it may surprise you that I'm not just looking to make financial profits from investments – which is precisely why I'd appreciate your advice.'

Laura explains that while she hasn't got a definite sum in mind, she is considering giving away a very significant proportion of her wealth. The auction of Frank O'Brien's stud business next spring will determine exactly how much.

'I'd gathered your husband was wealthy but perhaps not the extent.'

'Oh he was wealthy alright and as long as things go as I expect they will, soon I will have a very large bank balance.'

'So where do I come into all this? Are you going to give it to me?' he smiles.

'Ha. To be honest, the figure we're talking about is of great concern to me, not pleasure, as you might expect. No, I'm already flooded with more money than I could have dreamed of having, but the extra money next year is – funnily enough – not something I particularly welcome. In fact, I have nightmares worrying about worrying about it, if you get my drift.'

'I do get your drift – that would be a great responsibility.'

'It would, which is why I'd like to give a lot of it away.'

'I see.'

'God knows, I've wrestled with the ethics of all this wealth – and the ethics of high-performance horse breeding. Frank was a good man – and he was generous too, but let's not forget that his fortune was built on other peoples' weaknesses, gambling.'

'I'm not qualified to talk about the ethics of the breeding process of thoroughbred racehorses and their welfare during the process but I know there's a strong anti-lobby. But won't you be free from that after the sale?'

'There'll still be plenty of people who'll see it as 'dirty money' so I'll need to keep my radar up. Anyway, I'll feel a lot better using the money for good purposes. Which is where we came in.

'I have in mind an area that I'd like to explore but I need someone wise and trustworthy to tell me straight if I'm doing the right thing.'

'With respect Laura, you're the only one to judge that.'

'Can I just explain what I have in mind? I'm not after technical or financial help – just a wise head.'

Laura explains that she'd like to give a big donation to support abused people of all gender types. She's aware that there are already support systems in place for the victims of abuse, and wonders whether setting up a new charity would do more harm than good.

'Why don't you just give it to those charities and have done with it?'

'I would, but I'm concerned about how much of the money would actually be spent on frontline help.'

'I think you'll find that charities, by and large, do wonderful work, Laura.'

'It's a minefield Finn. I saw a story in the paper recently about a small charity that spent 80% of the money it raised on paying its staff salaries and admin. I wouldn't want that to happen.'

'I think that's a rarity, Laura. But of course, charities have largely moved towards the business model, haven't they? These days, charities are run pretty much like any other large business. So, they're vulnerable to certain costs, not least, paying top whack for top people who'll theoretically raise them bigger money. It's a difficult one, I do accept that.'

'I didn't realise how hard it is to give money away. It's a nightmare.'

'The only advice I can give to you, knowing you as I do, which is not intimately of course, is to write or type everything out and keep re-reading it. Keeping thoughts and ideas locked up in your head isn't conducive to clarity. It's a simple system that's worked for me all my life – and in my Navy days. Get your ideas down on paper and then you can see what you've got – or perhaps more importantly, what you haven't got.'

'Sounds very sensible to me.'

'That may not help you decide I'm afraid, but whatever you choose to invest in, Laura – I think you need to face the fact that you won't be waving goodbye to that financial burden – you'll just be moving it. I haven't helped you very much, have I?'

'Not so, Finn, you have.'

Laura thanks Finn for his time, leaves and sits in her car thinking everything over for a few minutes.

She realises that this is going to take a lot more thought and effort than she'd originally envisaged. Maybe it would have been better if Stephanie and Richard had got the lot.

She gets home to find Ali's van parked up on the drive. The inviting aromas of cooking greet her as she walks through the hall.

'That smells good – what's chef got cooking tonight?'

'Hi, I'm just doing some prep.'

She throws her arms around him and steals a very long kiss, as he stands helpless, spatula dangling from his right hand.

'I've been so busy with gigs lately, I thought that we should have our own little date night tonight. Is that OK?'

'If I drank champagne, I'd pop my cork,' Laura giggles. 'That's a lovely idea.'

'It's a good old-fashioned fish pie, I know you like that.'

'Yummee, can't wait.'

'How did it go with Finn?

'Good thanks. Much food for thought, pardon the pun. But I'll get there eventually. How bloody difficult does it have to be, to get rid of money. Whatever, I'll get there.

'Now have you had any more thoughts on the 'big promotional push' – if that's the right jargon?'

'Very good – you sound like a music biz pro.'

'I do think *Lavender* is a good choice. It's catchy,' she says as she wanders out of the room, still talking. 'I love Jim's voice – where's he been hiding that?'

'Yeh, it's turned out OK hasn't it ... I just hope the video will be as good.'

'I'm sure it will Ali boy! Have faith in yourself.'

Ali is capable of completely losing himself in music and the latest project with *Lavender* has been all-consuming. But unfortunately, his overwhelming burden keeps coming back to haunt him and it's not going to go away until he sorts it.

Suddenly even the thought of fish pie makes him feel sick and once again his stomach starts churning. He's not sure how much longer he can go on without some sort of meltdown. He's painfully aware that his father holds the ace card and has the power to destroy his relationship with Laura – and that terrifies him.

For God's sake, who would want to be associated with someone accused of rape?

42

It's early evening at Key Studios and Ali has called in to brief Jim on his plans for the single and video. Jim's busy working on one of his own tracks. His musical path is on a slightly different trajectory – more on the current chart music scene, in contrast to Ali's broader musical palate, but the pair of them work well together. Ali frequently reminds himself of how lucky he is to have Jim and is in awe of his technical engineering skills and accomplished instrumental work. He's also more than grateful for having, what he believes is, a world class recording studio, right on his doorstep.

The song, *Lavender*, has turned out particularly well and the pair have played the finished song to a small, select group of hopefully unbiased people, for comments. The feedback has been exceptionally good and it's endorsed Ali's decision to choose this song for a properly financed promotional campaign. Next on his list is the video.

'Yes, we've worked with some of the best, my friend; Maxx, Dua Lipa, U2, Beyoncé, Noel Gallagher – you name 'em, bud, we've done 'em.'

Ali has narrowed down a list of music video production companies to a shortlist of just three and he's a little nervous. Some of the prices he's seen are eye-wateringly expensive. Laura has provided him with a virtually open budget to make a topflight music video for his song Lavender.

Picking the right company is proving to be a minefield. Already, he's finding this guy way too cocky and over-familiar. Maybe that's what comes with stepping up a notch and playing with the big boys?

'Take a look at our platinum package, my friend – it sounds exactly what you need and if you sign up right now, we'll knock off a grand. That's an incredible bargain and you'll get the best deal in Britain today.'

'Sign up now? You're kidding. No thanks,' says Ali, 'I'm not buying double glazing.'

He rings off, disappointed and feeling a little foolish. He quickly decides to do what he should have done in the first place – ask an expert.

He realises that he's still in the amateur mindset of keeping a lid on the price and defaulting to feeling frightened. Time to think like a pro. Lesson learned. He'll call publicist Alvin Spear and take his cue from him. He chides himself for being so short-sighted.

He eventually settles on approaching the celebrated Mark Jackson, who's produced dozens of videos for name acts. He's an in-demand creative and was initially reluctant to take on the project. Until that is, Ali dropped Alvin's name into the conversation – and that of music executive, Stephen Gretsch.

Suddenly, he has a producer on board and Mark, having listened to the song quite a few times, is now happy to be involved. Ali is starting to feel the traction that Alvin was banging on about, beginning to kick in. He has a team of experienced professionals working on one of his songs and despite being conditioned into thinking that a music career is highly unlikely, he's now got a feeling of excitement, even optimism. Anticipation is in the air.

*

In Southsea, Ali and Laura are doing a check on his house – it's been a few days since he was last here. He's looking deeply into her eyes and pulling a silly face, still managing to keep his relentless family problems hidden away.

'I do love you Ali Kurmi. You're completely nuts.'

'Excuse me, where did that come from?' says Ali, 'I am most definitely not the only nut around here. You're right up there too.'

He straightens his face. 'I need to be honest with you. I'm a bit stressed out about this video; I don't want to balls it up. It's such a lot of money to be spending and such a good opportunity.'

'Stop worrying. If you're serious, and I know you are,' she says, heading off his indignation, 'it's something you need to get your head around.

'*When* you're successful, not if, you'll be living with phone number budgets all the time. Look at me, a humble printer's daughter, now having to cope with millions of euros or pounds. It's totally crazy. But I'm managing, and so can you.'

'Yeh, OK. I know I've got to get a grip and focus. I will, I promise. I'm working on it. '

'Good. Now then, I've got a surprise for you. I hope it'll take all this unnecessary stress away.'

'Sounds promising,' says Ali.

'You know I told you to keep Tuesday and Wednesday free next week?

'Well I've booked us some rock'n'roll,' she says, thrusting her phone at him.

Ali picks it up and focuses on a poster advertising The Rolling Stones' gig at Wembley.

'It's all fixed,' she says, gleefully, looking for a reaction.

Ali beams back. 'Wow, the Stones – are we going? I've never seen them live. How did you get tickets, they must have sold out ages ago?'

'Don't ask questions young man.

'The best part is that we've got VIP tickets and you'll get to meet the band too. Probably just for a split second, but that's better than nothing isn't it?

'AND we're going up by limousine AND we'll be collected AND we're spending the night in a suite at Claridge's.

'What's the matter? I've never known you to be lost for words, Ali Kurmi.'

'Wow, that's absolutely in-credible. It must be costing a fortune.'

'I knew that'd be the first thing you'd say. Don't spoil it. It's my treat. Come on let's just enjoy a bit of luxury for once – and a bit of rock'n'roll from the grandfathers of rock.'

43

'What can you tell me about him?' demands Stephanie O'Brien, from her Tipperary office.

'What do you need to know? He's the best, don't worry. He's young, but don't let that fool you. All these guys sound like they're fresh from their mother's teats, but I guarantee you, he knows what he's doing. All you have to do is say what you want, and you'll get it,' says the man on the end of her burner.

'I'm spending a lot of money here,' Stephanie says.

'You're asking a lot lady. You'll get what you want.'

'I want the lot!' says Stephanie. 'I want social media, legal agreements, bank accounts, phone calls, emails and all internet activity. Particularly her personal legal affairs. Can he do all that?'

'Sure,' says the man. 'Relax.'

'This isn't a one off, remember, it's ongoing – until I say, stop.'

'OK, I'll fix it then, yes?'

'Yes, for Christ's sake, just do it,' says Stephanie.

Stephanie has used a private investigator before, but times change quickly in the world of technology – and espionage. Instead of the old-fashioned concept of physical surveillance, these days the practice is almost exclusively conducted online. Enter spotty teenage hackers.

She has tentatively delved into the dark web and has found a contact she thinks is in Dublin – but in reality, could be anywhere in the world. He's fixed her up with someone to keep close tabs on Laura; someone who'll hack into her very being.

She's impressed with the organisation so far, even the payment method. She'll be funding the undercover work by paying a Dublin Company for "business advice". This way, multiple payments shouldn't arouse any suspicions – if anyone were to investigate. Nice and watertight, she thinks.

Stephanie's original PI could only come up with basic information about Laura's activities – and the odd photo posted by her friend Alice on Facebook. But nothing of great use to her. No, Stephanie is now being very thorough in her determination to bring down the woman she believes stole all her money. And ultimately, it isn't just surveillance work that she has in mind.

'What about the other matter? Can you deliver?'

'No problem, but let's talk about that when you're ready. One thing at a time.'

'OK, but you can guarantee it, can you? There's a lot at stake here. I don't want to spend the rest of my life in prison.'

'As long as you've got the money – there won't be a problem.'

'Good, I'll be in touch again soon,' she says sharply.

It's only a five-minute drive into town – and throughout the journey Stephanie's brain is whirling with excitement and anticipation, combined with a good helping of plain terror. She's set in motion a sequence of events that could be catastrophic, if she's not careful.

However, her objective is as clear as day in her mind. She knows precisely what she wants to do – she just needs more information before deciding on how to pull it off. A straightforward equation.

As she parks up outside another of her bars, The Railway, and heads inside, she turns her mind to immediate business matters.

One of her bar staff, a 19-year-old she took on in the spring, has proved too unreliable with her timekeeping and she's going to have to go. Stephanie is merciless with her staff, and despite the image portrayed by TripAdvisor's glowing compliments about the bar's friendly atmosphere, behind the scenes nothing could be further from the truth. The staff hate her, and will despise her even more when they find out that she's about to sack their chum Niamh.

Twenty miles away on the driving range at his club, Richard O'Brien is hammering the balls into the distance, still determined to improve his swing. He employs the club professional to better his game, so here he is today at the range, trying to iron out a few bad habits.

As well as target practice, he's mindful of the basics: grip, alignment, posture and ball position. He plays golf a lot and he's anxious to keep up with the people he plays with regularly. They don't hold any prisoners when they're all on the course.

He picks up his sand wedge for some short pitch shots and does his best to ignore his large pot belly, which is very obviously interfering. *It's only a stone or so*, he reassures himself. *I can shift that.* He's been telling himself this for months, but the weight stubbornly stays put.

Richard loves the game for many reasons. The fresh air, the company, the perceived exercise, the clinching of business deals, and the clarity of the mind that comes with all that walking and fresh air.

Right now, he is totally unaware of his sister's latest actions. He knows from bitter experience that his sister will get her way, one way or another. So why waste time and energy trying to contribute?

She's the cat with nine lives. She's taken mad gambles in her time but always seems to get away with murder, so to speak.

But who cares, he's thinking. Whatever she does, it's win-win for him. He's already happy with his inheritance and anything extra that Stephanie can grab, will be nice thick icing on the cake.

He breathes in, lifts the driver and follows through with his best swing of the day, smashing the ball as hard as he can. His sister is framed uppermost in his mind.

44

Alice and Laura are acting like two extremely naughty schoolgirls, whilst simultaneously trying to remain inconspicuous, amongst a crowd of mostly 18 to 25-year-olds. Not an easy task when you're both in your 50s, but they both look pretty amazing for their years and they're having a great time – without the help of any external stimuli, be it alcohol or any other fashionable concoction by mouth.

They're loving the music at Ali's local club, Ocean, even though they don't recognise a lot of it. They just watch the crowd and follow as best they can. So far, they've got away with it and haven't attracted any stares.

They're sitting at a small table at the back where they can just about hear themselves talk. Ali is behind his console, pumping out the beats, and the dancers love it. He knows exactly how often to talk – not a lot. Laura can't take her eyes off her man. She is glowing with pride and having so much fun.

Ali's not playing his speciality music tonight as he's standing in for another DJ, and he's doing pretty well, given that the playlists aren't his. He doesn't like to turn down work, especially when it's so conveniently local.

Laura turns to Alice.

'Do you know, when I got to Ali's place the other day, there was a little old lady with white hair, coming out of his house. She was only this high, bless her, and Ali was waving her goodbye, like an old friend. I thought, what on earth is going on here?

'It turns out she's a neighbour and Ali used to regularly walk past her house and see the back of this white permed hair in the window, apparently reading. Always reading, always in the chair. He couldn't help wondering what kept her so engrossed, day after day, and whether she was perhaps lonely. She appeared to live on her own and Ali tried to imagine what life would be like without having people to talk to. One day when he was walking past, she was coming out of her front door and she said hello to him and they got talking. Turns out she's a devout Methodist and the books she's buried in from dawn to dusk are all religious. She only socialises on Sundays at church and occasionally during the week. Anyway, they're now the best of friends and Ali has her round from time to time, hoping to offer a bit of company and a cup of tea. How's that for being a truly good person, Alice? What a fabulous thing to do.'

'That's lovely, I can't imagine many people doing that,' says Alice, almost shouting.

'That's the man I've fallen for. Look at him up there. I'm so proud.'

It's another late session and during a break before Ali's last set, he wanders over to the bar for a drink, still unaware of the ladies' presence. It is of course his usual, pomegranate and lime with ice and a straw. It's still noisy at the bar, so Ali doesn't bother trying to engage the staff in any goldfish-like conversation. No point.

He leans against the bar and does a casual sweep around the room. At the 120-degree mark he stops and slowly re-winds.

'What the …?'

'What the fuck's going on?' he says out loud, to no one.

He can see Laura and Alice pointing directly back at him from a table in the distance and they're in hysterics.

Confused, he walks determinedly towards them, avoiding the punters as he goes.

'You buggers. What are you doing HERE?'

'We've come to spy on you, Ali. We've come to check up on your secret lover.'

'What? You're mad. Have you been drinking?' he laughs.

'Of course not. This is a cheap natural high. Ali. We've been having a great time and you didn't even notice us,' says Alice, laughing.

Ali sits down.

'At least you can talk here,' he says.

'It's great, Ali. I just wanted to see you in action again. I like to know what I'm investing in,' beams Laura.

Ali leans over and kisses her, grinning wildly.

'Listen I've got another set to do. I'm so sorry. Thanks for coming. I'll deal with you later, madam.'

'Don't be daft, we're going in a minute – it's late enough for us old birds. We both think you're fab. You just get on and I'll see you tomorrow.'

Ali gives Laura another hug and a kiss and makes his way back to the console, chuffed to bits.

It's put him in a great mood and helps him try to forget about his horrendous family issues. Their relationship keeps getting better and better. He can't imagine what life would be like without her, now they've come this far. He shakes his head in amazement and wonders how he's managed to end up with such an extraordinarily wonderful person – and such a ridiculous situation with his father.

Ali Kurmi is seriously in love and having a better time than he could ever have imagined.

Like tonight's tunes, his heart is pumping along at 120 beats per minute.

He can't imagine what his father's heart rate will be, when he finds out about all of this.

Back to reality.

45

It's another sunny day and Ali has propped his kitchen door wide open, to let in the fresh air. He knocks back the last of his freshly ground coffee as he waits impatiently for his sister Rani to arrive. He inhales deeply through his nose and exhales slowly through his mouth. He's read somewhere, that this helps to calm the body and mind – and my God, he needs that right now as he prepares himself mentally to finally have everything out with his father.

Tonight he will call and to hell with the consequences. It's all gone on for far too long. Rani will no doubt have a few ideas on how he should handle it. She hasn't been down for a while and in her urgent phone call this morning, she sounded uncharacteristically serious and determined.

Ali is racking his brain, trying to guess why she's coming down at such short notice, and the vibe isn't good. He senses that it's going to be something that he's not going to like.

She's the only one who knows about Laura. It could be that. But why? He's insisted that she keep it a secret – that he will be the one to tell his parents, when it's the right time.

Is someone ill perhaps? Has one of his parents been diagnosed with something awful? He wishes Rani would hurry up and get here and put him out of his misery.

He's also made a possibly rash decision. Immediately after Rani's call, he rang Laura and asked her to join them this afternoon, so they can at last be introduced, convinced that his sister will take to her. But he's now wondering if that might just have been a little impulsive.

At last, his sister arrives and hugs him closely, kissing him on both cheeks.

'Hi Ran. You made it OK then.'

'Yes thanks, a bit busy at Guildford as usual, but I'm here.'

She walks in, immaculately dressed as usual, wearing the tiniest touches of makeup that subtly compliment her soft, natural complexion. As a busy mother of two, she manages to look after herself very well. Ali loves and admires his sister. A real new woman.

'What's with the long face then? Tea?'

'Ali, I've got some news that you're not going to like. I'm not even supposed to know about it myself, but Mum let it slip – you know what she's like, she can't keep a secret.'

'What, for God's sake, you're freaking me?'

'I don't know what you're going to do about this but it's going to affect you – and Laura.'

'What? They don't know, do they? You haven't told them?' says Ali, agitated.

Rani speaks slowly and deliberately.

'Dad has apparently arranged for you to meet a woman.'

'A woman? What sort of woman? What do you mean?'

'A woman for you, Ali.'

The moment of realisation ...

'Shit!' thunders Ali, leaping out of his chair. 'What. The. Fuck?'

'I'm so sorry, Ali. Please don't shout at me, I'm just the messenger. Don't tell them I told you or I'll be in terrible trouble.'

'The bastard. What the fuck is he doing? He's insane if he thinks I'll go along with that.'

‘Please calm down, you’ll make yourself ill.’

‘Tell me, what did Mum actually say? A bloody arranged marriage? No fucking way!’

Rani explains the little she knows, and says she felt compelled to bring him the news immediately.

‘I’m sorry. Thanks Ran,’ Ali says, quelling his temper. ‘Although thanks isn’t exactly the best word, is it? When did she tell you this?’

‘‘Only yesterday, when I went over.’

‘Was Dad there?’

‘No, it was just the two of us.’

‘Does Mum agree with him?’

‘I don’t know – I expect she does, but what can she do about it? She thinks the world of you Ali – we all do.’

‘It’s a funny way to show it. Do you know I was going to phone that bastard tonight. Yet again, he’s one step ahead. I hate him.’

After a short while, Ali manages to gather his thoughts and realises that the news is not that surprising, but now it’s happened, it has to be dealt with quickly – and without involving Laura.

‘Ran, I’ve got a massive favour to ask.’

‘What’s that?’

‘I’ve arranged for you to meet Laura this afternoon! She’s coming here. What have I done? But PLEASE, for God’s sake, don’t mention what you’ve just told me. If she found out about it, she’d run a mile. I have to stop this before it gets any further.’

‘I don’t think you can stop it, Ali. Dad’s already made the arrangements, apparently.’

‘What a bastard, he knows exactly what I’ll say. This is supposed to be the modern world we’re in, Ran. I can do what I effing well like. I have so had enough of it Ran. I can’t tell you. I could kill that man. Please promise me you won't say anything to Laura, please!'

'Whatever you say Ali. As long as you think it's the right thing to do. For the moment.'

'It is Ran. I need time to think, so we just need to act normally, OK?'

'I'll try. But I'm a bit of an open book, as you know. And listen, I can only stay a short while – I have to get back to collect the girls.'

'Of course, understood.'

The two nibble through lunch, with Ali still in shock, trying to keep off the subject. Their appetites have disappeared.

'Sorry, I can't eat with all this going on in my head. Ran, what am I going to do?'

'I wish I knew Ali. But knowing you, I expect you'll put up a fight. But if you do, you'd better be careful.'

Babe, this is my sister, Ran – Rani.'

'Hi Rani,' says Laura, as she steps into the living room. 'I've heard so much about you.'

She offers her hand, along with her million-dollar smile.

'It's all good too, you have a very good agent,' she grins.

'Nice to meet you too,' says Rani.

Ali is relieved to see a genuine smile on his sister's face as the two shake hands.

'Good lunch?' says Laura.

'Yes, er fabulous,' lies Rani. 'Up to Ali's usual standards of course. I do apologise Laura, this sounds incredibly rude, but I can't stay for very long, as I have to get back for the girls. They've gone to play with friends, and I can't be too late.'

‘I totally understand, Rani.’

‘I’ve got a few minutes though. So tell me, how are you settling into life in Hampshire? It must be very different to Ireland.’

Ali leaves the girls chatting and retires to his music room. Out of the blue, he has a new and even bigger problem. His father has moved the goalposts, and he’s now left with just one option – to walk. Leave the family and deal with the inevitable catastrophic fallout. His original plan, to ‘fess up about Laura, was risky enough what with his father’s threat to reveal the scandal, but the prospect of being forced into a marriage, changes absolutely everything.

If only he could ask her – Laura would know what to do. Ali completely trusts her wisdom and common sense. Already, she’s his rock. But he can’t possibly tell her.

He needs to get this over and done with, sooner rather than later, so, a showdown with his father it must be.

Fortunately, he doesn’t have to wait long for Bromley summons.

46

'Ali, please call me when you get this message. It's urgent. I'd like you to come up on Monday morning. Please confirm this as soon as you get this message.'

Ali has deliberately let his father's call go to voicemail. Fifteen minutes later, he calls back.

'Hi, it's me.'

'Good, thank you for calling back. I'll get straight to the point Ali; I want you to come up on Monday morning, please.'

'What for? I'm really busy.'

'Correct, you will indeed be busy – and you'll be busy up here. This is important and that's all I'm prepared to say at the moment.'

Ali is playing things carefully here. He doesn't want to let on to his father that he already knows what this is all about, but he also accepts that he needs to act normally and needs to show his familiar resistance.

'So, what's it all about? You don't normally ask me up on a Monday morning. I've got my own schedule you know.'

'Never you mind', says Javed. 'Just be here by 11 o'clock. You might be surprised to learn that I have something that I believe you're going to appreciate, so please make sure you're here promptly.'

Oh yeh? thinks Ali. *Appreciate? Fuck off father.*

Ali doesn't of course articulate these thoughts and reluctantly agrees.

OK, he thinks, just a few more days and it'll be over.

*

Jason Brand and two of his mates are walking down Toxteth High Street, past the gym and the Town Hall, in search of fish and chips. They find the only one open after 9pm. *Why do chippies close so early?* he wonders. Anyway, it's been a busy day and after lining their stomachs with starch and batter they're off to the club for a few bevies.

The music is thundering, as ever, and the three just sit, staring at everyone dancing. Jason loves this place and the physical hit he gets from the thudding bass frequencies. They're hypnotic and send him into – well, he doesn't really know what happens, but he likes the sensation. It's like being punched in the chest in a controlled way – being on the pain threshold.

Jason grew up on the tough Charleton Park estate, which is home to many people on the wrong side of the law – drug dealers, thieves, burglars – a whole breeding ground of discontent. There are safe houses for those on the run, and it was even rumoured at one time, that one house was used as a weapons store. Even the police don't seem to pitch up very often.

When Jason was growing up, everyone looked after themselves first and foremost, so the survival instinct kicked in at an early age. He also quickly learned to trust no one. They all let you down in the end.

His short temper frequently got him into fights but fortunately for him, he was a strong lad and usually came out on top. Not many people give Jason any grief – he's too volatile. Some think he's plain mad.

Jason has never met his father, but his mum has a good heart, so somewhere deep inside Jason there must lurk a tiny glimmer of good. But it doesn't often show itself.

For a time, he carried a knife. These days, he has a Glock handgun, which he handles lovingly and with deep respect and pride.

Boss Shaun is getting everyone to change their guns to automatic – a simple procedure thanks to Chinese technology. Things are on the move.

Back in the dance room, right now, Jason is switching his gaze between the dance floor and his phone – he can't stop thinking about his earlier conversation with Shaun – about the Indians. And what he's going to do to the guy who turned up at the house, when he gets hold of him. It's personal.

For the moment though, boss Shaun has new priorities and everyone has been told to cancel their plans and wait for his nod.

Jason knows they're getting into bigger business and expanding their work outside Liverpool. But he doesn't ask. He knows better and just waits for his instructions.

But that scumbag is still on his mind and he's not going to let it go – it's only a matter of time and he's gonna pay.

He stands up suddenly, knocking over the empty bottles on the table and pushes his way on to the dance floor, watched by his chums. The people on the adjacent tables look alarmed. Jason's mates look at each other and follow suit.

They're in the zone and tonight they're on the hunt for some female company.

47

When he was just 16 years of age Ali was accused of raping a girl, a schoolfriend. He did, at the time (and has ever since) vehemently deny the accusation. Fortunately, he was vindicated and the case never got to court – after the girl eventually confessed to making the whole thing up.

However, the damage was done and as is so often the case, mud sticks. Ali and his family were well aware of the likelihood of him being deemed to be "guilty" through association and duly battened down the hatches. Alas, their worst fears were manifested. The fallout was nuclear for the Kurmi family, and Javed Kurmi did everything possible to "manage" the scandal. He'd never admit it, but he was later accused by Ali of being more concerned about minimising potential harm to his own name and expanding business, than caring about his son.

Fortunately, social media was still quite young then, so there was an element of containment – heaven knows what would happen if the incident occurred today. The Kurmis breathed a sigh of relief when the excitement, if that's the right word, subsequently died down and they could start to get on with their lives again.

But it came at a price for Ali – he was brutally separated from his family, robbed of taking his 'A' levels and consequently, lost any hope of going on to university.

At just 16, he was packed off to live in Portsmouth, under the watchful eye of sympathetic family friends, for whom he subsequently worked at the local market, selling shoes. As Ali frequently quips – it was a soleless job.

It wasn't all bad news though, he was able to re-invent himself and concentrate on his big passion; writing music and developing his DJing – and Sudoku. A keen reader too, he devoured classic and contemporary literature, for pleasure. He didn't realise it at the time, but he was doing a half-decent job of educating himself – and enjoying it in the process.

Not one bit of this remarkable tale, does Laura know anything about.

He now realises, with the benefit of dear old hindsight, that keeping his dark secret from his lover could well prove to be a fatal mistake. But he's into the deception too deeply and will have to let it play out. It looks like his father's going to wreck everything anyway.

On top of the rape scandal, he now has to contend with the old man's intention to marry him off to a complete stranger. Likely scenario – he will lose Laura, his whole family, his planned music career, his DJing work, not to mention his good name. All his father has to do is leak Ali's rape accusation and social media will do the rest. Disaster.

Most people would never believe that a parent could even consider doing such a thing to a son. But Ali knows only too well what his father is capable of.

Right now, standing in the kitchen at Meon Lodge, with the unpacked shopping in his hands, Ali is finding it difficult to conceal all this anxiety. So far he hasn't aroused any suspicions and is trying with all his strength, to embrace the mundane.

'It would be so much quicker to buy everything online and have it delivered,' suggests Laura.

'Yeh, but I like to see what I'm buying,' says Ali. 'And I prefer loose fruit and veg to everything being hidden in plastic. You can't see what condition it's in, can you? And it's terrible for the planet.'

'Very true. Ali, I've never met a man who enjoys food shopping like you do.'

'I love it,' says Ali. 'Good ingredients mean good meals.'

'Don't I know it. Lucky me. Don't you ever get tired of doing all the cooking?'

'I don't do all of it.'

'You do most of it when you're here. Don't get me wrong. I really don't mind, you're a great cook and I love it, but I can cook too, you know. And I want to cook you something special. Have a think and tell me what you'd like. I've re-engaged with the kitchen since moving over here.'

'Of course, you had Mary doing all that, didn't you?'

'Yes, and I miss her so much. She was so lovely, a real friend as well as a housekeeper.'

'We'll have to invite her over,' says Ali.

'What a nice idea. I'll do exactly that. When we've got ourselves settled. That is – if we get ourselves settled.'

'Oh dear, I think I know what's coming.'

'Don't say that. It's just that I'm a bit puzzled as to why you still haven't told your parents, like you said you would. They can't exactly stop you from moving in here, can they now? It's your decision, whatever they might say.'

Christ, Ali is thinking, if only she knew.

'OK. Breaking news. I was going to tell you, but I've just been so busy – I'm going to Bromley on Monday.'

'That's great! Why on earth didn't you say something before? It's excellent news. Get it done Ali and whatever they say, we'll look after each other. We can do whatever we want, we have the means, remember. Anyway, I'm sure your parents will just want you to be happy.'

Oh yeh? thinks Ali.

'I want to move in here and get settled as much as you do. You know I do.'

'Then please Ali, go and get it sorted with your parents. Let's move on. Get into that vortex!'

Ali smiles, unconvincingly. He has a very bad feeling about the probable outcome of Monday's encounter with his father.

*

As luck would have it, the DJ has a busy weekend to occupy his mind. But back in Portsmouth, after a banging gig at Ocean, it all comes flooding back. Ali tries to sleep but is tormented by his predicament and fears that this perfect relationship is about to disappear, just as magically and as quickly as it manifested itself. He knew it was too good to last. He's deceiving the woman he's in love with and he hates it – and worst of all, it's not his fault.

In the end, he gives up, turns the light on, puts his earbuds in and seeks distraction.

He's a member of numerous Facebook music production groups and has spent hours on Instagram liking people who are in the same line of business – in the blind hope that he's doing the right thing to make connections, to further his career. Everyone says it's important to build up your social media.

Then he stops himself. All this will probably be over before it's even got started, if things go wrong next week. His amazing relationship with the stunning Laura O'Brien, his musical future – all his worldly dreams could go flying down the pan – and he shudders at the thought.

He's now in a Music Executive's Room in Clubhouse, determined to lose himself.

Clubhouse is a relatively new kid on the block on social media – it gives a live chat platform to anyone who wishes to convene a meeting with like-minded people, on any subject under the sun. Ali naturally goes for the music chat rooms.

They're usually modestly populated by 30 or 40 people all sharing advice and experiences – bonded with the same aim, of breaking into the music business. The majority of people on Clubhouse seem to be American and Ali has picked up quite a few bits of useful information from the groups, so he pops back from time to time.

Tonight, a guy called the Captain is in the chair, claiming he has some genuine experience in the business. He sounds like he has some tips to share and as is so often the case, it makes for depressing listening. It confirms what Ali already knows – that the music business has finally closed its doors on hopeful newbies and morphed deeper into big business, protecting the already-famous and having little or no care for nurturing new talent.

These days, the major record companies, of which there are only a handful left, are only interested in showbiz gloss and algorithms.

The Captain reveals that now, there are in fact, only three serious record companies left in the United States and all the other supposed independent labels, are just their subsidiaries. In other words, an even tighter closed shop. He's saying that THE ONLY way to go, is to do everything independently, forget record companies. Do it yourself – self-publish. Concentrate on getting those Instagram follows, Facebook likes and YouTube views. Build up your algorithms and keep posting bro. That's his upbeat but rather unhelpful advice. The Captain just happens to run a website that offers more of this kind of advice – for a modest subscription fee.

Ali removes his earbuds, saddened that the music business is populated with so many so-called experts preying on innocent wannabies desperate for a magical break. Now it's all about image rather than music, and newbie artists are being taken in by the illusion that they're making big progress in their relatively small social media pockets.

Then he smiles contentedly. The Clubhouse Captain might like to know that he has a long-term game plan and is poised to kick that off with the release of a great new single and a stunning music video. Ali feels that at last he's on the brink of something significant. He's got an inspired plan to write a musical and a possible TV drama. So, sod the Captain's doom and gloom and his sign-up fees. There's so much for him to look forward to and it's really happening.

Unfortunately, so is Monday in Bromley, and that thought brings his temporary high crashing back down to earth again. Come Monday, it's likely to be all over.

These dismal thoughts engulf Ali as he finally drifts off.

48

It's crunch day. The road back to Bromley is chocka this morning and every idiot driver in the south seems to be out, with the sole purpose of pissing Ali off. There's light rain too, the visibility is poor, and the wipers are scraping noisily on the windscreen. The radio is churning out a monotonous stream of similar-sounding processed tracks, the DJ is clearly in love with himself, and Ali's brain is all over the place.

It's years since he felt so miserable and there's not even a flicker of optimism to bring him any cheer.

Whilst driving, he goes back over the sequence of events that have brought him to this point today. The accusation of rape, the shame, the shock and indignation, the humiliation, losing friends, fleeing to an unfamiliar place with so many new faces, the necessary adjustment, selling cheap shoes at the open-air market at the crack of dawn every freezing morning and the violent work for his father.

But then he starts to think of the better things; his good friends, listening to music, playing the guitar, the piano, writing songs, recording in the studio, the joy of hearing his finished, mastered songs. His first DJ console, the new rig, the clubs, the sounds, the new single, the video, words of encouragement from one of the UK's top music executives – and topping the list, right up there, Laura O'Brien. He'll never forget that fateful day he met the most fabulous woman in the world.

That sunny day at Alresford, the clowns, the rides, the ice cream and all. Falling in love, the walks, the meals, the conversations, the

Isle of Wight, the Stones, the posh hotels and, oh yes, the beautiful sex.

That's where Ali wants his life to be.

And so, to "the now" on the nonstop road to Bromley. He is about to lose all that he's gained just because of an old fashioned, narrow minded, hypocritical fuck of a father who wants to follow an antiquated tradition? *Fuck off Father*!

'Coffee Ali?' calls Namita, from the kitchen.

'It's OK Mum, I'm good thanks. What's this all about, do you know?' he says, playing games.

'You'd better let your father explain.'

Ali is pacing around the living room, prepared for what's coming next. He's been rehearsing it over and over for the past 24 hours and it's not polite.

'Sounds ominous,' he digs.

'He won't be long,' says his mother, deliberately avoiding his question.

He looks around – and the room feels distinctly unfriendly – anything but a loving family hub. He feels like a stranger and plans to seize the initiative, get in first, say what he's rehearsed and leave as quickly as possible.

Unfortunately, his father beats him to it.

'Good morning', he says politely, striding in from the hallway, glowing with perspiration, as usual.

'Morning.'

'Thanks for making it on time. We've got a busy morning.'

'We have?'

'Yes, glad you've had a shave, that's good. Turn around will you.'

'Turn around? What's this?'

'You'll do fine,' mumbles his father.

'Sit down please. Good. As I said on the phone, I've something very important to tell you.'

The living room door quietly clicks shut as Namita prepares for the worst.

'Over the years, I've gone to an enormous amount of trouble to help you and I know you'll be surprised by this but I now want to help you even more. I want to help you settle down. Properly.'

'Settle down? I'm perfectly settled thanks, not that you'd know.'

'Just hear me out please,' says his father, sounding more pressing.

'I'm perfectly aware of what you went through in your teens, and you have to agree that we've all helped you in every possible way. We've supported you and provided you with everything you've needed from therapy to finance.'

'Yes Dad, and I've thanked you profusely on many occasions. But that doesn't mean ...'

His father interrupts again.

'I believe that now is the time for you to step back into the family again and play your part like your brother and sisters have been doing for a long time.'

'What the hell are you on about Dad? I'm not changing anything. I have a good career in corporate entertainment and I'm finally making headway with my music. And I've done all that by myself without you or anyone else's help. AND I do all your rotten stinking dirty work for you. Which is immoral and illegal.'

'Don't you dare talk to me like that, young man. You're in no position to argue.'

He pauses briefly to collect his thoughts and turns the volume down a bit.

'Ali, what you've been doing is not a career, it's playing at life. Playing is for children and you're not a child anymore. You're in your mid-thirties and it's already late for you to be finding a wife and settling down. Most people your age have been married for years and have families of their own.'

'A wife? If I want a wife, I'll pick my own.'

'OK here's what going to happen. In one hour's time, you will meet a very nice young lady doctor and you will spend time with her and you will be polite and you will get to know her.'

'What the fuck are you talking about?' yells Ali, wrong-footed by this unexpected already-arranged rendezvous. Everything he's rehearsed suddenly goes out of the window.

'What have you done?'

'It's time you got married and raised your own family, Ali. It's what we do.'

'I don't care 'what we do' – I'm bloody well not doing it.'

'Don't swear Ali, and don't raise your voice like that,' says Javed, raising his own voice.

'There's nothing you can do to stop me walking straight out of that door,' says Ali, pointing across the room.

'Ah, but there is. If you walk out of that door now, you walk out of your family, you walk out of that house in Portsmouth, you lose all financial support and you will lose your anonymity because your past will suddenly catch up with you.'

'You WHAT?' Ali thunders. 'My past will catch up with me? You'd do that? It wasn't even true!'

'I would. It's high time for you to finally grow up and take your place in the Kurmi family as a mature adult. Your family is more important than ANYTHING.'

Ali is speechless – for a few seconds and returns to his previous tactics.

'Yeh well, I'll just tell this doctor about the 'big secret' when I meet her. She'll run a mile. You didn't think that through, did you?'

'As a matter of fact, I did,' says Javed, very calmly. 'That's why I've taken such a lot of time to find the right woman for you. I've been honest with her family from the start, and they accept that everyone deserves a second chance and so they've agreed terms. They know everything.'

*

In resigned disbelief and misery, Ali finds himself sitting in a cafe in the middle of Bromley, ironically, not far from the Muslim Cultural Centre. At the moment, he's off anything Muslim and is trying to put his spinning thoughts into some form of comprehendible order.

His stomach is churning again at the thought of Laura sitting a hundred miles away in Hampshire, having no clue whatsoever, that her partner is about to meet another woman, theoretically destined to become his wife. He prays passionately for a miracle to magically whisk him away, back to the love of his life. He screws his eyes up tightly and exhales loudly.

At that very moment his anxiety is broken by the sound of a child that suddenly bursts into a maniacal screech that cuts right through the room. *Just like my nerves*, he thinks. Frazzled.

He wonders what kind of a world it is, where you say hello to a complete stranger, have a cup of coffee and discuss getting married. It's surreal.

Too late though, because Jiera has entered the building and she's looking around the room checking on her phone whilst doing so. She obviously has a photo of Ali. She spots him and moves uncertainly towards him, smiling shyly.

Ali's first impression is that she clearly likes green, a lot. She's wearing various shades of the colour from top to bottom. It's all very stylish and very sensible looking. She's quite a bit shorter than him, is wearing a hijab which covers most of her black hair and she has an intelligent, enquiring look on her face. She looks like a doctor, if that's possible.

He stands up politely and they shake hands.

'Hi I'm Jiera.'

'I'm Ali.'

'Good start, I suppose,' she chuckles.

'Are you here by choice?' she asks, looking closely at Ali.

'Er, I'm, here.'

'I see,' she says, sitting down. 'I think we might have something in common.'

Ali gives her a puzzled look. He decides to come clean straightaway and tells Jiera about Laura and the torment raging inside him, hoping that this tactic must surely put her off.

Far from it. To his complete surprise, she smiles sympathetically and begins to relate her own forbidden love story, and her own parents' subversive arrangements to get her here today.

'So, you don't want this either?' says Ali.

'No I don't! I've been completely manipulated.'

'Me too.'

They conclude that their parents have well and truly outsmarted them, and they sit forlornly looking out of the window, desperately searching for a solution.

'You're a doctor then,' says Ali, breaking the silence.

'Yes, I work at the Princess Royal – paediatrics.'

'I'm impressed.'

'And you, you work for your father?'

'Is that what you've been told? Yeh, I suppose so, sort of. But I'm really a DJ,' he says, seeing Jiera starting to smile.

'Corporate events,' he quickly adds.

'It's quite a big business and very successful I believe,' she says.

'Yeh it is, but to be honest I prefer the DJing. My father wants me to give it all up and come and work full time, up here.'

'And how do you feel about that?'

'Shit, to be honest,' says Ali. 'It's not exactly an interesting or satisfying career, is it? Renting out properties to students.'

Ali realises that he is talking to a very bright lady here.

'So, what do you do when you're not doctoring?' he asks.

'Lots. Cooking, reading, walking – but most of all, I run. I belong to a club, and we have great fun, running. I've done a few marathons including the London Marathon but the lottery system to take part here makes it difficult these days. I can see why, though. They need to control numbers and safety – and stop all the professionals taking it over.'

She pauses for a moment.

'What about you? Do have any interests, apart from DJing?'

'I cook, I train, I write music.'

'Oh, composing music?'

'Yes, and I'm currently in the process of releasing a single and a music video. I'm having a serious go at making a living from it. But it isn't easy.'

Ali notes a blankness in Jiera's face.

'I'm afraid music is not one of my strong points,' she says. 'I'm actually tone deaf. They tried to teach me the recorder at school, but I couldn't even do that. I can't sing a note – well I can, but you wouldn't want to hear it … but you've obviously got a musical gift, which is fantastic.'

Ali finds Jiera very easy to talk to and she's also very pleasant on the eye. In fact, she seems to be a very nice person. But for God's sake, what is going on here? They've spent the past 15 minutes "getting to know each other".

This can't be happening.

Two missed calls from Laura.

49

'So, what are we going to do about this situation we find ourselves in? They can't force us – not in this day and age,' says Jiera, finishing her now cold coffee.

'My father is having a good go.'

'Look, I hope you don't mind me bringing this up, but I know you had a very bad time when you were a teenager.'

Ali groans inside. *Oh God, she knows.*

'That's putting it mildly, yeh, I did. But as you say, that was a long time ago and it was all a load of lies. In the end, the truth did come out.'

Jiera has been told the gist of the rape story.

'Ali, I can't imagine what it must have been like.'

'She was crazy, that girl. But unfortunately, the damage was done. To be honest I haven't spent much time thinking about all that for quite a while. Until now, thank you dear father.'

'How bad is it with your father?'

Ali describes their very poor relationship and elaborates on the rape accusation that led to his banishment to Portsmouth.

Jiera is clearly genuinely horrified by his account and sympathises with him. She talks more about her own on-off love affair with another doctor, five years older than her. Her parents do not approve. Ironically, the pair have a great deal in common – and realising this, slowly begin to relax and begin to form a strategy to take on their parents.

'So are we agreed then? We're not going to let this happen?'

'Agreed,' says Ali, still a little confused by what is happening.

'No hard feelings?'

'No, absolutely not. I'm delighted, actually. But there is a complication for me. My father is blackmailing me into this and has every intention of ruining me if I don't go through with it.'

'Really? Why would he do that?'

'Because he's an odious, extremely unpleasant, manipulative man. If I refuse to play ball he will do his utmost to bring me down. He could basically ruin everything I love – first and foremost, my relationship with Laura. And just imagine, my name would be mud if the rape allegation got out. The personal and professional reputation I've built up over the years, would be wiped out with even the slightest suggestion of rape, if it got into social media. And my music career would also be blown out of the water before starting.'

'Haven't you told her about all this?'

'No, I haven't. I know I should have, but I didn't want to lose her when we first started dating. And then it got harder and harder to tell her.'

'Surely she'd understand if you told her now?'

'Mmm. Now, of course I can see that I made a big mistake in hiding it. But it's too late. What the hell is she going to think? Her boyfriend forgot to tell her about being accused of rape? I'm not too sure she'd be that understanding, do you?

'Well, can I tell you something? I don't agree. I think you have a very clear way of getting yourself out of this mess. I think we both have, if we play our cards right. Shall we have another coffee?'

Ali looks up again and smiles, encouraged.

'You're alright, you are. What's the plan Stan?'

What they haven't noticed, is the man in the corner scanning a newspaper and occasionally taking a bite from a sandwich. He's been watching them talking enthusiastically.

'I feel like I'm playing counsellor here,' says Jiera, 'but this could be the solution for us both. I suggest you call your father's bluff and tell all to Laura.'

'Really?'

'If you'll excuse me, from what you've told me, you two have a very solid relationship. She's older than you, right? Experienced in life … I'm pretty confident that she would handle the news OK. If she truly loves you. And wouldn't your father be risking his own reputation if he leaked the story on social media? Nothing has changed for him on that score.'

'That's a very good point. But I'd still be saying goodbye to my family. That's monumental too.'

'But wouldn't they come round eventually? Surely they would.'

'Not my father. My mother and siblings might.'

'Only you can decide that, then. You're going to have to, one way or the other – and soon.'

'OK,' says Ali, jolted by the immediate task ahead of him. 'What about you?'

'With your permission, I'm going to tell my parents that I didn't take to you and that I'm very unhappy about the violence involved with your father's work. I didn't know about that until you told me just now – but it's an even better excuse for me. I was just going to tell my parents that you weren't my cup of tea and that I wouldn't be able to trust you or feel safe with you. But what you've told me will make my case all the more convincing. Assault, for goodness sake!'

Ali starts to feel more optimistic. For what feels like an eternity, he's been struck down with doom and gloom, genuinely believing that his life with Laura will to come to an end.

Now, Jiera's surprising wisdom is giving him the strength to turn it all around. He successfully changed his life almost 20 years ago, so why can't he do it again?

'I need to buy some time, can we do that? Can we string this out for a couple of days?' he asks.

'Sure', says Jiera, 'take longer if you like. I can stall my parents, saying that whilst I'm not keen, I would reluctantly agree to a second meeting. Is that any good?'

'That's perfect, I'll do the same – it'll give me time to get organised. I'll somehow manage to string my father along. I just need time to talk things through with Laura.'

'So, depending on how it goes with you, we may or may not see each other again. Good luck!'

Ali knows very well that his proposed actions will mean that his father will certainly carry out his threat to cut all ties with him.

He's also going to take that huge gamble – that his father won't actually carry out his threat of spreading the word about the alleged rape on social media. Jiera's right; whilst hurting his son, Javed would also be damaging his own reputation. He is, after all, an incredibly vain and greedy man. And that is what Ali will pin all his hopes on and hope to God that his father is actually bluffing.

Whatever happens, it's all change in Ali Kurmi's life. A massive change – and the thought of finally being free from his father's shackles, to live his life with Laura, is now an indescribably exciting prospect.

'Jiera, I can't thank you enough. We've only known each other for less than an hour and it's like we're already old friends.'

Jiera beams widely and finishes her coffee, 'My pleasure entirely. Hey, before you go, let's swap numbers. We need to keep in touch, eh?'

Walking back to his van, Ali considers the conversation he's just had. She could so easily have been very different, someone who'd been unattached for so long, she'd jump at any opportunity to get married.

No, Ali boy – you just got lucky here. If you stay cool, this plan could really work.

As he walks confidently to the multi-storey car park, he checks his phone. Laura hasn't left any messages, but she's called twice.

He calls back. *Damn.* He leaves a brief voice message.

'Hi, I saw you called, call me back. I'll come straight over to you tomorrow morning. Love you.'

Laura will be anxious to know how the meeting with his father has gone but Ali isn't going to risk anything at this stage and certainly not on the phone.

Laura does call back, but Ali has switched his phone off again. So, she leaves him a message. 'Hi, I hope it went well with your dad. Please let me know. In the meantime, I've got some great news. I've been invited up to Birmingham by a lady who runs a freedom shelter for the abused up there. She's very kindly arranged for me spend a couple of days with them to see their set up. Sorry it's a bit last-minute but I didn't want to say no. I'll call you tomorrow evening from the hotel. Love you too – to the stars, the black hole and back! Mwa.'

'Shit, shit, shit,' spits Ali, 'this can't be happening. No, please. You can't go away now. Bloody hell.'

Just as he was beginning to feel optimistic and much happier, Laura unwittingly throws a thudding great spanner in the works.

What unbelievably bad timing. The very time he needs her with him, she's goes off on some trip and there is absolutely nothing he can do.

'It went OK then?' says Ali's father, looking hopeful as he and Ali reconvene back at the house.

'Dad, I told you at the beginning, that I am not marrying anyone until I decide to.'

He's being careful here. He doesn't want to arouse any suspicions – his father is a wily old man and he'd spot a conspiracy a mile off.

'Think carefully about that young man. The consequences if you don't are extremely serious, but I'm not going to go over all that again. You know the score full well. But tell me, you got on with Jiera OK, didn't you?'

'How would you know?'

'Did you?'

'She was very pleasant I suppose. But that's not the basis of a marriage.'

'It could be,' says Javed. 'It's certainly a good start. We'd like you to meet again, on Wednesday after you've both had time to think. I'm sure you'll make the right decision, Ali.'

Javed is confident that the second meeting will take place as his "eyes" at the cafe reported back immediately to say that the meeting looked very amicable.

'Right then,' says his father standing up, 'we're due at Basma's at five. I'm sure you can occupy yourself until then.'

Ali has just one thing on his mind. Talking to Laura. He'd like to head straight back to Portsmouth, but out of respect for his older sister, Basma, he'll attend and return in the morning, hoping with every part of his mortal being, that Laura will be back before the Wednesday deadline – and that she'll be OK with his revelation.

*

Basma has put on a buffet for the family get-together, so it's conveniently informal and there's less likelihood of Ali having to conduct any awkward conversations. He's quietly incredibly nervous about the plan he and his new friend Jiera, have set in motion, but he also feels empowered thinking about how life will be, if all goes well.

'I haven't talked to you for ages, how are things?' says Basma, moving over to sit by Ali.

'Good thanks, loads of work and the gigs are more corporate, so yeh, all good. You know me Bas, anything to do with music is good.'

'I was actually thinking more about how you are, you know, your well-being – we don't speak enough, do we? And I know you don't exactly see eye-to-eye with Dad!'

'I'm absolutely OK Bas, Portsmouth has been my home for such a long time – don't forget, I've lived there for longer than I lived up here. It's a fab place, I've got good friends and apart from the shameful work for our dear father, I love my life. It's all I want to do. You should come and visit me more often.'

'I will. I must make time. Are you still writing songs?'

'Yep, I love it. And producing.'

'You never let me hear your music, Ali, why not?'

'I don't really think you'll like it. You like chart music.'

'I'm sure I would. I'd like to listen to what you do.'

'OK I'll send you a link – but I don't want your opinions, OK?' he says laughing, 'I'm a shy and sensitive creative.'

He looks over towards his father to see if he's listening in. He clearly is and Ali straightens his face again. Basma and the others know nothing at all about their father's ultimatum.

My God, when all this kicks off, the shit is really going to hit the fan and I'm really going to miss these people – well, most of them.

Ping goes his phone – a text from Jiera.

'All going to plan here. Good luck. Hopefully won't have to see you Weds!'

50

Ali comes to the end of the motorway and is greeted by the familiar view of the English Channel in the distance. Soon, the iconic Spinnaker Tower and the “lipstick” building, as it’s affectionately called locally, come into view and whilst the scene is welcoming, his mind is awash with crazy thoughts – and being home fills him with trepidation. God knows what his blood pressure must be.

He spent yesterday evening trying to call Laura but kept getting her voicemail. She must have a stack of missed calls from him – so why isn’t she responding?

He’s got less than two days to get everything organised. But what is he thinking, for goodness’ sake? He’s not even sure how she’s going to take all this. Perhaps she’ll be horrified and feel betrayed by his deception. It doesn’t bear thinking about. Anxiety begins to smother him again as he contemplates the worst.

He walks up the path and clumsily unlocks his front door and steps in, glad to be back and immediately tries calling her, yet again.

This time, she answers and is taken aback by the gushing urgency in his voice.

‘Laura! Thank God! Thank you so much for answering babe. I’ve been going crazy, not being able to get through to you. You wouldn’t believe what’s been happening, not in a million years.’

‘My goodness, what in heaven’s name is wrong? What’s happened? Is there a problem?’

‘Oh babe – where do I start?’

'I'm here Ali, just calm down and tell me slowly. I'm sorry I had to go away but it was too good an opportunity to turn down.'

'No, no, no, I get that – it's not that. Nothing is your fault. It's just incredibly unfortunate timing. I've got something absolutely huge I need to talk to you about, and it can't wait.'

'Then for goodness sake, tell me now. Is it your father, did it all go wrong?'

'I need to talk to you face-to-face,' he says, becoming agitated.

'Can't it wait until I get back on Wednesday? If not, just tell me now.'

'God, NO!'

Ali's anxiety and frustration suddenly boil over and he lets out a huge uncontrolled yell.

'What on earth is wrong Ali? What the hell was that?'

'Please forgive me. Please, I didn't ...'

'What is it Ali? Please tell me, you're scaring me now!'

Ali starts to sob, and it's come from nowhere. He never cries, but right now he's unable to articulate what's in his head and heart and all his feelings pour out of him, in the form of gushing tears.

'I'm SO SORRY ... I can't even speak; I'll have to call you later ...' he splutters, clumsily ending the call frantically stabbing his phone with his fingers.

The tears continue to flood out in a torrent and he rolls over onto his bed. He hammers his pillow, swearing angrily, completely losing it.

In Birmingham, Laura looks at her phone in astonishment, shaken by what she's just heard and immediately calls back. The phone keeps ringing but to her frustration and dismay, Ali doesn't pick up.

She ponders over what to do next. She's in a very awkward situation. She's driven over a hundred and fifty miles in rotten weather, she's tired and is due to meet her hosts who have gone out of their way to accommodate her.

She doesn't want to be rude to them, but they'll just have to understand. Ali is more important.

She calls him yet again, but his phone still keeps on ringing.

Damn it, what the hell is going on?

Ali is lying on his bed, still weeping, stunned by his outpouring of emotion. He picks up the book on his bedside table and hurls it against the bedroom door, in a rage.

'I'm finished,' he yells. 'I am totally fucked!'

His front doorbell is now ringing. He ignores it and lies there, trying to control his frantic breathing. He's almost hyperventilating and he begins to feel light-headed. Oh God, not again. The bell rings again.

'Fuck off,' he shouts.

It rings again.

'Argggh!' he screams and pulls the pillow over his head.

At 3 o'clock he awakens, befuddled, reaches instinctively for his phone and sees the list of missed calls from Laura. There's a voice message too. He calls in and Laura is sounding distressed and says she's on her way back and will be driving straight to Portsmouth.

He spots the mute button in the on position. *Oh, no what have I done?* He does some quick calculations and works out that she'll probably arrive within the next hour.

Oh my God, she'll be furious.

He stands up, stretching his arms above his head and shakes his whole body – checking in the mirror as he does so. It's a broken, crumpled vision.

He needs to pull himself together quickly and get his story into some sensible, coherent order to explain everything. That is, if she'll listen. There's so much at stake. What's she going to say after driving all the way back from Birmingham – having only just got there? She's going to be so angry.

Christ alive, could things be any worse than they are right now on Planet Ali?

He really doesn't think so.

At almost exactly 4 o'clock, Laura is standing there on his doorstep, looking pale and frightened. He lunges at her and hugs her with such vigour, she nearly topples.

'Wo there, let me come in,' she says. 'You nearly had me over.

'So pardon my French, what the fuck is going on? What happened up there?'

Ali looks blankly at Laura – he looks terrible, his eyes are swollen from all the crying. Laura's never seen him like this.

'Ali, I've been so frightened. What have they done to you?'

'Please don't leave me, I beg you. I love you Laura, please don't dump me. I'm so sorry.'

'Hey, hey, hey ... you're not going to lose me, but you do owe me one hell of an explanation. I've driven nearly 300 miles and cancelled a very important appointment. I am knackered. So please let me in, let me go to the bathroom and for God's sake get me a cup of tea before I fall over.'

They sit down together and now, more composed, Ali slowly and painstakingly gives his account of the previous day. After what seems like an eternity, Laura places her hand on his knee.

'I cannot understand for the life of me Ali Kurmi, why you didn't tell me all this before. What on earth must you think I am?'

'I thought you'd leave me. First, it was the allegation – and as if that wasn't bad enough, out of the blue along came the marriage idea. It's been a nightmare. And it's not my fault!'

'Listen, I've shared all my dark secrets with you – all the terrible things I've done – and believe me, there have been plenty. Why in God's name didn't you think you could share your nightmare with me? That's what love is all about Ali, having unconditional trust in each other and no lies.'

'I've never lied to you babe.'

'I know, but there is such a thing as lying by omission, isn't there?'

'I wanted to tell you all along – as we were growing closer but I was falling so crazily in love with you, I didn't want even the slightest thing to spoil our relationship. I was scared you might dump me. Can't you see that?'

'I suppose I can. But I have to admit I'm disappointed that you couldn't tell me everything.'

'Does that mean we're finished? Please don't say that. I can't possibly live without you.'

'Alli Kurmi. You are a very foolish and naive young man sometimes. Clearly, you still don't fully understand and know me. Come with me.'

'What?'

'I said, come with me.'

'Are we ... are we OK?'

'Stop asking questions and do as I say; you need to clam down and chill out,' says Laura, 'I'll tell you exactly what I think. And I'll tell you exactly what we're going to do.'

'Feeling better?' asks Laura.

'Much,' says Ali. 'What time is it?'

'9:30,' she says, reaching for her phone on the bedside table. 'And I'm hungry.'

'How did we manage to sleep, for God's sake?'

'Are you serious? We've both had an horrendous couple of days. You certainly have.'

'Horrible,' says Ali.

He sits up next to Laura and puts his arm round her shoulder and pulls her closer. He loves the softness of her body against his and he adores her natural scent. He could quite happily make love all day. Laura gently rubs her breasts against his side and looks up at him.

'Right, Mr Kurmi, we need to make some plans, don't we? Get you prepared. But first, let's get this clear once and for all. So, there can be no arguments.

I love you, Ali. I don't care about any false allegations of rape and I don't blame you for your father's actions, OK? Is that absolutely clear?'

They dress and go downstairs. Ali pulls a pizza from the freezer and turns on the oven.

'I'm sorry, only got frozen.'

'That's fine, I could eat anything right now, to be honest.'

'So we're good then?'

'We certainly are, as far as I'm concerned. But no more secrets, eh?'

'Promise.'

'You don't mind committing to an ageing Irish hag?'

'You're kidding me.'

'I'm 17 years older than you Ali Kurmi. One day you'll look at me and I'll be old and you might regret the things you're saying now.'

'Never. Never, never, never. Never,' says Ali.

'Sure?'

'Yes, you old hag.'

They forget about cutlery and plates and start to devour the pizza straight from the oven.

'OK, it's time to get down to the practicalities of all this. All we've done is agree our intentions. You, young man, have still got Wednesday to sort out. That's going to be a traumatic day for you.'

'Not any more, now that I know we've got a future, that's everything, it's all I need.'

'But what about your mother and father? Do you think they really will disown you?'

'That's what I expect, yes.'

'And your brother and sisters?'

'I honestly don't know what the others will do. Rani'll be alright, maybe Basma.'

'I have to say, I'm deeply impressed with how you and this girl, Jiera have got yourselves organised. And so quickly. Can you imagine where we'd be if she actually wanted to marry you?'

'Don't. Don't. The thought is appalling. But yeh, luckily she's really OK.'

'What a masterstroke, Mr Kurmi. So, she's going to tell her parents on Wednesday that you've been assaulting people as part of your work?'

'Yeh, she's going to big that up. Her parents know about the rape accusation but clearly my father hasn't told them the full truth – details about what we do to keep tenants in line. They wouldn't want their daughter marrying a thug and a law-breaker, would they?'

'Brilliant,' says Laura.

'What you have to get your head around, is that you're actually in a very strong position. You no longer have any money worries. You're already standing on your own, without the need of financial support from your father.'

'Yes, that still bothers me a bit, I have to say.'

'Oh come on, don't bring all that up again. Don't worry about any of that. I've already told you, I never had money, not that long ago. It's still new to me, so we're both pretty well in the same position. Let's explore wealth together. Like winning the big prize in the Euro Millions.'

'Ha. That doesn't usually go well, does it? The winners usually implode within six months.

'No seriously … that's amazing.'

'Alright, I'm absolutely shattered, and you must be too, so let's just curl up, go to sleep and really get things going tomorrow.'

Laura turns the light out and they cuddle up together with her clinging to him – spooning.

'I love you, Laura O'Brien,' whispers Ali.

'I love you, Ali Kurmi.'

'You did shower, didn't you?'

'ALI …!'

When I'm getting tired and down
You're always there to bring me round,
When I'm falling outta line,
I turn to you and feel just fine,

In the darkest hours of the night,
lying in bed just waiting for the light,
I reach out my hand and then I feel alright
Cos my baby's got my back
And I'm right on track – I'm back.

51

Today, Wednesday, is another huge day for Ali. He seems to be having rather a lot of them at the moment. As far as his father is concerned, he is scheduled to meet Jiera for the second time, but if all goes to plan they will simultaneously reveal to their parents, that they are incompatible and the meeting will not happen. The result, they believe, will free them both to be with their chosen partners.

Ali will use this as his long-awaited moment to finally sever all ties with his father. No more beatings, no more long car journeys with his cousins, no more hours of remorse, no emotional debt and no guilt.

However, such freedom will come at a huge price. He already knows what will happen at today's meeting. His father never likes to lose anything – arguments or money, so Ali believes he will be told to march.

Javed Kurmi is sitting in his office, staring at the letter he's just opened. No stamp, no postmark, ordinary printer paper, a buff brown envelope – nothing to indicate its origin. It's just one sentence and consists of the worst racist profanities that he has ever seen. He is taken aback by its sheer vulgarity and violence. He's so shocked, he's just sits motionless and silent.

This letter has completely ruined what should have been a good day, before it's started. Should he do what any right-minded citizen would do and immediately report it to the police? Or does he need to exercise a bit of caution?

Javed has never openly committed any crimes, but he knows very well that he's frequently crossed the line to get his own way when "certain situations" have demanded "certain actions". He doesn't want anything to upset the running of his property empire that he's worked so hard to establish.

But who in Allah's name would send anything so rampantly racist and disgusting as this, he wonders?

It doesn't take long for his furtive brain to return to the Liverpool riddle. The boys ran into trouble at one of their properties and Javed was warned by a friend to leave it alone and not investigate the incident. Could it really be anything to do with that? Why would a drugs gang in Liverpool feel the need to scare a property businessman in the south of London, after all this time?

He decides to hold back on calling the police and carefully folds the letter again, replacing it in the envelope and slides it slowly into his desk drawer, trying to avoid fingering it too much.

Not knowing, is alarming Javed. Alarming him a lot.

After several long minutes, his thoughts return to his immediate priority, his son. He pulls himself together. He's confident that he's finally corralled Ali into towing the Kurmi line and as an unexpected bonus, he's even managed to find a very decent marriage prospect that his son might even be pleased about.

Deep in thought, he makes his way home and calls to his wife Namita as he opens the front door.

'I'm home, any chance of a tea?'

He's still trembling a little after receiving that letter and needs to steady himself before Ali arrives.

He says nothing to Namita about it and settles himself in his chair, in the living room. Shortly, he believes his family will be considerably strengthened, thanks to his actions.

Family, he repeats to himself, *my family*.

He looks around the room slowly and realises that he rarely stops still long enough to appreciate his own living space. Come to that, he's not he even sure he knows his own wife any more. What are all these cheap and vile ornaments dotted around this room? They're everywhere – over the large marble fireplace and in various places along the fitted bookshelves on the other side of the room. Small creatures, buddhas, miniature vases, bowls, and countless other unidentifiable ceramics.

Namita is also a big reader. Mostly rubbish, in Javed's opinion. She's filled the house with books. Loads of them. She always buys the hardbacks, but Javed can't understand why she never recycles them at the charity shops. She just keeps on adding to her collection, adding to all the clutter.

He doesn't complain though, it's all innocent enough and most importantly, it keeps her from meddling in his affairs.

Whilst the fun and excitement evaporated many moons ago – the two have been married for a long time and have so far managed to co-exist without any major fallouts. These days, Javed considers his marriage to be more of a business arrangement, than a relationship. Anyway, the woman he married has lost her looks and she's carrying more weight now. Physical attraction is just a distant memory and even the thought makes him shudder. She feeds him well and keeps the house running and that's just how Javed is happy to keep it.

Now then, back to today. He finally gets to square things up with his son.

He hasn't forgotten Ali's impudence earlier this year, when he insulted him in front of the whole family, during lunch. It was unforgiveable – the last straw as far as he was concerned. From that moment, his mission has been to show Ali, indeed everyone, that he is the boss in the Kurmi family and that insolence like that, will not be tolerated.

Today, he is confident that Ali will finally have to accept returning to Bromley, marrying a good, professional woman, start a family and put all his efforts into developing and consolidating the family business.

'What on earth is going on in here?' shouts Namita, bursting in.

'You two can be heard three streets away. Please stop shouting. Both of you.'

'Leave us alone please,' snaps Javed, attenuating the volume and turning back to Ali.

'Do you realise what you're saying here young man? Have you not thought about the consequences?'

'Of course I have, I know exactly what I'm saying and it's my final decision, and there is absolutely nothing you can do that will change my mind,' says Ali, with the calm confidence he has gained from carefully planning this moment with Laura.

And he feels even more empowered, knowing that he will leave this room, this house, this family – and the bastard still won't know anything about her.

'Oh I'm afraid there is. If that is your final decision, there's a very great deal that I can do that will make you come to regret this day very much indeed.'

Ali's blood is now on the move – and the indignation, frustration and anger suddenly start to build. He can't resist the opportunity to have the last words – and stares fiercely into his father's eyes.

'Forever the bully, eh? No, the brute, the sadist, even. Well you can keep your rotten job, keep the house in Pompey and cut me off in every way you choose – but you will NOT force me into any marriage – or force me to do *anything* I don't want to do. It's over. We are finished.'

'You will not talk to me, your father, in this way – you will listen to me.'

'A father? You call yourself an effing father? You're just a waste of space. A fat, selfish, monstrous pile of egotistical shit – even your own wife hates you. But again, you're too self-absorbed to even notice. Mind you, you probably couldn't give a shit anyway.'

'How dare you speak to me like that!'

'And just for the record … you have no idea what you did, when you threw me out all those years ago – you were just looking out for yourself. Did you really think that throwing money around would magically solve all my problems? What I needed was my family. My mother, father, brother and sisters. But what did you do? You took it all away and sent me off to live with complete strangers. How could you ever believe that was the right thing to do? You abandoned me and left me to rot. Out of sight – out of mind. And as we're talking about the others – you do realise they all hate you, too. They really do. Go on, I dare you. Ask your family what they really think!'

Forehead now awash with perspiration, Javed suddenly stands up and screams, snarling at his son, and raises his arm in rage, ready to lunge.

'Yeh, go on hit me, do what you do best. Go on, Dad.'

Javed holds his arm in the air and at the point when he's about to strike his son, he somehow manages to check himself and instead, shrieks.

'Get out! Get out of this house, now. And don't you ever set foot in here again, go.'

Ali picks up his bag, stares at his fuming father and walks slowly to the door without looking back. He feels in complete control and doesn't even give his father the pleasure of slamming the door.

His mother, Namita comes out of the kitchen into the hallway looking shocked and dismayed.

'Oh Ali. What have you done?'

'No, Mum what have you done? I'm going now. I love you, Mum. Goodbye Mum.'

'Ali ...'

*

Ali is sitting in his van with the engine ticking over – trembling. He texts Jiera: *Job done here. It's all over. Good luck at your end. Speak soon.*

He takes a deep breath and slowly moves down the road, a few metres from the Kurmi residence.

'You'd have been proud of me. I did it,' he says, clicking his seatbelt and adjusting the hands-free cradle.

'Oh Ali, are you alright? It must have been terrible. Did he react as we expected?' says Laura anxiously.

'He did, and a lot more. An awful lot more.'

'OK, don't tell me now, just get yourself home and tell me all about it later. But please Ali, drive carefully. You're bound to be shocked after all that.'

'I'll be fine. This is just the beginning and it's all good. I'll go to Portsmouth first to collect some things – I don't trust that bastard. I'll call you from there.'

The drive back can take up to three hours, depending on the traffic. Today the roads are good, and Ali spends the time going over what his actions this morning are actually going to mean.

He's still floating on adrenalin and feels a real joy at the thought of being liberated from a routine and a mindset that has controlled him for years. How on earth did he stick with it for so long? He shakes his head in bewilderment at his own inertia.

Again, for some inexplicable reason, driving through Portsmouth, the place somehow feels different.

As he walks up the path to his front door, he crosses his fingers, hoping that he can still get in. The key goes into the lock OK, and it turns. He's in. Phew. He bends down to collect the pile of letters and junk mail and walks through to the kitchen.

He thinks of Laura in Wickham and quickly texts to say he's arrived safely. He shivers with excitement. Strangely enough, he doesn't feel any sadness at the prospect of leaving Portsmouth, where he's lived for so many years. He's consumed totally by the love he has for Laura and the thrill of their future which will be very different to anything he's experienced so far.

He looks at the mail. One of the letters stands out. It's a buff envelope with no stamp but it doesn't look like a bog-standard mailer. He opens it and unfolds the paper inside.

His jaw drops in horror and he just stares at the paper. Its content is shocking – racist and deeply threatening. Disgusting doesn't come near it.

He turns the letter and the envelope over in his hand. Who could have sent this? And why him? Suddenly, he is filled with terror and instinctively checks every room in the house for any sign of disturbance. Nothing. Could the person who sent this, get in? He's not going to hang around here on his own long enough to find out. He has just one aim in mind, to fill his van as fast as he can and get the hell out of the place.

His mind goes into overdrive as he processes what he's just seen. How could anyone send a letter containing so much raw hatred?

Is it someone he knows, for fuck's sake? Is it another unhappy student at one of the properties? Would a wronged student go this far? Maybe it's someone at the club – maybe one of those nutters who spiked his drink? He's at a complete loss.

Luckily, Ali's life isn't cluttered. Most of his possessions consist of his clothing, DJ gear, cookery books, his kitchen knives and his musical equipment. Those are his priorities and he'll risk leaving furniture and other items for the time being and hope he can get them later. Now though, it's a question of getting everything together as quickly as possible and leaving.

That bloody letter. What in God's name is that all about?

*

It's late afternoon and Ali parks his van on the drive at Meon Lodge and leaves everything inside it for the moment. He's confused, angry and scared. A single, anonymous letter, has turned his feelings of elation back into a mire of uncertainty and fright. This is so unfair.

He lets himself into the hallway, wiping his feet as he goes and calls out to Laura who comes running down the stairs, looking thrilled to see him.

'At last! At bloody last!' she says, hugging him tightly round his neck whilst smothering him in kisses. He almost chokes. 'Steady on babe.'

'Sorry, I've been so worried about you. I can't tell you. But look at you! You've done it – you must tell me everything. Now.' She grabs his hand and pulls him into the living room.

He relates the morning's events, going into every bit of detail to illustrate the extent of his father's scheming and nastiness. Then he pauses, before pulling out the anonymous letter and placing it slowly on the coffee table.

'What's that?'

'I'm not sure I want you to see this.'

'Why, what is it? I knew there was something wrong when you walked in.'

'It was in my mail when I got back to the house earlier. Be prepared, it's scary.'

'Let me look at it. Who's it from do you think?'

'I don't know. A crazy racist, that's for sure. It calls me a black c..t, tells me to fuck off back to India and says I'm going to have my black testicles sliced off slowly with a blunt serrated knife.'

Laura is dismayed and puts her hand to her mouth.

'Oh my God, let me see.'

Ali carefully holds the letter up by its edges for her to read.

'Oh my God. I've never seen anything like it. You really must report this to the police, they're so hot on this kind of thing nowadays. You can't go round looking over your shoulder for the rest of your life. You need to do something about it not only for yourself, but everyone else too. These people disgust me – they should be locked up and the key thrown away.'

'OK. Whatever you say.'

'Get on to the police right now Ali – and if you must go straight back to Portsmouth, then so be it. This is so not right. You have to confront racism and violence – I know what it's like believe me. Remember, I'm Irish.'

'Why is this happening to us? We didn't do anything wrong – did we?'

*

Inspector Kate Hussein from Portsmouth police makes it very clear that they are treating Ali's letter very seriously indeed. Ali's giving a full statement after previously handing over the evidence.

He's questioned closely about the work he does for the family letting business and about his DJ work as they try to identify possible motives. The only worrying factor is that similar letters have not been reported elsewhere in the city. The exhibit will be examined for fingerprints and traces of DNA.

'We're going to need a full list of all your tenants in Portsmouth. Can you arrange that?'

'Ah, that might be a problem,' says Ali. 'My father who owns the business – and I – er, we've just fallen out, so it could be a bit tricky.'

'I see. Well, I'm afraid that we're going to have to insist. We'll need your father's contact details please.'

Ali swallows hard and provides them with his father's phone number and business address.

The Inspector thanks Ali for his time and says there may be a wait before the lab results come back – and confirms that they'll be in touch with any developments.

Ali quietly hopes that their enquiries will lead to a dead end and that the incident will be placed on file and that will be that. Any digging around into his father's affairs could uncover a whole can of worms at the very time he's trying to extricate himself from anything related to his father and his "work".

But on the other hand, who the fuck is it out there gunning for him?

52

It's almost Christmas and Alice and Dave are having dinner with Ali and Laura at Meon Lodge. Ali is in charge of the kitchen tonight and Laura is sous chef. They often cook together and work well as a team. They both love their food and their culinary interests and cultures continue to merge.

'This is gorgeous,' says Alice. 'What's it called?'

'Aromatic Lebanese Chicken,' says Ali.

'I love it – what's that unusual taste?'

'Probably nutmeg or perhaps sumac,' says Laura.

'The aubergine is really good – normally it's too mushy for me. But this is just the right texture.

'You can tell it's good because Dave isn't saying anything, are you Dave? He's got his nose in the trough, haven't you David!'

Dave attempts to smile whilst continuing to eat enthusiastically.

'Thanks Alice,' he says sarcastically. 'It's delicious and deserves my full attention! I must have the recipe Ali, and we can serve this at the wine bar. It's fabulous.'

'So you two, what's new? Ready for Christmas?' asks Alice.

'I think so,' says Laura. 'I think we'll just have a quiet time, given how frantic we've been. What an understatement that is. Anyway, I've got plenty on my plate – and Ali's been doing a lot DJ work, haven't you babe? And I must say, writing some really good songs. We're trying to put all the negative stuff behind us.'

'Yes, how is the music going?' Alice adds.

'All good thanks. For the past couple of months, I've been doing quite a bit of writing and recording and I'll be in the studio over the next few weeks. It's got me through everything, to be honest.'

Dave joins the conversation. 'What a talent – a great chef and a great songwriter!"

'Ha. Thanks very much. I'll email you the recipe.'

'I hope you don't think I'm prying, but all that business with your family must have been traumatic?'

'It certainly was, and there were times when I thought I'd had it. Correction. That *we'd* had it. But someone was clearly smiling down, because amazingly enough, we're still together.'

'Don't you worry my love. You two are rock solid. You'll be OK,' says Alice.

'I even managed to squeeze a song out of it. Isn't that terrible?'

'True inspiration, eh?' adds Dave.

'I guess so. I've called it *Fatal Equation* and it's about a passionate but doomed love affair. In other words, it's about me and Laura, if things had gone the other way and if we'd been forced to break up. I tell you, for a while I really thought that would happen. Anyway it's the full Disney – an epic. The song was written from my heart, 1000%.'

'It's a Shakespearean tragedy,' quips Laura. 'It's very dramatic – you'll see what I mean, if and when our little genius here, lets you hear it.'

'So, what about your family, Ali? You're now estranged, yes?'

'Sadly, we are and it was bloody awful, but I didn't have a choice, Dave.

'How could I even contemplate losing this gorgeous being?'

'You were under huge stress, babe – and yes, there were a few mistakes along the way, which might have lessened the crisis, but let's focus on the positive. We, no *you*, got through it and here we are, intact and stronger than ever,' says Laura.

'Here, here,' Alice and Dave concur.

'I look forward to hearing it. Music is so important to you isn't it?' says Alice.

'It is. I live and breathe it, 24/7, and I can't get enough of it. Luckily, I'm with someone who totally gets that.'

'Where does your music come from, who are your big influences?' asks Alice.

'Everyone I've ever listened to and liked, I guess. I absorb everything. But I really admire the pioneering spirit of The Beatles – well before me, of course,' says Ali, 'but I totally get them, because they didn't stick to anything. They constantly pushed the boundaries of style and I love that idea. I wouldn't dream of comparing myself to them in any way, but I love their sense of adventure and exploration.'

'You're about to make a video, aren't you?' says Laura.

'Yeh, soon. I've got a really good producer who's agreed to work with me.'

'Which song is it?' Alice asks.

'*Lavender.*'

'I don't know that one do I, is it new?'

'Quite new. It's a bit of an experiment.'

'How's that then?' asks Dave.

'I don't want to bore you …'

'Not at all,' says Alice, 'you could never bore me Ali!'

'I tried to write it spontaneously – almost like the first ideas that came into my head. Normally I spend a long time polishing it all up as I write but I wanted to create something – if you like – inspirational and instantaneous.'

'It turned out well then?' says Dave.

'It did, hence the video and single. We're going to have a go anyway.'

Ali continues, 'But I am realistic about it. The odds are still stacked against me. I think the song is as good as quite a lot out there. It just needs to be heard by the general public – that's the hard part. It's not for serious die-hard music fans. It's a simple happy feelgood track to sing along to.'

'Can't wait to hear and see it,' says Alice.

'Yes, cheers,' says Dave, raising his glass.

Two hours later they're all still at the table.

'Come on, let's go into the other room, my bum is starting to hurt,' says Laura.

'You've done this so well,' says Alice, looking around their sitting room. I love the colours, especially the deep reds and gold that you've got here and there. Very classy. And I love those long velvet curtains. Fab. It all looks so different in this light.'

'Thank you,' says Laura.

'You're quite the socialite now, aren't you?'

'I wouldn't put it exactly that way but I do have some nice friends now, yes. You have to make the effort, don't you? We also get on very well with next door which is both wonderful and a relief. They're not on top of us exactly, but it's comforting to know that there are friendly faces nearby, should you need them. They love Ali."

'What about the pool? I've brought my cozzie.'

'You're welcome any time. But perhaps not straight after Lebanese Chicken!

'I swim most days and I love it. It keeps me fit,' says Laura.

'Well you look good on it, my love.'

'This room is a very happy room,' declares Alice, looking round. 'I could feel it the first time I walked in. The vibrations are good.'

'Oh really?' says Dave. 'I can't hear anything.'

'Stop it you, I have a side that you know very little about, Mr Draper. And I'm not joking. All rooms have vibrations. Surely, you've experienced that yourself? What about when you bought your house or the Wine Bar, for that matter? At decision time when you settled on it, I bet it was the 'feeling' you had, that swung it.'

'I'm sad to say it was money that was a pretty big consideration when making the decisions. But now you come to mention it, you could be right. You must tell me more about your other side.' he says mockingly.

'OK, you asked for it. I love talking about this and you'll have to forgive me if you've heard me say all this before. Do you believe in a bigger picture, Dave? No jokes please.'

Dave looks puzzled.

'What do you mean?'

'Do you believe in a greater being?'

'God, you mean? No, I'm not religious.'

'I don't mean that.'

'Oh my word Alice, what are you doing.' says Laura. 'You do realise you've started a conversation about religion in my house, don't you? Religion and politics are banned at social gatherings here. It always ends in tears.'

'Yes, but you know what I'm talking about Laura. Come on, own up. You're very spiritual.'

She turns back to face Dave again and enthuses.

'Listen, I don't accept that the wonders of our world and beyond, are random. You just have to stop and think about the sheer enormity of our universe, and you'll very quickly come see how complex and incredibly clever and intricate it is. Words don't do it justice. I just believe that something intelligent is behind it all. I know you've heard me banging on about this before, but it's so interesting, don't you think? Surely, the world, the universe and creation has crossed your mind at some stage? Or do you just take it all for granted?'

'No, I don't at all and I don't mind talking about it again. It's not actually a subject I've touched on for a very long time. Probably, since my student days. But I will give you one thing. Whilst I trust the logic of science – and it usually guides my beliefs, it's still learning, itself, isn't it? Not everything can be explained away by science. So, in answer to your question, I have an open mind, I suppose is the answer.'

'That's a good answer!' says Alice.

She goes on to talk about her own interest and how it's led her to many unusual places in her quest for knowledge. She says that she believes in some form of afterlife and that she regularly visits a medium who has given her convincing evidence – at least, to her – that life exists after death. She says she's had messages from her father and her grandmother.

She even went on a course at the Arthur Findlay College of Mediumship at Stansted where the celebrated medium, the late

Glyn Edwards, was at the helm – to explore the possibility that she might have some mediumistic abilities herself.

'Have you?' asks Dave. 'Can you see dead people?'

'Sadly no, nothing yet. But I'd love to, wouldn't you?'

'No, I wouldn't!'

'I meditate as often as time permits and I try to let my inner self unfold. I truly believe that the world would be a better place if everyone stopped to meditate every day. We should all sit quietly and try to shut down – even for a few minutes. It's fabulous when you get the hang of it. But it is something you need to work at. It's like anything, practice makes perfect.

'You find that the people who poo-poo it, have usually spent just five minutes trying it, failing of course because they're impatient and then declare it a load of old rubbish. They're fools.'

'This is going to sound very cheesy,' says Ali, 'but I believe in a greater being, for sure.'

'Oh no!' shouts Laura, interrupting and sensing what's coming.

Ali stares at Laura. 'Look who he, she, they – created for me!'

Laura screeches, 'Argh, Ali that is so ghastly. Horrible. I've completely gone off you!'

53

It's a typical, cold January day, one that is almost over as soon as it's begun. Grey skies every day and still a bit too early to be looking forward to Spring. Even stepping out of the house on such days makes Laura think again.

She's catching up with her occasional employer and advisor, Finn O'Donnell, at Wickham Wine bar. She's very fond of this man who has helped her to get on her feet since she settled in Hampshire – it's not been a huge amount of work, but so far she's enjoyed everything Finn has asked her to help with. During the winter months, it tends to be residential team building exercises and Laura's enjoyed the challenges and meeting a wide range of people. Finn has also given advice on her long-term financial plans.

He is very taken with her, recognising and admiring her considerable intelligence, strength and independence. It's not surprising that he likes to include Laura in his team – her charisma shines brightly, and her presence adds much gravitas to his events. And she's bloody good at the job.

'How's the big philanthropic project coming along?' he asks.

'Good question, I've spent many days researching it, and to be honest, the more information I collect, the more confused I become. Being a benefactor is not as straightforward as you might expect.'

'I completely understand. I think I suggested that you might find this when we originally talked about your ideas.'

'You were right Finn. It was my intention to help abused people by setting up a charity but I'm beginning to think that it's a bureaucratic nightmare and probably not the best way forward after all.

'Whichever idea I come up with, it always means involving and trusting a lot of people I don't know and whilst I think I have a reasonably generous opinion of humanity, one has to accept that there are a lot of people out there who are, to put it bluntly, cretins on the take and not suitable at all. Avoiding *them* is my concern,' she says. 'But I suppose you must place trust in people at some stage – or nothing would get done, would it?'

'You're expressing exactly the same concerns that most business leaders have, Laura. This is why leadership isn't all it's cracked up to be. Time and time again I've spoken with business folk over the years and one after the other, they all come back saying almost exactly the same thing. Running a business is the easy part. Handling the staff and all their problems is the hard part.'

'So what would you do, if you were in my position? If you don't mind me asking.'

'Not at all. I'd have the same concerns, I suspect. So, why don't you think big – but small?

'I haven't put that very well. What I mean is, why don't you think big with the concept but think smaller about its delivery? Go local even. That way, you could keep an eye on things and oversee what you're doing, at a level that suits you.'

'What a good idea! Keep it local and more under control,' Laura repeats.

'I know you said you were keen on helping abused people, but perhaps you could broaden the idea a little. What other things fire you up Laura, really get you going?'

'Well, I couldn't have children and the reason I mention that, and this might be an idea, is because I underwent fertility treatment that didn't work. It was a while ago, but here's the point; I remember talking to one of the consultants, who said that throwing money at fertility treatment machines is not the most effective and best use of resources BUT funding the *training* of staff, to learn how to use that equipment, would be a much more effective idea. Even then can you believe it, they had the technology, but they didn't have the trained staff to use it.'

'That sounds like a cracking idea to me. I'd look into that.'

Laura ponders. 'But it would mean jumping through all the hoops and all that damned bureaucracy that already strangles the NHS. I'm really hoping to avoid that if I can.'

'OK then, step even further back,' says Finn. ' You clearly like children?'

'Like them? I love them. That's why we were trying all those years ago. It was the very reason my first marriage failed.'

'Well you might be on to something there then. How about helping less fortunate children? Not through the usual channels, but in your own way.'

'What are you thinking?'

'Scholarships. Fund children's education – those who can't afford it. Help them to reach their potential levels. It doesn't have to stop at academic achievements either.'

'Go on.'

'It could be as simple as funding the training of a talented young horse-rider who shows signs of Olympic potential – that should resonate with you. Funding educational school trips for children whose parents can't afford them. Funding students through university. There must be a million ways your money could help youngsters who would otherwise never blossom, simply because their parents aren't well off.'

‘What a brilliant idea. Scholarships. Superb.’

‘It would certainly deliver for you in many ways, wouldn’t it? ‘

‘The more you talk, the more I like it. And it’s manageable too, isn’t it? Thank you, Finn.’

‘If you do that Laura, you’ll have every school in the county wanting to be your best friend!’

‘It’s a great idea, Finn. You’ve given me a lot to think about.’

‘Pleasure. Now, please tell me, how is Ali getting along?’

*

Thirty miles away in the middle of the New Forest, Ali and Jim are standing, frozen to the core, trusting that producer Mark Jackson knows what he’s doing. They’re being watched from a distance by a group of ponies that has wandered in to see what the fuss is all about. Ali wonders how on earth they can live outside in these conditions for the entire winter. Thankfully, there’s little wind today which is one tiny compensation.

Mark has made videos for a host of names in the pop world and is tasked with making one for Ali’s song, *Lavender*, all thanks to Laura. Jim sings the track and the pair plan to release it under Ali’s Coolstar brand.

For a guy who regularly mixes with superstars, Ali and Jim find him very friendly and approachable. Working with him only emphasises the barrier that divides professionals and wannabes. Only when significant cash and connections come into play do such barriers disappear.

‘Don’t worry boys, this is the hardest part. The rest will be more comfortable, I promise!’

Wrapped in a giant puffer jacket and multi-coloured scarf, he turns to his small team to discuss the next shots. Mark has already explained his ideas, but they still seem a bit – er, surreal to Ali.

The video references the lavender flower, but quite how that fits in with the middle of the New Forest on a freezing cold day, with not a flower in sight, let alone a lavender bloom, leaves Ali perplexed.

'It's OK, I do trust you,' says Ali, 'I think.'

As the main vocalist on the track, Jim is being asked to mime to the song over and over again, line by line, sometimes phrase by phrase. Close-ups, distance shots, walking shots, you name it, Jim is doing his stuff over and over. All against background scenery that wouldn't look out of place in an old black and white war film shot in Northern France. Très noir.

The shooting schedule is four days but, thankfully, the next three will be split between the warmth of a studio somewhere in East London and Jim's recording studio, inside the church. Ali and Jim are soaking it all up and making the most of the experience. During breaks, they quiz Mark about his work in the music business and listen to his anecdotes from working with name acts. Mark is professional to a T and very wisely avoids any gossip or casting any aspersions on anyone he's worked with.

The guys are loving getting a real taste of the big time, as most un-signed artists can only dream of making a music video at this level.

Thank you, Laura.

54

Ali and sister Rani have stayed in touch, despite their father's insistence that Rani should make no contact with her brother. It's been quite a while since Javed Kurmi banished his son into the wilderness, but Ali and Rani have determinedly maintained phone contact throughout.

Today, Rani is visiting her brother at Meon Lodge, in secret, for the first time and Ali's showing her round. Laura is out but expected back later.

'Ali, this place is amazing. I had no idea.'

'It's brilliant, isn't it?'

'It's huge.'

'Six bedrooms. And the pool.'

'A pool?'

'Yep. That was no. 1 on Laura's shopping list.'

'Where is it'?

'At the side. I'll show you in a minute. Would you like the grand tour?'

'Of course.'

As they walk around, they catch up on Rani's news about Ali's nephew and niece, school, Rani's husband, Shahed – and their Mum.

'How is she?' asks Ali.

'She's fine. I know she'll eventually come round, give her time. She's in a difficult position with Dad.'

'She needs to stand up to him. He treats her like shit.'

'We both know that's not going to happen, don't we?'

'I suppose so.'

'And Dad?'

'What do you think? Business, business and more business. Oh, and yes there is a bit of news, he's thinking of working from home three days a week – for a trial period.'

'My God, what does Mum think about that? Ha, that is so funny.'

'Not a lot.'

'It won't work of course. What about Bas?'

'She'll get in touch soon, you'll see, she's your sister.'

'I won't hold my breath.'

'She will. Just hang in there.'

Rani looks round and spots Ali's guitar on its stand.

'How's the music and the DJing going?'

'Great thanks. We've made a video for one of the songs – it's being edited now.

'DJing? These days I'm just doing the corporate gigs – which is all very nice. I still love doing it so for the moment I'll keep doing it. Why not?'

'I hope you don't mind me asking – all this,' she says looking around, 'all this was paid for by Laura?'

'Yep. She's funding my music too. And she's working on her own project, which is absolutely amazing.'

'It's a lot to take in isn't it? I don't quite know what to say.

'This …' she says, looking round the room, 'is totally amazing. I'm so happy for you Ali. Give me a hug.

'So Laura's rich?'

'She is – and there's a lot more to come.'

Ali explains Frank O'Brien's international status in the horse breeding world and the forthcoming sale of the stud by the trustees.

'We're talking buckets of money. Not just a couple of million.'

'I had no idea, Ali. You'll need bodyguards.'

'Don't. Right now, we're looking at a security system for here, so you're not far off the mark. When the stud sale happens, God knows what form of low life might get to hear about it, so you're right, we need to be protected.'

'Talking of which … have you heard any more from the police about that letter?'

'Oh God, that. No, not for ages. I knew it would come to nothing.'

'Scary though, getting something as vile as that.'

'Yeh, and it's weird that Dad had a similar one, on the same day. That's freaky.'

'You haven't had any further letters then – or phone calls?'

'No, nothing. Thank God.'

They move back downstairs.

'Laura plans to use the money for good purposes. She's had loads of ideas, but I think she's settled on helping children with scholarships. She'll tell you all about it when she gets back I'm sure. She's incredibly motivated and driven.'

'She sounds like a good woman Ali. You're a very lucky man. And she's alright being the banker?'

'Absolutely, we thrashed that out a long time ago. We decided then, that money isn't going to define us. That sounds a bit posh, doesn't it? Anyway, we're going to enjoy it responsibly – and do some good into the bargain.'

They're back downstairs.

'Now, let me show you the pool. Through here.'

Ali leads Rani into the TV room which is dominated by a huge wall-mounted TV screen, assorted comfortable-looking chairs and a very new-looking cream carpet.

'You'll have to take your shoes off I'm afraid. House rules!'

An hour later, Laura returns and glides into the kitchen, looking the picture of elegance in a camel cashmere Armani coat.

'Laura, hello. You look amazing.' Rani stands up and they exchange kisses on both cheeks.

'I love your house. I've just had the tour.'

'Oh good, how nice of you to say that, Rani. Are you well? You look wonderful.'

'I try, but I have two extremely needful children. Life can be demanding at times.'

'It sure can. Your brother would probably agree with that too! I'm so proud of him.'

'Me too. I hope he's OK?'

'He's fine Rani. And before you ask the question ... I love that brother of yours with all my heart. He truly is the love of my life. Nothing and no-one will come between us, I promise you!'

55

'That bitch. That money belongs to us.'

Stephanie's bitterness and anger has intensified over the past few months and it's something that has alarmed her brother. Richard has little idea of what his sister is presently up to.

'What's the matter now?' he asks, on his latest visit.

'Never you mind. I know exactly what I'm doing.'

Through her contact on the dark web, Stephanie hired the services of a hacker to spy on their stepmother, and she's been getting regular reports. This, coupled with a watchful eye on social media and other illegal methods, has yielded valuable information. It's helped her to make a final decision that she certainly won't be sharing with her brother.

'Well, the auction is coming up in May, we haven't got much time left,' he says.

This immediately irritates his sister.

'What do you mean *we*? It's *me*. There is no *we*. What are you doing about anything, my useless fat fart of a brother?'

'You won't let me help.'

'Just as well, you'd only fuck things up.'

'What are you up to Steph?'

'How dare you even ask. You do nothing to help – but you'll be a very happy man if I get you more money, won't you? Yes, you will. More funds for your miserable scrawny life. Sod off, why don't you? Go play birdies, bunkers and balls.'

Richard glares back at his sister. 'Sometimes you're *such* a nasty piece of work ... just don't do anything we'll regret.'

Stephanie and Richard have felt cheated from the outset. Despite having already received a great deal of money as beneficiaries of their father's estate, they're angry that the sale of the stud business by the trustees – as laid down by their father, will mean disproportionally more money for Laura.

They soon discovered that there was nothing they could do to legally oppose their father's wishes and since then, Stephanie has been making her own plans.

What Richard doesn't know, is that his sister is planning something far more extreme than getting a bigger share of the sale. She's lost patience with her brother and intends to expand her own business interests which would elevate her from a moderately successful local business owner – to a national franchise seller. To make this big jump, she needs a great deal of money and Laura O'Brien, who only stepped into their lives seven years ago, is taking a massive slice. She believes that this is her money by right and she now thinks she's got a watertight plan to get it all back.

With the help of her "contacts" she now has a remarkably clear picture of Laura's new life in England. She knows where she lives, knows all about her toy boy lover, his father's business, the family split and all about that hocus pocus witch, Alice Kingston.

Working on the campaign without her brother already seems to be paying dividends and she's only just begun.

The letters that Ali and his father received and the ensuing police investigation caused a huge amount of confusion and much pointing of fingers. Oh yes, she liked that a lot and it was a mere taster of things to come.

However, not everything is in her control. What isn't going down at all well with Stephanie right now, and is beginning to panic her, is Laura's ongoing fixation with giving all their bloody money away to spotty children and other low life in fecking England. What does she think she is doing? How dare she?

The sale of her Daddy's stud farm is now not far off and she's running out of time. Armed with the knowledge that Laura still has to get any personal legal matters in place, she's ready to put the final part of her plan into action.

She snatches at her phone, confident that she's made the right decision. Now there's no going back.

56

Ali and Jim are buzzing at the studio today. Things are going well with the current slow track, *I'm Waiting For Midnight.*

'Loving the string parts, mate,' says Jim.

'Yeh, they sound OK, don't they? I knew they would, once we got them on to the track in here.'

Ali's on a creative roll and has accumulated several songs ready for the studio production process. He continues to prepare them on software at home and then brings them to the studio where he and Jim turn them into finished master recordings. *I'm Waiting For Midnight* is the latest.

They play the track again, in full.

'Ian's a pro, isn't he? What a singer.'

'He's done a lovely job. Note perfect and from the heart,' says Ali, banging his chest. 'Not easy to achieve in the studio. You gotta have e-mo-shun, bro!'

'It sounds like it could come from a West End show.'

'Or a Marks & Sparks Christmas Ad. Now that would be good.'

Writing songs and producing them with Jim and other great musicians and making top class professional recordings, is Ali's idea of bliss.

Since the split with his family and a new loving harmony that he now enjoys at home with Laura, he's on fire with creative ideas that will keep him busy for months to come.

Laura is making plans for later in the year. The solicitor handling the trustees' legal side of the Frank O'Brien stud farm sale, says he's confident of a very successful outcome and that she – and Frank's children – can expect a very substantial pay out, after a hefty tax bill, of course. No figures are being quoted yet, though.

She has plenty of ideas to put the money to good use and as well as developing her own plans, she's encouraging Ali to really go for his musical dreams, whatever the cost.

Today though, she's going to concentrate her attention on best pal, Alice. She's invited her round for coffee with the intention of offering her financial backing, to expand her beauty business. Whenever she's mentioned it in the past, Alice has always batted it away, clearly feeling uncomfortable.

'I've mentioned this before,' says Laura, 'but you very carefully change the subject whenever I do – you wily old witch. But this time I want your attention, Ms Kingston. Let's talk about your business. Have you ever thought about setting up your own salon in the village?'

'A witch, eh? And no, I haven't really. I'm quite happy as I am. I've got things just as I want them at home. I know it's a bit tight on space, but it works, and I manage to turn in a reasonable profit. Why change it?'

'You're underselling yourself, that's why – and I'd like to help you, if you'll let me?'

'I don't want your money Laura.'

'Come on, don't be ridiculous. You're so much more than a talented beautician, Alice. Your spiritual beliefs and motivational ideas, not to mention your counselling skills as a mentor to me – they're all part of you, and you need to be putting them to full use. Have you ever considered expanding your work into something more holistic?'

'What are you saying exactly?'

'Sorry, that sounds very airy-fairy. I don't mean to. But what about setting up a centre that offers what you do now but much, much more. For example, alternative medicine, reiki, reflexology, laser treatments, hair removal, eyebrow tattooing, permanent makeup, that sort of thing. You could even have evening groups and workshops for your mediumship. The list goes on. But you get my drift.'

'Blimey Laura, where do you get all this inspiration and energy?'

'What I'm offering, is funding.'

'You must be kidding. All that would cost a fortune.'

'Alice, I have a lot of money and soon I'm going to have even more. I WANT to help you. You've done more for me than anyone in the whole world. If I can't give *you* something, well I give up!

'I know properties don't come up very often in the Square, but I have heard rumours that the deli has been struggling for a long time. That's an amazing space.'

'I don't know what to say, Laura. Can I have a think?'

'Of course. That's the whole idea. But I truly believe it's a great idea and you would be so good at it. You're an inspiration too and you ought to be sharing that more with more people. And think about the space you'd reclaim back at home.'

'I'd have to get some more qualifications … oo er.'

Laura has only lived in the area since June last year, but she's made a concerted effort to contribute to the community. She's already gained a good reputation for being a "do-er" and as ever, once people meet her, they're usually enchanted.

The local community centre which draws on a very scattered population, has already benefited from a number of generous donations and Laura has also given her time too, which many see as more precious than cash.

It's barely Spring and Laura is thriving on her new life in England. She now has an accountant, a solicitor, a new home, her own swimming pool, money – lots of it – a part-time job she loves, nice friends and exciting plans for the future. All this with her beautiful and talented young man at her side – she's never felt better.

*

Ali has received an urgent call from Dom, his old pal and occasional employer at Ocean. Dom was reluctant to give any details on the phone but he said it was in Ali's best interests to attend a meeting at the club. Intrigued, Ali readily agreed, spotting a good excuse to drive his new car which is still a novelty.

He's taking the longer scenic route, over Portsdown Hill, down into Portsmouth, through the city and along the seafront – and he can't resist the temptation to drive down his old road.

This was his stomping ground for so many years, his home, workplace and playground. He turns into his old street and slowly drives past his former home which looks exactly the same as it always has. He has no idea what his father has done with the property but there are no visible signs of life or any obvious changes as he drives by.

He feels a pang of guilt as he crawls past Mrs Walker's house. He slows down further, to see if he can see her little white permed head in the window – and wonders how she is. He used to enjoy her visits, chats and cups of tea. He did manage to say goodbye to her before leaving but he still worries she might be lonely.

Then it's into Albert Road, which buzzes all year round, with businesses of every imaginable description. Some come and go but largely speaking they do well and the area thrives through diversity.

Ali is looking forward to catching up with Dom. The club manager's always had a soft spot for Ali and came to his rescue the night of the drink spiking episode, which could have turned out very badly for Ali. Dom and Becky were both there at his bedside when he needed support and whilst he's not gigging regularly at Ocean now, Ali still does the occasional night when Dom is desperate.

He parks up at the club and checks in on the access system. Dom appears and they make their way back to his office.

'So how are things Al?'

'Pretty good thanks.'

'Missing all the gigs here?'

'Yeh, yeh' smiles Ali. 'You still have the pleasure of my talents from time to time.'

'How's that lovely lady of yours?'

'She's fine, thanks.'

'And the music?'

'Really good. I've got a music video in production and I've got a publicist.'

'Wow, impressive. I wish you luck with all that Al. You're a clever guy – you deserve success.'

The pair walk through the empty club chatting about Dom's never-ending staffing problems and arrive at his tiny office on the first floor.

'Sit down mate. I have to confess that I've told you a bit of a white lie. I'm afraid there is no meeting.'

'OK …?' says Ali, slowly.

'I hope you won't think I'm interfering and I know that you and Becky broke up a long time ago …'

'Becky? No, I don't mind, why do you mention her? We didn't break up – we weren't an item in the first place.'

'OK, but you were close at one time, weren't you, as friends?'

'Yeh, we were. What's this about?'

'Well, I'm very worried about her, Al. I saw her the other day for the first time in a while and she's clearly having a really difficult time, and I was wondering if you'd consider popping round to see her.'

'Why me? What's the matter? Is she in trouble?'

'It's not my call, Al – not my place to say. But she very deliberately asked if I'd seen you. You need to see her for yourself. You'll see what I mean. She needs help and I think a visit from you would cheer her up a lot.'

'This is all very strange, if you don't mind me saying. You bring me down to Portsmouth for a non-existent meeting, and tell me that Becks, an old friend I haven't seen for months, suddenly needs my help. Why me?'

'I can't say Al. Trust me on this. Please would you go and see her? She's not working and she's still at the same flat.'

'This is very odd but OK, if you say so. I suppose I could pop round as I've come all this way. It would be good to see her actually.'

'Good man. You won't regret it, I promise.'

Ali makes his way back to his car, deeply puzzled. All very awkward too. He hasn't spoken to Becks since last summer when they went their own ways. He's now thinking that perhaps a phone call or two might have been a good idea just to check on her well-being. But he's had so much on his plate since then, he's hardly had time to think about it.

It's a peculiar feeling, heading towards her flat – once again stirring up emotions and memories of his recent life here in Pompey.

He gets to the door and knocks gently. It opens.

'My God. Ali, what are you doing here?' says Becky, looking genuinely shocked. 'No, don't tell me. Dom sent you.'

'Is that a baby I can hear?' Ali jests.

'Do you want to come in?'

'Sure, that's why I'm here.'

Ali is taken aback by Becky's dishevelled and ashen appearance. She looks washed out and the flat is incredibly untidy – mostly covered in baby accessories.

'What the fuck's going on Becks?'

'Rather a lot, as you can see. I have a baby!'

'Blimey, that was quick. How, what, why?'

'I got pregnant Ali.'

'Doh. I can see that. Was it intended?'

'No, it wasn't! Not at all. Would you like to see her?'

'A her? Yes of course.'

'Won't be a moment.'

Becky goes into the bedroom to collect her little bundle, returning with a big smile that transforms her face back into the one that Ali is more familiar with. She pulls the blanket from around the baby's face and shows her to Ali.

Ali looks intently and smiles broadly as he looks at the little being in front of him.

'This is Olivia.'

'Hello Olivia,' says Ali, gently touching her face with his little finger.

'Say hello to your daddy, Olivia.'

Ali is now sitting down, his heart pumping faster that an Olympic athlete's.

'What the fuck, Becks? Tell me what's going on here, please.'

'Here, hold her. There you are, like that. That's it. For God's sake, Ali!'

'Becks, I don't know what to say. I'm speechless. She's beautiful.'

He looks up. 'She's mine, I mean, ours?'

'I was going to tell you, really. I was trying to work out the best way. It's been so difficult.'

'Why didn't you tell me for God's sake? Have you been on your own the whole time? '

'Jane and Linda come round lots. So does Rita. They've been great.'

'Oh, Becky.'

'When we last met that night last summer, and you told me about Laura, I didn't know I was pregnant. Honestly. It was a couple of weeks later that I noticed things were a bit different, you know, inside. I did the pregnancy test after the penny dropped, and here we are nine months later.'

'And she's definitely mine?'

'Ali. I never screw around. It was only you. And look at her, there is a clue there you know, if you look at her. She certainly hasn't got a white daddy!'

'Fuck me, fuck, I still don't know what to say! What about your parents?'

'Ah well, there lies a bit of a problem.'

'When I told them I was pregnant they didn't say much, but they immediately came down here to help. I thought. But as soon as they got here, they promptly told me that I should get rid of it.'

'What?'

'Yeh, my dad said that having a baby would ruin my life. Ruin my career prospects and ruin any chance of settling down in a good relationship. My mum who usually has plenty to say, just sat there nodding. I suppose I get what they were saying but I wasn't going to get rid of my baby. I couldn't do that. Anyway, when I refused, they just left and apart from the occasional awkward phone call I haven't had anything to do with them since. I have to admit I did say some pretty awful things to them, but they still abandoned me. Can you believe it?'

'Oh no, that is awful.'

'Thank God I've got good friends who've supported me throughout. Bless 'em. My little sister has been down too – she helped me the first few days after I got out of hospital. And social services are involved too; they say they won't interfere, but you know what those types are like. Mind you, they have kept their word so far and just keep an eye on me. I'm sure I'm not the only young mother in Portsmouth without a partner!'

'Holy shit Becks. That's terrible. You should have called me, I'm her father.'

'I know, I know – and looking back, I wish I had. But after a while, it got harder and harder to do that.

You had a new life with a new woman; you left the area, and I genuinely didn't think you'd want the burden. I had this romantic notion that I could give birth and look after the baby myself.'

'I haven't even asked how old she is, she's tiny.'

'Three weeks today!'

'What? My God,' says Ali, chuckling in disbelief.

'Listen Ali, I haven't changed my mind. I'm still more than happy to look after Olivia on my own. I made the choice and I'm sticking with it.'

'If you think I'm going to walk out of that door and leave you two behind, you're crazy. I'm in. I mean it.'

Becky smiles, looking relieved, 'What about Laura, what do you think she's going to say?'

'Oh God, I know. But I can't keep any more secrets from her. I've already put her through hell and back with my family. She's been so understanding. Now I'm going to bring this news to her – on top of all that.'

'Perhaps you don't have to?'

'Oh I do Becks, and I'll just have to face the consequences. I'm done with lying. Whatever happens, I'm not going to leave you two in the lurch. And that's final.'

57

Ali drives back to Wickham via the most circuitous route he knows. He's had plenty of shocks in his lifetime but this latest one really has come out of the blue.

One thing he's learned from the recent crises, is not to keep any more secrets – they always end in tears. So, he will bite the bullet and take ownership of today's shock news, straightaway. Not that he didn't for a very short time consider hiding it. It was probably only a split second but his default seems to be to cover things up and avoid anything awkward or confrontational. Thankfully, he cancelled the thought and he'll come clean and tell Laura everything. God knows what she'll think about her boyfriend fathering a child with another woman.

Although his relationship with Laura is less than a year old, they've been rock solid from the start. They've both weathered traumas – together and apart, so Ali's hoping this latest revelation won't cause any structural damage to that closeness.

Once again, he shakes his head in disbelief. Out of nowhere, he has a child to look after. A human life that he will need to invest in, for the rest of his life. His own flesh and blood.

Why the hell didn't she tell me? he wonders. Until he realises that he is hypocritically accusing Becky of hiding things from him – the biggest culprit of all.

'I've seen this face before Ali Kurmi, and it usually means trouble. What have you been up to, you naughty boy? Should I make some tea?' asks Laura.

It's late afternoon and the couple are standing in their kitchen. Laura pulls up a stool and sits down.

'It's another big one, babe. And I didn't see it coming.'

'What now, in heaven's name?'

'I'm a father!'

'You're a what?'

'I'm a father to a three-week-old girl!'

'Please Ali, explain. You're not making any sense.'

'Becky was pregnant and I didn't know anything about it.'

'What? But that was a long time ago, last year.'

'I know but when we split up, she was apparently almost two months gone and she says she didn't know.'

'Why didn't she tell you when she found out?'

'That's the first thing I asked.'

Ali relates the conversation he had with Becky.

'I suppose I understand what she was thinking, to a certain extent. But to keep it a secret from you for all this time. I'm not so sure about that. I'm staggered.'

The pair sit silently for a few moments digesting the enormity of the situation.

'You certainly know how to liven up a dull afternoon young man, don't you? That's a lot to take in. My word.'

'Are you angry with me?'

Laura looks to her side, at nothing in particular, for just a moment, to think.

'Do you know Ali? … I'm not … actually. On the contrary, you may be surprised to learn that I'm absolutely delighted.'

'What?'

'On the Kurmi-Richter scale of seismic shocks, I'll give this a modest five. Yes babe, I think this is great news, not bad news.'

'How do you come to that conclusion?'

'You know very well that I've always wanted children, but can't. And I haven't shared this with you, but I've secretly been worried that one day you'll regret us not being able to have our own children. Please don't protest, hear me out … at some point in the future, I guarantee, it will occur to you. BUT, look what happens out of the blue? Today, our prayers have been answered! And you, my beautiful Ali – should be thrilled,' she says, becoming more excited.

'Wow. I wasn't expecting that. The surprises just keep on coming. The universe is very busy today. Anyway, let me double-check. You're OK with this?'

'Yes!'

'I still can't take it all in. God, can you imagine what my parents would say? It's almost hilarious.'

He kisses Laura on the forehead whilst gently squeezing both her arms. She looks at him and mouths a kiss.

'I won't be long. I need to freshen up and get my head around it.'

Ali takes his time in the shower and as the hot water flows all over him, he continues to think about today's news. Not that long ago, he'd be freaking out about it but today he's surprised at how calm he feels. A warm swirl of contentment flows through him and as he dries himself off, he starts to enjoy the thought that he's actually a father. He's also hugely relieved that Laura has not just taken the news well, but is actually fully embracing it. While dressing he looks upwards and says "thank you" out loud. He looks in the mirror and checks himself up and down.

Yessss.

Over dinner, the pair talk excitedly about the baby and Ali tells Laura everything he knows.

'As you've never actually met Becks, perhaps you'd like to come down with me and put that right?'

'Of course, I'd love to, but I'd check with Becky first. I might not be welcome. The baby's only three weeks old and I suspect she's still adjusting mentally to having a child – as well as all the physical business that women keep quiet about after having children.'

'Agreed, I don't want her to think we're barging in and taking over. Let's just go down and offer any support we can. Are you OK about the er – um, rather scary financial implications of all this?'

'Absolutely, we'll give Olivia the best possible start – and we'll support Becky, if she'll let us.'

'Christ Laura, I love you so much, you are the most beautiful person God invented. I love you.'

'To the black hole and back?' says Laura, laughing.

'Yes and further. I'll give her a call in the morning.'

'Don't forget, I've got you to myself on Thursday and Friday. From lunchtime. Remember.'

'Yes, I know, what are we doing? Going somewhere special?'

'Maybe. It's a surprise and I'm not telling. Anyway, we've got even more to celebrate now, haven't we? You are a clever boy, Ali Kurmi.'

Laura is in no doubt about the strength of their relationship, but she's wise enough to know that it still needs to be constantly worked on and nurtured. This latest news about Ali's baby has the potential to change the so-far straight trajectory of their fairy-tale journey, but she's fully confident that they're a good team, both moving in the same direction.

She's been trying to come up with a surprise treat for Ali and it's proved to be a difficult task – but she's finally settled on an idea she hopes he'll really enjoy.

He's passionate about food but has never sampled Michelin-standard cuisine. So, she's treating him to an overnight stay at celebrity chef, Carla Patterson's hotel in the New Forest, The Three Chimneys. Carla ticks the Michelin box and her hotel has a fine reputation for its accommodation and its food. It's fairly local, so Laura has booked them in.

The fact that the hotel boasts a luxury spa has, of course, nothing to do with it.

58

Ali leans in close to the bathroom mirror, pulls both eyelids down and grunts. He turns his head to the right and then the left. He's never gone for the George Michael look – the five o'clock shadow. Too much work to keep tidy; so, clean-shaven it's always been.

He's had a restless night, hardly surprising under the circumstances. To wake up one day and discover that you're the father of a three-week-old child that you knew nothing about, is understandably mind-blowing.

He shaves, brushes his teeth, smiles to check them and walks back into the bedroom.

'How are you my gorgeous daddy-o?' says Laura teasingly, from somewhere under a pillow.

'Are you still OK with all this?'

'Of course,' she says surfacing, doing her best to wake up.

Ali stares at her, amazed at how she always manages to look stunning first thing in the morning. Her tousled hair and sleepy eyes are so incredibly sexy, and his first urge is to get undressed again and get back into bed with her.

This morning though, he has something else on his mind, his daughter.

'Why don't you call her – go down and see her on your own? You won't be happy until you do. And I don't blame you. Go on, get down and see your daughter on your own. You and Becky have a lot to talk about.'

'OK, I think I will, if you don't mind. Thanks for being so good about this. You-are-incredible. As always.'

'Listen, this is all good for me too, you know. I love kids and I can't wait to meet Olivia. We're all going to have such fun. Well, maybe not just yet but we will soon. I have plans. Put the coffee on. I'll be down soon. I need one before my swim today.'

Laura steps into the kitchen in her dressing gown, after her twenty lengths. Her hair is combed back, and she looks sleek and toned.

'Did you get through?'

'No, it's turned off.'

'I don't blame her, but you'll get through eventually. When you get there, remember what I said. That we'll support them both from now on. Becky mustn't feel she's on her own with this. Try and find out what she immediately needs, and we'll get things sorted. I'm so excited about all this. And invite her over; if she'd like a break and a bit of pampering, I can help. A night or a week, it doesn't matter. I don't have a diary full of commitments, so it's all good.'

Ali finally gets through and he's out of the door like a rocket and driving back to Portsmouth.

On the way, he takes the opportunity to make a couple of calls. He wants to speak to the scheming Dom, to say thanks; but first he calls his sister, Rani. He needs to shout about his joyful news to someone. Sadly, it's not something he can share with the rest of his family. They don't even know about Laura, let alone Becky and a child.

'Guess what, Ran? I'm a dad.'

'You're a what? Don't be ridiculous, Ali.'

'I am. I've got a three-week-old daughter. She's called Olivia.'

'Let me get this straight, you and Laura have had a baby? She didn't look very pregnant last time I saw her.'

'No, not Laura. Becky!'

'What? You and Becky have a daughter?'

'Yes, isn't it wonderful?'

'Wow, Ali, where did that come from? And what the hell does Laura think about it?'

Ali spends the rest of the journey telling Rani the full story, and on a cheerful note, they arrange to speak again later in the week. His call to Dom will have to wait.

He arrives in Portsmouth, finds a space, parks the car and walks up the stairs to Becky's flat with a slight swagger.

'How are you both?' he says cheerfully, making room on the sofa.

'Tired. I'm always tired these days.'

'How does Olivia sleep?'

'Better than me! She sleeps really well, but I'm up several times to feed or settle her.'

'Well done you. I'm still trying to take all this in.'

'I'm sure you are Ali. Believe it or not, so am I. I'm so sorry.'

'Don't be ridiculous. Why are you apologising? Have you registered the birth yet?'

'No, I haven't, it's something I have to do it this week, so you could come too, if you want.'

'Of course I will. Now then. I've told Laura.'

'Oh dear, what did she say?'

'No, it's all OK. She's actually really happy.'

'Yeh? How's that then?'

Ali explains Laura's problems with fertility and outlines her IVF back story in Ireland.

'Gosh, what a life she's had. The poor woman. I've heard bits and pieces about her but it sounds like you've got yourself a whole lot of woman there.'

'I love her to bits.'

'Listen, I hope you don't mind me stating the obvious – she's a lot older than you, isn't she?'

'And?'

'Well, you know … '

'No, I don't. I just know that we're good Becks. We clicked at GO. She's amazing and I dunno, we just work well together. We love each other very much – in every way. It's really quite sickening.'

'You're very lucky.'

'I know I am,' says Ali, grinning.

'Anyway, I want to be a hands-on dad. And support you financially.'

'Wow, I truly thought I was going to do all this on my own.'

'No way, all you had to do was say. Don't worry, we'll get it all sorted. What's the situation with the flat, by the way?'

'I'm OK at the moment, but wait a mo, if you contribute to looking after us, that might mess up the council subsidy?'

'Don't worry about that. We'll look into it.'

'I can't risk being homeless.'

'Of course not. That won't happen, so please put it out of your mind. We'll be very careful, I promise. Now, is she still sleeping, can I see her?'

'Wait a mo.'

Becky comes back with Olivia.

'She's so beautiful. And so small. She looks like you,' says Ali.

'She's definitely got you in her too, as you can see,' she smiles.

'She better had.'

'How's all this going to work do you think? It's going to take quite a chunk of your time isn't it? Is that going to be OK with Laura?'

'I've told you, she's fine. We're both strong and we trust each other completely. Laura knows I'd never do anything to upset her. She gets it. As I said, she wants to be involved too, if you're OK with that?'

'Yeh, I suppose so.'

'Look, there's a lot to work out but let's not rush it. Let's do things methodically – one thing at a time.'

'Thank you. That's all I can think of to say. Thank you.'

'Can we take her for a little walk? It's quite nice out there. Down to the sea front?'

'Give me ten minutes.'

'Don't hurry,' says Ali, looking into his daughter's eyes with a love and passion he's never felt before – and very different to the love he feels with Laura.

He takes a deep breath, looks up and exhales slowly and contentedly.

Thank you.

59

'This place is quite something,' says Ali looking out of the suite's windows. 'It's even got a pantry and a hob.'

'I don't think we'll be needing that – we're dining in style tonight. I hope,' says Laura.

'Do people really do their own cooking on their wedding night? Crazy. This is seriously, wonderfully OTT.'

They're settling into the honeymoon suite at The Three Chimneys in the New Forest.

'Why not? We don't waste money. I think we've been very sensible with everything. I don't have any guilt anyway. I don't spend a fortune on clothes like some ladies. I'm certainly not a slave to haute couture – I think I'm more Monsoon and Zara, don't you know? Well, perhaps a little Armani!'

'I wasn't suggesting we waste money – I'm just trying to get used to the idea of spending it, I think. I prefer this to Claridge's. It's less intimidating.'

Laura howls with laughter.

'You sound like a seasoned executive traveller, Ali … Okay yah!'

'Don't get me wrong, I could get used to either place.'

'Well, almost the first thing I'm going to do is take advantage of the spa – I quite fancy a dip and a sauna.'

'Almost the first thing?'

'You know the rule, young man.'

Laura turns her back on Ali and theatrically undoes her jacket, places her forefinger under its collar, twirls it and tosses it on to the dark pink chaise longue. Then she slowly and titillatingly pulls her blouse up over her head and throws that on the chaise too, whilst shaking her hair back into shape.

'Oh my God,' says Ali, 'fasten your seatbelts, ladies and gents – and everyone else.'

He takes a running leap across the bed and tries to grab Laura with outstretched arms.

She quickly steps back, out of his range, as he crawls closer across the bed.

'Be a good boy Ali, please.

'Oh my word, Ali – you are a *very* good boy!'

'This is like having dinner in a large sitting room, isn't it? Quilted chairs, round tables and subtle soft furnishings. Very posh. Do you like it?' asks Laura, looking around admiringly.

'Yeh, it's cool.'

'So what do you fancy?' she says, perusing the menu.

'I'm going for the Dover Sole, I think. I once had that under the Tancarville Bridge in France! It was one of the best plates of food I've ever tasted. Just the fish and a simple butter sauce with a couple of tiny new potatoes. It doesn't sound very exciting but it was incredible. What are you going to have?'

'I like the look of the guinea fowl.'

They order their food and Laura nibbles at a breadstick.

'This is a very good time to take stock of things, don't you think?' she says.

'We've been together since last July. Everyone laughed, didn't they? A 52-year-old woman and her toyboy.'

'People are too quick to judge, in my view – they haven't got a clue what they're talking about. And frankly, it's none of their business. We make our own choices, don't we?'

'We certainly do Ali. Anyway, I'm a *very* happy bunny. Are you?'

'I am a very happy bunny. Now I have two women in my life. And there's no competition between them!'

'Exactly, it's something we hadn't planned on, but I don't see it as a problem, do you?'

'Not with you standing by me, no. Obviously it's going to take some of my time away from me – and of course there's the financial consideration too.'

'On that subject, let's talk money again. I want you to be absolutely clear in your mind that money will never ever be an obstacle or barrier between us. There is no sense of who pulls the weight and who doesn't. That is irrelevant. We are a couple who happen to have a fortune at our disposal. I think it's actually very healthy to talk openly about money. More people should do it. It's nothing to be ashamed of. After all, it governs every aspect of life on the planet, doesn't it?'

'It sure does.'

'Right then, we'll get to Becky and Olivia in a minute, but first, you. You must carry on with your music plans. You've got the *Lavender* video and song to release this summer and others to prepare, haven't you?'

'Yeh, the publicist wants me to build the *Coolstar* brand. And I'm going to push songs for TV syncing – and there's the idea of the musical.'

'That's brilliant. Your songs are good and I'm not just saying that. And looking at the longer term, how about you setting yourself up with a studio or whatever you need, in the barn/stable block?

It'd be ideal and you deserve more than a converted bedroom to make your music in.'

Ali's eyes glisten. 'Seriously?'

'Yes, why not? You can physically go out to work!'

She looks at Ali with her wide, perfect, white-tooth smile.

'Are you still happy DJing?'

'I am. As you know, the gigs aren't regular but they're good ones, when they come up.'

'Well, keep that up because it's good to do things you enjoy – and you really do enjoy it, don't you?'

'I do.'

'And so to Olivia and Becky.'

'You say she's renting from the council? We need to get her into her own place, soonest. Can you check that she'd be up for that? Meanwhile, I suggest that tomorrow we set up a regular payment to her and I think you should agree with her exactly how you're going to spend time with your daughter in a way that suits you both. As you're not living together, it's going to need some thought so it's important you get it right at the very beginning, so there can be no loss of expectation.'

Ali stares across the table in wonderment.

'You are so impressive babe. Just listening to you speak, your simple logic – and always being one step ahead – I'm so in awe.'

'This guinea fowl is gorgeous,' says Laura, smiling and changing the subject, 'and judging by your plate and the lack of fish on it, you liked the sole?'

'Fabulous. I think.'

'Good as France?'

'Do you know, we were talking so much, I almost forgot about the food. Isn't that dreadful?'

'Not at all, we've got a lot on our plates!' says Laura, grinning widely again.

'Very good! Yeh, the sole was très bon, merci cheri. Just as well, given how much it cost!'

'There you go again, Ali. Bloody money. You're so prosaic.'

'It's just as well we don't drink alcohol, isn't it? I could fill my van with petrol for the price of a bottle of wine here.'

Laura signals to their waitress for another bottle of mineral water.

'I can't imagine you being drunk, says Ali.

'Why would you want to do that?'

'You once said, drinking actually helped you.'

'Let me make this perfectly clear – I was in an extremely bad place each time I got into serious trouble with drink. Mentally, yes, it did help in the very short term, but it wasn't any kind of solution to the bigger, longer-term problems. If anyone who drinks, even moderately, stops for one moment to consider it, they'd realise that it's only the first few sips of alcohol that give you a buzz. Afterwards, you're just chasing that initial high – but you never get there! You just drink more and more and end up with a new, even worse problem, on top of the first one. Depression.

'It's very hard to describe but don't ever go there. It's a bad place. Believe me.'

The waitress arrives with the mineral water.

'Shall we talk about something more cheerful?'

'Our birthdays are coming up soon, aren't they? Our first together. We must do something,' says Ali.

‘Agreed, we could do something combined, couldn’t we, as they’re so close together? To be honest, there’s such a lot going on right now, I don’t really want the fuss of organising anything complicated, do you?’

‘Definitely – let’s just have a nice quiet meal. I’ll cook something really special.’

‘That would be lovely. Perfect. I’d be happy with a boiled egg.’

‘You will not! You know, I still can’t get my head around all this. So much has happened in such a short space of time. I’m going to be so busy.’

‘And that’s absolutely fine with me. I’m busy too. There’s one thing that I’m definitely looking forward to getting out of the way – the dreaded stud sale.

‘All my longer-term plans hinge on that going through. I’m happy not to be involved, to tell you the truth. Anything to do with Richard and Stephanie is to be avoided at all costs. Their silence is actually a bit ominous, come to think of it. I’m surprised they’ve haven’t been causing trouble. I’m scared to even think about them, in case I trigger something negative.’

‘Just how bad were/are they?’

‘You really want to know?’

‘I do.’

60

Seven-years-ago

'Silver Beeches' stands in some twelve acres of grounds outside Tipperary and has been home for Frank O'Brien since he hit the racing jackpot fifteen years ago. It was always a happy family home, until the day Catherine O'Brien, Frank's dear wife, lost her battle with cancer.

Her drawn-out demise was painful – and after her death, Frank struggled to look at a life without his beloved partner. His children were of little help, internalising their own grief and anxieties, doing little to help console their father.

That was to be expected really. Frank was a caring husband, but completely consumed by his passion for all things horses. He freely admits that he could have spent more time with his children when they were growing up – and indeed later. They'd flown the nest by the time he and Catherine moved to Silver Beeches. He seldom stopped to spend quality time with them. Catherine did all that and it seemed to work and no one complained.

Today, Frank is still at his happiest inside his racing cocoon and it's where he dwells for most of the time, mentally and physically. Some might call him selfish. Frank prefers the epithets, passionate, focused and driven.

He certainly enjoys his acclaim and willingly turns out at major functions and events whenever called upon and he has deep pockets for charitable work. His work, not surprisingly, involves a fair amount of continent-hopping with his mentor and friend, Joe Kelly, expanding his business empire, not to mention his bank accounts.

Frank O'Brien is a hugely successful man who embraces his fame and wealth and enjoys life to the full. He brims with likeable self-confidence and likes to think that he's master of his own destiny. However, last month an extraordinary thing happened.

He met another woman. He wasn't looking, it just happened.

Whilst his grieving for Catherine had eased, he hadn't been on the lookout for a new companion.

So when a bright young journalist arrived on his doorstep with a photographer one day, to write a story for the Dublin News, he thought little of it.

But strolling through the house with this very attractive bundle of positivity, Frank was enchanted. He was particularly taken with her beckoning eyes that indicated a different, mysterious and probably wonderful world behind them. He was immediately attracted to her.

He found himself in the most unusual position of having trouble in finding words.

In just a few short minutes Frank O'Brien had been smitten.

*

'Thank you all for coming, dinner will be served soon, and in anticipation of that, thank you Mary, as always.'

Frank is standing in front of the mantlepiece, glass in hand.

'Mary is more than housekeeper, she's the backbone of this house, thank you my dear.'

Mary politely nods and retreats to the back of the room.

Frank has organised a dinner with his children and their spouses, along with Joe Kelly and his wife and other friends – to introduce his new friend, Laura.

To be honest, Frank isn't quite sure how to describe Laura to his friends just yet. He knows it's too soon to start using the word 'girlfriend' – for fear of being rebuked by his children, particularly Stephanie. He's aware that they wouldn't look kindly on any attempt to replace their late mother, in any shape or form. He's playing things very carefully. He thinks.

Stephanie steps forward and looks absolutely beautiful. She's clearly gone to some trouble for the occasion, with her hair up and looking the picture of charm and elegance. Her husband Séan stands one pace behind her to the right, looking anxious.

'Stephanie, this is Laura.'

'Hello Stephanie, pleased to meet you,' says Laura, shyly.

'Pleased to meet you too, I'm sure,' says Frank's daughter, with an expressionless face. 'This is my husband, Séan.'

Frank turns again.

'This Laura, is my son Richard and his wife, Sarah.''Hello,' says Laura looking at each in turn. They smile weakly.

God, this is awful, she thinks. Laura is not getting anything back from these people. She's met enough folk in her career as a journalist and has had to win plenty of difficult ones round, but she senses that this evening is going to be a real struggle.

The group moves into the large dining room with its huge windows looking out on to the gardens.

'So, what exactly is it that you do?' asks Stephanie, who is now sitting diagonally opposite Laura at the dinner table.

'I'm a journalist,' replies, Laura.

'Someone has to be, I suppose.'

'Stop it, Steph,' says her husband from her side.

'Sorry, I'm sure. It's just that I liken journalists to the prawns on your plate – scavengers on the ocean floor hoovering up all the fish shit. No offence intended, of course.'

'None taken,' lies Laura, ambushed by the sheer rudeness.

'What do you do?' she quickly asks, looking for a *touché* moment. 'Your father says you run a bar.'

'I work in leisure,' she snaps, 'I've a chain of bars and clubs. It's boom time here just now.'

'I'm pleased to hear it. How long have you been in that line of work?' asks Laura, trying to rescue some form of conversation.

'Quite the investigative journalist, isn't she?' says Stephanie, turning to her husband again, who looks away, embarrassed.

'Why on earth would you want to know that, then?' she adds.

'Stephanie!' her father reprimands. 'I heard that. Stop it immediately, please. Laura is our guest.'

The room suddenly quietens.

'I'm sorry father, I'm sorry Laura,' she says, turning back to face Laura with the warmth of a crocodile.

'Please, good friends, continue your meal; it's a lovely evening and we're here to enjoy ourselves, good health to you all,' says Frank, raising his glass, whilst glaring at his daughter.

On Laura's right, sits Joe Kelly. As soon as he sees Stephanie muttering to her beleaguered husband, keeping his voice low, he whispers.

'I'm afraid you'll have to get used to that kind of thing. She's a cruel being, that one. She's never been completely right in my opinion, but when her mother went, it was like she underwent a character transplant. Overnight almost, she turned from being plain nasty into a complete monster.'

'Frank did say she'd probably be a bit difficult to begin with, but I have to admit, I wasn't expecting that.'

'Hard hats required,' Joe chuckles, feebly.

After the meal, which continues without any further interruptions, Frank takes Laura to one side.

'I'm so sorry, you really didn't deserve that. I knew she might be a little awkward, but that was downright rude and uncalled for. Unforgiveable. I should have sat nearer to you. But Joe looked after you, didn't he?'

'Yes, don't worry, he's always nice to me.'

'Was she rude again during the meal? I couldn't hear everything.'

'Not to me. We didn't speak again'.

'I'll have words, rest assured. I'm very sorry that happened. I hope it doesn't put you off, you know, us.'

'Don't worry Frank, I've been stung by a few scorpions in this career of mine. I've learned how to handle myself.'

'She took her mother's death very badly,' says Frank, attempting to offer some form of explanation, 'but this deep, dark, cold streak she has, none of us knows where that's come from. It's a mystery. But enough is enough, I'm going to have it out with her once and for all.'

'I'm sure she'll come round, given some more time. I understand what it's like to lose your mother, it's major stuff.'

'That's very generous of you, but you don't know what my daughter is capable of, and to be honest, neither do I.'

61

Damn it, says Laura to herself, closing her phone.

She's just received a call from Ireland to say that the long-scheduled stud sale is being put back a month. She's going to have to wait longer, to develop some of her plans – or more to the point, put Stephanie and Richard behind her.

She's standing in the guest room that she's picked out for Becky and Olivia. It's warm and bright with gentle green colours and looks out on to the main garden at the rear of the house.

Outside is looking good, and is getting some seasonal attention from two gardeners and Laura's crossing her fingers that she's chosen well with the company she's trialling, to maintain it.

There's a pond and a small, railed paddock to the right, near the barn-come-stable block, which is already allocated to Ali, for his music.

Looking round, she thinks their guests will like the room. It's got a relaxed feel about it and it'll give Becky a good chance to have a breather from urban flat life.

She's already been looking at properties in the Southsea area of Portsmouth. Becky is going to need somewhere to live soon and rather than waste money on paying rent, Laura will offer to buy a property for her to use, rent-free. They're family anyway, well almost, and investing in property is never a waste of money.

She's thinking even further ahead, too. As Ali will no doubt be spending more and more time down in Portsmouth, there's a good argument for having some sort of base there for him, too. This idea though, will remain a secret for the moment and will be a surprise for him later.

She's a little nervous about meeting Becky and isn't going to overwhelm her with her well-meant ideas and plans. She reminds herself that Becky is also the girl her man was sleeping with, before she came along – and can't suppress some faint feelings of jealousy.

Ali, Becky and baby Olivia arrive just after noon and they're piled high with bags and baby paraphernalia. Becky looks around as she stands by Ali's car.

'You live *here*?'

'I do, welcome to Meon Lodge, Rebecca,' smiles Ali. 'Let's go in. I'll bring all this stuff in, after you've said hello to Laura.'

The door opens wide as they climb the steps.

'Hi Becky – it's lovely to meet you.'

Ali looks on with pride as he sees Laura, hand outstretched to greet Becky who is holding Olivia, straddled on her hip. As always, she looks effortlessly immaculate.

'Nice to meet you, too,' says Becky, clearly impressed, and opening up her own big smile. She manages to find a free hand.

'So, this is Olivia,' says Laura, 'she's so cute. Come in both of you, make yourselves at home.

'She's gorgeous, Becky. Aren't you clever? So quiet too.'

'I don't know about that, you wait.'

'Come on through, let's go to the kitchen. Would you like something to drink before lunch?'

Phew, good start, thinks a relieved Ali, now laden with baby bags. So far, so good.

'I've put everything up in the room,' he says, re-joining the ladies who are deep in conversation.

'You didn't tell me Becky was a trained solicitor, Ali.'

'I'm not allowed to practise without doing more exams and two years of work experience, but yes, I got the degree.'

'Still, it's fantastic to have that under your belt. Do you think you'll ever use it?'

'I don't know what's going to happen with anything to be honest, now this young lady's come along. I've spent the past couple of years trying to make up my mind. Now it's been made up for me, it would appear.'

'I'm sure you'll come to a good decision when you're ready – it's an option at least. Right, let me show you around and take you to your room. We haven't got a proper cot I'm afraid, but you've brought a carry cot with you, haven't you?'

'Yes, we're fine thanks.'

After lunch, Laura suggests that Becky and Olivia relax and do as they please. She's thoughtfully arranged to go down to Wickham to create some space for her guests.

'Ali will look after you but I expect you could do with a little rest, couldn't you?'

'Ooh, that would be lovely,' says Becky, feeling a lot more comfortable.

'I'll take 'Liv for a walk,' Ali enthuses.

'OK, see you all later,' says Laura.

She is off to the estate agent in the village, to try and find out more about the deli, in the Square, which has finally closed its doors. There are no boards up outside it yet but she's been keeping an eye on it. She still believes that it would make a fabulous base for Alice, to expand her beauty business.

Ali waves Laura off, delighted at her effortless ability to juggle multiple projects simultaneously. She says she needs to be busy all the time and she certainly is. His brain would simply seize up if it was left to him. Multi-tasking is not his forté.

Before going for a walk, he WhatsApps Jim Sexton at the studio.

'Hello, is that the star of the international hit *Lavender* by any chance?' putting on an American accent.

'Hello Mr Kurmi!'

'Hey, guess what? I'm a father.'

'You're a what?'

Ali relates the complicated story of his unexpected gift of a daughter and after the initial shock subsides, Jim is delighted.

'Congratulations mate. Unfortunately, Stevie Wonder beat you to it, didn't he?'

'I beg your pardon?'

'If you're thinking of writing a song about your baby, he beat you to it. *Isn't She Lovely*, is *the* definitive baby song.'

'Gotcha. I'm a bit slow on the uptake today. Got a lot on my mind.'

'I bet you have,' says Jim. 'Give my love to Becks, by the way. I haven't seen her in ages.'

'I will, she's here as I speak. Somewhere here. I'm in on Tuesday, aren't I?

'Yes sir. We must wet the baby's head. I'll order the lemonade …'

'Indeed. See you then.'

Back in the house after a stroll, with Olivia now snoozing, he settles down to enjoy a few minutes of Sudoku on his phone, but almost immediately, his eyes start to close and he soon nods off.

The next thing he hears is Becky's voice.

‘She’s so nice, Ali. Laura, that is. Oh, I’m sorry, did I wake you?’

‘No it’s fine, I must have drifted off.’

‘So did Liv. Look at her, isn’t she just amazing?’

Becky moves closer and peers lovingly at their sleeping daughter.

‘Laura’s nothing like I expected. She’s very beautiful. I’m not being rude, but why hasn’t she been snapped up by some rich man somewhere?’

‘Thanks a lot, pal.’

‘You know I didn’t mean it like that. She’s incredible. And the two of you just met at a gig?’

‘Yep. And you ain’t seen nothing yet, Becks, she’s really up for all this. We both are. Will you let us?’

‘I’m still a bit confused. All this,’ she says looking round, ‘it’s hard to take in. One minute I’m in the flat – the next I’m here, in a luxury home. I love it, mind you – the vibe is so friendly and happy. In fact, can I move in?’

‘Look, if you feel a bit uncomfortable with all this money flying around, I get it; but try seeing it this way. All we’re doing is getting you settled – providing a platform, to give you some practical help and Olivia a decent start in life. It can be as temporary or as permanent as you like, it’s up to you.’

He straightens his back. ‘I still can’t believe your parents by the way … what they’ve done to you.’

‘No, neither can I. But I remember telling you ages ago, that I felt there was always something odd about their relationship. Do you remember? They never really behaved like a loving couple throughout my time at home.’

'Yes, I do. But it's bloody awful, Becks, no excuse. They should help you, unconditionally,' he says, immediately recognising the personal irony of that statement – and not for the first time.

'Well, they haven't, have they? Never mind, it's their loss. Me and their granddaughter. As you would say … fuck 'em! We both seem to be in the same boat, don't we? Effing useless parents.'

'You never know, they might come good one day. But we're concerned about the now, aren't we? We're going to help you, for as long as you like. And you never know, you might find yourself in the position of being able to complete your law exams. A nice new man could come along into your life.'

'I don't think so. I can't see that happening.'

'Yeh, well I didn't expect all this with Laura, I promise you. Anyway, you know what I mean. Don't feel restricted by us Becks, we won't get in your way at all. As long as I can see Olivia on a reasonably regular basis, that's all I ask. To play my part in raising my daughter. What do you say?'

They fist bang.

After dinner and an hour or so of TV, Laura announces that she's off to bed.

'I've got a busy team-building weekend ahead. Birmingham isn't far but I've got quite a bit do before I go tomorrow.'

'Let's hope this visit is longer than your last one!'

'Very funny, Ali Kurmi!'

Ali explains to Becky how he dragged Laura back from a fact-finding mission to Birmingham, just as she'd arrived there.

'It was a crisis though, wasn't it?'

'OK, I'll give you that, but don't repeat it.'

'What time are you meeting Finn?' asks Ali.

‘We’re meeting for dinner at the hotel and it’s an early start on Saturday. Don’t forget, you and I have a busy morning tomorrow,’ says Laura, looking at him hardly.

‘Are you going to be alright on your own over the weekend?’ Ali asks, looking concerned.

‘I won’t be on my own, Finn will be there.’

‘You know what I mean.’

‘I’ll be fine. I can look after myself.’

‘I know you can, it’s other people I worry about. There are a lot of folk out there with poor intentions and I don’t want you anywhere near them.’

‘What are you doing there, if you don’t mind me asking?’ says Becky.

‘I’ll be solving a murder! Not. I work part-time for an events company. We do corporate functions and team-building events. It’s a crime investigation weekend for a load of merchant bankers.

‘God, that sounds horrendous,’ says Ali. ‘Now you really have worried me.’

Don’t be silly. Rest assured, it’s not exactly my scene but I like supporting Finn, the organiser, and it sounds pretty harmless to me. Anyway, they’ll all be concentrating on whodunnit.’

62

Laura is being introduced to three former police officers at the hotel, just outside Birmingham. It's a typical chain hotel at the higher end, enormous and completely devoid of any warmth or individuality. It's an early start and she's glad they travelled up the previous evening. Finn is at the helm and delivering his post-breakfast welcome speech and running through the agenda with his team.

A large group of city bankers have gathered for a crime-solving weekend and they're expected to turn themselves into detectives and forensic scientists for almost two days. Finn's former police officers are there to assist and to add credibility.

Laura is general factotum again which suits her very well and after the briefing, she's off to welcome the three HR executives from the banking company, who commissioned Finn to organise the event.

Finn is hoping that these people will sit back and let his team get on with the job. But you never know until the day, very often, so he's keeping his fingers crossed that they won't interfere too much.

Laura brings them in from reception; two men and a woman.

One of the men introduces himself as Charles, who immediately offers his hand and smiles at Laura for just that split-second longer than appropriate. But long enough for Laura to clock it. He's certainly exuding the confidence of a senior executive and quickly irks her even more, after introducing his two colleagues dismissively. *Cruel, she thinks. What is it, with these pompous types, are they really that thick-skinned?*

After the introductions are over, Finn confirms the programme for the weekend and they disperse, in readiness to reconvene in the conference hall at ten o'clock.

Laura joins the delegates for the introductory presentation, but decides that solving pretend murders isn't for her and slinks back to the large reception area and refreshment bar to go over the arrangements she and Ali have put in place for Becky and Olivia.

'This the down part isn't it? The waiting around,' says Finn, who joins her for a coffee a few minutes later.

'Anyway, I can see you've got plenty to occupy yourself with,' he says, nodding at her tablet.

'Is that OK Finn? If there's anything you need me to do, just say.'

'No you're fine my dear, hopefully this should run like clockwork. I can't foresee any likely problems.'

He puts his coffee down and groans. 'Argh that's awful. Horse piss. You'd think they'd get it right wouldn't you? A simple cup of coffee.'

'Perhaps you need something a little stronger Finn?' says Laura, with a grin.

'Don't tempt me my dear, the sun'll be over the yardarm soon! Anyway, all good on the home front?'

Laura decides that it's probably too soon to reveal her and Ali's latest news about the baby.

'We're fine thanks. Settling in at last I think. It's a big house!'

'I'm envious – it's a grand place and I'm sure you'll both be happy there. How is Ali?'

'He has a music video and a song being released in June, so that's keeping him busy.'

'Sounds impressive. Do we get a preview?'

'I think they're holding it back until the last moment for greater effect,' says Laura.

Laura likes being around Finn and enjoys his old-school subtle wit. She has complete trust in his professionalism – and his friendship. He successfully manages to combine the two – a rare talent, she thinks. He really does know his stuff and can hold his own with any of his younger competitors.

'OK, if you need me, I'll be at HQ,' he says with a wink – and off he goes.

'See you later.'

The day passes slowly, but it gives her the opportunity to look deeper into the possibility of funding scholarships. The idea appeals to her more, the further she delves. It would require a fair amount of continuing input, but she knows herself well enough to accept that being busy is essential for her mental and physical well-being. So, it all feels pretty good.

Grateful for the freedom to have this time to research, she also understands that she's still on-duty all day – and that includes meal times.

She and Finn are joined for dinner by Charles and his two assistants Denise and Richard. Charles, it seems is in the mood for enjoying himself tonight, and by the time the third bottle of champagne is uncorked, the conversation around the table becomes a great deal less formal.

Laura is familiar with such scenarios, being a non-drinker, and is already anticipating the inevitable slurring of words and loud laughter that comes with people drinking heavily. They think they're being so funny and clever but in reality, they are so not.

Charles and Richard have dropped the formalities of company rank and appear to be swapping extremely lewd jokes, as Laura and Denise try to converse. The pair talk about their respective jobs and touch on home life. Then the heckling starts, as Charles and Richard start interrupting them with unfunny wise-cracks.

Finn is in a tricky position. He's wise enough to watch his own intake of alcohol and can only internally grimace at what he sees and hears, unfolding in front of him. He can't upset the people paying him for his services, but he also has a duty of service to protect his own staff. He hopes that things won't deteriorate any further.

Laura, Finn and Denise are horrified to hear the way Charles and Richard are now talking to the waiting staff, who have been charming and tolerant all evening. They're no doubt used to being treated poorly by thoughtless patrons, but tonight is intensely embarrassing and there's no excuse.

Finn even pulls the young waiter to one side, slips him a twenty pound note and quietly apologises for his two guests, who are still howling at each other's jokes.

Eventually, Charles stands up, wobbling – and thanks Finn and Laura for the meal and their company and disappears to the bar with Richard in tow.

Thank God, thinks Finn.

'Thank God!' *says* Finn!

'Here's to that, Amen,' says Laura.

'I'm *so* sorry,' says Denise.

'Don't worry my dear,' says Finn, 'we're used to it, but are you OK?'

'I'm fine thanks, I'm used to it, too. Unfortunately.'

Laura's room is unspectacular but comfortable – like the other 300 here, no doubt. She sits on the bed. Apart from that very unpleasant dinner experience, it would seem that the day has gone very well, not that she's had much to do. Hopefully, by 4 o'clock tomorrow afternoon, she and Finn will be on their way back to Hampshire.

She undresses, reads for a short while, yawns whilst turning off the light and drifts off.

She has no idea what the time is, but in her half-consciousness, she can hear a tapping at her door. Is she hearing things, she wonders? The tapping continues. She switches her bedside light on and gets out of bed and puts on her dressing gown. The tapping doesn't stop.

'Who is it?' she whispers.

'It's me.'

'Who's me?'

'You know very well.'

'I do not. Go away.'

Christ, thinks *Laura, it's that slimy Charles character. What the hell am I going to do?* She heads back to pick up her phone.

The knock on the door is now much louder and Laura dashes back.

'Who is it please? Could you go away or I shall call reception.'

'Come on, I know your type. Fucky-wucky. Open up, I know you want some fucky,' comes the slurred, lecherous voice.

Laura slides the safety chain in to place and opens the door slightly. To her horror, there stands the younger of the two drunks, Richard – and he's standing there, flies undone, exposing himself. The vision is appalling. She slams the door shut again, grabs her phone and calls Finn who's in a room two doors down. In under a minute, she can hear his voice outside the door talking firmly to the very drunk Richard.

'Come on young man, make yourself decent, for God's sake. This is a serious matter and if you don't come with me, you're going to find yourself in very big trouble.'

Laura opens the door on the chain again and sees Finn steering the hapless drunk towards his own room. *I'll call you very soon*, Finn indicates, waving his phone.

She considers phoning the police. *No, I'll wait for Finn - he'll know what to do.*

Fifteen very long minutes later, her phone pings with a text.

'Respectable?'

She replies with the thumbs up emoji.

She opens the door cautiously, Finn enters and motions towards the mini bar.

'Do you mind if I do?'

'Of course not,' says Laura, opening it up. 'Whiskey OK?'

'Anything,' says Finn.

'What did you do with him?'

'He's gone. He won't bother you again. I'm so sorry you had to endure that. Are you OK?'

'I'm OK, if a little shocked,' says Laura.

'I'm sure you are. God's honour, that's the first time anything like that has happened on my watch,' he says, 'not that that's any consolation. Do you want to report it to the police? You're perfectly within your rights and I'm happy to back you.'

'What do you think?'

'Your call my dear.'

'What would you do?'

'Well, it's a bit different for me. But if you want my opinion, I'd say that the man is not a threat to the public. I've seen many complete idiots like him in my Navy days. What he needs is a good bollocking, threatening with dismissal and sending on his way. Trouble is, his boss wasn't much better, was he?'

'I'll do anything you advise, but I suppose if we make a fuss, it could affect your business?'

'It might, with that company. But that's not the point. You must decide.'

'I tell you what, let's just forget it. Yuk, that picture I've got in my head of him standing there thrusting his ... ugh, it was revolting. I just don't want to see that man ever again. And I really don't want to go through it all again multiple times with the police.'

'I'll see to it Laura; you won't see him again. I know how to handle this. Leave it with me.'

63

'I'll kill the bastard if I ever get my hands on him,' spits Ali. 'People like that should be strung up by the balls, if they've got any to get hold of.'

Laura is not long home and has run through the previous night's incident and the joint decision between her and Finn to let the matter drop.

'You should have reported it immediately.'

'I knew you'd be angry, I was too. But I was never in any danger, I promise you that. Finn was there incredibly quickly. The guy was just drunk.'

'But he could easily have harmed you, raped you.'

'Believe me, he wasn't in any state to be able to do anything like that, let alone attack me. If he'd been a real threat, I promise you, I would have phoned the police straightaway.'

'Are you absolutely sure? It's still not too late.'

'Finn and I debated it and we decided against it. We both think the guy and his boss are two of a kind. Privileged, self-opinionated idiots who can't hold their booze. Like kids behaving badly. They were completely pissed. I don't think they're anything sinister, just complete prats.

'If I felt he was going to be a danger to other women, I would've called it in. Finn handled it brilliantly; he got hold of the boss first thing this morning, who was actually horrified to discover that his colleague had done such a thing. You know, at first, I thought it was *him* banging on the door, but no, it was his very immature and embarrassing junior. Anyway, the guy vanished into thin air, so I presume he was packed off in disgrace. The boss actually thanked Finn for not reporting it. SO, it all turned out OK for everyone in the end. Oh, and the event itself went very well too. So, no harm done and it's business as usual.'

'OK, but I'm very unhappy about it. I wish I could have been there to look after you, but well done for handling it, I'm really proud of you.'

The two hug.

'Anyway, he had the ugliest penis I've ever seen.'

Ali coughs. 'What did you say?'

'Ha, ha. I didn't know penises could look like that.'

'What was wrong with it, for fuck's sake?'

'It was bent - upwards.'

'Laura!' Ali splutters.

'It's called Peyronie's disease. Pay-roni.

'I looked it up.'

'You did what? It sounds like an ice cream vendor!' says Ali.

'What search term did you use to get that information, for heaven's sake?!'

Laura pushes Ali over on the settee and mock-punches him.

'Stop it, stop it,' Ali says, still laughing.

Laura straightens herself and adjusts her blouse.

'I much prefer a normal penis, like yours,' she adds. 'It was a horrible shock, believe me.

'Anyway, changing the subject quickly ... how was your weekend? I left you to it on Friday.'

'Yes, all good. I took Becks and Olivia home yesterday. They had a great time here and she's incredibly grateful about what we're doing.'

'Oh, that is good news. The standing order's set up so now we need to concentrate on finding her somewhere decent to live. Are you happy with everything?'

'I'm *very* happy. I can't believe how all this is working out and that's completely down to you. Saying I love you, doesn't get near it. I mean it.'

Laura smiles, at which point her phone rings, and it's Finn.

'Fine thanks, thank you for calling. No, not all – we did the right thing, I'm sure of that. Yes, it was a bit of a scare but as I've just said to Ali, I didn't feel in any real danger.'

They chat a little more and Laura reassures Finn that it hasn't put her off working with him.

*

'This is nice, what do you reckon? Better than the others, don't you think?'

Laura is touring prospective properties in Portsmouth with Becky; the pair having already whittled them down to a shortlist and this is the last one they're viewing.

Ali is absent, busy recording in the studio across the harbour in Gosport, more than happy to let the girls sort out the property business.

'The rooms are a good size and I do tend to prefer older properties. They were built better and as long as they've been maintained, I think they're a better buy. Well, it's like that in Dublin, so I suspect it's the same rule of thumb here.'

'Yeh, I love it,' says Becky, swaying with Olivia in her arms.

'Do you want some time to think about it?'

'No, this is perfect. I thought this would be the one. Great for the shops too – and the seafront is pretty close. I don't know what to say, Laura.'

'You don't need to say anything Becky. We want you to be comfortable and stress-free.'

'It's in pretty good condition too, so I won't have to do any decorating,' says Becky, looking round the room.

'I'm sure you'll want to add your touches at some stage, but there's no hurry, is there?'

'Look Laura, I've been thinking about all this. I'm still a bit bewildered to be honest, and you giving me a flat is incredible but you must let me pay you some rent.'

'You don't have to think about that now Becky.'

'I'd like to, if you don't mind. In fact, I insist.'

'OK, we'll sort something out, but don't worry now. Let's get the flat first. Apart from the survey I'll get someone to check over the services, just to be sure that everything's nice and safe. Let's get together very soon and do a spot of online shopping for the essentials you're going to need, much as I hate it buying remotely. Some things need to be seen and touched!'

'You're incredibly kind.'

'Leave it with me. We'll have you in here in no time. There's no chain and we're cash buyers.'

They say their goodbyes but instead of going home to Wickham, Laura waits for Becky to disappear round the corner with the pushchair and then reaches into her bag for another set of estate agent details.

She's smart enough to realise that Ali will want to spend a substantial amount of time with his daughter – and rather than risk any awkwardness between them, she's come up with what she considers to be the perfect solution. Another property. It's a good investment and once again everyone wins.

She already has her hopes pinned high on the house she's off to see in Merridean Avenue; so all being well, today should be a very productive day.

64

There are six sitting around the table at the New Bengal, in Toxteth. It's Shaun James's immediate team and he's decided they need to let off some spicy steam after a few very tense weeks. The table is crammed with more food than this bunch will ever get through.

Shaun always over-orders but no one would dream of making the point – he's the boss. He never picks up the tab either, so it's never a cheap night out for any of them.

He likes his chicken tikka dhansak and mushroom bhaji with pilau rice – and dipping into everyone else's dishes. By the end, when he's stuffed to bursting point, he probably hasn't a clue what he's eaten. It's a ritual of gluttony that he loves and never seems to suffer from.

Jason Brand is sitting to his right. He's had a haircut – a side shave and undercut. It looks menacing – just how he wants it. He's doing OK at the moment, enjoying the unofficial position of Shaun's right-hand man.

They're all enjoying themselves and the mood is light. Some big changes have been taking place over the past nine months and Shaun and his team are ready and prepared for their next business development, county lines trafficking. They've got a bit of catching up to do but they've sorted out their differences with other interested parties and it's now full steam ahead.

It could have been a very different story, given the near-disaster last summer.

They'd set up an important, delicate meeting with Brian White, to negotiate a truce and to explore the idea of working together.

It was planned meticulously, the venue was top secret and secure but just as they were about to talk, a complete stranger knocked on the door and freaked Brian into thinking they'd been set up.

It's taken nine long months to win back his trust and move things on and Shaun hasn't forgotten how damaging that knock on the door was. Neither has Brian White.

One of his conditions is for Shaun to eliminate that black bastard.

*

I'm Back is the latest Ali Kurmi song to get the full treatment in the recording studio – and today, Ali and Jim are working with pedal steel guitarist, Leo Smith, to add a country texture to the song.

Jim is doing his usual tidying up of the music files, removing unwanted notes, cleaning up the tone, adding a plugin for reverb and a touch of compression here and there. There's a lot that Ali can follow but an equal amount he hasn't got a clue about. Which is why he's here, paying a professional to do it for him.

'Sounding good now, isn't it? Nice one Leo!'

'My pleasure dear sir,' says Leo.

'Good decision,' says Jim, beaming. 'Liam's vocal is great, too – he's got that natural country drawl – there's nothing artificial about it. It's funny how so many country artists in the UK try too hard to sound like they're American and end up sounding sound completely naff. Liam's cool though. Good lyrics, too.'

'I'm really pleased. It's another one of my real life near-misses,' says Ali, remembering all too clearly, the fallout with his father, and how it had threatened his relationship with Laura.

'It didn't happen though, did it? Just like *Fatal Equation.* You always catastrophise in your songs young man.'

'Ah, but the best songs come from the heart don't they.'

'Does life mirror the song by any chance? All happy families now?'

'It does, thankfully,' says Ali. 'The past few months have been extraordinary. If you put it all in a book no one would believe it. But it's all true.'

Three and a half thousand miles away in New York, Curtiss Jackson and his Music Advisor Helen Garcia of Endera Productions are looking at Ali's Facebook page and Instagram account. Helen happened upon the Coolstar song *I Keep Walkin'* which she thinks will fit perfectly into Curtiss's docudrama.

'His website is cool too,' says Helen, 'but he's a newbie from what I can see.'

'So the song, is pretty anonymous then?'

'Yeh, just a few hundred YouTube views, virtually nothing on Spotify.'

'Excellent,' says Curtiss.

'Shall I make some enquiries, publishing and the like?'

'Yeh, I want that song for the closing sequence. It would be perfect. See what else he's done while you're at it.'

'Will do.'

Helen puts in the call.

'Hey, is that Ali Kurmi?'

'It is. Can you hear me?'

Ali waves frantically at Jim, signalling him to turn the track off.

'Yes, I can. Pardon me, I'm Helen Garcia from Endera Productions in New York City. Hey.'

'Hi Helen.'

'I got your details from your website, Coolstar?'

'OK right, how can I help?'

Ali is looking manically at Jim, trying and failing to mouth what's going on.

'We're in post-production for a film and we'd like to include your song, I Keep Walkin' by Coolstar if you're agreeable and it's got clearance.'

Ali gently clears his throat, and answers as confidently as possible. *How do Americans manage to sound so incredibly cool*? he's thinking.

'Yes of course.'

'Do you have a publisher?'

'No, I don't.'

'Oh, that's cool. Is it registered with Performing Rights?'

'It is and it has an ISRC code too. It's all organised.'

'Excellent. I get the impression Ali, if I may call you that, that this sync licensing might be a little new to you?'

'It is, to be honest.'

'That's cool. Well, we'd be prepared to offer you the standard deal plus we'd want 25% of the publishing, which shouldn't be a problem as you haven't got that set up. Anyway, our legal people will deal with all that if and when. Are you still on for this?'

'I'm very interested, yes. What is the film?'

'Sure. It's a docudrama about a famous hiker over here who died in mysterious circumstances and it covers the subject of *thru-hiking* generally, that many folk know very little about. It's a powerful story, Ali.'

'Wow, sounds amazing.'

'Can I ask you; do you have a showreel or something similar so we can listen to more of your work? You never know.'

'If you give me your email address I can send you a link to my private account on SoundCloud – there are about 20 finished songs on there – all ready to go.'

'Perfect Ali, send it over. We'll be in touch. I'll text you the email.'

'Thank you Helen.'

'The pleasure's mine, have a great day. Oh, and … I just love that guy's voice!'

Ali slowly turns and slides down the wall and onto the studio bench, in shock and delight.

'Fuck me man, did you hear that?'

'Good news by the look on your face.'

'It bloody well is. That was a TV company in New York. They want to use *I Keep Walkin'* and maybe some other songs!'

65

Wickham Horse Fair always takes place on May 20th, unless it's a Sunday. Travellers from all over the country take over the Hampshire village square for two days, to buy and sell their horses or cobs, and it seems, anything equine.

It's a spectacle that's also enjoyed by the locals and other onlookers – and today, Alice, Dave, Laura, Ali, Becky and Olivia are behind the barriers marvelling at the row of huge horse buttocks lined up outside the pub – all manes and feathers with intricately plaited tails.

Ali is pointing them out to Olivia and Becky.

'Look at that,' he says, as Olivia gurgles.

Suddenly, to their side, from nowhere, there's a loud clattering of hooves, as an enormous horse pulls up sharply from a trot with a saddle-less rider wearing a white T shirt and jeans. He turns the horse's head round with gusto and dramatically trots back off again.

Olivia's face lights up and she points at the horse.

'Aren't they big, Liv?' says Ali.

Dave shouts across to Laura, 'a bit different to the horses you're used to, Laura.'

She smiles back – *if only he knew …*

'Let's go round to the fair,' says Alice.

As they walk, Alice explains, 'the locals are split on all this. Most are happy enough but there are some crusty folks who look down their noses at the event. But they never show up, so who cares. I like it. It's fun, isn't it?'

The road has been closed to allow bareback riding and sulkies or carts to ride up and down. There are big groups of hefty looking males chatting amongst themselves and no one knows whether they're trading or just having a good chat.

The atmosphere is friendly and everyone attending the event seems to be enjoying it.

The group moves though the square, past all the market stalls and into Dave's wine bar. It's packed as usual and noisy with animated conversations.

He moves two reserved tables together.

'Good business with the fair, I bet, Dave?' says Ali.

'Yep, I'm very happy thank you.'

They settle down with drinks, nuts and crackers.

'A lot's been happening for you two since I last saw you, hasn't it?' Dave ventures, motioning towards Olivia.

'Bit of an understatement Dave – there's been an addition to the family. Take a bow Olivia!'

'And Becky, of course,' beams Laura.

Dave smiles at Olivia. 'She's a beauty,' he says, 'I'm very happy for you all.'

Laura turns to Alice. 'Ali's got some great news about his music, haven't you?'

'Yeh, I suppose so.'

'You have. Don't be so coy. An American film company is going to use one of his songs – maybe more.'

'That's great,' say Alice and Dave in unison.

'Which one?'

'*I Keep Walkin'*,' says Ali.

'Is that the one with the harmonica?' says Dave – and Ali nods looking pleased.

'Yeh, I know the one. Great track and great singer. So, what does this mean exactly?'

'I don't know yet to be honest Dave, or how long it'll be before it comes out. It's for Netflix and it's what they call a docudrama. But yes, I'm really chuffed because it means the song will be heard all around the world. My publicist is very happy too.'

'Oh yes, of course, you're releasing your video and single soon, aren't you?' says Alice.

'Yeh, so it's all happening at once. But I'll wait to see *I Keep Walkin'* on air, before getting too excited,' says Ali.

'Very wise.'

'What about you, Laura, how are your plans shaping up?' asks Dave.

Alice affectionately squeezes his knee under the table. The pair are getting on very nicely.

'I'm getting a good idea of what I'd like to do,' says Laura.

'I can't quite remember how much I've already told you, but my ideas have changed from my original plan. I've decided that I'd like to help young people realise their potential – with scholarships. I had one myself and for that I'll be forever grateful. So, it feels kind of nice and natural doing that.'

'Great idea,' says Dave, 'no doubt there's a lot of work and red tape involved in something like that?'

'You're so right – and that's my big thing. I hate wasting money on paying pen pushers and bureaucrats. But I'll get there, somehow.'

Laura motions with her hands, 'What about yourself Dave, are you happy here?'

'I am, yes. I've got a good team at the moment and I like to think they enjoy working here. I'm sure it's the reason we do quite well. Happy staff, happy customers. We have a lot of regulars, so we must be doing something right.'

'Whenever I come here, it's a great atmosphere,' says Laura.

'Now, has Alice told you about her plan?'

'The new salon? She has actually, but it's not definite yet, is it?'

'Not quite. Every time I'm in the Square, I pass the old deli with my eyes tightly screwed up, hoping to God it hasn't been sold. It would be perfect for her. I don't know if she's told you, but I'm waiting for the sale of the family stud in Ireland. It should have taken place around now but it was postponed for a month. Hopefully though, it should all be done and dusted soon and we can all get on with our plans.'

'I should imagine the sale will be on a grander scale to the one here today in Wickham!'

Laura snorts at the contrast. 'That is so funny, hilarious.'

'She can't wait to get going – she's bursting with ideas about what to do there.'

'Bless her. She'll make a great success of it, I know. She has many talents, does Alice.

'What about you two, things are good, yes?' asks Laura, keeping her voice down. Alice is speaking to a friend who's wandered over.

'Yes, we rub along together quite well, generally speaking,' Dave smirks.

'Alice deserves to be happy. She's the most giving person I've ever met and she has a huge, warm heart. I love her to pieces,' says Laura.

'She's very special, I agree and I'm very fond of her. Do you share some of her more, how shall I put it, her more esoteric beliefs? I like to think I have an open mind, but I do struggle with some aspects of Alice's thoughts and philosophies. She's brimming over with excitement when she talks about her spiritual interests and it's quite hard to follow what she's saying.'

'What do you mean, that she believes in life after death?'

'Yes, that sort of thing, and reiki and spiritual healing, it takes some believing, doesn't it? Well, it does for me.'

'It can seem very strange, I know. Some of it is still a mystery to me too, in all honesty. I mean I've never had a sense of being close to dead people and being able to communicate with them. That's a step beyond me. But I do believe in energy that we might not yet understand. I think some people are able to tap into that more easily than others. I think Alice is one. I've also heard some extraordinary healing stories that can't be scientifically explained. The boundaries of science are being extended all the time after all, aren't they? Hard to explain, isn't it?'

'I'm afraid it is. But I do respect her though.'

'That's wonderful, Dave. That's all she wants, I'm sure.'

The subject returns to Laura's plans.

'Alice did tell me about the fly or flies in the ointment,' says Dave.

'Oh, you mean Stephanie and Richard, my adorable step-children. Is it possible to divorce or disconnect with step-children? I doubt it, but I'd like to completely cancel them, I can tell you.'

'Pretty bad then?'

'Yeh, pretty bad. They were horrible to me from the word go. Frank, my husband, did his best but they weren't having it. They just took an instant dislike to me. The trouble is though, it's a bit more sinister than that. Stephanie *really* hates me and even after Frank died, she was venomous. I was at rock bottom and she continued to pile the pressure on me. It was actually very scary.'

'And now?'

'Now? That's a very good point. I don't know, in all truth. The sale of the family stud is coming right up and I haven't heard a word about them, or from them, in months. I doubt if they even know where I am – or anything about Ali. My God, if Stephanie knew about Ali, she'd go ballistic, I tell you.'

'She sounds ghastly.'

'She is and it's no exaggeration. To be honest I'm worried about the sale because there's so much money involved, many millions, Dave. It's a big deal.'

'That does sound very scary.'

'It is and I'll be very, very happy when it's all over. The stress is not pleasant. It proves yet again that money doesn't automatically mean happiness – it isn't the answer to everything.'

'I'm sure all will go smoothly for you, Laura. You deserve it. Your plans are wonderful and you both deserve peace and happiness. I'm sure it'll all work out OK.'

66

'Are you one hundred per cent sure you want this?'

'Completely sure,' replies Stephanie.

'This is serious stuff lady. There's no going back, once you give the go-ahead,' he warns.

'I'm not stupid. Can he do the job? Properly, I mean?"

'Listen lady, I've put a lot of time into this for you and you're really starting to piss me off; you're dealing with pros here, so cut the shit or you can find someone else to do your dirty work.'

'Sorry, I just need to be sure.'

'As long as you don't change your mind again – it'll work. We know the location – we just need the date and time.'

'And he, she, they – are you sure they can do this without leaving any evidence? Nothing that will lead back to me?'

'Nothing. I keep telling you lady, you're dealing with experienced professionals. And believe me, the less you know, the better it'll be for you.'

*

'Ali, have you got five minutes?' Laura calls up the stairs.

'I'm going out and there are a few things I need to run past you.'

'OK, I'll be down in a mo,' comes Ali's distant reply.

Laura has just received a call from her local solicitor with some good news. She's decided that she can't keep her little secret any longer and is dying to tell Ali that whilst sorting out Becky and Olivia's accommodation in Portsmouth, she's also been house-hunting for them. A pied à terre for when she and Ali need to be in Portsmouth.

Ali sidles into the kitchen looking at his phone.

'Still hard at work?' asks Laura, knowing Ali's sudoku look.

Ali smiles sarcastically.

'Babe …'

'And I know that tone', says Ali.

Laura giggles.

'I've got something to show you,' she says, in a little girl voice.

'Oh yeh?'

'Look at these, will you.' She places a set of estate agent details on the island and swipes her hand across them. 'There.'

'Becky's?'

'No, take a closer look.'

'OK, what am I supposed to be seeing?'

'It's a bloody house, Ali. In Southsea.'

'Yes …'

'It's ours. You fool.'

'What do you mean, it's ours?'

'Look, you'll need to be in Portsmouth often and rather than have you driving backwards and forwards or having to sleep on Becky's sofa, this is the solution.'

Ali pauses to take it in and then looks directly at Laura.

'Wow. I hadn't even thought about all that stuff.'

'Take a look Ali, it's a semi and not that far from the seafront,' she says, enthusiastically.

'And you've actually bought it?'

'Yep, just completed this morning. Just put the phone down. No. 29 Merridean Avenue is now ours. Everything's gone through. I spoke to the solicitor and all we have to do is go and collect the keys.'

'Let me have a look then.'

He studies the details and keeps grinning and looking up at Laura.

'Three bedrooms, huge bathroom, large lounge and dining room, kitchen, utility room … garden.'

He pulls her closely into him and they stand there hugging each other tightly.

'I adore you,' he whispers in her ear.

'And I adore you.'

'What about Alice's shop?'

'That's all OK too. I'll proceed with that after the stud sale goes through. Please God that it does, and doesn't get delayed yet again.'

'Have you heard anything on that?'

'I had an email from the solicitor in Ireland yesterday and it didn't mention any problems.'

'OK. Once again, fingers crossed. This house looks really good, and it looks in pretty good condition?'

'Yes, not bad at all. It'll need decorating to our taste but it's good enough to move in to. So, I'm going to be busy.'

'Blimey, you're only halfway through this place.'

'I know, but you have to adapt to circumstances; and as you know, I like to be busy. This place can wait. But we need Portsmouth to be up and running, sooner. There are a few things I need to check out for safety's sake – like plumbing, heating and wiring. The boiler's a bit old but I'll get it all checked. So that's what I'm going to be doing for the next few days, sourcing plumbers and electricians. What about you? What's on today?'

'I've got a Zoom meeting with Pete about the single and video. Talking of which, guess what? Mark isn't going to use the footage we shot in the New Forest. We froze our testicles off for nothing! I guess that's the music business for you. He wants to shoot some more footage on Stokes Bay and at the church.'

'Your *Ozone* beach.'

'Yeh. Anyway, I'll be talking to Pete – he's being paid to do most of that stuff, so I just need to find out if there's anything I need to be doing too. I don't want to waste this opportunity. This and the Netflix deal means things are slowly beginning to move. I have to confess that I'm feeling just a bit excited. It's very uncool to say that, but for fuck's sake, Laura, this could be brilliant.'

They kiss passionately and Ali runs his hands down her back.

'Er no, Ali, not now. There's too much to do. Later, eh?'

Ali takes hold of Laura's hands.

'Look, I know you've got an incredible amount on but just stop for a moment and think about what you've done in such a short space of time. It's actually extraordinary,' he enthuses.

'You've uprooted, moved to a new country, fitted in brilliantly with a totally new community, you've bought a fabulous new home – no, three homes, and one with a bloody indoor pool! You've made friends, got a part-time job and you've found the love of your life. For fuck's sake Laura. And yes, last but not least, *everyone* loves you. All that in just one year.'

'I know, I know it's amazing when you line things up like that. But the very bestest of bests – the most important part of it – is you babe. A gorgeous, kind and talented man, who's successfully fought his demons, handled a very nasty family situation, writes amazing music and is the best specialist DJ in the country. That's not bad either. Oh yes, and a dad too!'

'We're a good match then,' says Ali.

'I reckon so!'

'What about the dreaded Stephanie and Richard, should we still be worried about them? They seem to have disappeared.'

'I know, that worries me. They were on at me all the time back in Ireland but since I got here, nothing. I do find that odd. She's such a conniving creature. Even now, I don't trust her.'

'But what can they do? The sale's going through, isn't it? And the legal stuff about the will and the Trust, they can't argue with that?'

'No, thankfully, they can't.'

'Well, stop worrying. In a month's time we'll be saying cheers and wishing good luck to both of them. We'll raise our glasses and mentally send them blasting off into the sunset – or better still, into the fires of hell.'

'Right, let's go and get those keys. Your car or mine?'

67

Laura is in her work gear, hair up and carrying in boxes from her car. She and Ali now own two properties in Portsmouth – completion on this, the latest one, 29 Merridean Avenue, went through without any hitches and it's time to roll up the sleeves and get it ready for habitation. This is their Portsmouth base.

Her first target is the kitchen and she won't be happy until she cleans it thoroughly – her way. It might look clean, but she's fussy and makes no apology for attention to hygienic detail. She doesn't want any unnecessary accidents or bugs.

As for décor, she wants to take advantage of the natural light from the house's south-west facing aspect, so nothing dark and dreary. She'll go for curtains rather than blinds and there'll be carpets in most of the rooms. Laminate is definitely out – it had its noisy day.

She stands at the living room window and looks out. They're in a good position near a bend in the road, it's quite long and links the common, by the seafront, to the shopping area at the northern end. The shops are decent, useful ones and there are a couple of restaurants that look worthy of sampling.

She's about to fill the kettle for a cup of tea, when she hears a knock at the door.

It's Becky, with pushchair and a gurgling and happy-looking Olivia.

'Hi Becky, your young lady looks like she's in a good mood. Come in, both of you.'

'I just thought I'd pop round to see if you need any help?'

'That's sweet of you Becky. I'm just trying to get a feel for the furnishings. We need all the basics; white goods for the kitchen, sofa, dining table, beds, lights and another set of kitchen equipment. If I'd had the presence of mind, I should have doubled up everything when we were buying everything for your place. Well, some of the things – how silly is that? So back to online buying it must be, and hope for the best.'

'It'll be lovely, when you've got the furniture in, I can just picture it. I thought I might be able to help but I can see that's a bit premature. But do let me know when you start having stuff delivered. We're not far away and I can just pop round.'

'I know Becky, thank you so much. Come to think of it, there is something you could do. Are you around tomorrow morning? Would you be able to let the plumber in?'

'Sure, no problem.'

'That would be fantastic. Finn has got a meeting late morning, that I need to go to, but I'll have a problem if the plumber is late. He probably won't take more than a couple of hours. It's just a routine service for the boiler and radiators. I've tried them and they seem to work OK so he shouldn't be here very long.'

'That's absolutely fine with me. Better to be safe than sorry, eh?'

*

'Am I speaking with Mr Ali Kurmi, please?'

'Yes, you are, who's that?' says Ali, putting his guitar down, his heart pumping faster at the sound of another American accent.

'Ali, may I call you that? It's Bob Speke from Top Tune Publishing in Los Angeles. I hope this isn't a bad time to call.'

'Not at all,' says Ali, his heart still fluttering in anticipation.

'It's first thing in the morning here but I guess it's way later there. Anyhow, Ali I got to hear some of your music via Helen Garcia of

Endera Productions. I believe your song *I Keep Walkin'* will be in Curtiss' new film?'

'That's right.'

'I like that cut very much, great sound and a great hook. Anyway, you know how things are in this business, things are passed between people, and recommendations count for a lot. It's the way we do things here.

'I like your music, Ali. I'm particularly interested in your heavier tracks and I love one in particular, *I'm Back*. That's got a real Nashville vibe, hints of Luke Bryan maybe. I dunno. And I like *Homeland* – that could be a big song Ali, in the right context. The lyrics are mighty good and with the way things are in the world that could really catch the mood of people who have lost their homes. Great song. Could become an anthem. And then there's *In Paradise*. Wow. Why did you write that please? It's real powerful. I thought I was at a stadium show.'

'Well thanks. Yeh, that's exactly the idea of the song. I wanted something triumphant and grand – and at the same time very emotional. It's not intended for Top 40 radio, obviously.'

'You did that son, you got it damned right, if that's what you intended.'

'Now, I haven't said why I'm phoning. I don't want you to make any sudden decisions but I'd like you to think about a publishing deal. I agree with you, your work is probably not for today's kids – it lends itself more to syncing opportunities, which is exactly where I come in. You may or may not have heard of our company but we have a fine track record in placing songs on major networks and films and commercials. Let me tell you more, if you have five minutes.'

'I do,' says Ali, keeping as cool as he can.'

Ali is beginning to recognise a bit of forward momentum on his musical journey. Several good things have happened in succession. Whether it's as a result of his efforts, simple good luck or the much-debated law of attraction, he isn't going to overthink it and intends to maintain it, whatever it is.

He'd prefer to concentrate on creating and producing songs, but the current musical world demands that composers and performers are marketing experts too. Only the rich and very famous get to delegate those tasks and focus on their music. Ali consoles himself with the thought that whilst he may not be famous, he's getting a sniff of that life thanks to Laura's cash injection.

'Woh, that smells a bit ripe, Ali-babe ... you haven't got a problem, have you?'

'Ah, you're home,' says Ali, looking up.

'It's cauliflower – I'm par-boiling it.'

'Phwa, it is isn't it. What are we having?'

'Mustard cauliflower-cheese – with cumin, curry powder, cheddar and parsley.'

'Lovely, now don't tell me where the recipe comes from, I couldn't possibly imagine!'

'Yep, Yotam, the man. '

'I look forward to it. Have you had a good day?' she asks, leaning across to kiss him.

'I have, but it just got even better.'

'Ah, you're so sweet. Good job I love you, isn't it?'

'You don't love me as much as I love you.'

'I do.'

'You couldn't possibly! Right, enough of that. You asked if I've had a nice day. I have. I've had another call from the States.'

'The production company?'

'No actually, this was a music publisher, in Los Angeles.'

'Ali, that sounds really exciting. What did he want?'

Ali explains that the man called to offer a publishing deal and that he was very flattering about Ali's songs.

'I'm a bit cautious. It sounded great but I need to check this guy out and find out more about his company. I don't want to rush into anything I might regret. Remember, I've waited for this moment for years and I'm going to be very careful.'

'Very sensible, but you never know, it could be the start of something.'

'I hope so.'

'I saw Becky today, by the way. She says, hi.'

'Everything OK?'

'Yes, she's kindly agreed to go round tomorrow, to let the boiler man in.'

'I'm glad you two are getting on. She's a good girl and she doesn't deserve all that shit from her parents. Still, she's got us now, so sod them.'

68

Meon Lodge, the O'Brien-Kurmi residence, is now partially surrounded by scaffolding. The decorators are here and the exterior of the house is getting a facelift. Laura has already bonded with the two guys and they're clearly impressed with her. Ali can sense it in their white boiler-suited body language when they're around her. He's getting used to living with a woman who always turns heads.

'I have a suggestion, Ali Kurmi,' says Laura, in the kitchen.

'Yes ma'am.'

'Going back to what we discussed at the Three Chimneys, we've got our birthdays coming up and Friday next week is a big day in my life – and indeed, yours. The stud sale. The estimated value as of today, is … go on, guess?

'No idea.'

'€2 billion. But it could be a lot more – or a lot less. What do you think of that? We get half.'

'Please God, let's get this over and done with,' says Ali, shaking his head, 'that amount of money is beyond my comprehension.'

'Amen to that. Now, whatever we think about it, it's an extremely important day and we both want to draw a line under it. So, I want mark the occasion and our birthdays with a little party. Just close friends. God knows it's a modest thing to do and we should celebrate, not apologise.'

'Good idea.'

'Check your diary. Let's do it next Thursday, in Portsmouth at the new house, when everyone is most likely to be available. It can be a house warming too.'

'Even better,' says Ali. 'I'm clear. Who shall we invite?'

'Let's see … you, me, Becky and Olivia, Alice and Dave – Thursday is Dave's day off. And I'd like Finn and Samantha to come too if they can. So I reckon a lunchtime buffet would be the best idea. We'll buy in some ready-made food, which will be less hassle, and we can all enjoy ourselves. What do you think? I'm thinking Ottolenghi Direct.'

'You're kidding me. Will they deliver down here? I'll check it out. I think that's a brilliant idea.'

'I want to do a proper party in this house too, at some stage. There are so many people we need to invite but that can wait a little while longer. Let's keep this celebration to the select few. I'll text them and get it all moving. It'll be fun.'

Ali smiles with admiration and love.

'Come here, Mr Kurmi. You haven't got to be anywhere right now, have you?'

'Jim's popping round later to give me some advice about the studio project outside.'

'Brilliant idea. What time's he coming?'

'4 o'clock.'

'Lovely,' says Laura taking hold of his wrists and pulling him towards her.

Ali immediately kisses her on the lips and the two stand there lingering over their building passion. Still kissing and glued together, Laura edges him towards the hall. They only pause when they reach the stairs and again Laura looks directly into his eyes and leads him by the hand up the flight destined for their bedroom.

'What about the painters?'

'Scared of showing your undercoat?' she giggles, mischievously.

In their bedroom, Ali starts to unbutton his shirt but Laura takes over, pulls it off and gently rubs her hands over his chest, smiling and kissing it as she does so. Ali reaches for her trousers and she wriggles teasingly until he catches hold of her zip and pulls it down.

Laura responds in the same way, unzipping Ali's jeans slowly and deliberately.

He lifts her blouse and reaches behind to undo her bra. The pair kiss again, and fall onto the bed. Now completely naked, Laura pulls both of her legs up in a welcoming gesture for Ali, who needs little encouragement and in moments the pair return to their familiar state of rhythmic bliss.

'What are you thinking about?' says Laura, nuzzling into Ali's temple and kissing him.

'That you are the perfect lover.'

'So are you.'

'Please God or Allah ... whoever, don't ever take this woman away from me. I would rather die.'

'Don't say such things Ali, be careful what you wish for.'

'I wish I could stay inside you for ever! We fit together so well.'

'It was wonderful. So, you still love me then, do you?'

'Stop that. I don't have the words.'

'You don't need any words for this. I'm so happy right now. For you and for me. As soon as next Friday is out of the way we can really chill and start to enjoy ourselves. We've both had such a lot to deal with in the past few months. No small matters either. Big life-changing issues. I genuinely believe that we've earned a happy and peaceful time ahead. There are so many things we can enjoy – as well as our work. We should go on holiday for a start. What about it? Our first holiday! Where would you like to go?'

Ali rubs his chin exaggeratedly. 'I've always dreamed about the Caribbean – you know, one of those palm beaches that stretches away into the distance – with that unreal blue sea and white sand. Somewhere nice and hot. But to be honest, Bognor would be fine as long as it's just you and me.'

'Then consider it booked, Mr Kurmi. Butlins in the Bahamas, here we come!'

69

Joe Kelly is breaking into a sweat at the stud in Tipperary. Not from physical exertion – but from the tension surrounding the imminent sale of one of the horse racing world's biggest assets, the late Frank O'Brien stud.

It's been his world for the past 15 years or so and his part in the story is more than likely coming to an end.

He and his huge team are preparing the stock and facilities for the sale. The horses of all sizes and ages need to be presented in their best possible conditions. The foaling units need to be checked and re-checked, ditto the farrier quarters. There's all the stud transport that needs sorting. The quarters for the 24/7 staff, the gallops, the paddocks and pastures, the tack rooms need to be cleaned and organised, the yearling training areas, the list is endless.

Contractors have been working around the clock on the site for the past two weeks and they're still busy all over the place.

And Frank's daughter, Stephanie, has been hovering around, interfering and poking her nose in, asking unnecessary, stupid questions. It's painfully obvious that she hasn't a single care for the horses or the staff – she just wants to sell up and run off into the sunset with the cash. A lot of cash. Joe exhales loudly.

Frank expected this and he was well-prepared. The business is in good shape thanks to Joe and the trustees – and stands to do well in the sale and Joe will too. Frank looked after that. But it will be the end of an era and unusually for him, Joe finds himself a touch emotional, despite knowing that this day has been approaching for a long time.

The emotions are mixed though and he finds himself in an awkward position. He wants to honour his late friend's wishes but it's placing a huge amount of pressure on him to get everything just right. Hopefully, most of the staff will keep their jobs; but personally, Joe isn't holding his breath. In reality though, he doesn't actually mind which way it goes for him. Like everyone else concerned, he'll be glad when the whole affair is over.

*

In Bromley, Kent, the temperature has gone sky high. Javed Kurmi has just heard news about his son and he's absolutely furious. This afternoon, he overheard his nephews discussing Ali and his wealthy girlfriend and left them no option but to spill the beans. Hammad and Kamran have never seen their uncle so angry.

'What wealthy girlfriend?'

Javed's daughter Rani, had perhaps acted naively, when telling her cousins about Ali and his new life with Laura in Hampshire. She believed she'd spoken to them in confidence.

Ham and Kam have visited Portsmouth a number of times since the family break up – including clearing out Ali's old house, prior to letting.

On one such visit, they were approached in the street by an elderly lady, who it turns out, was a neighbour and something of a friend to Ali. She'd asked after Ali and Laura's well-being.

The two seized the opportunity to glean as much information as possible – and at a later meeting with Rani, had shared the details of the encounter.

Rightly or wrongly, Rani who was finding difficulty in keeping silent about her brother, for some reason, chose to tell them Ali's story. She trusted the pair to remain silent with their new knowledge.

This afternoon, thinking they were alone in the office, they talked about Ali and his new life. Unfortunately, Javed was very much present, working quietly in the room next door, and overheard snippets of their conversation.

He burst into the room and demanded to know the full story. Shocked and dismayed, Ham and Kam had no option but to share all the information they had.

Angry and feeling betrayed, Javed slammed his hands down on his desk and left in a rage.

*

In Tipperary, the ever-cool Stephanie is being pestered by her exasperated brother who wants to know what is going on with regard to Laura.

'Stephanie, I have a right to know what you're up to. The sale is next Friday.'

'A right? You have no right.'

'Stephanie, *what* is happening? *What* are you planning? I want to know – now!' he says, slamming the door shut behind him.

Stephanie shudders, surprised by her brother's sudden outburst.

'What's the point? You'll get your money whatever happens, so why should you worry.'

'Because anything you do my dear sister, worries me. It worries me a lot and I want to know what you are doing. Right now.'

Reluctantly, Stephanie tells Richard everything she's put in place.

His facial expression changes to a look of horror as he listens.

'You stupid woman. You fucking idiot. Cancel it right now. I mean it. It won't work and we'll both end up in prison. I demand it or I'll go to the Garda now.'

'Go on then, I dare you. You're the fucking idiot. The moment you tell the Garda they'll have you in cuffs. You are 100% complicit in this. Like or not you're in this right up to here. I'm sure you don't want to go to prison, do you, you nasty, nasty, oily little creature.'

*

Shaun James has a great deal on his plate at the moment, including raw scotch bonnet chillies, and whilst he revels in the thrill of expanding his operation outside Liverpool, he still hasn't got used to the agreed truce. After years of constantly watching his back, and the backs of his teams, he's hard-wired to be extra vigilant at all times. Old habits die hard.

But now, he finally has time to settle that score. He's called Jason Brand over to his favourite bar to give him the go-ahead.

'You OK?'

'Yeh,' grunts Jason, 'OK thanks.'

'Drink? '

'Yeh, why not?'

'Peroni for my friend, please,' he calls to the barmaid.

'Like chillies? Here, try one.' He pushes the bowl at Jason, giving him no choice and knowing well the very likely outcome.

'Christ, that's fuckin' hot,' says Jason desperately wiping his mouth in vain and in complete shock.

Shaun is in stitches. 'Ha! No balls. Did you know Jase, that chilli should really be spelt with just one L?'

He swivels on his seat to face Jason.

'Christ, you should see your face, Jase!'

Jason looks at him blankly.

'Right my friend, time to complete our little plan down south.'

Jason, still burning, smiles knowingly, he loves a sniff of blood.

'Yeh, understood,' he says, smiling to reveal his trade-mark teeth braces.

'Good boy, Jase – you will be richly rewarded my son. Your uncle Shaun will look after you. Have another chili.'

70

Ali and Laura look down at the massive hall from the balcony. As far as corporate summer balls go, this is the biggest he's worked at. It's London. The ceiling is festooned with long strips of lace-like material, offering a hint of the Bedouin – mood lighting enhances the exotic atmosphere.

There are dozens of large round tables stretching away on both sides – each seating twelve people. The noise is deafening, not surprising given that the guests are now on their desserts and much champagne has already been consumed.

Ali never ceases to be amazed at how caterers can possibly turn out high quality food for such vast numbers. Despite his keen interest, he keeps well away from the kitchens, knowing how frazzled the atmosphere usually is in these places.

Tonight, is an agency gig and it's the first time Laura has accompanied him on one of his corporate shows. He has actually been given his own dressing room and the organisers have also made sure that he's fed properly. The DJ usually comes low down the pecking order, so this is a turn up for the books.

When they arrived, the agency rep said she'd do what she could about an extra meal for Laura, and hey presto, here they are, with their own three course spread.

'Decent crockery with knives and forks, too,' notes Laura, impressed.

'You have that effect on people,' says Ali, kissing her forehead.

A very strange scraping and banging sound is coming from the door – followed by a series of short erratic knocks. Ali and Laura look at each other, puzzled.

'Hello, just coming,' says Ali, as he crosses the room and opens the door to find a tall, attractive woman, probably in her forties, cleavage on full show, heavily made-up and clutching an open bottle of Moet et Chandon.

'May I join you?' she asks.

Ali starts to laugh.

'I'm afraid I …'

'I'm sure you can find time for a little drinkie with me, can't you, young man?'

'I'm sorry madam …'

'I've always liked people like you,' she says, slurring her words, clearly blotto.

'Like me?'

'Yes, I like a dark man, very erotic …'

The door flies open wide behind Ali.

'Can I help here? What is it you want, dear lady?' says a very straight Laura.

'Ooh er, get you Mrs Snot. Who – the - fuck do you think you are?' stutters the unwelcome visitor. 'I'm his wife!' snaps Laura.

'His what? Oh, no … I tell you what. Go and fuck yourself – and you, fuck you too,' she spits at Ali.

'Well that's charming, isn't it?' says Laura, watching as the woman waddles along the corridor just missing the walls as she goes, presumably back to the bar.

'I seem to attract drunks.'

‘Silly woman. And that was racism by the way,’ Laura adds.

Thankfully, the gig itself goes without incident and Ali’s guest set of 80s disco classics goes down a storm with the huge crowd. At the end, he’s mobbed by his new fans who all beg him to continue and play more of their favourite tracks. Ali just smiles, enjoying all the attention and when the set finishes, makes his way back to Laura. Gig complete, they prepare to leave.

‘Have you got everything?’ says Laura.

‘Yeh, so they tell me!’

‘Ha, Mr Kurmi.’

‘I just want to say goodbye to the organiser before we go – I’ll see you out the front.’

‘I couldn’t drive through London like you do.’

‘I’m not too fond of it myself, especially if I have to come during the day. At least it’s quiet now.’

‘True, and we’re not in the van. That would’ve been awful.’

Ali looks at Laura and smiles in delight.

‘It was great having you there tonight.’

‘I enjoyed it. I really did. Apart from that stupid woman. What would have happened Ali Kurmi, if I hadn’t been there, eh?’

‘What do you mean?’ says Ali, half laughing.

‘She was after you, big time.’

‘I know, you get them occasionally. Not often, I’m pleased to say.’

‘Have you ever been tempted?’

‘What?’

‘You know, to have a quick one? It would be very easy.’

‘Hang on, are you testing me here, or something?’

'No. I think it's quite sexy, actually. And I saw all those younger women at the end. You could have had your choice there.'

'What is this?' protests Ali.

'Nothing. Just saying.'

'Listen, the only sex I want is with you. Not some scraggy old drunken whore. Have you got that?'

'Yes sir. Yes, I have. And that was the right answer by the way.'

They laugh and continue down the A3 towards Hampshire.

'You know that woman was being racist, don't you?'

'So you said. Just rude, I think,' says Ali, 'she was pissed. If she'd said it when she was sober it would have been different.'

'Yes, but there are plenty of folk who would have reported her for that.'

'I know. I've been lucky I suppose. Lucky in that I haven't ever had any really nasty confrontations. Apart from that foul letter I got, that is. Generally, most people are nice to me.'

'That's because you are nice, babe.'

'You can't change nations' collective minds overnight,' Ali continues. 'It'll probably take a generation, maybe more. And don't forget, it isn't limited to white Europeans. Anyway, these aren't usually active racists, they're just folk who've been raised in a predominantly white environment. It's not exactly their fault, is it? It's just that countries are more multi-racial now. Thanks to oil and the jet engine. But let's not go there!'

'I totally agree ...'

'No, racists are nasty, deliberately aggressive hate-filled people. They're the ones to worry about – not pissed, ignorant folk who haven't caught up yet.'

Laura quietly smiles, impressed by Ali's wise analysis. However, she's noticed that throughout he's been constantly checking in his rear-view mirror.

'What's the matter babe? What's going on behind? You keep looking in your mirror.'

'I don't like to alarm you and it could be my imagination.'

'What?'

'I'm not sure. It's just that the car behind, has been following us for ages.'

'Are you sure?' says Laura, turning round.

'Yeh. It's got very distinctive LED sidelights and it's been behind me for the past half hour. It could easily have overtaken but it didn't.'

'It is a main road, Ali.'

'I know. It's just a feeling.'

'Look', there are services coming up. Let's pull in there and see if it follows us.'

'OK.'

Two miles down the road, Ali signals to come off and immediately the car behind follows suit.

'It's coming off too.'

'OK, don't panic, it's still probably nothing.'

'Hallelujah, divine intervention,' says Ali. 'Lookie here.'

He slows down rapidly – and amid the sparse row of cars in the parking area, is a police car. Ali immediately pulls in beside it, leaving one parking space between the vehicles.

'How lucky is that? Did the car follow us in?'

'I don't know – I couldn't see.'

'Let's wait here for a few minutes, just to be sure.'

There are two policemen sitting in the adjacent car, with hot drinks and keeping an eye on the forecourt. Ali looks over and smiles as they raise their heads and look back at him expressionless.

'Evenable,' he mouths clumsily.

'What?' snorts Laura.

The policeman winds down his window. 'Is there anything I can help you with, sir?'

Ali opens his window too. 'No, nothing I was just' er. I'm just about to go to the toilet.'

Laura sniggers again. Ali tries to poke her.

'You alright sir?'

'Yes I'm fine.'

'Would you mind stepping out of your vehicle, please.'

'Really?'

'Yes please sir.'

The policeman steps towards Ali. 'Have you been drinking sir? Have you taken any prescribed or other sorts of drugs?'

'No, of course not. No, I don't actually drink. Or take drugs.'

'Could you step forward one pace sir, thank you. Please take a deep breath, fill your lungs and blow in one continuous breath through this mouthpiece, please.'

Ten minutes later, Ali and Laura are slowly pulling away from the car park and driving along the slip road back on to the A3.

Laura is the first to burst into laughter.

'Oh Ali, that was SO funny. You should have seen your face. You were in a total state of panic!'

'I wasn't.'

'You were! You're so funny. You must have a huge guilty conscience.'

'I don't even drink.' says Ali, beginning to laugh.

'Hilarious.'

'Any sign of that car?' says Ali, being more serious.

'No, can't see it. I'm sure it was nothing.'

'I don't know about that. I've still got a funny feeling about it. I'm sure it was tailing us.'

'Well, why would anyone want to do that? And who for goodness sake, who would have known we'd be on that road at *this* time?'

'Yeh, you're right I suppose. I just get paranoid occasionally. Don't forget, I've upset quite a few people over the years.'

'Yes, but that was then. Things are very different now. Our future only holds good things Ali Kurmi. Remember that.'

71

Laura knows that Thursday is a bit of a weird day for a lunch party, but today is the only day she can get everyone together. She's determined to do something special with her friends and loved ones to mark her and Ali's imminent birthdays, their new properties – and the auction.

It's the usuals; Alice and Dave, Becky and Olivia, Finn, Samantha, plus Jim and his partner Emma.

Lunch has been bought in and was delivered this morning, direct from Yotam Ottolenghi HQ in Notting Hill, London. Laura had to use a taxi in the end, but what the hell, it's a special occasion.

Ali has been inspecting the spread with uncontrolled excitement. Crushed carrots with rose harissa, butternut squash with ginger tomatoes, kale tahini-caesar with za'atar chickpeas, porcini mushroom pilaf with sweet spices. And the rest. He can hardly contain himself.

The sun is in and out, the temperature is warm and their guests arrive around noon. After a brief tour of the house, drinks in-hand, the buffet is uncovered and the assembled friends, intrigued and delighted, help themselves. The music's on, the atmosphere is relaxed and even baby Olivia gurgles happily in her pushchair.

The buffet tastes as good as it looks and no one is shy about going back for seconds.

'Speech, speech …' Dave starts the chorus around the room.

'Come on Laura, let's be having you.'

'Oh dear, do I really have to?'

'Of course you do,' says Dave.

'Here, here,' come the echoes.

'Whoop. Whoop.'

Ali looks at Laura with pride and nods at her encouragingly. Every day he spends with this beautiful woman his love gets stronger and the heartbreak of his broken family, fades further into the background.

Laura has restored his self-esteem and given him the encouragement and confidence to develop and expand as a person, as well as his musical talents. He's not just a very keen songwriter and DJ, he's a wiser soul, and a loving father with a wider perception and purpose.

There are so many things he now feels are possible to achieve – not just for him, but for his beautiful daughter and his most incredible partner, lover and mentor, his complete inspiration, Laura O'Brien.

'Funnily enough, I would like to say a few words. All of you here are the most special people in my life,' says Laura.

'Whoop, whoop.'

'Stop it, I'm serious, Ali and I have our birthdays on top of one another, no rude jokes please … and the dreaded bloody auction is tomorrow – so we wanted to have a little celebration in our new little house. And here we are! There are so many things to be thankful for right now.'

She looks towards Ali.

'I've found the most wonderful, kind, thoughtful and talented man. Ali Kurmi, you are absolutely everything to me. Thank you for sticking it out with this ageing Irish witch!'

'Hubble bubble,' Ali heckles, stirring with his hands clasped.

'And we have the lovely Olivia here, the apple of all our eyes. What an absolute joy she is – and blessed with a beautiful and loving mother. Here's to you Becky. We're all with you. With you both …'

'Here, here.'

'We wanted all of you to come here today because you're *all* so special to Ali and me in so *many* ways. So, thank you: Alice, Dave, Finn, Samantha, Becks and of course Olivia. And thank you Jim and Emma.'

'Bravo – well done,' chimes Finn.

'I think you all know about my past – not just the recent past, but going way back to my early days, happy days as a child, but blasted into oblivion by my parents' accident. My first marriage, how it all ended so badly. And yes, my very, very bad time with the booze.'

She looks towards, Alice.

'My wonderful saviour and life-changing friend, Alice here … without you, Alice, I can say for certain that I wouldn't be standing here in Portsmouth right now. Alice, I love you – more than I can describe. Thank you.'

'Oh Laura. You don't have to thank me – that's the whole point of life, isn't it? Helping one another along. Not many of us get to sail through without a care in the world; we're here to be challenged. Life's about mistakes – lots of them, and wrong decisions, consequences, ownership, responsibility and most of all, love.'

'Seconded,' says Dave, who has fallen completely for Alice.

'It's all about the rough and tumble, the heartaches, the pain and the desperation. That's living and it's all about experiencing that and learning from it and turning all those negatives into positives. That's our test here on earth. In my humble opinion. Laura, you're a wonderful example of all that, in action. You are an evolved spirit, my dear! Truly.'

Laura is beaming. 'Love you,' she mouths, 'thank you so much. A year ago, none of this was even on my mind. I had no idea when I opened the front door of my rented house in Wickham, forgive this corn, that I was stepping into a completely different and wonderful future.'

'Whoop, whoop.'

'Seriously, all that ghastliness after Frank's death – and the distant past, it slowly and magically, started to disappear. When I came here to Hampshire, it really was closing one door and opening another. The door isn't quite locked on Ireland just yet, but come next week it should be, God preserve us. And then it really will be full steam ahead.'

She turns back to Ali. 'Ali, coming back to you again – I'm so proud of you.

Especially your scrambled eggs. Never knowingly over-cooked! 'But seriously, leaving your family behind to make a new start has been so painful for you and all those unhappy years working for your father. But just look at you now. Unrecognisable. A father too, can you believe? And at last, your wonderful music is being recognised. Here's to you, my gorgeous Ali Kurmi.'

'To Ali,' is the chorus around the room.

'Speech Ali, speech.'

'Really? I mean *really*? I couldn't possibly follow that. I'm not as eloquent as Laura. I just write the lyrics.'

'Whoop, whoop.'

'... And the tunes! I'll start with raising a glass to you Jim – and your fine studio. Without your amazing talent my songs would just be crude doodles on my PC at home. Cheers mate and thanks for helping to turn them into half-decent masters!'

Jim just smiles, not wishing to be drawn into the limelight. Emma nudges him affectionately.

'You all now know my hidden scandal – the scandal that shouldn't have been – and thank you all for being so understanding. I came here to Pompey when I was just 16. I didn't know what the hell was going on. I had all those accusations thrown at me, and for so long I just had to take it, without being able to defend myself. I can't describe how awful that feeling was. However, things did come right and my parents, bless 'em, didn't think I could handle the stigma and packed me off out of the way. My father said it was for my own good, but as I've since discovered, it was more for his benefit and his fear of damaging his business reputation. That's why I ended up here. BUT. As Laura and Alice keep telling me, everything happens for a reason and I guess that's true 'cause I wouldn't here talking to you now without all that shit having happened. Pardon my language Samantha.'

'I've heard far worse,' says Samantha, half-smiling and looking accusingly at Finn.

'Anyway, I've experienced an amazing and completely unpredictable sequence of events. If somebody is controlling our every move from somewhere out there in the universe, they're either genius' or raving mad. Either way, I don't care. It happened – and it's brought me to this point and, all of you, thank you for being in my life and ... Laura, thank you for being my lover, soul mate, teacher, best friend, sous chef – and banker! And to everyone in this room, long may we all thrive in love and happiness. Oh, and happy birthday babe. Almost.'

Everyone cheers.

'Hey Ali. Wow! Good man,' says Becky. 'Where did that come from? That really *was* a speech!'

Ali bangs is chest with his forearm.

'Here Becks, right here!'

'Right you lot,' says Laura standing up. 'It's a lovely day and a bit of sea air will do us all the world of good. Please do me a favour – all of you, go for a walk on the front, while I get things straight here and have a tidy up. Head for the pier and I'll catch you up in a few minutes.'

'No way,' says Alice, and is quickly joined by Becky, Emma and Samantha.

'It's fine, it's fine' says Laura holding up her hands up, emphatically.

'Leave me to it, please, it'll only take a short time. Then I'll come and find you. It's all disposable apart from the dishes and the cutlery. And they can go straight in the dishwasher. Go on with you. You know I'm a control freak, so humour me. Be off. The lot of you. The ice creams are on me.'

The group assembles on the pathway outside and makes its way slowly down the road towards the common. Southsea common occupies a lot of seafront real estate and separates the housing and guest houses from the long shingle beach, that faces the English Channel and the eastern end of the Isle of Wight.

Ali never tires of walking here, as there's something new to see every time, whether it's the people or the weather. Whatever, he's happy that he hasn't completely severed ties with Portsmouth, his adopted home city.

The group is now strung out across the common, making for South Parade Pier.

'Shit.' says Ali to Becky.

'What's the matter?'

'I've left my phone at home.'

'You don't need it do you?'

'I know, but I never go anywhere without my phone!'

'You're as bad as the kids,' says Becky.

'Ha, you can talk, you're glued to yours too. I'll just nip back and get it. It'll only take a minute. I'll catch up with you.'

'OK,' says Becky, and continues pushing Olivia across the dry brown grass.

The others who are in front, turn enquiringly.

'It's nothing, he's gone to get his phone. Doh! Carry on. He'll catch us up.'

They get the message and continue towards the Pier.

Laura, looks around the room, relieved to see that it's surprisingly tidy.

Ali's iPod is still playing tunes and is now featuring his epic song, In Paradise.

Laura stops for a moment, turns up the volume to listen closer and realises that she hasn't properly appreciated the song until now. Tears start to well up in her eyes. She's genuinely moved by the lyrics and the mood of the song. She is so proud of Ali.

With the song still playing, she loads everything washable into the dishwasher and looks around to make sure she's got everything before starting the machine.

Oh dear, she mumbles to herself, *he'll be back for that*. She spots Ali's phone on the sideboard. She knows her man inside out and he will not part with his phone under any circumstance. She picks it up.

'Can you see him yet? Shall we go on to the pier?' Finn shouts out to Becky, who's bringing up the rear with Olivia and Alice.

They've slowed their pace to allow Ali to catch up, but there's no sign of his reappearance yet.

Then, they suddenly stop in their tracks, halted by a deafening bang and flash of light.

'WHAT the hell was that?' shouts Alice, looking back over the common.

'It sounded like a bomb, and did you see that huge white flash?' says Becky.

'Christ, that was really loud,' Dave shouts.

'Didn't sound like fireworks,' says Jim.

'Probably the Naval Dockyard,' says Finn. 'They're always doing pyrotechnics or similar.'

'Look at that!' says Samantha, pointing to the houses to the rear of the common. 'Look at that smoke.'

'My God, what's that?' says Becky, staring at the huge mushroom of cloud now rising.

In the distance, people start moving towards the source of the smoke. Some break into a run. It's not that easy to see from where Becky and Alice are standing, but one thing is for sure, something serious has just occurred.

'What do you think it was?' says Alice, looking at Finn who's now not so sure he was right about the Dockyard.

'That smoke isn't coming from the Dockyard,' he says, 'it looks like it's coming from … surely not.'

Oh my God, says, Becky shrieking. 'You don't think … it couldn't possibly be anywhere near the house, do you? Here, look after Olivia will you,' she says, thrusting the pushchair towards Alice.

'Becky, where are you going?' cries Alice.

'To have a closer look,' she says, as she runs off in the same direction as everyone else.

As she hurries back across the common, steadying herself as she goes on the uneven turf, more and more people are moving in the same direction. In no time at all, the sirens begin. A lot of sirens, echoing noisily over the common like screeching crows. Soon she can see several police cars, ambulances and fire engines racing along the Parade in the same direction as the milling people.

She picks up speed, and by the time she reaches the end of Merridean Avenue, policemen are stretching tape across the entrance and telling people to keep back. More police further down the road itself, are ushering confused residents, emerging from their houses, to make their way back to the junction. An evacuation is under way.

The sirens eventually stop shrieking and apart from the soft hum of conversations there's a brief surreal silence across the area. The natural light has been dimmed by a massive cloud of dust.

Becky can feel her heart pulsing strongly and starts breathing heavily.

Then the mayhem begins again.

'Please, please – what's happened?' she yells at no-one in particular.

The two policemen remain silent and only when Becky screams directly at one of them, does she get a response.

'All we know, Ma'am is there's been what we think is an explosion in this road,' the policeman says holding a finger to his earpiece.

'Which number? says Becky, desperately. 'My family is in there.'

'I'm afraid I can't say,' says the policeman, truthfully. 'Please keep back madam, please.'

Becky shouts as loudly as she can, 'Ali! Ali are you there? Ali Kurmi! Laura!'

There is of course no reply. Small groups of bewildered people, mainly residents, are looking back up the road, unable to process what has just happened.

Alice, Dave, Jim, Emma, Finn and Samantha arrive with the pushchair and Olivia, looking shocked.

'Any idea yet?' says Alice?

'No, just that there's been an explosion and there's no sign of Ali. Oh, Alice it can't be, can it?'

'I don't know,' says Alice holding Becky tightly, trying to stay composed, but deeply shocked.

All they can hear now is the throbbing sound of the emergency service vehicles' pumps and equipment swelling and ebbing. The hub of the action is just out of sight, round the bend. The flow of evacuees continues.

'Please God, no,' says Alice.

'There's nothing you can do madam,' says one of the policemen, 'as soon as we have any information, we'll let you know.'

She looks round at the crowd that's gathered at this end of the road. Many are tapping at their mobile phones searching for any information – but of course it's far too soon.

'There's nothing we can do, he's right,' says Finn, 'it'll be exactly the same at the other end of the road. I think we're just going to have to wait.'

'I've tried phoning,' says Becky, 'Laura's is dead and Ali's goes to voicemail.'

They stand waiting for news for several painful minutes.

Eventually, a more senior police officer, an inspector, arrives and talks to the constables and they look over towards Becky and the group. He comes over.

'You have relatives here in Merridean Avenue?'

'Yes, no.29,' says Becky.

The officer's face is expressionless but Alice senses something ominous.

'I can tell you that there has been an explosion at the premises of no. 29. The house appears to have been completely destroyed by an explosion. At this stage this is just conjecture of course. We'll get the full picture eventually. Do you know if anyone was occupying the house today?'

'Yes, Laura and Ali.'

'Could I have their full names if you know them, please.'

'Laura O'Brien and Ali Kurmi.'

'Thank you,' says the Inspector writing down the names.

'Oh my God,' says Alice putting her hand to her face in horror. Do you think they were inside?'

'I'm afraid madam we cannot say at this stage. The explosion was very large and there's a huge amount of damage so it'll take time for the engineers to carry out tests. If you give this officer your contact details, we'll do our best to let you have any information, when we get it. You did say you are relatives, didn't you?'

'Yes, yes,' shouts Becky, pointing towards the pushchair, 'this little girl is the man's daughter. Is there no sign of them – he's in his 30s, jet black hair and he was with his partner, Laura – she's in her 50s – has long brown hair. Have you seen them? They were there.'

'I'm very sorry madam, I can't say anything for sure at this time,' he says, swallowing hard.

Becky and Alice slump to the pavement, howling with grief. They look desperately at each other and at Finn and Samantha, tears rolling down their cheeks.

'Ah, Laura …' Becky wails in desperation and resignation, her usually pretty face transformed into a contorted, anguished vision of pain and grief.

'No. No. No!' she cries, 'he only went back to get his phone. And Laura … oh my God!'

'I'm very sorry Madam.'

Becky and Alice hold on to each other, broken and mouthing unformed words at their sobbing friends.

The Inspector adjusts his steel-rimmed glasses on his nose, looks down and clears his throat. He turns and walks slowly and solemnly away from the tape, rubber-gloved hands at his side, back down the road towards the dust – and the remains of what was once, 29 Merridean Avenue.

72

'I can't thank you both enough …' says Laura.

'That's alright, love. I'd make you a tea but the power's gone,' says the lady. She turns to look at Ali. 'Are you OK? Sorry, I don't know your name.'

'It's Ali, and this is Laura – we moved in recently just up the … er, up the road,' says Ali, bewildered, and trying to look out of the window. 'Thank you for being so kind.'

'That's OK, mate,' says the man, 'least we can do.'

'What's going on? What the hell happened?' says Laura, shivering, looking at the man.

'I don't know, love. It sounded like a bomb, and next thing I know, there's bits of brick all over the shop.'

'We saw you outside – you two're lucky to be alive,' says the lady.

'My ears', says Laura, placing her hands on them. 'They really hurt.'

Ali puts his arm around her shoulders. 'It's OK babe. We're both OK. Sorry, what are your names?'

'I'm Debbie and this is Mike.'

'Thanks again,' says Ali. 'All I can remember is this huge bang and this amazing blast of wind. We went right over – nearly took off.'

'I reckon you can thank that van out there, mate. You were bloody lucky,' says Mike.

'Do you know what it was?' asks Ali.

‘Gas maybe?’ says Mike. ‘I can’t think what else. It happened just around the bend on the right from what I can see. The police and fire people are everywhere.’

‘That’s where we live!’ says Laura. ‘Oh God. Ali.’

‘I’m so sorry, love,’ says Debbie. ‘I think we’re all lucky to be alive. Are you sure you’re not hurt? You should get yourselves looked at anyway – you may feel alright now but you never know.’

‘Everyone’s moving down to the common,’ says Mike. ‘I think we’re being evacuated.’

‘What about the alley?’ says Debbie. ‘It’ll be safer and it goes up the road to the shops.’

‘Yeh, let’s go that way. The road’s full of debris.’

‘Thanks – I mean it,’ says Ali.

‘That’s OK, mate. Truth be told, I’m a bit wobbly meself. But I really think we should get going. It might not be safe here. Let’s just go – come on, Debs.’

They all stand up and move towards the back door. Mike reaches into his back pocket.

‘Oh, I nearly forgot, is this yours? I picked it up when I came to get you.’

Mike hands Ali the battered phone – glass cracked and looking very dead.

‘Thanks, yes it is,’ says Ali, wiping the broken screen on his jeans.

At the top of Merridean Avenue, the area is now a major incident scene – strobing blue lights colouring the drama. Laura and Ali are sitting inside one of the ambulances. Laura passes the water bottle to Ali.

‘Thanks,’ he says, taking a huge gulp. He holds up his phone. ‘I think this little bugger might have just saved our lives.’

'Oh Ali, what the fuck was all that? Was it a bomb? We've lost our new home – and your lovely car.'

'They think it's probably gas – the boiler maybe.'

'What? I only had that looked at the other day,' says Laura, indignantly.

'I don't know, babe. But I'm sure they'll find out.'

'And where are the others? I hope they're alright. They must be going crazy.'

'Unfortunately, this is buggered,' he says waving his phone. 'But look here babe – we're alive and that's all that matters. We both could have been blown to pieces. If you hadn't come out to meet me at that precise moment, you'd have died. My God, someone or something is looking after us.'

'We'll have to get a taxi back to Wickham. My God Ali, we are SO lucky. Some of these other people have lost their homes too and they don't have anywhere to go.'

'The police are already sorting that out and the council people are here too. They've got our address and I've told them that for a while we won't have phones. But I think mine might work if I can recharge it.'

'Somehow, we've got to let the others know we're OK. Becky will be going mental if she thinks anything has happened to you. I know Alice's number off by heart. I've called her a million times over the years. Can we borrow a phone from someone?'

'Laura! Is that you? Really?' yells an astounded Alice. 'Are you guys OK? Oh my God! That's amazing.'

She waves excitedly at the reast of the group who are looking expectantly at her. She grins at them and gives the thumbs up.

'Where are you? OK, we'll come the long way round and find you. Yes, we're all OK. Sort of. We've just heard what happened.'

'It's awful, Alice. The whole house is gone – and the car. It's just a miracle we weren't killed. It was such a big explosion. The police say we're the luckiest couple on the planet.'

'Are you sure you're OK?'

'We're just a bit shaken and just want to go back home to Wickham, and try to get our heads around it all.'

'Of course, you must be stunned. We'll take you home, don't worry.'

'Thank you, Alice. We've got the bloody stud sale tomorrow, for goodness sake. I just want it all to go away.'

'Forget about all that – it can wait. Focus on the now. We're on our way.'

'Come here, you,' says Ali, pulling Laura towards him. He cups her face in his hands and looks deeply into her eyes.

'Laura O'Brien, I love you SO much,' he says, kissing her gently on the lips.

'I know you do …'

'I will never, ever let you out of my sight again – not for a millisecond.'

'Oh Ali …'

'I'll look after you, I promise.'

'You just did babe. You saved my life.'

They kiss again.

'This is just the beginning. No more bad things. I love you.'

'To the black hole and back?' she smiles.

'Yeh, all round the universe, into the vortex and back again.'

POSTSCRIPT

Stephanie O'Brien, sitting at her office desk in Tipperary, gets a ping on her phone, heralding the arrival of a text. The message is short – just five words: 'Look in the usual place.'

She opens her laptop, realising her hands are shaking. She finds a hyperlink to a news website.

Breaking News: **Portsmouth Gas Blast – Miracle Escape.** Stephanie looks at the dramatic photo and story in disbelief and very soon, rage.

In Toxteth, Liverpool, Shaun James gets the call he's been expecting. He listens closely, glares and shuts his phone with an angry slap. He reaches for the bottle opener and yanks the top off another Peroni. *Fuck.*

Javed Kurmi and his wife Namita are thinking about turning in for the day, and as usual they catch the regional news bulletin before doing so. The story of an explosion in Portsmouth is the main story. 'Oh, how awful – those poor people,' says Namita. Husband Javed, uninterested, just grunts and wipes his brow with his handkerchief.

Hampshire Police's Detective Inspector, Paul Davies, is finishing his shift and looking through the day's paperwork. He picks up the explosion report, reads it through again, raises his left eyebrow and shakes his head. *Lucky buggers.*

ACKNOWLEDGEMENTS

This book is part of the Fatal Equation trilogy – a novel, an album and a TV Drama treatment.

Thanks to Ian Bartholomew. He sowed the seed and set me on this satisfying creative journey.

I never dreamed I would write a novel. Initial bewilderment soon became an unmissable experience. Not that different from writing songs actually – having the confidence to allow inspiration to take you over.

Thanks to Peter Robson, forensically vigilant and champion of the Oxford comma.

Thank you, Nick Bowen. It was my passion for writing songs that triggered the book idea. You are a superb musician, engineer and producer. I couldn't have done this without you and all at Quay West Studios. And a further thank you for the cover design.

Thanks to the many fabulous musicians and singers who contributed.

Musicians: Nick Bowen, Alex Long, Graham Preskett, Mike Hugg, Ian Duck, Jack Turnbull, Daryl Nash, Joe Smith, Jamie Wilson, Jim Cutts, Chris Welch, Teddy Edwards, Alex Wilson and John Rennie.

Singers: Liam Wakefield, Ian Bartholomew, Nick Bowen, Alan Finlan, Erin Newman, Paige, Lily Garland, Millie Claxton (Wren), Phil Cottrill and Amba Tremain.

Tracks from the storyline, are available to download and stream.

FATAL EQUATION by Coolstar [www.coolstar.uk]

ABOUT THE AUTHOR

Gethyn Jones

Gethyn spent 30 years as a producer, presenter and journalist – primarily in BBC local radio and latterly in commercial radio and community TV. He's also an accomplished songwriter and producer, having been part of JUGG Music which, in its day, provided music for a variety of BBC and ITV programmes.

He has provided media training to senior military personnel and in 2003 set up his own web design company.

Fast-forward to 2018, determined to find a place for his music, he began work on the trilogy, Fatal Equation – a music album, TV drama proposal and novel.

Gethyn lives in Hampshire, UK with Ros and Dibble.

www.gethynjonesauthor.com/

Fatal Equation – The Music

You can listen to a selection of Ali's songs by COOLSTAR on all major streaming platforms. An EP is available to download from the usual sources.

Listen to Ali's songs by Coolstar now.
Go to: www.coolstar.uk

Printed in Great Britain
by Amazon

21188995R00220